Praise for *Her Sec*

"Compelling characters, heart-stopping suspense and an ending that blew me away. *Her Secret Son* is an unbearably tense page turner that I devoured in one sitting. Make room on your bookshelf for this gripping thriller!"
　　　—Heather Gudenkauf, *New York Times* bestselling author

"An engrossing mix of suspense, grief, and family drama, *Her Secret Son* is a powerful tale of the lengths parents will go to care for their children and ultimately, the true meaning of family."
　　　—Kimberly Belle, international bestselling author of *The Marriage Lie*

"McKinnon creates tenderly drawn characters, ordinary people thrown into haunting situations, and turns up the heat. Promise, you won't see all the twists coming!"
　　　—Kaira Rouda, *USA TODAY* bestselling author

"An intricate tangle of family secrets...with unforgettable characters who bring this heartbreaking and chilling story to life."
　　　—K. A. Tucker, *USA TODAY* bestselling author

"McKinnon skillfully balances suspense with emotional depth.... I raced through this gripping, heart-rending tale of secrets and lies all the way to the stunning conclusion."
　　　—Laura McHugh, award-winning author

"Warning: may cause sleepless nights and a frenzy of page-turning.... High-stakes family drama at its finest."
　　　—Paula Treick DeBoard, author of *The Drowning Girls*

"McKinnon continuously ratchets up the stakes to a stunning conclusion you won't see coming. Emotionally tense and brimming with secrets, McKinnon showcases love in all its purity and peril."
　　　—Mindy Mejia, author of *Leave No Trace*

"You won't be able to put this book down until you've unraveled the mystery surrounding this family. And you will root for them with every page."
—Robyn Harding, international bestselling author of *Her Pretty Face*

"With skillful storytelling, McKinnon keeps us guessing to the end."
—Roz Nay, bestselling author of *Our Little Secret*

"The perfect blend of taut suspense and heartbreaking family drama."
—Emily Carpenter, bestselling author

"A smoldering domestic suspense, full of chilling secrets that will knock you sideways."
—Jennifer Hillier, author of *Creep* and *Jar of Hearts*

"McKinnon does it again, weaving a twisted tale of lies, secrets, and conflicting loyalties that culminates in a surprise ending that I did not see coming!"
—Jill Orr, author of *The Good Byline*

"Riveting...vivid and surprising."
—Shannon Kirk, international bestselling author

"Immediately captivating, shattering and poignant."
—Marissa Stapley, bestselling author of *Mating for Life*

"You'll race to the end."
—Karen Katchur, author of *River Bodies*

"A read-in-one-sitting book that deals with family, love, and the fragility of trust. Dark and compelling."
—Karma Brown, bestselling author of *The Life Lucy Knew*

"A masterfully twisty tale fraught with suspense."
—Wendy Heard, author of *Hunting Annabelle*

HER
SECRET
SON

HANNAH MARY McKINNON

mira

mira

Recycling programs
for this product may
not exist in your area.

ISBN-13: 978-0-7783-5126-9

Her Secret Son

For questions and comments about the quality of this book, please contact us at
CustomerService@Harlequin.com.

BookClubbish.com

Printed in U.S.A.

To Mum & Dad and Joely & Co—with a lorra love!

Also by Hannah Mary McKinnon

THE NEIGHBORS

HER SECRET SON

"The truth is rarely pure and never simple."

—Oscar Wilde

CHAPTER ONE

They say the lucky ones experience an incredible, life-defining moment, a moment they can point back to as the second everything changed. Maybe it was sitting down on the bus next to a stranger who became the love of their life. Or witnessing the birth of a child they were told they'd never conceive. Perhaps getting that elusive break the day the boss had the flu, launching a career that, until then, was only the stuff of dreams.

And then there are the others. People like me, who have life-shattering moments instead. We're the ones who want to believe we've had more than our fair share of bad luck, enough misfortune to last multiple lives over. We get comfortable, believe nothing else can go wrong because fate has already played with us the most, seen how far we can be stretched and bent, twisted into the shape of a pretzel before becoming brittle and shattering into a million pieces.

For me, one of these moments came late one Friday morning as I stood in Harlan Gingold's dark, wood-paneled study, the musty air closing in on me. I pulled at the neck of my sweater in a futile attempt to cool down. I'd forgotten how warm he kept this room, as if he secretly longed to be a gecko under a heat lamp and pretend he was somewhere far closer to the equator than the outskirts of Albany, in upstate New York.

His study smelled of expensive whisky and Cuban cigars, wizened fingers left to linger in an ashtray. A stereotypical rich man's man-cave, complete with leather armchairs and gold-lettered law books Harlan no doubt cited by heart when he valiantly fought—and usually won—his cases in court, something he'd done for longer than I'd been alive.

We were going over the quote for the pool house extension and elaborate backyard revamp he'd promised his wife for the spring. While he checked the details again, running an index finger down the page, I tried to ignore the buzz of my mobile in my back pocket. Harlan was the kind of man who commanded nothing but your undivided attention. In this case I couldn't blame him. Not with the amount of zeros he was writing on the deposit check my bosses had sent me to collect.

My phone rang a second time. While Harlan put the final flourish on the paperwork with his thick Mont Blanc fountain pen, I slid my mobile from my pocket and glanced at the screen. My neighbor's number. Nothing unusual in itself. Mrs. Banks often called for a hand around the house—putting together yet another of her bookcases, repairing the front door, unblocking a sink. Nothing that couldn't wait or would justify the lecture about people's dependence on technology Harlan would no doubt dispense if I answered.

"There you go, Josh," he said as he handed me the check.

"Thanks," I said. "I'll see you next month?"

"Yes. I've no doubt you'll do a great job, as always. My yard has never looked better. Those Fraser firs were the talk of the street when they were lit up for Christmas. Even Ivan was impressed."

I grinned, thinking I'd enjoy ribbing Ivan about not paying the compliment forward. I wouldn't give him too much of a hard time. He'd become my best mate since we'd met a few years back, and since then he'd pointed a number of his friends and colleagues my way, including the firm's biggest cheese and Ivan's uncle, Mr. Harlan Gingold himself. When I'd told Ivan I owed him one, he'd cheerily replied, "Better make it a big one, whatever it is," before graciously settling for a pair of football tickets I'd got on the cheap.

Harlan accompanied me to the front porch where he shook my hand as I ignored the ongoing buzzing of my phone. He lifted his nose toward the dark gray, early March skies, swirling with ominous fast-moving clouds, and breathed in deep, nostrils flaring. "Something wicked this way comes," he said. "You'd better batten down the hatches, son. You Brits aren't used to our snow. Tell that lovely wife of yours to keep you safe."

I didn't bother reminding him Grace and I weren't married, or argue that, despite my strong British accent, I'd lived in the US for twenty years. I was only too familiar with the legendary winters. For crying out loud, the city competed in the annual Golden Snowball Award, although it regularly lost to Syracuse. As Grace once said, upstate New York was where lake effect and nor'easter storms mated, making trillions of snowflake babies, and everyone's life beneath a frozen misery.

When we'd said our goodbyes, I finally pulled my phone from my pocket and trudged to my truck, glancing at the darkening skies, thinking Harlan's prophecy could turn out to be the understatement of the season. Not that I'd mind a blizzard, within reason, anyway. It was Friday, the weekend gloriously stretching out ahead of us. As far as I knew, work didn't need me, and Grace hadn't mentioned any special plans. So what if we couldn't leave the house? It would mean a family weekend; Grace, Logan and I huddled under the blankets in front of the TV, eating popcorn and watching movies, exactly the way we liked it.

If I'd known what was actually coming, how my life was about to be forever, indelibly changed, I wouldn't have grabbed my mobile so hastily. I'd have taken a few moments to savor how my life had become simple again, full of uncomplicated, innocuous decisions. I'd have mulled over my mundane lunch choices. Thought about which film Grace and I would watch once we'd tucked Logan up in his bed. What Grace and I would do to each other later, after we'd headed upstairs, too. I'd have enjoyed the excitement building in my gut when I pictured the ring I'd hidden at the back of my sock drawer, a gold band solitaire I'd saved up for over the last year in the hope Grace would say yes this time.

But I didn't do any of that. Instead I unlocked my phone, looked at all the missed calls from Mrs. Banks and dialed voice mail. My brow furrowed as I listened to her message. She sounded unusually high-pitched and grating, breathless, even, as if she were in the middle of a ten-mile run. A feat in itself considering she was in her midseventies and walked with a stick.

"Josh, it's Mrs. Banks," she said. "There's been an accident. Can you call me? *Please*. It's urgent. Call me now."

I pushed a hand against the truck to steady myself. Perhaps her grandson had put his soccer ball through our bathroom window again. Or maybe the mangy dog who'd been hanging around the house, the one I'd caught Logan feeding his breakfast to, had dug up the tulip bulbs Grace replanted twice already. Although I grabbed hold of both ideas like a shipwrecked man to driftwood, I knew from Mrs. Banks's voice it was more serious. Way more serious. My next thoughts went to Logan, peppering my brain like fully automatic gunfire.

He's hurt. Grace can't call. She's with him. She told Mrs. Banks to phone. How bad is it? He's only seven. Christ! What's going on?

When I tried to hit redial, I missed the button four times, my fingers—thick and limp as raw sausages—impossible to maneuver. Finally I pressed the phone to my ear, and Mrs. Banks picked up on the first ring.

"Josh! Oh, thank goodness." Her voice sounded shakier than before, and I could barely make out her words with the crackling and whooshing of the wind in my ear.

"What's happened?" I said, an icy hand sneaking its way down to my stomach, grabbing hold of my innards and yanking hard. "Is Logan okay? Where is he? Has he—"

"It's not Logan… It's…it's…"

Saliva collected in my mouth as Mrs. Banks stopped talking. Just as I was about to shout into the phone, demand she tell me what was going on, she very quietly said, "It's Grace."

My stomach lurched, threatened to empty itself right there on Harlan's driveway. I'd been so sure Logan was hurt, I thought I'd misheard, but she said it again. "It's Grace."

I opened and closed my mouth three times, my tongue refusing to form a single syllable until I finally managed, "Is she okay? What happened?"

"I was drinking my coffee by the window—" Mrs. Banks's voice sped up, an out-of-control freight train barreling straight toward me "—when I saw Grace taking out the garbage and… and, oh, Josh…she slipped on the steps." Her words came out garbled now, making it harder for my brain to process what it already struggled to decode. "She went down."

"Where is she?"

Mrs. Banks's voice fell to a strained whisper, as if she were pressing a hand over her throat, trying to keep her next sentence inside. "When she didn't get back up, I—"

"Where is she?"

"—ran over and…and…" Her voice tailed off, the last syllables gobbled up by a sob. "We're outside. The ambulance is here. And the police. You need to come home. Please, come home *now*."

"But Grace is okay? Has she broken anything? Can I talk to her?" Silence. "Mrs. Banks, *please*. Is she okay?"

More silence, a whisper. "I don't think so, Josh. I really don't think so."

Yes, this was one of those life-shattering moments, an instance I'd point to in the future and say it was the second everything changed. And I was right.

Except that worse—far, far worse—was still to come.

CHAPTER TWO

The drive home shouldn't have taken more than fifteen minutes, but every traffic light had a personal vendetta against me, changing before I'd made it through, mocking me as if they were obnoxious, red-faced security guards.

I gripped the steering wheel hard and reminded myself for the millionth time I was supposed to check the steps and the driveway that morning. I'd remembered when I'd been halfway to Harlan's, had decided not to turn around, hastily scribbled *SALT* on a note instead and stuck it in the cup holder. Although I grabbed the paper, scrunched it into a tiny ball and stuffed it in the side of my door, it continued to burn a hole in my forehead straight to my conscience.

I made a hopeless attempt not to picture what waited for me at home, but the images came all the same. Grace's arms bent at unnatural angles. Feet twisted backward. Kneecaps bulging. Back shattered. I tried to shake the images, but they remained hot-glued to my brain. Was she in pain? Conscious? Able to walk? What if she couldn't move at all? It took everything I had to keep my eyes on the road, telling myself getting hurt wouldn't help anyone. Grace and Logan needed me now more than ever.

When I arrived at our short street, the weathered bungalows and towering oak trees glistened in a mix of red-and-blue lights from the ambulance, fire engine and police cars. Uniform-clad figures moved with less urgency than I'd expected, and I allowed myself to breathe; Grace had to be okay if they weren't rushing. But when I leaped out of the truck and ran to the house, hope melted away faster than a freak snowstorm in June.

I saw the blood first. A dark, sticky pool on the third step. Smears of it across the concrete, some reaching the bottom of the snow pile I'd made the day before, which had softened and hardened again overnight. Bandages, compresses and whatever else the first responders had used splattered with red, and abandoned in the driveway.

My gaze moved to the fluffy puppy slipper discarded on the ground, the pair with the brown eyes and pink tongue Logan gave Grace for Christmas, and which she'd insisted were the only thing that kept her feet warm. And then my eyes finally landed on the sheet-covered body on the ground.

"No!" I yelled the word over and over as I lunged forward. "No! No! *No!*" until it came out as nothing more than a quiet moan. I noticed Mrs. Banks only when her thick arms went around my middle and she buried her head in my chest.

"Oh, my Lord," she said as I propped her up, or maybe she held me. The laws of physics made no sense anymore. "Oh, my sweet Lord."

Someone else put a hand on my shoulder. "Sir?"

The police officer was minuscule, her head barely above the top of my shoulders, but her dark, oval eyes, framed by long lashes, were full of concern. Her skin, porcelain smooth and fair, was a stark contrast to the dusky circles underneath her green glasses. She looked at me and I nodded, absurdly hoping she'd tell me there'd been a mistake. I wasn't the person they were looking for. She had the wrong house. The wrong family.

"You're Mr. Joshua Andersen?"

After I'd nodded again, or maybe I hadn't stopped, more of her words followed. They swirled around my head as if I were underwater, her sentences stubborn waves pounding my skull, searching for a way in. I looked at her name tag, which read J. Hiraoka, watched her lips as I tried to decipher what she was saying until, very suddenly, my hearing and focus all returned at once, as if I'd pressed some magic unmute button and had turned up the volume too loud.

"...autopsy will confirm, but we believe it was severe and fatal head trauma from falling on the steps," Hiraoka said as she looked at me, her blinking slow and deliberate, unoffending.

Had she learned that at the academy? Taken "how to blink appropriately" lessons for when she'd have to deliver bad news? The thought made me want to laugh. Put my head back and let rip at the sheer ridiculousness of it, the craziness of the entire situation and the mere suggestion my Grace could be deceased. Laughing wouldn't have been an entirely abnormal reaction. People do all kinds of irrational things when they're confronted with death.

"I'm so sorry for your loss, Mr. Andersen," Hiraoka said, but when I still didn't respond she continued, "Sir? Do you want to sit down, sir?"

"I have to see." My voice came out foreign, so alien I wondered if I'd spoken at all, so I said it again. "I have to see Grace."

Hiraoka and Mrs. Banks, who still clung to my arm, exchanged a glance before the police officer walked me the six longest steps of my life, while my neighbor stayed behind. All that time, right up until the sheet was removed, I tried to convince myself it wasn't true. Couldn't be true. But there she was; my perfect, beautiful Grace, her long, red hair framing her face, as it always did, a fiery sunset. She looked asleep, lips slightly parted, as if, any second now, she'd open her green eyes, sit up and point a finger at the hidden camera across the street.

"Look, look, it's over there," she'd say. And I wouldn't be mad. Even though it was the sickest joke she'd ever played on me, I wouldn't be angry at all. I'd hug her, wag a finger at everybody around us because they were all in on it, and they'd chuckle, too, even after I called them a bunch of bastards.

Yes, I'd do that. All of it. If only she'd *just wake up.*

Grace lay there, her body eerily still. As I kneeled to kiss her, tears running down my cheeks spilled onto hers. My nose filled with the sweet scent of her favorite apple blossom shampoo, and I inhaled deeply until I thought my chest would implode.

How could someone who still looked so perfect be gone?

"Grace," I whispered. "No, baby. Don't go, please don't go. We need you. I need you here with me, with Logan." When she didn't open her eyes, didn't move, my heart pounded— wild horse hooves in my chest—as the sweat trickled down my back despite the fact I felt completely frozen, inside and out. I couldn't be next to her, didn't want to see her like this, but as I tried to get up my legs buckled and I stumbled, worked hard not go down again.

Hiraoka's hand went under my elbow, her grip surprisingly strong. "Mr. Andersen, why don't we get you inside?"

As I shook her off, swiping my face with the back of my hand, the desire to wrestle her to the ground bubbled to the surface. I opened my mouth to scream at the pint-size police officer, demand to know how she, old Mrs. Banks, the first responders and everybody else in my *fucking* driveway was very much alive when Grace lay there on the freezing ground, a slipper missing. How was it they got to live when she didn't? It wasn't rational, I knew, and thankfully my brain, which must've disconnected itself from my heart in a desperate act of self-preservation, commanded my hands to stay glued to my sides.

"I don't want to go inside," I said, the sentence somehow escaping my clenched jaw, my voice gruff, tired, defeated. "I have to get Logan."

"Your son?" Hiraoka said, and I nodded, gave my head a shake, left the officer's quizzical look unanswered until Mrs. Banks jumped in.

"Grace's boy," she said, her cheeks flooding, and she dabbed at them with a damp, mascara-stained tissue. "Oh, the poor little soul. He'll be at school and—"

"I have to get him. I have to tell him…" My shoulders slumped. "Oh, Jesus, what am I going to say?" The tears came again as I imagined Logan's face, smiling and excited to be picked up early, only to learn our lives would never be the same.

"Do you have any other children, Mr. Andersen?" Hiraoka said.

"No…" I said. "No. It's the three of us."

"Is there someone you can call?" she said. "Your parents? Ms. Wilson's? Another family member who can come over?"

"No," I whispered again. "My parents…they died a long time ago. My sister's in New York, I think, on business. And Grace's family…" I closed my eyes. Ever since we'd met, Grace had insisted that particular can of tangled, slippery worms stay nailed shut, but I'd be duty bound to open it somehow. Her parents—wherever they were—would need to know about their daughter, too. Looking at Hiraoka, all I said was, "It's complicated."

"And Logan's biological father?"

"He's never been in the picture," I said, my voice low.

"I see…"

"I'm Logan's dad." I put a hand to my chest, the words coming out louder than I'd intended. "Me. Have been for five years. But he's only seven and he needs his mom. How will he—"

I couldn't ask how Logan would cope. It was too reminiscent of what I'd gone through when Mom and Dad had died, and I'd been sucked into a cluster of rabbit holes, each one deeper and darker than the next, and from which I'd barely returned.

Hiraoka nodded and pressed her lips together, no doubt trying to avoid sticking her foot into other areas of the murky mess that represented Grace and my familial ties. It wasn't the officer's fault. Most of that particular landscape was scattered with hidden land mines even her miniature, boot-clad toes couldn't avoid.

"Shall I fetch Logan?" Mrs. Banks said as she rubbed my shoulder. "I can—"

"Thank you, but I have to… I should be the one to—"

I stopped as two paramedics knelt down next to Grace, wanted to etch her face into my memory before they took her away. I knew how the images faded—quicker than morning mist in the sun. It had been almost two decades since Mom and Dad passed, but for the longest time already, the pictures weren't as sharp. "Where will she go?" I said. "Which hospital?"

"I'll find out, sir." Hiraoka walked over to her colleagues, their faces set in identical expressions, their voices low and tone subdued.

When another pity-filled glance landed on me, I gave in to the churning waves of emotion throwing me up and down, left and right. My legs crumpled beneath me, and as I slid to the ground, burying my face in my hands, all I could think of was Logan, and what would happen to us now.

CHAPTER THREE

We buried Grace fifteen days after the accident, but it might as well have been fifteen years. It felt at least that long since we'd spoken, I'd touched her skin, heard her laugh, or listened to her read Logan's latest dog book with him.

The silence in the house had become deafening. The whole place filled with an oppressing emptiness, making it barren, utterly devoid of happiness, as if all the joy had been sucked out of the walls and carried away with the bitter winds.

The longest Grace and I had ever spent apart was a week, on the one occasion I'd made it back to England, money and time not permitting other trips. Now, at the grand old age of thirty-five, years of solitude stretched out in front of me like a wanton path to hell.

I'd been hiding in the kitchen for the last five minutes, resting my hands on the sink and staring out of the window as I listened to the hubbub from the people who'd come back to the house after the service. I closed my eyes and exhaled deeply, reminded myself it was so much worse for Logan. When my sister planted a soft, hesitant kiss on my cheek, I pretended to busy myself by rinsing a cup I'd only just washed.

"How are you holding up?" Lisa said as she rubbed my back, something she'd done when we were kids and I'd showed up in my big sister's bedroom, terrified by another nightmare.

"To be honest, I'm not entirely sure."

"Me, neither. I still can't believe it. Poor, poor Grace...and Logan. And *you*." When her swollen, big blue eyes welled up again, she turned away for a moment to wipe them. "I wish we had a finite amount of tears," she said, "because surely we'd have used them up by now."

"Have you spoken to Ivan?" I said.

"A little." She nodded, bit her lip. "I'm glad he came back."

A smile teased my lips upward, although it felt like I was wearing a Halloween mask where the holes for the eyes and mouth didn't line up properly. "Steady on, did I hear you say something positive about my best friend? That's a first."

She frowned, took a sudden interest in rearranging the already alphabetized spice rack. "I meant I'm glad he's here for you. He was about to board a flight to Texas—"

"I told him he didn't need to come back right away."

"Sure he did. He's known Grace longer than either of us. You said it yourself. You're best mates. You would've done the same."

"Would I?" I snapped, my cheery facade a crumbling old stone wall in the English countryside, thrashed and beaten down by the rain.

"Course you would. You'd have dropped everything, too," Lisa said, her attempt at defusing the tension before it mushroomed only too obvious.

"Easy to say when you're the one with the offensively large paycheck. And you'd know all about that, wouldn't you?" The muscles in my jaw worked overtime as I spat the words. These days I was ever-ready to pick a fight; fair or unfair, I didn't seem to give a shit.

Another frown crossed Lisa's face, but it disappeared in an instant when she put her arms around me, pulling me closer when she felt me resist. "Is that the best you can do, baby brother? Because you can lash out at me all you want. I'm not going anywhere."

My shoulders dropped as the desire for another argument with my sister, the person who'd done nothing but be there for me since…well, *forever*, slunk out of my chest and disappeared. "Why am I being such an asshole?" I whispered. "Honestly, I'm a total bastard to you and Ivan these days, and—"

"I don't think that," she said. "And I'll bet you anything he doesn't, either."

I looked at her, almost challenged her and called her a liar before letting it go.

"The service was lovely, wasn't it?" Lisa held up a hand before I could answer. "And I know it's bloody ridiculous to say because there shouldn't have been one in the first place."

It was true. It had been lovely, as these things went. I'd even managed to get up and say a few words without breaking down again. The sky had cleared, and by the time we'd said our final goodbyes to Grace, the sun shone, making the snow-covered trees glisten like something out of an ironic, two-faced fairy tale.

Now here we were, a few dozen people, Grace's colleagues from Ruby & Rose's Bookshop, my bosses, Ronnie and Leila, a few friends and neighbors, some people from Logan's school. All dressed in somber colors, speaking sotto voce, crowded into our little rental home with its quirky, now inappropriately jolly blue-and-orange kitchen, trays of prepackaged sandwiches and the odd homemade dish on the dining table. "Need You Now,"

Grace's favorite Lady Antebellum song, was playing softly in the background.

"I talked to Logan earlier," Lisa said. "He told me all about why dogs have wet noses. Something to do with it cooling them down, apparently."

I tried another smile, felt it fit a little better this time. "Yeah, he's still obsessed. Before Grace—" I swallowed the jagged lump in my throat "—before she left, he begged for a puppy at least five times a day."

"Poor kid. It's a shame about your allergies, but you remember how bad they were." She grabbed a dishcloth and dried the cup, stared out the window. "He seems to be handling the whole situation incredibly well."

"Better than me." I looked at my sister, studied her furrowed brow, her head tilted to one side, her thick, blond, wavy hair falling past her shoulders onto her tailored suit and slender frame. She'd driven back from New York within hours of me calling, and had refused to leave my side since, comforting Logan, helping with the arrangements, making decisions about flowers (lilies or roses), music (classical or contemporary), coffins (oak or elm) and urns (aluminum or pewter) when I couldn't speak, let alone make a coherent choice.

"He's an amazing kid," Lisa said. "Incredible."

I leaned over and peered through the kitchen doorway. Logan stood near the dining room table, from the looks of it wishing he were anywhere but there. He'd already changed into his puppy-print pajamas and held Biscuit, a four-inch, dark-brown-and-beige stuffed dog I'd given him a few years back, and which had become his forever friend. Grace had patched Biscuit up so much it barely held together. With the tatty thing firmly clenched under his arm, Logan looked even more lost and vulnerable, exactly how I felt—hollow, insignificant, like someone had scooped out my insides as if I were a jack-o'-lantern and left me on the deck to rot.

When I caught his eye, I gave him a small wave. He raised his hand, turned and walked to the front door. A few seconds later, he reappeared outside the kitchen window and sat down at the little mosaic table Grace had salvaged from a charity shop and spent hours cursing under her breath while she repaired it. As he put his head in his hands, a fresh rush of guilt coiled its way around my middle, squashing me tighter than a belt half a dozen notches too small.

I often joked I'd fallen in love with the brown-haired, green-eyed toddler a good few beats before I'd fallen for his mom. Both Grace and I considered the fact I wasn't Logan's biological dad—and had missed the first two years of his life—a mere technicality. We'd never hidden it from him, had agreed we'd be completely honest about everything. Except for the Easter Bunny, the Tooth Fairy and Santa; we weren't monsters. But now I had an awful, despicable secret I couldn't shove into the category marked "keeping childhood magic alive."

The salt. I didn't know if Logan had heard Grace remind me about it that morning, and I hadn't told him I'd forgotten, which made me a liar by omission, and a coward by default. I hadn't admitted it to anyone else, either. Not Ivan, to whom I'd regularly spilled my guts since he'd decked me with an impressive right-hook when we'd first met at the boxing club, and definitely not Lisa. I couldn't face watching the way she felt about me transform into abject disgust again, exactly the way it had when our parents had been killed. She'd denied ever thinking that their deaths had in any way been my fault, said it had never crossed her mind when I'd accused her again—in another of my drunken moments—of secretly blaming me. I disagreed with her pushback, but had kept my mouth shut from then on. Sometimes face value is your only friend.

"Josh?" Lisa's hand was on my arm. Had she been talking all this time? Had I answered? I didn't recall words coming from my mouth. Then again, I didn't remember much of the last two weeks; the lack of sleep and unbearable roller coaster of emotions had anesthetized most of my brain the way booze used to. Maybe that was why, so far at least, I'd resisted the urge to drink.

"Do you want to rest?" she said. "I can tell everyone to leave. They'll understand."

I shook my head. "No, I can't sleep."

At least that was true, and Lisa being there was a relief, and I was grateful to her, Ivan, whom I'd last seen talking to Ronnie in the living room, Mrs. Banks, who'd checked in on me daily, and everybody else who'd dropped off cards, flowers and enough casseroles to last until summer. But, and this made my selfish prick levels skyrocket to never-before-seen levels, at times the sympathy was overwhelming, stifling—a thousand woolly blankets piled on top of me in a heat wave.

All I wanted was for everything to go back to normal, for Grace to burst in through the front door with a bottle of her favorite nonalcoholic margarita mix in her hand, a smile on her face and another cheesy movie suggestion we'd pretend-argue over, a fight she always won.

I rubbed my hands over the five o'clock shadow. Until that morning my cheeks had no longer been covered in the trendy stubble Grace found "hot," but a prickly mess she'd have bugged me to shave, or at the very least questioned why I was impersonating a hedgehog. Even after I'd got dressed, I'd still barely recognized myself in the mirror. The only suit I owned hung off me as if I'd borrowed it from my granddad. My hair needed a cut in a bad way—I'd long abandoned trying to stop it from sticking up at gravity-defying angles—and its mud-brown color

looked dull and faded, the graying at my temples more promi-
nent, or distinguished, if Lisa was to be believed.

The worst thing was my eyes, which Grace had always said
were her favorite feature. They'd morphed from an amber-
come-chestnut color, to watery, bloodshot spheres. It was a
wonder Logan hadn't darted out of the house yet, yelling at the
top of his lungs that he was living with the bogeyman.

"Hey," Lisa said. "Are you sure you don't want to lie down?"

"I can't," I said. "If I do, I won't stop thinking about stuff.
I...I just don't know how I'm going to cope. What's going to
happen to us now and... I'm sorry I—"

"Don't apologize," she whispered. "Really, I mean it."

"I need a bit of air," I muttered and pushed past her, escaping outside through the back door. I closed my eyes, filled my
lungs with the crisp, mid-March breeze, silently pleading with
Grace to appear, tell me what to do, and an instant later, a familiar hand slipped into mine.

CHAPTER FOUR

"Logan." I knelt down and put my arms around all forty-five pounds of him—he'd always been on the skinny side—and squeezed hard. He smelled of gummy bears and cupcakes, with a tiny hint of dirt, in my mind exactly how a seven-year-old boy should. When I let him go, his bottom lip wobbled, stretching across his teeth as he spoke.

"I want Mom back."

I pulled him closer, worried we'd shatter into pieces if I hugged him any harder, bounce off the deck like marbles, scatter all over the backyard and disappear into the frozen grass.

"I know, kiddo," I whispered as I stroked his hair. "I want her back, too."

The pain rushing through me and the need to appear strong fought one another as if they were a pair of heavyweight champions. Thankfully, this time, the latter won. I rubbed his arms with my hands. "Why didn't you put on a jacket? Aren't you cold?" Stupid, irrelevant questions, all things considered, but Logan was gallant in his response.

"Not much," he said quietly, shaking his head and shivering all the same. "I don't want to be inside anymore. Everyone keeps asking if I'm okay and they pat my head. I'm not a German shepherd, or a Great Dane, or—"

"A poodle?" I offered.

He sighed. "Definitely not a poodle. Mom thinks they look weird."

I managed half a smile, my mouth still not quite getting there. "People do it to me, too."

Logan's smooth forehead turned into a crinkly frown. "They pat your head?"

This time a small laugh made it all the way out from between my lips, a sound I'd all but forgotten. "No, they keep asking if I'm okay." I shrugged. "I tell them I'm fine…"

"But it's a lie?" Logan's eyes went wide with mutual conspiracy.

"A complete lie."

"I lie to them, too," he whispered, dropping his chin to his chest, crossing his arms tight. If he made himself any smaller, he'd risk falling through the cracks in the deck. "But you and Mom said I shouldn't. You said it's bad."

"I don't think she'd mind about that little fib, though," I said as he burrowed under my arm and snuggled up to my chest. "I don't think she'd be mad at all."

"Do you think she's mad because I ran away?" he said. "When you came to get me?"

I kissed the top of his head. "Nope. I told you, it's all forgotten. It's fine."

Not a little fib, because it hadn't been fine at all. After Grace's accident I'd driven to Logan's school, fighting back the urge to scream and shout in the truck, trying to calm myself and prepare what I'd say, rehearse it in my mind. Pitiful, because how the hell do you prepare for that? My adult brain could barely comprehend what had happened, and now I had to tell a child? There was nothing I could possibly say to make the situation any better, and with a glance in the rearview mirror I'd taken in my blotchy face that had aged ten years in about an hour. Logan was a smart kid. One look at me and he'd know.

I'd pulled up at the school, rang the obligatory front entrance buzzer and waited, my fingers tapping an indecipherable rhythm on my thighs. The first snowflakes fell as the wind lashed my body, blew my jacket open, which I made no attempt to close. Glacial temperatures had little effect on the grieving. I was already numb from the inside.

"Hello, Josh." Vickey *with an e* Longo, the formidable school secretary, greeted me with a smile when I walked in, but it soon withered when she took a second look at my face. "Are you alright? My goodness, what's wrong?"

She cried when I told her, fat drops spilling over her immaculately made-up cheeks as she whispered how she'd talked to Grace just the other day about helping out with the upcoming book fair, and how Grace, as always, had been happy to oblige. "You know how she loves volunteering here, and her books," Vickey said, and cried some more.

The principal came out of his office, too, Mr. Searle, an impossibly tall, skinny, bald man, with an Adam's apple you could cut yourself on. Soon more people surrounded us, telling me how sorry they were. The only thing I could say in return was, "Can you please call Logan?"

"Dad!" He ran up and threw his arms around my waist when he arrived in the office, knocking the wind out of me as his head thudded into my belly. He didn't notice the small crowd standing around. Didn't detect what I knew they were all silently thinking, what I'd thought whenever I'd read about similar tragedies, or seen them on the news. *Thank God that's not us.* They'd all hug their loved ones longer that night, maybe not argue about whose turn it was to set the table, or who'd forgotten to pick up their socks.

"Am I going home already?" Logan's eyes lit up. "Mom didn't

say. Are you taking me for ice cream?" He'd have eaten frozen treats while sitting at the North Pole on an iceberg if given the chance. I'd joked about him being half bear, called him "my little cub," and he'd replied, if anything, he was half dog. I swallowed hard as I remembered Grace laughing, saying, "In that case I'll put some dog treats in your lunch bag tomorrow."

After Vickey had ushered us into her office and left us alone, I knelt in front of Logan and opened my mouth. All my words stubbornly remained at the back of my throat, bashful children refusing to come out, so I pulled him in for another hug.

"Da-*aad*. What's wrong?" Logan tugged my sleeve when I let him go, poked my chest with a fingertip, pushing harder when I didn't answer, his voice going up a notch. "Dad? Dad?"

I told him. Watched as his young brain connected the dots, his eyes widening at first, then his brow knitting together as he listened. The pain carved itself into his face, like nails into soft wood, and I couldn't breathe as I watched the transformation from happy and innocent to grieving and despairing child. Logan threw his arms around me and sobbed, quietly at first, his desperate howls becoming louder, his words an indecipherable jumble of syllables and tears.

I held him, whispered "Everything's going to be okay, I promise Logan, shh, shh, I promise, I've got you, I've got you" over and over until he pushed me away, bolted out of Vickey's office, down the corridor and out of a side door, with me following behind. For a skinny seven-year-old he was fast, had already been hailed one to watch in track and field, and by the time I got outside, he'd disappeared.

We'd searched for ten minutes, yelling his name, shouting for him to come out. Vickey, Mr. Searle and some teachers went through the classrooms in case he'd sneaked back inside, while another group of us hunted the playground.

Finally I located Logan underneath a bush at the far end of the grounds, his lips and fingertips a slight shade of blue. It took me five minutes to talk him into taking my coat, and another five until he came inside, by which time our teeth played their own clattering symphony, and we were too exhausted to do anything but go home.

Logan slept in my bed for over a week, wouldn't leave my side, but then he'd insisted on going back to school the day before the funeral. I'd told him he could stay home as long as he wanted, although secretly I'd been a little relieved. I was ashamed to admit I couldn't afford to take much more time off; we needed the money. Lunch made, bag packed, and he'd got on the bus before turning around and asking me if I was sure I'd be okay at home alone. In my book, that made him the bravest person I knew.

"Want a hot chocolate?" I said to him now, pulling him close.

"If I have one," Logan said, his huge eyes reminding me so much of Grace's it almost took my breath away, "will it make me feel better?"

"For a moment, perhaps," I said. "Maybe if I add marshmallows and chocolate sprinkles. And if you go to the den and close the door, you can watch TV and avoid more head patting. I'll come and find you when it's ready."

Logan hugged me and whispered a thank you in my ear, before disappearing into the house. I gave myself a few seconds, walked around to the front door, buying time to prepare myself to face everyone inside. It turned out people were ready to leave, so I saw everyone out, repeating *thank you, thank you for coming, yes, she was a wonderful person, yes, it's such a tragedy*, until it made me want to yell at them to get the fuck out of my sodding house. The advantage of everybody's pity was that I could be the rudest wanker on the planet, and it was perfectly acceptable. At least today. What happened tomorrow, and every day after, would be a different story.

CHAPTER FIVE

Ronnie patted my shoulder on his way out, but his sister, Leila, who everyone knew was the real boss of their company, wasn't quite ready to leave. "Again, we're so sorry for your loss," she said, half a beat later adding, "Can we have a quick talk about Monday's project?"

"I don't think we should do this now, Leila," Ronnie muttered, shooting me an apologetic look before feigning an interest in his shoes. Not his usual pair of mud-encrusted, steel-toed American Worker boots, but shiny brown loafers that made me wonder if he might try to sell me insurance. "Can't it wait?"

"We're already behind schedule," she said, and I almost expected her to chastise me for the inconvenience of Grace's death, but she smiled tightly, adjusting the cuffs of her navy blue suit. She didn't look comfortable out of her work jeans, either. "Ronnie will text you the details of where we need you Monday morning, okay? It's a straightforward job, but I need to know if I can count on you. Otherwise I'll get someone else."

By now I was used to Leila and Ronnie Thompson, twins and owners of L&R Homebuilding & Landscaping Services.

When I'd joined their team as a general laborer a few years ago, I'd asked why they hadn't called their company Thompson Twins in honor of the '80s pop group. Even hummed a few bars of "Hold Me Now." Ronnie had laughed, Leila hadn't. Later, after she'd left, he swore she'd ripped any sense of humor clean out of herself while they were still "womb mates," before trying to get to his, too. As far as dominant twin theories went, Leila took hers to beyond another level.

"I'm sure it'll be fine," I said.

"Great, I'll text you tomorrow." Ronnie clapped me on the shoulder again and scooted his sister out the door, closing it behind them.

The living room was empty now, and I took a few moments to savor the peace and quiet before remembering why everybody had been there in the first place. I made my way to the kitchen, and heard Mrs. Banks's voice as I got closer. She was a sweet lady, but had a tendency to overstay her welcome and break into rambling monologues if she had a drink and the chance, and even though Grace and I hadn't seen her much lately, she always knew our business, anyway.

I stopped outside the doorway and peered in, trying to get a glimpse of the victims Mrs. Banks had managed to corner. One of them was Ivan, who stood right next to Lisa, a sure indication of how miserable she felt. Under normal circumstances she'd never have let him anywhere near her. Ever since I'd introduced them she thought he was, and I quote, "A bigheaded Scandinavian tree who thinks he's a Nordic god."

As I watched them leaning against the kitchen counter with generously filled glasses of wine and juice in their hands, a surge of anger shot from my toes right up to my crown, red-hot lightning flowing through my veins. I'd been to a few wakes in my time, enough to know people ate and drank as a way to celebrate a life. But it felt inappropriate. The bottles of cheap wine

I'd vowed I wouldn't touch a sign of disrespect toward Grace. She deserved champagne, barrels of Veuve Clicquot, not the low-cost pseudo-plonk I'd bought in bulk despite my sister offering to pay for something fancier, and the promise she'd take what was left with her when she went home.

I tried to clear my mind, thought about disappearing upstairs as Lisa had suggested, but remembered my promise of a hot chocolate.

"Well, I think he's a marvelous man," I heard Mrs. Banks say, and I leaned in.

"He most definitely is," Ivan replied, his entire body, all six foot six of pure muscle, nodding in agreement.

"He was outside for hours with Logan last fall," Mrs. Banks continued. "Taught him how to fly his big kite. It was such a pleasure to watch."

Ah, so I was the "marvelous man." I remembered the day clearly, Logan running as fast as his toothpick legs would carry him. Up and down the street, over and over, until Mother Nature herself had rolled her eyes and taken pity on us, sending a gust of wind, pulling Logan's purple-and-white-checkered kite so hard, he'd almost become airborne. It was one of my favorite memories, another I'd stuffed into my full-to-the-brim, but now shattered heart.

"You'd never know he isn't Logan's father," Mrs. Banks said, her voice low.

It was something she'd commented on before, to Grace and myself, probably anyone who'd listen. I knew she meant it as a compliment. Mrs. Banks wouldn't have been capable of saying anything nasty if she'd jabbed herself in the eye with a pointy poker.

"He really is a marvelous man," she said again, her head bobbing. "They were such a wonderful couple."

"The very best," Lisa said, and I suddenly recalled Grace joking about Mrs. Banks fancying me, how she'd looked at my butt as I'd reached for the pasta when we ran into her at the grocery store one day. I had to say, the flattery had been relative.

"Did I tell you about when I first met Grace?" Mrs. Banks said, her cheeks flushed, her eyes slightly glazed. She didn't wait for an answer, and I stayed hidden in case she stopped talking about Grace if she saw me. "It was November… Which day was it? Let me think… It was…hmm…never mind. But the weather was horrific. Rain for weeks on end, the kind where you wonder if you'll wake up with your bed floating down the river." She chuckled briefly, pressed on. "I knew someone was moving in because the girl who lived here was subletting cheap as chips to a friend of a friend of a friend while she went backpacking around Australia."

"That's nice…" Lisa said, but her expression told me she was wishing Mrs. Banks would get to the point. It had been a long day for all of us, and from the bags under her eyes, Lisa looked about ready to collapse.

"You think so?" Mrs. Banks said. "Never saw the appeal myself. Too many creepy-crawlies." Ivan and Lisa nodded politely, and she continued, "She never came back, the girl who lived here, I mean. Met a German fella at Ayers Rock so Grace took over the lease in the end. Anyway…" She finished her wine and held the glass out to Ivan, who dutifully refilled it, but only quarter-way. I licked my lips, closed my eyes for a moment, reminding myself of my long-standing promise not to do something stupid.

"November eighteenth," Mrs. Banks said with a snap of her fingers. "That's when it was. My grandson's fifth birthday. How could I forget? I'd finished speaking with him on the phone when I saw Grace. Poor girl was drenched trying to get something out of her car."

Lisa fake-coughed, glanced at her watch. "Well, I think it's time to—"

"When I rushed outside to help, I realized she couldn't get the baby seat out," Mrs. Banks said, as if she hadn't heard, or decided to ignore Lisa's objection. "We didn't know the new tenant had a baby, but I didn't mind. This old street needed some youth and, my goodness, was he ever cute. All chubby cheeks and big eyes, so adorable. But Grace seemed lost. My gosh, she held Logan as if he were a bag of boiled potatoes."

She must have seen Lisa's and Ivan's raised eyebrows because she quickly added, "Some of us take to motherhood instantly, you see, and with Grace, well, there was a little delay, is all, it happens sometimes. And she was a wonderful mother. Truly."

I'd heard enough, was about to step inside the kitchen, but Mrs. Banks's next question hit me as if it were a torpedo. "What do you suppose will happen to Logan now?"

"What do you mean?" Lisa said.

"Well, I wonder about Logan's real father. Won't he—"

"Josh *is* Logan's father, Mrs. Banks," Ivan said. "He's—"

"I mean biologically," she replied, "because—"

Within a heartbeat I was in the room. The three of them froze before they looked at each other—not me—the guilt of gossiper's tongue spreading across their faces in various shades of red and pink.

"Need to get Logan a drink." I crossed over to the cupboard and pulled out his favorite mug, a puppy face complete with pointy ears and shiny black nose. As I dug around for the cocoa, Mrs. Banks broke the stifling silence by mentioning something about the weather.

I turned around, slammed the tin on the counter. "To ensure there's no doubt in anybody's mind," I said as the flush on Mrs. Banks's cheeks deepened. "Logan's my son."

She exhaled sharply. "I'm sorry, Josh. I didn't mean—"

"Grace knew if anything ever happened to her I'd look after him," I said, cutting her off more sharply than she deserved. "He's my family. My *son*. And nobody's going to take him away from me. *Ever.*"

My chest heaved as Mrs. Banks made her excuses and Ivan shuffled her out of the kitchen. When Lisa put her arms around me, held me tight, I rested my head on her shoulder, trying not to cry, right up until Logan came looking for his drink.

CHAPTER SIX

The house now empty of guests, and the steady din of voices gone quiet, Logan surrendered to his exhaustion, letting Ivan carry him to bed—providing the hall light stayed on and the bedroom door was left ajar. Since Grace had gone, Logan screamed like a crazed demon whenever he woke up in the middle of the night, engulfed in the dark. The first time it happened I'd leaped out of bed and sprinted to his room before I was properly awake. My small left toe had gone an eggplant shade of purple, and bent slightly to the left from where I'd whacked it on the door frame.

After Logan had settled in bed, Lisa, Ivan and I went to the den. Some mindless reality show with overtly plastic people played on the television with the sound turned down, but none of us could be bothered to retrieve the remote and switch it off completely. I disguised my yawns, rubbed my eyes when neither of them were looking. Going upstairs would end in a repeat performance of me flopping around, impersonating a fish on a pier, periodically staring at the clock, wishing it would move faster before remembering I had a whole lot less to get up for in the morning.

"When are you heading to Texas?" I asked Ivan in an attempt to stay awake.

He waved a hand, and in his deep, gravelly voice said, "I canceled the trip."

"You didn't have to—"

"Relax, pal, not everything's about you, you know." He winked. "Harlan agreed I can manage everything from the office. I'll go later, if I need to. Besides, we've got a new client here that's merging with a big local company, so I'll be traveling less for a while."

I sighed. "I appreciate it. Thanks for being here."

"Wouldn't have it any other way. Someone's got to watch out for you." Ivan put his paddle-sized hands behind his head and stretched out his legs. He was so big he could bench press me if he wanted, had threatened to do so once at the boxing club when he'd been on a mission to impress a girl. I'd refused. He thought it was because I had no desire to become a human gym prop, which was true, but I'd also heard the girl whisper "dumb jocks" under her breath as she'd walked by.

"Okay if I stay here tonight?" he said, and I nodded.

"I'll stay, too," Lisa said. "You take the den, Ivan, and I'll bunk with my baby brother. But I have to go to the office in the morning. It'll be quiet over the weekend so I can catch up. You don't mind, do you, Josh?"

I'd known their company would end soon. Life went on, people had things to do, including Lisa. Out of the two of us, my sister had always been the brainy one, the grounded one, the one who had her shit together. Unsurprisingly she'd excelled academically, started her own architectural firm, won prizes and become the latest darling of the cutting-edge design world. I loved her for it, at times hated her, too, in the way only siblings understand.

I pulled my shoulder blades together in attempt to loosen the knots in my back that made me feel about three times my age. "What time are you heading out?"

"After breakfast. I promised the munchkin I'd make waffles," Lisa said, exchanging a look of concern with Ivan. "Uh, do you think you'll be okay on your own for a few days?"

I considered the question for a moment. Logan would be at school after the weekend, and I had to work. Hopefully Ronnie would arrange my schedule and keep the jobs simple so I could ease myself back in after two weeks away. I looked at Lisa. "I'll be fine."

"You could stay with me for a while," she offered. "I've got the spare room."

"Or with me," Ivan said. "I'd be happy to put you both up."

I shook my head. "Thanks, but all our stuff's here, and it would be a nightmare getting Logan to school on time."

"He's seven. Does it really matter?" Ivan said.

"Routine." I tried to keep the what-do-you-know tone out of my voice. I'd felt the same not that long ago—nothing easier than parenting someone else's kids. "Routine's the best thing for both of us right now."

"Hold that thought," Lisa said, getting up. "Back in a sec."

"You're not off to the loo again, are you?" I said with a grin.

"Shut up, Dad." Lisa laughed and disappeared into the hallway.

"I nicknamed her Baby Bladder once." I smiled at the memory. "Dad would tell her to go before we left the house and I swear, every single time, she'd ask him to stop within ten minutes. He always said she was…wait for it…taking the piss."

Ivan grinned. "Somehow I don't think she'll appreciate you telling me that."

When Lisa came back she sat down again, but kept shifting in her seat, biting her thumbnail, a telltale sign she was about to say something someone wouldn't be happy about.

"What is it?" I asked, looking from her to Ivan, unrealistically hoping whatever she was thinking had nothing to do with me at all.

"I'm really sorry about what happened in the kitchen, with Mrs. Banks…"

Ivan nodded. "That *real dad* thing was way out of line."

I took a deep breath. "Her timing was shit, but she didn't know I could hear and she didn't mean any harm. Besides… she has a point, doesn't she? I mean, I'm not—"

"Let's not talk about this now," Lisa said.

"Why not? Let's face it, I'm not his legal guardian, am I?" I snapped, my hot-air balloon temper swelling.

Lisa knew the warning signs all too well. She'd rarely heeded them when we were kids—much to Mom and Dad's despair—but the way she now looked around the room, anywhere other than at me, sitting on the edge of her seat as if she wanted to lunge for the door, I could tell my sister was actually flustered.

"Maybe we should change the subject?" she said.

"Or I should speak to a lawyer." I pressed my fingertips into my thighs, brought my temper back from rolling boil to gentle simmer. "What do you think?"

"I think I'm a lawyer," Ivan said.

"Yeah, but you do corporate law, not family," Lisa said. "No offense, but I think Josh should find out his rights about Logan from someone who's specialized."

"It can't be that complicated, can it?" I said. "I've been his dad for five years, and I—"

"Didn't arrange anything with Grace," Lisa said quickly. "Not legally."

"Lisa," Ivan said, his tone far more gentle than I'd have expected. "We really don't need to get into it. The funeral was today. He doesn't have to—"

"But she's right," I said. "I do need to find out where I stand."

Lisa looked at me. "Don't get mad, okay, but I made a few calls. Without any kind of legal guardianship, Logan's dad—"

"Who cares about him?" I threw my hands up. "The guy's never been around. Hell, Grace didn't even think he gave her his real name."

"But her parents—"

"She didn't speak to them in years, Lisa." I crossed my arms, sat back in my chair. "You know what the situation was, what kind of people they are. Grace told you last year. We talked about it right here, in this very room, remember?"

Lisa's words were less urgent now. "I know, I know."

"Have you tried to find them?" Ivan said. "Her parents, I mean."

"No luck yet," I said. "I've Googled a ton and made phone calls, but so far I've come up with nothing. I didn't exactly have much to go on."

"But how will you tell them about Grace?" he said.

"I don't *know*." I took a deep breath, reminding myself neither Ivan nor Lisa were the enemy. "I'll have to keep looking."

"Or don't bother," Lisa said.

"I can't do that," I said. "She's their daughter."

"That's right," she said. "But I'm petrified they'll want Logan when they meet him."

I rubbed my eyes, wishing they'd stop stinging so badly, knowing the remedy was sleep, something I hadn't done properly in two weeks, didn't think I'd ever do properly again. "Honestly, that scares the shit out of me, too," I said. "All the more reason for me to look into guardianship, right?"

Ivan put his fingers in a steeple under his chin, resting his elbows on his thighs in a let's-pretend-I'm-a-shrink-not-a-lawyer sort of way. For whatever reason, it really pissed me off. "Maybe you should—"

"Hey," I muttered. "I know I said I'd discuss it, but can we stop for now?"

"Sure," Lisa said quietly. "But you know we're just trying to help."

"Well, thanks, Captain Obvious." I shut my eyes, exhaled for a few moments, finally holding my hands up in surrender. "Sorry, sorry. I really don't mean to be such a huge shit."

"No problem, man," Ivan said. "You're not being a huge shit."

"Maybe a small turd," Lisa said with a smirk. "Sometimes."

"Thanks, sis. I love you, too." My lips twitched upward for an instant but collapsed again. The smallest of grins made me feel like a traitor to Grace. I dug my nails into the armrest, felt the pudgy stuffing bulge beneath my fingertips. Fight or flight. *Fight or flight.*

"It's late," I said, pushing myself up.

Lisa reached out and grabbed my hand, her skin warm, her touch reminding me how alone I was. I pulled my fingers away.

"Night, Josh," she said.

Without looking at them I walked out of the den, throwing what I knew was anything but a casual "See you in the morning" over my shoulder, and headed into the hallway, stopping when I heard my sister's low but urgent whisper.

"I really hope he speaks to someone," Lisa said. "Sooner rather than later. Will you recommend someone from your firm?"

"Of course I will," Ivan said, "but give him time to breathe. The last thing he wants is—"

"No, the last thing he wants is for Logan's dad or Grace's

parents to show up and battle him for custody. Because we both know he could very well lose."

My intestines turned themselves into a knot, as if they were a mass of Christmas lights taken down too hastily and shoved in a box with the promise of doing a better job next season. I had to sort out the guardianship; I wanted to. Becoming Logan's dad had been something I'd dreamed of since I'd met Grace, but now it also meant accepting our lives had changed forever, that she'd never come home, she really was gone.

I headed upstairs, pretended to be asleep when Lisa sneaked in after a while. Hours later sleep still hadn't come. Those tangled Christmas lights had moved north, became multicolored fireworks going off in my head. They accepted to be silenced only once I'd crept to the kitchen and guzzled a pint of ice-cold milk while trying to ignore the open bottle of Chianti on the counter, and staring at Grace's photograph, wishing she'd come home.

CHAPTER SEVEN

Sunday disappeared amid a domestic blur. Logan needed help with his math homework, a mountain of dishes had to be washed, the food from the wake frozen, the booze thrown away, clothes folded, dust bunnies sucked into the depths of the vacuum cleaner… It all had to be taken care of, whether I wanted to or not, but at least it occupied a large part of my brain.

Well before I was ready, Monday morning arrived. Time to get up, go to work and rejoin a world that had carried on as normal, and looked exactly the same, regardless of the fact every bit of our tiny universe had imploded.

While Logan was still in bed I made his lunch, poured myself a cup of tea and pulled out my phone. I skimmed through the contacts, muttering some expletives when I misspelled the name, my ridiculous impatience working me up some more. These days I had everything at the touch of a button, a flick of a screen, and it still wasn't fast enough. "Shut up, Josh," I whispered, hit dial and continued reprimanding myself for being a middle-aged fart a decade too early. As I prepared to leave a message, a real, live voice answered.

"Harlan Gingold speaking."

Grace had once described his name as "the most perfect, lawyer-y name ever" and joked he should rent it to *Law & Order* for huge royalties. The name had made me smile ever since—until now. This was something else, another little detail that would never feel the same.

"Harlan, it's Josh Andersen," I said. "How are you?"

"Josh. I'm well, thank you. I'm so sorry I couldn't make it to the funeral, but I hope the flowers arrived. It's such a tragedy. Grace was delightful, simply lovely."

"Yes, they did, and she was. Thank you." I clambered for more appropriate words. Accepting people's sympathies still made me feel inadequate, as if saying *thank you* wasn't enough, made me appear ungrateful somehow. I looked at my watch: seven fifteen. "Sorry for calling you this early."

"Don't worry. I've been at the office for an hour. Besides, you know what I always say—lawyers are like the fire department. Handy to know how to get hold of them. Hopefully—"

"Never required in an emergency," I said. "I remember."

Harlan paused for a moment. "In that case, should I presume your call isn't about the pool house extension?"

"No, it's about Logan, I—"

"Is he alright?"

"Yes, he's fine, but, well, you said in your card I could call if I needed anything…"

"Anything at all. Tell me how I can help."

"Well, the trouble is, uh, financially speaking, I don't know if I can afford—"

"Please, Josh. Don't worry about that. Tell me what you need."

I exhaled, hoping the force would decrease the weight on my shoulders. "I've been thinking about my rights for guardianship, or adoption. Would you have time to talk me through the options?" It felt more urgent than ever now, my laissez-faire attitude from a couple of nights ago long gone. Lisa would be happy. "As soon as possible, please."

He tapped on his keyboard, clicked his tongue. "I'll rearrange my schedule and meet you today at noon, if you're amenable? Although it can't be for more than thirty minutes at most, but it'll give us a chance to get started."

I thought about work, decided I'd duck out for an hour. Ronnie would understand, and Leila didn't have to know. "Yes, please. Thank you very much. Should I bring anything?"

"Well, we'll definitely need Logan's birth certificate but—"

"His birth certificate?"

"Yes, that'll be an absolute must."

I rubbed my chin, unsure where the document might be, but certain Grace had kept it somewhere safe. "I'll do some light digging."

"No rush. I'll have Shirley email you a list of the other items we'll require," Harlan said. "Don't worry about bringing them in today. I understand how these things take time. We'll start discussing scenarios. I'll see you at noon?"

"Yes. Thanks again. I'll see you later."

I hung up and looked out of the kitchen window. Logan sat on the swing set he'd helped me build last summer, his boot-clad feet scraping the ground, head bent forward, Biscuit stuffed under his arm. He must have slipped outside while I was on the phone. How hadn't I heard him open the door? Even from this distance I could tell his cheeks were pink from the cold, from crying, or both. Either way it wasn't good. I knocked on the window, but Logan didn't raise his head and moved his shoulders closer to his knees.

I grabbed my boots and jacket, opened the back door, the crisp grass crackling under my weight. When I sat down on the swing next to Logan I kept quiet, a trick Grace used, the theory being he'd talk when he was ready.

"Why did Mom leave?" he said a minute later, staring ahead of him, his voice tiny.

"I wish I had an answer, kiddo." I pulled my jacket tighter, tried to stop the wind from going directly for my soul. "She wasn't supposed to, and she didn't want to, I promise."

"But she fell."

"It was an acci—"

"She's so *dumb*!"

"Logan, she was—"

"*Fucking* dumb! I *hate* her!" He glared at me, challenging me to say something about his choice of words—ones I'd never heard him say before, didn't even realize he knew. When I didn't reply he leaped off the swing, stomped to the door and yanked it open. "I *hate* you, too!"

"Logan!"

He stood still, his hand on the door handle, shoulders rising up and down with every fast breath. I said his name again, but the exhaustion in my voice made the word come out as a pathetic protest, traveling no farther than my nose. I wanted to reprimand him, tell him to apologize to Grace and me, but when he turned around and I saw the hurt in his eyes, my anger pooled at the bottom of my boots and sank into the ground.

"What?" He raised his chin, narrowed his eyes in another act of defiance.

Seven thirty. My energy reserves for the day already spent. "You need to eat breakfast."

"I'm not hungry!" He disappeared into the house, the door banging shut behind him.

My grip on the swing tightened. I was ridiculously unprepared for this, for the entire situation. Anyone could see I was about as well equipped as a Formula One driver pulling up to the starting line in a soapbox.

I sat in the cold, gently moved back and forth until my legs protested that they'd stay bent at the knees until summer if I didn't get up. It wasn't until the sugar-dust snowflakes settled on my boots that I finally went inside, where I found Logan curled up in the den, fast asleep with Biscuit and Grace's photograph wrapped in his arms.

CHAPTER EIGHT

When Logan came to the kitchen twenty minutes later, he sat down at the table without saying a word. After a bowl of cereal, he worked his way through two pieces of peanut-buttered toast, rubbing Biscuit's threadbare ear between his index finger and thumb, something he hadn't done since he was five.

I didn't mention what had happened outside, fully aware that made me a chicken. Then again, and although it had been a while since I'd attended school, I still remembered getting to class, fuming from something that had happened at home— Lisa hiding my left shoe, Mom asking me for the twentieth time if I'd done my homework, Dad telling me to leave my sister alone and stop snapping at Mom—and it usually ended with me in some kind of playground brawl I'd started simply because I was pissed.

So I said nothing to Logan, and except for the sound of crushing toast between his teeth he made no noise at all. When I couldn't stand it any longer, we engaged in a dance of placated attitudes, watching our manners, being overly polite, desperately pretending everything was fine.

Would you like more milk, Logan?

Yes, please.

With chocolate?

Yes, thank you.

You're very welcome.

It was so well coordinated and smooth, I expected someone to jump out and present us with an Emmy for outstanding choreography. Grace would have called me a "typical man," said I was stuffing the feelings to the bottom of my gut, not letting any of them out. She wouldn't have been far wrong, except I knew if I gave in to my emotions, there was a high probability I'd never make it out of the door unless someone scraped me off the kitchen tiles and molded me back together again, the cracks and repairs visible for everyone to see.

I put the milk in the fridge, for the first time registering the bare shelves, and made a mental note to go shopping, buy fresh food I couldn't face preparing, let alone eating. When I turned around, I caught Logan looking at me, his eyes shiny with tears. I walked over, hugged him and whispered, "I love you, kiddo," and blinked hard when he said it back.

After I'd waved him off on the bus, I decided to risk being a few minutes late for Ronnie and locate the birth certificate. Harlan said it wasn't urgent, but I wanted to get things moving. Back in the den I sat at the desk, traced a finger over Grace's writing on a pink love note she'd hidden in my lunch bag, and which I'd stuck on the computer screen.

ILU, Josh.

Now, forever and always.

Grace xoxoxoxo

As I touched each letter, every *x* and *o*, I hoped some of her soul would somehow flow up through my fingertips and straight to my heart. For the thousandth time I thought how we'd never have the opportunity to say goodbye. No chance of whispering a final *I love you*. Grace's last words to me, which she'd called out as I'd left that morning, were, "Don't worry about the garbage. I've got the day off. I'll take it out." No hidden meaning there. Nothing would ever give me any kind of comfort, or make me think, *At least I got to say how I felt one last time*. Her last words to me only represented the stark reality of life, and how quickly it could all be snatched away. I shifted in my seat, made my brain move, too, as I looked around.

We were total organizational opposites, Grace and I. She, meticulous and neat, binders and folders color-coded, carefully labeled, her financial history that went back exactly five years. Me, piles of old and new receipts in no particular order, barely held together with giant bulldog clips, haphazardly stuffed into the bottom drawer of our battered, old wooden desk. I could have pretended there was a system to my chaos, but how I'd ever located anything Grace needed without sending in a professional search party—fully equipped with shovels, axes and headlamps—remained a mystery to both of us.

Two minutes into my quest and I was ready to cry victory when I opened the binder labeled Personal Docs, immediately locating Logan's up-to-date immunization records from Dr. Minhas, and a birth certificate.

"Yes!" I said, but dropping my fist when I saw it was Grace's, not Logan's, and despite riffling through the rest of the binder, I came up empty-handed. Logan's birth certificate wasn't the kind of document Grace would leave anywhere. Knowing her, she'd have kept them both together, especially considering how particular she was. I looked at my watch, set myself a fifteen-minute time limit and pressed on.

I turned the pages of Grace's files and notebooks. Rooted

through cupboards and shelves. Stopped when I located an old, crinkly paper bag, tucked away at the very back of the cupboard behind a Tupperware of old maps and a stack of Grace's ancient, dusty cassette tapes, which hadn't moved since we'd met. I emptied the bag on the floor, pushed the bits of torn-up paper and an old Christmas card away and stared at the photographs I'd never seen before, or knew existed.

They were terrible quality, grainy and dog-eared, printed on cheap paper. There was no particular order to them, either, half a dozen baby pictures shoved together. I leafed through them, soaked in Logan's toothy grin, him sitting in his high chair with a fist full of blueberries, taking what must have been some of his first wobbly steps and him crawling on the floor. I frowned, wondered why Grace had never shared them with me, but was running out of time. I opened the Christmas card, cursing as the glitter from the red-and-green candy cane fell into my lap and stuck to my fingers.

Dear Grace,

We think of you often and wish you the happiest of holidays.

Love, Mom & Dad xxx
PS. Here's our new number, please call.

This was it, my chance to tell Grace's parents what had happened. More important, an opportunity to connect with someone from her past, people who knew her years before I did. So what if they didn't get along when she was alive? They'd have anecdotes to share, memories I could borrow, a restorative glue to cover my heart. And I needed that glue.

Before I could change my mind, I hastily dialed the number and waited, holding my breath. Instead of Grace's mom or dad picking up, an automatic message kicked in, telling me the line was no longer in service, which meant neither the card, nor the number, were recent.

My fifteen minutes were long up, and after all that, despite the sea of paper debris that made the room look as if a paper-hating burglar had busted in, I'd made no progress. If anything, I'd been catapulted back to the beginning, sailing past square one, and well beyond that, too.

CHAPTER NINE

By now I was seriously behind. I reluctantly gave up my search, fired off an apologetic text to Ronnie about being late on my first day back and drove to the address he'd sent. It was a street in a part of town with nothing but McMansions, each driveway built for a multitude of brand-new, shiny vehicles. We'd done the remodel of the client's master bedroom two winters ago, but Ronnie had said they no longer approved of the shade of gray they'd chosen for their carpet, and wanted it replaced—all five hundred square feet of it—with another, almost identical.

As I parked the truck, I wondered what it must be like, when money was no object. It made me envious, sure, and it also felt as if a giant magnifying glass was being held up to all of my failings. It was my own problem. Grace had never cared about my lack of qualifications, or been particularly interested in money. She loved working at Ruby & Rose's, her favorite part when she turned yet another reluctant kid into an avid reader, saw them come back, excited to devour more of the intricate worlds and unforgettable characters she'd introduced them to. She'd run the shop for a couple of years now, and her job had paid okay. Like so many, we managed between the two of us, although "managing" had never been my intention, certainly not when I was growing up.

I'd had visions of grandeur for my career, plans long abandoned since they literally went down the drain with the booze. While I was smart enough to understand money didn't buy you happiness, I also couldn't imagine how it would possibly hurt during shitty times such as these.

Truck parked and locked, I walked to the front steps, slowing when it dawned on me the Chevy Silverado on the left side of the driveway belonged to Leila. The job was basic, and I hoped she wouldn't stick around all day, or, better still, maybe Ronnie was inside because he'd borrowed her truck.

I'd never quite warmed to the Thompson Twins. While Leila had an incredible knack for design, a great business head and could sweet-talk the most nervous of customers, as soon as she spoke to her employees, she transformed into Cruella de Vil. On the plus side, she and Ronnie made sure my hours were consistent, and when the landscaping work ran low over the winter, they always needed help on renovations and flipping houses.

As I got to the top step, the front door opened and Leila walked out. She raised her eyebrows, then looked at her watch. "Did you get lost?"

"I'm sorry," I said. "Had to get Logan to school. I sent Ronnie a message."

Leila didn't have children, but Ronnie's four girls under the age of ten probably meant she knew school didn't start this late. "You should've sent me one, too," she said. "Our clients expect punctuality. So do I. Being on time sets us apart from the competition. You know that."

"Yes, and I'm usually early. *You* know that." When her eyes narrowed, I forced a smile and added, "It won't happen again. Anyway, has the project changed, or—"

"No, they wanted input for their backyard kitchen."

As she talked, I found my mind pinpointing the exact moment I'd become destined to build outrageously expensive outdoor kitchens that would be used only a few months a year, and not having the money to buy one instead.

I was eleven, had fallen into a bad crowd at my school in England whose behavior culminated one Tuesday afternoon when four of us stole a car. None of us knew how to drive properly, and we'd had pints of cider before we jumped the curb, almost sending a group of seniors to the hospital, or, as the police had told my parents, the morgue.

When a transfer to the US office in Albany came up at the insurance company Dad worked for, both he and Mom grabbed hold of it like Charlie Bucket to his golden ticket for the chocolate factory. Lisa thought going to study architecture at an American university would be *awesome*, and even put on a ridiculous accent until she noticed the original one garnered far more attention. Me, on the other hand, a gangly, sullen fourteen-year-old, moaned the idea of moving halfway across the world was "absolute total crap." Despite vowing I'd hate America, I settled in quickly, loving the school and making friends—ones my parents approved of—finishing near the top of my class every year, getting two full scholarships to uni.

It was in the middle of an advanced calculus lesson, three months before the end of high school, when Lisa showed up. "It's Mom and Dad," she'd whispered, tears running down her face. "A lorry…it jackknifed and… Oh, Josh, they didn't make it. Mom and Dad didn't make it."

Right there, in the middle of the high-school corridor, was the life-shattering moment that made the next decade of my life unravel. Nobody was surprised when I failed my engineering course and lost the scholarship, not considering how I drank myself beyond oblivion most days in an attempt to make myself either entirely numb, or synthetically happy. I hated myself even more when I became jealous of Lisa, who finished her degree in architecture and joined the ranks of a prestigious firm whose name I couldn't be bothered to remember.

When I blew the small amount of money from my inheritance on a plane ticket to Sydney, I thought I'd leave my excess baggage behind, but I didn't, despite bumming around, working odd jobs for cash under the table. When that finally ran out I called Lisa, who agreed to give me money only if I spent it on a ticket back to Albany, where I worked odd jobs and collected even more of an alcohol problem, a slew of traffic tickets and a DUI. By the time my thirtieth birthday loomed, I could barely look at myself, knew if I hadn't been such a selfish, reckless teenage asshole, we'd never have moved to the States and my parents would still be alive—and I'd felt that way almost up until the day I'd met Grace.

"Have you listened to anything I've said?" Leila's voice dragged me back to the front steps and the fifty shades of gray carpet I was supposed to care about.

"Sorry," I said. "You want me to—"

Leila's hands went to her hips. "Look, I know it's only been a couple of weeks, but you need to focus. I said you have to finish this job by three. The clients are leaving town."

"Uh, that's going to be a problem. I have an appointment at twelve."

"Did you text Ronnie about that, too? Why didn't you tell me? I'd have rearranged."

"It's a last-minute thing. A meeting with the lawyer. About guardianship for Logan."

Her jaw muscles clenched, making tiny, sinewy movements as she considered her response, gracing me with a curt, "I see."

I'd rarely asked for time off, had taken only a total of three sick days in more than five years, each day justified, and unpaid. Ronnie's famous mantra was *sick days are for wimps*, which he'd proven by going to the office every day after he'd broken his leg in two places, needed a dozen pins, earning him the nickname Iron Man.

"How long will it take?" Leila said.

"About an hour. I'll come back—"

"No, it's fine." She may as well have told me to go fuck myself. "Take the afternoon."

"But I don't need—"

She waved a hand, effectively dismissing and shutting me up, and walked down the steps to her truck without another word. Taking an unpaid afternoon was something I could ill afford, but challenging Leila and pissing her off even more wasn't an option. I pushed the door open and stepped inside, hoping the day wouldn't get any worse.

CHAPTER TEN

The next few hours were spent busting my ass, laying most of the carpet in an attempt to redeem myself with Leila. When I made it to Gingold, Garner & Greene's offices with ten seconds to spare, Harlan's assistant, Shirley, who always sported chunky necklaces that could drag her to the depths of a swimming pool, ushered me into his office, told me to make myself at home.

When Harlan walked in, he grabbed my hand. "Josh, good to see you. Have a seat." He gestured to the tawny-colored, gold-studded leather chair opposite his desk, and I sank down, grateful to give my body a rest.

As he took out a yellow legal pad and one of his expensive pens, I wiped my hands on my thighs. I always kept a clean pair of sneakers in the truck and I'd changed into them earlier, but although my feet were clean, my frayed jeans and paint-splattered shirt definitely looked out of place amid the spotless oak desk, rows of shiny books and immaculate fish tank quietly bubbling in the corner.

Harlan was an older gentleman, about the age my dad would have been if he were still alive, with deep-set wrinkles around his eyes and a full head of dusty blond hair—the color where you can't quite tell if it's the original, or a more recently acquired silvery hue. From the little I knew about him as a lawyer and a client, and from what Ivan had said about the way his uncle ran the firm, Harlan wasn't one to make the "blue collar, white collar" distinction. As far as he was concerned, without the people who'd made the desk he sat at, or the building that housed their offices, he'd be out of a job.

"I know I've said it before, but please accept my sincerest condolences," Harlan said as Shirley brought in two cups of steaming tea. She put them in front of us before leaving the room, shutting the door softly behind her. "I'm sure asking how you and Logan are is premature, but not doing so would be callous, in my opinion. So, how are you both?"

I wrapped my hands around my cup, warming my fingers on the porcelain. "We're coping. It's, uh, an adjustment."

"I completely understand. I felt that way when my first wife passed."

"Of course, Ivan mentioned it. I'm so sorry."

"As am I. Pancreatic cancer, twenty-five years ago." He paused. "I wish I could tell you getting over losing your spouse is a fast and simple process, however, I'd be misleading you. What I can say is it gets easier with time…a lot of time."

I wondered if he'd told himself that in the hope it would eventually become a self-fulfilling prophecy, but I didn't ask in case he said it hadn't worked. To busy myself I put my cup down and retrieved some paper and a pen from my backpack.

Harlan clasped his hands together, gave a quick nod. "Alright, let's talk about Logan."

"Well, it's simple, I think," I said. "I want to become his father. You know, legally."

"I understand," Harlan said. "Before you arrived I had a look at your file to refresh my memory. It's a good thing we put the domestic partnership agreement together. I'd forgotten."

"It was a few summers ago," I said. "After we got talking about it in the yard."

"Well, I'm glad we did," Harlan said, "because, in its infinite wisdom, the great state of New York doesn't recognize common-law marriage."

I nodded, remembering the discussion I'd had with Grace about a week after she told me she still didn't want to get married, probably never would.

"As far as I'm concerned—" she planted a kiss on my lips, slipped her arms around my neck "—we're already husband and wife. I don't need a ring or a piece of paper to prove it."

"Well, that's not what the law says." It hadn't dawned on me until later that I'd perhaps not quite taken the most romantic of angles, but a practical one nonetheless. "If anything happens to you, I wouldn't be considered next of kin."

"Course you would," Grace said. "We're common law."

"I don't think that's true," I said. "I've looked into it and—"

"But why does it matter? We're young and healthy." She squeezed my hand. "Stop worrying. Nothing's going to happen to either of us, okay?"

I'd bugged Grace for ages. Finally convinced her to at least speak to Harlan with me. When he told her I was right, if something happened to her, her parents would be legally recognized as next of kin, she blanched.

"I don't want anything to do with them, even if I'm dead. *Especially* if I'm dead," she said, and finally agreed to a domestic partnership agreement we'd signed a few weeks later.

When Harlan gently cleared his throat and asked if I was okay, I realized he'd probably been speaking all this time but whatever he'd said, I hadn't heard. Leila was right about one thing at least; my focus was shit these days.

"Did you put anything in writing about Logan?" Harlan said. "Or discuss the situation?"

It was another conversation I could recall almost word for word, one that had happened even before I'd brought up the domestic partnership. We were lying in bed early one Sunday morning. Grace had been woken by the rain belting against the bedroom window, and decided if she couldn't rest, neither would I. I'd been in the middle of a dream about driving a motorbike down a deserted and dangerously curvy road when Grace had lulled me back to reality by pressing her soft, naked breasts against my back.

The sex had been slow and gentle, with her on top doing most of the work, me hardly able to open my eyes and grateful she was happy to take control. Afterward she'd rested her head on my shoulder and pulled the covers back over us with a contented sigh.

I stroked her arm, her skin soft and luxurious as a velvet robe. "That was unexpected."

She laughed gently and ran her fingers over my chest. "Unexpected but...hot?"

"Always hot," I said, pulling her closer still.

"Well, you were there for the taking..."

"Apparently."

"I couldn't resist." She sighed again, and despite it still being dark, I knew she was frowning. "I need to ask you something."

"And you thought having Sunday morning sex would be the best way to butter me up?" I kissed the top of her head. "Okay. Yes to anything you want."

Grace didn't laugh this time. "No, and this is serious."

I reached for the light and flicked it on before propping myself on my side, looking down at her. "What's wrong?"

"Nothing's wrong."

"You look like someone's died."

"That's as good a segue as any, I suppose."

My throat went dry. After my parents passed, I'd built myself a cocoon of resilience, told myself if anybody else close to me died, I'd be able to handle it because I'd survived before, however barely. Looking at Grace, I knew if something happened to her, my protective bubble would instantly burst, and I hoped Death had already had his or her fill of Josh's plate of misery, that I'd be left alone until I was an old grandpa. As all this swirled around inside my head, and I studied Grace's face, my gut turned itself inside out.

"Baby, are you ill?"

"No—"

"Because whatever it is, we'll beat it. I'll be there every step of the way and—"

"No." She shook her head. "I'm not sick, Josh. It's about Logan. And before you ask, he's not sick, either. I need to know what you'd do if I died. What would happen to him?"

"I'd take care of him."

"Really?"

"Of course I would."

"But you've only known us a little over a year. I don't expect you to make that commitment when you're not his—"

"Please don't say father. That's semantics."

She touched the Big Dipper–shaped set of freckles on my stomach with her finger. "Are you sure? Because I promised to keep him safe, always and forever. And if, for whatever reason, I can't keep that promise, then I have to make sure someone else will."

"Grace—"

"It can't be my family, or his...dad. So if you're sure, I mean really sure, will you promise? Will you look after him, no matter what?"

I kissed her gently on the forehead. "I promise. No matter what."

Grace exhaled, seemingly satisfied. "Thank you."

"But it's irrelevant, anyway," I said in an attempt to lighten the mood, "because Brits have fish-and-chip grease in their veins, not blood. Ask Lisa, she'll tell you. I'll be dead before I'm fifty. You'll live to a hundred and ten with all the kale and quinoa you eat."

Grace's head snapped upward, the glint in her eye telling me my comedic skit had come too soon, so I added, "We could ask a lawyer to put something in writing. Make it official? I could ask Ivan's uncle. I'm seeing him next week about a project."

I felt Grace stiffen, exactly as she had when I'd asked her to marry me. Admittedly, we'd been seeing each other for only six months, weren't living together and I didn't have a ring when I'd dropped to one knee in the middle of an ice-cream shop. Unsurprisingly, she'd said it was too soon. After that I'd quickly understood Grace didn't like to rush things, or easily let people get close, which was why her presenting me with a house key a few months later had meant even more. I'd officially moved in a year after we'd met, and another rebuffed marriage proposal followed on her birthday. I'd remained hopeful there was some truth in saying "third time's a charm," but had decided I'd give her more than enough space until I asked again.

"I don't want to get a lawyer involved," Grace said. "And that's final." She kissed my chest, reached over me and switched off the light, pressing herself against me once more, rendering me incapable of further debate.

The sound of Harlan tapping his pen on his notepad whisked me out of the memory and back to his office. He'd taken off his glasses, polished them with a fluorescent-green cloth as he observed me. "Should I assume there's nothing in writing?"

With an apologetic shrug I said, "I promised Grace I'd look after Logan, and that hasn't changed. He needs me. I have to sort something out."

"Very well," Harlan said. "Now, you've been involved in Logan's life since he was two... What about the biological father?"

"Well, it's a bit...complicated."

"Josh," he said gently. "Please rest assured I'm not here to judge."

"Grace only knew his first name," I said quietly. "And seeing it was…less than a one-night stand, she thought it might've been fake."

It wasn't a story I'd shared with anyone before, how Grace went out with her work colleagues from Portland one balmy summer evening, ended up having sex in the park with a guy she'd met at the restaurant that night and never saw again. It had never been my tale to tell, but now, I wondered, at some point would Logan have to know? If it was this uncomfortable speaking to Harlan about it, how impossible would it feel to discuss it with Logan as he grew from boy to man? He'd have questions about who his father was, be it for health-related issues, his background or simply to *know*. The problems that could affect Logan in the near and distant future—physical ailments, mental illness—and the immensity of the situation made it difficult for me to breathe.

"Grandparents?" Harlan looked up from his notepad, half a page already scribbled in dark blue ink, his handwriting indecipherable swirls. I'd yet to mark a single thing on mine.

"No… Grace and her family were the definition of *estranged*. She hasn't spoken to them in years. Certainly not in the time I've known…*knew* her." I looked out the window. It had started to rain, and the gray fog hung low in the sky, intent on devouring entire rows of buildings, making the room, and my mood, darker still. "Grace didn't talk about them much. I've tried to contact them, but I haven't found them yet." I exhaled, shook my head. "Do you have a prize for the most messed-up family? I bet we'd win."

Harlan smiled and put down his pen. "In my line of business, I see all kinds of things. Like I said, I'm not here to pass judgment, but to help." He paused, read over his notes. "No birth father, no grandparents to argue they've been a constant in Logan's life…well, I'm cautiously optimistic of the outcome when we apply for guardianship."

Relief—a sensation I'd all but forgotten—invaded me. "Nobody's going to come and take Logan from me?"

He gave me a quizzical look. "Such as Child Protective Services, you mean? No, they might make an inquiry, but they'd have no reason to take him from you. You're the only stable factor in his life. There'd be no benefit, or logic, in putting him into any kind of care."

"And what about adoption?"

"It's more complicated and time-consuming but not impossible. We could start with guardianship."

I took a deep breath and exhaled slowly, rubbed the back of my neck, its touch like a cold, damp washcloth. "I'll feel better when it's official."

"I'll push to have the application wrapped up within two to three months, once we have all the documents."

I pictured the den covered with papers and open binders, the contents of the bookcases askew. A thought, thin and slippery as an eel, darted through my mind, but it was too quick for me to grab hold of and sped back into the darkness. "I'll get everything together."

"Wonderful. Send it all to me when you do."

We continued with small talk about landscaping, the terrible weather and how much he was looking forward to his pool house extension, until Shirley knocked on the door, announcing the next client's arrival. Harlan stood and shook my hand. "We'll get things arranged as quickly as possible, and, Josh, I'm doing all of this pro bono—"

"I can't accept—"

"You can, and you will." Harlan smiled. "I'm afraid that part is nonnegotiable."

CHAPTER ELEVEN

The nagging thought about the den returned almost immediately after I'd walked out of Gingold, Garner & Greene's offices and back to my truck. By the time I got home, it felt as if it had latched itself to my body and taken root, spreading throughout. An image popped into my head, the paper bag with the photographs I'd found as I'd searched for Logan's birth certificate, and my subconscious kept whispering in my ear that something wasn't quite right.

I drove home slowly, parked the truck and opened the front door, shed my boots and coat like a snake would its skin, abandoning them in the middle of the hallway as I wandered to the den. My feet dragged as if I'd poured concrete around them, my brain deliberately trying to delay me from seeing what was there. What *wasn't* there.

I pulled out the bag, emptied it on the desk and examined the photographs of Logan one by one. Instead of my heart swelling with pride as I looked at them, it shriveled away, almost disappeared from my rib cage completely with a tiny pop.

The oldest picture was of Logan at three months old; it said so on the back in Grace's elegant hand. There were none of him before, maybe because she'd been a single mom, short on time, no family or grandparents to help out or fuss over her baby boy. Except Grace had told me she hadn't any photos at all, not a single one before Logan was eighteen months old; they'd all been on a phone she'd lost.

"I never backed them up or printed them," she'd said. "And it sucks I can't show you a picture of when I was pregnant. You wouldn't believe how big my boobs were."

I looked at the photos again. There definitely weren't any of her pregnant, or otherwise. Maybe she'd forgotten all about the bag. After all, she'd laughed about her terrible case of baby brain, said she could barely remember her own name after Logan had arrived, regularly found her keys in the fridge and almost put a load of clothes in the dishwasher until Mrs. Banks—who helped out with babysitting Logan in the early days—asked her what she was doing.

As I put the pictures back in the bag, I picked up the shreds of what I'd dismissed as blank scraps of paper that morning. Most of them were plain white, but I now noticed some had bits of printed letters on them, light gray and faded, made by one of those ancient dot-matrix printers I'd once seen in my school's aging computer lab. I laid the pieces out on the desk and set to work, fitting them together like a jigsaw puzzle. Despite missing a few parts, three words became clear enough to decipher.

TELL NO ONE.

I stared at the words, felt my brow furrow as I read them a fifth, sixth time.

TELL NO ONE.

Tell no one…*what?* My mind raced through the possibilities. Why would Grace print that? What did she mean by it? What was it for? Was the note torn up and stuffed in a bag of forgotten photos because it meant something, or nothing? Had someone sent *her* the message? Or…my shoulders dropped. The note must have been part of a treasure hunt Grace made for Logan—she did them every year for his birthday and for Easter, and sometimes just because. This had to be a discarded clue, one she'd probably printed at Ruby & Rose's. They had all kinds of ancient stuff in that shop, probably long-redundant printers, too. Yes, of course. That made total sense. Although how it had ended up with the photos and the card, I really didn't know.

I picked up the bits of paper and, after a moment's hesitation, threw them into the garbage. The message was irrelevant now, and I didn't want Logan to see it, not if it would upset him. Besides, I had one mission that afternoon, and one mission only.

Impatience quickly turned to frustration and culminated in anger as I searched the rest of the house for Logan's birth certificate. No nook or cranny was spared. Cookbooks in the kitchen were flicked through and held upside down, and entire spider villages from the cupboard under the stairs now lay in silky tatters on the laminate floor. Even Logan's plastic tubs filled with Lego and army men hadn't stopped my unnecessary attack. And still—nothing.

As I shoved the multicolored blocks back in their place, I wanted to kick myself for not asking Grace about these things when she was alive, for not begging her to tell me every detail about her past. In the very beginning, she'd given me the abridged version of her history. She'd grown up an only child near Waterville in Maine with strict parents she'd never really got along with, but whom she assumed would still have her back, despite their differences.

As her trust in me grew, she shared more of her story in little dribs and drabs, told me about the abuse she'd suffered—albeit not in great detail—and how her parents had blamed her for it. On the day after her eighteenth birthday she left home, when she was sure her parents couldn't force her back. She'd moved to Portland, worked in coffee shops and diners, then for accountants and insurance brokers until she'd had Logan and decided to come to Albany, happy for the change of scene. I'd always suspected it was more, maybe something to do with Logan's dad, but I'd been reluctant to press her for details when she clammed up, and I'd decided she'd tell me what she wanted me to know, in her own time.

I should've kept her awake at night instead of accepting there was no urgency, that we had all the time in the world, but Grace had always said her life had only truly begun when we'd met, and I'd laughed at the *über*cheesiness of the line. It had given me the warm and fuzzies regardless, because I felt the same way about her and Logan.

I sank down on Logan's comforter and picked up the framed photograph from his bedside table, the one of him, Grace and me. It was a classic selfie taken a few months after I'd moved in, the three of us smooshed in close enough to fit the frame, part of Grace's arm visible in the picture. We wore baseball hats on backward, so the shadows didn't cover our faces, and we stuck out our tongues. That had been a fun day. A barbecue in the backyard, the three of us. We'd stayed up late, gorging on burgers and hot dogs, drinking pop and juice until the sun set and the cool air made them snuggle up to me, my arms around them, their heads on my chest.

"I love you, Josh Andersen," Grace had said later that night as we lay in bed after we'd made love. "You're the best thing that's ever happened to me."

I'd stroked her arm, running my fingers through her soft red curls. "Don't tell Logan," I'd whispered. "He'll kick me out."

Grace laughed softly. "Very funny. You're both the best thing that's ever happened to me… He called you Daddy today, did you hear?"

"Yes, I did."

"Why didn't you say anything?"

"I didn't want to make a big deal out of it in case it was a fluke."

Grace kissed me on the cheek. "You're such a softie."

I'd insisted we shouldn't make a fuss when, in reality, I absolutely wanted to. Logan had always called me Josh, pronounced it *Dsos* at the beginning, and although I'd never have admitted it, him using my first name for over a year had stung way more than it should have.

I put the picture down as a sudden surge of anger sped to my heart. If Grace had agreed to marry me, or sort out the legal stuff for Logan, it would all have been taken care of now. Yes, I'd still be an emotional, heartbroken, sniveling wreck, but at least the logistics would be fine.

Running a clammy hand over my even damper face, I immediately cursed myself for thinking badly of Grace, whispered "I'm sorry" at the photograph and turned away before I imagined any judgment in her two-dimensional eyes.

I shook out my arms, reminded myself I needed the birth certificate, and the movement kicked my brain cells into touch because an idea hit me. I grabbed my phone and searched for hospitals in Portland, Maine. A few came up, so I plumped for the first.

"Maine Medical Center, how may I direct your call?"

"Uh…" I hesitated, unsure how to explain I needed documents for a child who wasn't mine, and who may or may not have been born in their hospital.

"Hello?" the voice said, with a sprinkling of annoyance. "Can I help you?"

"I need to speak to someone about birth certificates."

A few clicks later, and I was connected to a man whose voice was so smooth and deep, he could have been Barry White. I explained what I needed, but before I got to the part about not being Logan's dad, he cut me off.

"I'm afraid you have to contact Portland city hall for birth certificate copies," he said.

"You don't keep them at the hospital?" I hoped the desperation in my voice would make him offer up the certificate and email it to me, pronto.

"I'm sorry, sir, but Portland city hall and—" His next words were muffled, an exchange going on between him and another person in the background. "My apologies," he said, his voice clear again. "You have to contact the city hall in the town where the mother was *living* when she had the child."

"Are you sure there isn't another way? I'm kind of desperate here and—"

"My apologies, sir. That's the best I can do."

I mumbled a quick thank you and hung up.

Grace had only ever mentioned living in Portland when she'd had Logan, and we'd never visited. I'd suggested it exactly once, asked if she'd take me there and show me her old haunts, but she'd shaken her head, said she had no interest in going back, ever, there was nothing there but memories of a shitty past. Her tone had been firm, her words so final, I hadn't made the suggestion again. If she'd lived in a suburb or a town on the outskirts of the city, she'd never mentioned it. Then again, when people asked me where I was from I always said London, England, when it was actually Fulham, which people rarely knew of. But I'd told Grace. I'd told her everything.

I found the number for Portland city hall and dialed, got passed around a few times before being connected to a soft-spoken clerk who introduced herself as Julia Fesenko.

"I'm so sorry for your loss," she said when I explained what I needed.

"Thank you. Uh, so do you think you can help me?"

"Believe me, I'd send you the certificate right now if I could," Julia said. "But I'm afraid we'll need a certified copy of your domestic partnership agreement. And if you're not exactly sure where your son was born, or where your partner lived at the time… Hmm, this is tricky—"

"There must be something we can do," I said, the frustration building. "Please. Can't you find a way to help?"

"Well…you could ask the court to request the place of birth…or… No, wait, I know," Julia said. "You need to call Maine Vital Records. A friend of mine works there, Noreen Zuckerberg. No relation to Mark, much to her dismay. She's the supervisor there. She'll definitely know what to do. I'll give you her direct line."

I made a note of the number with one of Logan's colored pencils, pressed the tip down so hard it snapped. "I'm trying give my boy some security, you know? How complicated can it be?"

"I understand, and I'm sorry, truly I am," Julia said. "Best of luck."

I hung up, redialed, thankful when Noreen "no relation" Zuckerberg picked up straight away. She listened quietly as I went over my request again, and I crossed my fingers.

"You'll have to demonstrate direct and legitimate interest in the child," Noreen said. "And we'll need a notarized letter from the courts saying you're applying for legal guardianship, and that's why you want a copy of the birth certificate."

"How do I—"

"Your lawyer should be able to help you with both of those," she said. "You can give them my contact details if they need more information."

"And how long will it take to get a copy?"

"Of the birth certificate? If you bring the request to us in person, about ten minutes. But you said you're in Albany, New

York? That's a little far…but once we receive the application in the mail you should get a copy in around seven to ten days."

"That long?"

"Tell you what," Noreen said with an audible smile, "I'll make a note to expedite it. You could ask your lawyer to courier the request to us, too. That'll speed things up even more."

Progress, at last. I thanked her and hung up. Logan's bus was due back in fifteen minutes, which meant I had time for one last call, and a few seconds to silently thank Leila for giving me the afternoon off after all.

"Great research, Josh, well done," Harlan said after hearing about my phone marathon. "You're doing my work for me. I'll let you know what I need, get the details together and we'll courier everything to Vital Records. Don't worry, everything's going to work out just fine."

After we hung up, I sat on the bed for another five minutes, staring at the photograph of me, Logan and Grace. My throat became a little tighter as an uncomfortable voice slowly clawed its way from the pit of my stomach and up to my brain, where it softly whispered everything wasn't going to work out fine. It wasn't going to work out fine at all.

CHAPTER TWELVE

As the next few weeks passed, Logan and I fell into a semiroutine. Mrs. Banks offered to pick him up at the bus stop after school, and he spent an hour or two at her house until I got home. Ronnie and Leila weren't thrilled when I told them I wanted to start work after seeing Logan off on the school bus for a while, and Logan moaned about spending so much time with "the old lady who smells of foot cheese." As a result I felt like a punching bag, swinging back and forth, anticipating—and unable to duck away from—the next hit.

At home I'd ask Logan about his day, but all the nudging and encouragement didn't garner more of a response than, "It was okay, I guess." When I asked if he wanted to talk, he said no, and disappeared upstairs to read one of his dog books, or listen to the radio station he and Grace had always played. That left me in the kitchen, blankly staring at the open cupboards, rustling up another meal neither of us wanted.

In those moments I pretended Grace was on a girls-only vacation, imagined her somewhere hot and exotic, her long, perfect legs stretched out on a beach filled with fine, white sand, where there was no internet access or phone reception. I told myself she'd be back soon. Grace would walk in, face glowing, bursting with stories she couldn't wait to share. Never mind that the only people aside from Lisa, Ivan and me she'd socialized with were her bookshop colleagues at the occasional after-work event, and even then she'd come home, kick off her shoes and say, "I shouldn't have bothered. I missed you."

Sometimes the vacation illusion turned out to be a trap, for example when Logan had come to me in search of clean underwear. Taking care of the mundane chores continued to feel wrong, and I could hardly swallow down the big ball of anger about the world still turning regardless whether Grace was in it or not.

As I took note of Logan's mild disgust when I told him he'd have to recycle a pair of dirty underwear for the day, I grabbed our clothes from the hampers, the towels from the bathroom, and threw them into the washing machine, color sorting be damned.

It was only when I got home later that I'd grasped what I'd done. I yanked the damp items out of the machine, searching for Grace's shirts and blouses, pushing them up against my nose, but all I could smell was budget brand detergent. I'd cried, sat on the floor in a heap, clutching cold clothes to my chest, sobbing silently so Logan wouldn't hear.

Later, when I couldn't sleep, I'd kicked the covers off and flicked on the light, only to find Grace's sleep-shirt in a crumpled bundle at the very bottom of the bed. It was her soft, yellow one with a faded cartoon bee and the words *Just Bee Awesome* underneath, the one she'd pull on before bed if she was tired, and leave off when she wasn't, an unspoken invitation.

I'd grabbed the shirt and slept with it on my pillow ever since, but it didn't smell of her anymore, taking on the fragrance of my shampoo instead. People always said how much they missed their loved one's voice or laugh or touch, and while it was all true, why hadn't anyone mentioned the scent of their skin? Consequently, I couldn't bear to dispose of any of her things, including her puppy slippers, which I'd cleaned and returned to their rightful place; under the chair in the bedroom, ready for her to come home, take off her shoes and sigh as she slipped her feet into the fluffy warmth.

My brain played tricks on me, too. Whenever I saw an old, green Ford, for a fraction of a second I thought it was Grace, and the same feeling invaded my heart every time the phone rang, making me think it could be her, that she hadn't ended up on the steps, the morgue, the funeral home, the crematorium.

I shuddered, grabbed a pack of spaghetti from the cupboard and filled a pot with water. Grace and I had never properly discussed what was to happen to us if we died. From what I knew it wasn't the kind of thing most people our age talked about, with the exception of Lisa; my ever-organized sister had everything planned, right down to her shoes. In contrast, Grace had only once mentioned being cremated, not buried.

"I don't want to become worm food," she'd said with a grimace. "I want you to scatter my ashes in the ocean somewhere. Bali, preferably, so I can travel the world for all eternity."

I'd laughed, said she'd be fish food instead, and in retaliation she gave my arm a gentle punch and told me she'd make sure I ended up mixed into a vat of asphalt if I didn't shut up.

After the accident, and with Lisa's help, Logan and I had picked a light blue urn with silver butterfly etchings, and eventually there'd be a headstone at the local cemetery where we could visit. But I wanted to follow Grace's wishes, so I'd kept part of her ashes in a small wooden box that I'd placed at the bottom of her cupboard. Going to Bali wasn't an option, so at first I'd thought of taking them to Portland, until Lisa said I couldn't because Grace hated it there, and suggested waiting until Logan and I went on a trip somewhere.

"You'll both need a break at some point," Lisa had reasoned, and she was right, although how I'd fund any kind of vacation was another question. Money had already become tight without Grace's salary, which was why I'd accepted Mrs. Banks's offer to look after Logan for free again, despite his protests.

"I don't want to," he'd said.

"How come? She used to look after you when you were little."

"I want to be with you," he'd wailed, clutching Biscuit. "Why can't you be home?"

I'd had to explain it wasn't a luxury we could afford; I needed the work, we needed the cash. I'd asked him not to tell Lisa. This was a private affair, something between us, and I'd meant every word. While I loved my sister, there was no way I'd end up her charity case again, the little brother in need of another handout. No, I had to handle this financial crisis on my own.

I added salt to the boiling water, fished around the cupboard for a jar of tomato sauce before realizing I'd forgotten to buy some. Even though I couldn't be bothered eating, Logan needed to, although I knew he'd find the prospect of limp, buttered spaghetti for the second night in a row completely unappetizing. I made a note to be more organized about meals in future, and was just about to stuff the pasta into the saucepan when the phone rang.

"Hey, you," Lisa said. "How are things?"

"If I say they're okay, will you believe me?"

"No."

"Then best you don't ask. Are you still at work?"

"Yeah. No rest for the wicked, right? Crap, hold on a sec."

As I pressed my ear to the phone, I heard Lisa opening a

door and a familiar voice in the background greeting her. "Is that Ivan? What's he doing at your office?"

"Oh, one of his clients wants his house renovated so he's introducing us."

"He never mentioned it."

Lisa laughed. "Do you live in each other's pockets now? He doesn't have to tell you everything. Anyway, that's not why I called. Have you found Logan's birth certificate?"

"No, not yet."

"Okay, here's a thought. What if you called the Social Security Office with his number? They might be able to give you some details."

"You think so? I'm not his legal guardian—"

"*Yet*, and maybe. It can't hurt to try. Look, I've got to go, but think about it."

I pulled the boiling pan of water from the stove. Lisa had a point, and maybe it would avoid the entire Vital Records thing. Decision made, I headed for the cupboard under the stairs where I'd seen a purple file marked "Taxes" Grace had stuck in a box with some old clothes, probably because we'd run out of room in the den. She'd always insisted on doing both of our returns, which suited me fine. Although a wunderkind at math, I'd long decided tax returns were akin to mythical creatures—best left to the experts for fear I'd mishandle them. I opened the file, my confidence soaring, certain this would yield the information. When I flipped to the return's corresponding page, my mouth dropped.

Grace's hadn't listed Logan as a dependent.

That wasn't right. *Couldn't* be right. Maybe it was a one-off, and she'd forgotten to add him for the previous year, although the possibility of her making that kind of a mistake was exactly zero. I riffled through the papers for the year before. And back another. And again. The result was the same. Neither Logan's name nor his social security number was there. *Why?*

I clambered out of the cupboard before the walls closed in. Just like the photos I'd found, there had to be a logical explanation, but my brain fogged up, making whatever it was impossible to grasp. I needed time to think, time to breathe. And to hell with money being tight. I needed to get out. I couldn't deal with this. Not now.

"Logan." I stumbled across the hallway, calling up the stairs. "Want to see a movie?"

Moments later his head popped over the banister. "On a school night?"

I forced a smile, made my voice sound lighter than Cool Whip. "You'll be in bed by eight thirty. Come on, Granddad, we can have a burger."

"And ice cream?"

"Definitely."

"Yes!" Logan pumped his fist. "Thanks, Dad, I love you."

That single sentence was enough to slow my pulse, make everything fade away for a second as a tiny fragment of my shattered heart slotted back into place. Only nine hundred and ninety-nine thousand, nine hundred and ninety-nine to go. And yes, I was counting.

CHAPTER THIRTEEN

P icking a movie turned out to be easy. Logan had raved about the new superhero film weeks before he'd caught a glimpse of the trailer, and I had to admit it took my mind off things for a couple of hours. Still, I kept glancing at him, watched him wiggle his feet, listened to him plunge his hand deep into the bucket of popcorn and whisper, "Get him, Spider-Man, get him!"

The good mood continued right up until the lights came on, and we filed out into the lobby, where Logan's grin evaporated as he put his head down and mumbled something.

"What's up?" I bent over, trying to hear over the hubbub of the crowd.

"Dylan." He made big eyes at me, hid a hand in front of his chest and pointed to the right.

"Is he from school?" I asked, and Logan gave a nod. "You two don't get along?"

"No," Logan whispered. "But it's okay. It doesn't matter. Can we go?"

"Kiddo, what's wrong?" When Logan hesitated I said, "Has he been bothering you?"

He grabbed my arm. "Don't say anything, Dad. He hates me. You'll make it worse."

Well, that did it. I stomped over and tapped a petite brunette, Dylan's mother, I assumed, on the shoulder. "Excuse me," I said, the fake smile on my face tighter than the size-six shoes my mom insisted I wear one summer despite me being a seven-and-a-half. "Can I have a word?"

When the woman turned around, her smooth skin, button nose and baby blue eyes caught me off guard. She didn't look much older than the kids. "Yes? Can I help you?"

"Dad, please." Logan tugged at my jacket. "Don't."

I ignored him and put a hand to my chest. "I'm Josh, Logan's dad."

Her eyes flitted to my son, and she seemed to grow at least an inch taller. "I see. I'm Cecelia, Dylan's mother." She sounded wary now, her hand moving slowly to take her boy's, guiding him behind her.

"Look, can I ask you to make sure Dylan leaves Logan alone?"

She cocked her head to one side, raised her eyebrows. "Leave *Logan* alone?"

I looked at Dylan with his messy hair, not one cowlick, but three and teeth too big for his face. The little shit was probably a master at getting his naive-looking mom to believe anything. She was in for a fun ride when he hit puberty if he was lying his ass off at the tender age of seven. Takes one to know one and all that.

"Could you get Dylan to back off, please? Logan's been through a lot at home already. He doesn't need any more at school."

"But—"

"I really appreciate it, thanks." I turned to leave, but not before I clocked her wide eyes moving from me, to Dylan, to

Logan and back again, or the crocodile tears miraculously rolling down her son's chubby cheeks.

"Dad," Logan whispered urgently when we'd moved a few
steps away. "I said not to."

I looked at him, ruffled his hair. "You tell me if he bothers
you again, alright?"

"Alright," he said, and chewed his bottom lip.

"Want to watch another movie tomorrow?" I said. "We can
stream one at home. What about the one with the singing pen-
guins? Or was it dogs?"

"Pigs!" Logan beamed, his encounter with the school bully
already forgotten. "But can we get an ice cream now?"

"After all that popcorn?" I grinned. "You've got hollow legs.
Come on then."

When we walked across the lobby, the mere sound of someone calling out my name made my fists clench as if they were
on remote control. I knew who it was, and it was too late to
turn around and go the other way.

JD Marino moved toward me like an overgrown spider, arms
and legs long and spindly, his trademark grin plastered on his
face. A dark-haired girl, dressed in a skimpy blue outfit barely
reaching the top of her thighs, hung off his tattoo-covered arm,
and she pouted, shaking her long, glossy mane as he grabbed
me by the shoulder.

"Josh. Good to see you, man. Good to see you." He sniffed
and looked down at Logan. "He yours? Weird. Never pegged
you as a family man. This is Lorna."

Raising a groomed eyebrow she said, "S'up?" and I didn't
bother with an answer.

"Fuck man, where you been hidin' at, bro?" JD said. "You
just sorta—" he blew on his fingers as if he were performing a
magic trick "—disappeared."

"Needed a change," I said. "And watch your mouth in front of my kid."

"Sorry, bro." JD held up his hands. "We should hang sometime. Reminisce over—"

"Not my scene anymore. Hey, Logan, let's get that ice cream."

JD held on to my arm, moved in close, his mouth by my ear. His grip tightened some more, the smell of stale cigarettes and alcohol wafting up my nose. "Come on, man. Let me buy you a Jack's or three. We miss you—"

"No." My eyes narrowed as I shook him off, stared him down until he backed off.

"Alright, alright. You know where to find me when you change your mind. You always did, sooner or later." JD stepped back, his lips twitching into a smile as he took Lorna's hand. "C'mon, baby, let's split."

Logan, who'd been silent during the entire exchange, looked up at me. "Who was that?"

"Someone I knew from a long time ago."

"I don't like him."

"Me, neither."

I struggled to push the memories of my drinking with JD at a plethora of watering holes with various degrees of rancidness to the back of my mind, forcing myself to remember how hard the fall afterward had always been instead. That was the trouble with booze, the glossy overlay it created, not only distorting your vision and emotions, but also the memories, making them bigger, better, louder and entirely more fun.

We'd met at a bar one night, JD and I. Two lonely drunks joining forces, banging on about our issues together, quickly committing to spending all of our money on, and most of our free time with, our third party friend, Jack Daniel's. The fact the two of them shared initials wasn't lost on us; we took it as a sign and regularly paid adequate tribute.

JD's wife was pregnant when we met, but as he spiraled downward, so did his marriage, and by the time I climbed out of the hole I'd drunk myself into—while he insisted on continuing his exploration to the depths and beyond—he hadn't seen his kid in at least a year.

Lisa took an instant dislike to JD, blamed him—unreasonably in my opinion—for the fact I couldn't hold down a job and was still bunking on her couch. "You went out with JD and you're pissed. *Again*," she said, hands on hips, sounding exactly like our mother. "That's twice this week and it's only Tuesday. Did you drive? You did, didn't you? You promised you wouldn't. You're going to kill someone, you moron."

"It was one drink," I lied. "What's your problem?"

"My problem is that *you* have a problem, Josh," she said. "You're screwing up your job. You're screwing up your life. Get your shit together, you asshole."

It wasn't her most eloquently put argument, and I wish I could say a stern talking-to (or ten) from my sister had been effective, or that her kicking me out of her flat multiple times over the years had worked. In reality it was getting busted for a DUI that did it. Being handed a suspended prison sentence and hours of community service finally made me understand how badly I continued not only to let Lisa down, but the memory of my parents, too, how ashamed they'd be if they were still alive. Suddenly, the prospect of prolonging my stay in Loserville became so unappealing, I decided to claw, crawl and beg my way out, vowing I'd never return.

With Lisa's help, I channeled my addiction in a different direction, went on a health kick and joined AA. It wasn't easy. Deciding—believing—I was worth saving was the hardest choice I'd ever made. I stumbled and fell at first, but picked myself back up again, had a sponsor for the longest time until he moved away, by which time I felt confident enough to fly solo. I hadn't touched a drink in over two thousand days. Two thousand and seventy-one, to be exact. But now, standing in the middle of the popcorn-scented lobby, for the first time in years the allure of a glass of Jack's slid its arms around me, a sultry temptress, whispering in silky purrs all the things she'd do to me if only I gave her another chance.

Thankfully, Logan babbled all the way home, telling me about his art project, a collage of a dog—"Duh, Dad, what else?"—and I tried to focus on every word, a necessary distraction from the encounter with JD, and all the good memories, because there had been plenty of those, too, that still played on my mind.

"Did you know some huskies can live outside, even if it's minus seventy-five?" Logan said. "Mr. Shapran told me. He knows lots of stuff about dogs."

"You really like your teacher, don't you?" I said, watching Logan in the rearview mirror.

"Yeah. He's nice."

I waited, as casually as I could, said, "What's the scoop with Dylan?" Logan put his head down and when I asked again, he refused to look at me. "Has he hurt you? Because if he—"

"*No.* He hasn't."

"You sure? It's not right for him to pick on you. Nobody has that right. Look, we've spoken to his mom, so tell me if he bugs you again. Promise? As soon as it happens. Straightaway when you get back from school."

Logan murmured something under his breath.

"What was that?" I put the indicator on to turn into our street. "Kiddo, I didn't hear."

"I said you're never there after school."

"Logan, we decided Mrs. Banks—"

"No." He shook his head, crossed his arms. "*You* did. Because Josh decides everything."

I frowned. "That's not true, and why did you call me Josh?"

Logan shrugged, and when I thought it was a simple case of him being grumpy and overly tired, and he wasn't going to answer, he very quietly said, "You're not my real dad."

The air left my lungs as if he'd thrown a punch harder than a grown man. Somehow I managed to wait until I'd pulled into our driveway and cut the engine before turning around. "If by real dad you mean biological dad, then no, I'm not, but I *am* your dad. You know that."

"People say you're only looking after me because you have to," Logan said.

"Who said that?" When Logan didn't answer, I pressed him some more. "Was it Dylan? Did he tell you that?" A moment's hesitation, a slight nod. "The little... You can't listen to him. You're *my* boy, you always have been, ever since I met your mom. You're my *son*, okay? Don't let anyone tell you anything different. Because they're wrong and I love you."

Logan looked up, wiped his mouth with his sleeve, and when he put his hand down I could see the quiver in his lips. "Pinkie promise? Even...even when I said I hate Mom, and you? And I said that bad word outside... I'm sorry, Dad. I didn't mean it. I'm sorry."

It seemed to take forever to unbuckle my seat belt and clamber into the back, but when I got there I put my arms around him, and he buried his head in my shoulder.

"I pinkie promise," I whispered.

"I d-don't h-hate her," Logan sobbed, his chest heaving. "And I d-don't hate you."

"I know you don't, I know," I said, my poorly glued together heart cracking again. "I promise I'm not looking after you because I have to, but because I *want* to. We're family."

"But what if—"

"No buts. Ignore Dylan, because he's being a jerk. Listen, I went to see a lawyer. Do you know what that is?"

Logan sniffed. "Ivan said they keep people out of jail and make lots of money."

I laughed softly. "Yeah, Ivan would say that, wouldn't he? But the lawyer I saw helps families figure out what to do. We talked about me becoming your dad. You know, officially. With a piece of paper that says so."

Logan pulled away, eyes wide. "You can do that?"

"Yes, we can." I squeezed his arm. "How about this? You go to school, have fun, work on your husky project and let me worry about the grown-up stuff, alright?"

"Will you pick me up from the bus?"

"I can't, I'm sorry. I have to work. But Mrs. Banks—"

"I don't want Mrs. Banks," Logan whispered, the words coming out muffled as he pushed them past his trembling lips, "I want you."

"Okay, shh, shh. Only tomorrow, okay? Just this once."

How could I say no? Ronnie had asked me to get materials from the wholesaler after work, but Logan was more important. An hour wouldn't make any difference. I'd go when Logan came home, take him with me and use the opportunity to talk, get him to open up more.

"We'll get through this," I said, kissing the top of his head, as he cried softly into my jacket again. "I'm not going anywhere, I promise. I'll always be here for you."

God, how I wanted to take his pain, bundle it into a ball and push it down my throat so he never had to feel it again. One of my few talents was repairing stuff. Dented cars, broken walls, damaged toys… But what good was any of that when I couldn't fix what needed it the most?

CHAPTER FOURTEEN

"Last card and out!" Logan threw the ace of spades down with panache, his grin triumphant. We sat at the kitchen table playing cards after getting back from an unsuccessful trip to the wholesaler because I'd forgotten Ronnie had said they'd close early.

We'd eaten a dinner of fish sticks, instant mash and peas and, in Logan's case, a bowl of rocky-road ice cream. Hardly haute cuisine, but I hadn't put up a fight on his choice of dessert, decided not to remind him of Grace's rule that ice cream was a weekend treat only. With the way his pants sat below his hip bone, I was glad to see him eat anything. I'd even emailed his teacher, asked if he could make sure Logan didn't throw any of his lunch in the trash. Mr. Shapran had replied almost right away, promised he'd look out for him, told me not to worry, but I couldn't help it. At least Logan had said everything had gone okay with Dylan all day, so I hoped my talking with his mom had made the kid back off.

"You win, *again*?" I smiled at Logan. "That's three in a row. I'm rubbish."

"Yup," Logan said. "And next game it'll be four."

"Fighting words, eh? Bring. It. On." I reached for the scattered cards, but my hand stopped midair when the doorbell rang. "Get ready to lose," I called over my shoulder as I walked to the front door and pulled it open, my smile immediately transforming into a confused frown when I saw Harlan on the doorstep.

"Good evening, Josh," he said. "I hope you don't mind my stopping in. I was in the neighborhood and I thought it best to see you in person."

"Do you have good news?" I said, ushering him in as Logan wandered into the hallway. "Logan, this is Mr. Gingold. He's the lawyer I told you about, the one who's going to help us."

"Hello," Logan said.

"Pleased to meet you." Harlan shook his hand. "Your father and my nephew Ivan have told me so much about you, it feels like I know you already. I hear you love dogs."

"They're my favorite."

"Mine, too," Harlan said. "Alas, my wife prefers cats, so we have two of them."

"I want a dog," Logan said. "But Dad won't let me."

Harlan laughed. "I'm sure he has excellent reasons as to why that's so."

"Tell you what, Logan," I said before he launched himself into an hour-long justification about the acquisition of a four-legged friend, "why don't you watch TV in the den and I'll come in when we're done."

He disappeared down the hallway, and I took Harlan's coat, motioned for him to follow me to the kitchen. "Excuse the mess," I said, feeling more than a little self-conscious about the dirty dishes on the counters and the pile of laundry on the floor I hadn't got around to stuffing into the machine. "I'm still finding my feet. Can I get you anything?"

"A glass of water, please, and there's nothing to excuse." Harlan sat down at the kitchen table as I filled a glass for him, and I watched him open his leather briefcase and pull out a folded piece of paper. He drummed his fingers on top of it. "Josh, I'm here because—"

"Da-*ad*. The TV's not working properly," Logan called out. "Can you come?"

"Excuse me," I said to Harlan before slipping out of the door, sorting out the remote and reminding Logan about the rules for privacy. "Sorry about that," I said, as soon as I was back in the kitchen. "So, what did you need to see me about?"

Harlan looked at me. "We have a problem."

If he was after my attention, he got all of it. It felt as if I'd been pulled upright by a puppeteer, the invisible strings so taut, they threatened to snap. My body held perfectly still, waiting for my commander to determine my next move. I opened and closed my mouth, said, "What kind of problem?"

Harlan tapped the folded piece of paper still under his fingers. "Are you sure you gave me the correct details regarding Logan's birth?"

"Yes. Why?"

"Let's go over them again to be certain."

He grabbed his notes, and as he read them back to me, I found myself nodding, saying "Yes, yes, that's right, yes" until he'd finished.

Harlan leaned in. "You're sure Grace had Logan in the state of Maine?"

I closed my eyes for a moment as I recalled not only the conversations I'd had with Grace, but also what she'd told Logan. He'd gone through a phase of asking her almost every day for a baby story, giggling when she told him about the times he'd peed in the bath, or redecorated the wall with blueberry purée, listening closely when she described the day he was born in a hospital in Portland. *Maine.* Doubt tried to wriggle through the cracks of my mind, but I pushed it away.

"Positive," I said. "I mean, not the exact hospital, but you said it didn't matter. Why?"

Harlan danced around the question, a short pas de deux. "Could you be mistaken? Confused it with somewhere else, another state, perhaps?"

I shook my head. "No. Maine's the only place she's lived other than here. Can you please tell me what this is about?"

"I heard from Vital Records." Harlan slid the paper across the table.

I picked up the letter and unfolded it, the note trembling between my fingers as I read it a few times before saying the words out loud. "No record found."

The sentence entered my ears, but my brain seemed incapable of processing it. Instead it bounced off my skull and fell to the floor in a nonsensical heap at my feet. "No record found at the hospital? Or in Portland?" I said.

Harlan paused for two beats, blinked. "No record found in the entire state of Maine."

My left eye twitched and I pressed my palm over it to make it stop. "But…wait…what? You're saying there's no record of Grace having Logan anywhere in the state of Maine…at *all*?"

"I'm afraid not."

"That's ridiculous. It's not possible. They must've got it wrong. Lost the file or the record or something. Happens all the time, right?"

Harlan smoothed down his tie. "No doubt it's some kind of misunderstanding. Maybe Grace meant a different Portland? Oregon, perhaps? Or elsewhere? I ran a quick check, and there are towns and cities called Portland in multiple states, and abroad. There's one in New Zealand, Ireland, even Canada and Australia. I had no idea."

This was all news to me, but I knew Grace had said Maine, not Oregon. Not Texas, Alaska or wherever the hell those other Portland places were in America, and she'd definitely never mentioned another country. Was this another mistake? How could I possibly stuff this into the same category as the misplaced photographs and the error on the tax returns, both unusual, but—until now—somehow justifiable?

"Take a while to think things over," Harlan said. "Maybe one of Grace's old friends can fill you in? But, Josh…you have to understand, without knowing where Grace had Logan and without a birth certificate, well, the guardianship application is going to be—"

"Difficult?" My hollow laugh echoed around the kitchen.

"I'd have to caution you *difficult* is a generous assessment." He pushed back his chair and got up, a fatherly look of concern on his face. "I'm sorry I didn't bring better news. Why don't you call me when you've made progress on your end? And in the meantime, I'll see if I can figure out a way to help on mine."

After he left I leaned against the front door, breathing deeply, barely managing to stop myself from bashing my head on the glass repeatedly. Once my hands stopped trembling, I headed for the den. I sat next to Logan, who was on the sofa with Biscuit under his arm, watching cartoons, and I wished I could be seven, too, cuddle my stuffed animal, oblivious to the grown-up problems around me.

"Logan, did I ever show you where I was born?"

"Uh-huh."

When his gaze didn't move from the television, I switched it off, passed the tablet to him and pressed the home button. "Want to show me?"

He opened a map, deftly moving his fingers across the screen. I was no technophobe, but if I hadn't known any better I'd have sworn he'd arrived with a device in his hands. "London, England," he said proudly. "You said I should look for the squiggly snake river."

"Yes, that's right. The River Thames." I paused. "What about your mom? Do you know where she came from?"

He moved the map to the west, zoomed in. "Waterville, Maine. She hated it there."

"And you? Where were you born?"

He traced his finger down the highway, all the way to Portland. Maine. "Here."

"You sure?"

"Uh-huh. The same as Stephen King. He wrote a book about a dog who got rabies. But he lives in Bangor now. Mr. King. Not the dog. He's not real."

When he reached for the remote and looked at me, I nodded, and he continued his show, bouncing in his seat and laughing. In contrast, I sat with my entire body glued to the sofa, heart pounding, mind racing, the increasing tightness in my chest making it impossible to breathe.

There was no longer any question, not a single shred of doubt Grace had lied about where she'd had Logan, not only to me, but to him, too.

The next question was *why*?

CHAPTER FIFTEEN

My brain was still a mess by the next afternoon as I tried to reason with logic, make excuses for what I'd discovered, attempted to convince myself it was all a giant mass of confusion. Each way I turned, every story I told myself, had the same outcome. Grace *lied*.

If that wasn't enough to deal with on its own, Ronnie had given me an epic bollocking about not getting to the wholesaler on time, and once Leila had found out, she'd had a go at me, too. Ronnie and I were now in the middle of a discussion with a client about a basement renovation, him rattling off ideas, me working hard to listen and write everything down. When my mobile rang, I pulled it from my pocket, saw it was Logan's school. Damn it, every time I got a call I couldn't help but expect the worst, and I couldn't imagine a time when that would change.

"I have to take this," I said to Ronnie, walking to the back of the room, sliding a shaky finger across the screen. "Hello?"

"Mr. Andersen? It's Mr. Shapran, Logan's teacher. This isn't—"

"What's happened?" I knew I'd struggled to contain the panic in my voice because Ronnie and the client looked at me, talking in hushed whispers.

"He's fine, don't worry," Mr. Shapran said. "This isn't an emergency, but, well, we need to talk about some issues that have been going on. Is now a good time, or...?"

Anger pushed all of the worry away. I wasn't panicking anymore, I was seething. "Is it Dylan? Has the bullying started again?"

"Oh." Mr. Shapran paused. "You're aware?"

"Yes, I'm *aware*. Logan told me."

"Well, I appreciate this has been an incredibly difficult time for him...for both of you..." He sighed, paused for a moment. "The number of incidents have increased dramatically these past few days. I've tried to handle it directly with Logan—"

"That's great, and I appreciate it, I do. But what about Dylan? How will you make that kid stop? Do you want me to come to the school?"

"I'm sorry?"

"Have you spoken to his parents? I met his mother, so—"

"I, uh, think you may have some misinformation."

"What do you mean?"

Mr. Shapran's hesitation made me want to crawl into the phone and yank the answers out of him, and I was about to repeat myself when he said, "Dylan isn't the one doing the bullying, Mr. Andersen. Logan is."

"*What?* That can't be right. Are you sure?"

"Yes, I'm afraid so. Logan admitted everything," Mr. Shapran said. "He's been calling Dylan names, taking his things, pushed him down. He deliberately tripped him in the playground today. I was there, so he couldn't talk his way out of it. It wasn't an accident."

"But I don't understand. Logan's never been aggressive. Never."

"I know, I know," Mr. Shapran said. "He's a great kid and it's completely out of character. Look, normally I'd have to involve the principal, but given the circumstances...well, can we handle this, together?"

"Yes, yes. Where's Logan now?"

"Back in class. He seems fine. So is Dylan, and I'm sure it's a question of them getting under each other's skin, but we need to put a stop to it now." He paused again. "Mr. Andersen, I can't pretend to understand how you and Logan are feeling, what you're going through...but on the other hand, we can't have him going around getting into fights."

I imagined how my parents must have felt when they had similar conversations with my teachers, although there'd been no excuse for my behavior, other than boredom. We talked for another few minutes, figuring out "strategies" as Mr. Shapran called them. By the end we'd agreed I'd speak to Logan to reinforce positive behavior and choices, and Mr. Shapran would update me every week on how things were going, more frequently if necessary.

Ronnie and the client had headed upstairs at some point during the call, so I hung around in the basement for another minute, trying to sort out the jumble of thoughts that made my head feel like it was stuffed full of insulation.

No need for a degree in psychology to work out where Logan's anger came from. It was exactly how I'd felt when Mom and Dad had died. Alone and abandoned, furious at everyone and everything. I'd lashed out, too, got into fistfights I'd provoked for the hell of it. One of them had been with a guy a head taller than me, twice my width, and not nearly as drunk. The reminder of that particular brawl was permanently etched under my chin, a thin, D-shaped scar from where his hefty monogram ring had split me open.

After that, Lisa suggested grief counseling, and I'd instantly shut her down. I didn't need it, I was fine. In reality I had zero intention of baring my soul to a stranger, expose any of my ugly truths. It was far easier pretending everything was okay, even if nobody believed me. But I'd been eighteen, not seven, and despite being that much older than Logan was now, I'd derailed. It wasn't something I could let happen to him.

I took a few minutes, surfed the web and found a number for free grief counseling services for children, and dialed. "And you have custody of your son?" the woman said once I'd explained the reason for my call.

"No, but I'm in the process of becoming his legal guardian."

"Ah…well, can his current guardian call us? I'm afraid it's necessary to arrange—"

I hung up, clenching my phone so tight I thought I'd shattered the screen, and headed upstairs to the kitchen where Ronnie and the customer were finishing their discussion.

Ronnie looked up. "Can you help with the supplies from the truck?" Once outside, he closed the front door and turned to me. "Is everything alright?"

"Yeah, yeah. School stuff with Logan. It's fine."

"You sure?"

I pinched the bridge of my nose. "Yeah, it'll have to be."

"You were on the call forever and, well, I can't afford for you to take off again. I need you here. On the job."

"Honestly, Ronnie, it's fine."

He looked at me. "You should know Leila's grumbling. She thinks you're—"

"When doesn't she grumble? Quite frankly, I don't give a shit what Leila thinks right now." When his eyes narrowed, I knew I'd gone too far.

"Sure she can be a pain in the ass," he said, "but you're talking about my sister, and your boss. First of all, get your act together, and, in the future, keep those comments to yourself, yeah?"

"Crap, you're right, that was out of order. Sorry, Ronnie."

He looked at me. "Don't let me down on this job, Josh, okay? *Don't*."

I worked in a frenzy to get everything done, including the extra bits and pieces the client added to the list after Ronnie had left. I phoned Mrs. Banks, asked if I could be an hour late, which meant by the time I got Logan home and washed, it would almost be his bedtime.

Lisa texted me late afternoon, too, said she'd stop in around eight for a "chat," which Captain Sub-Text translated as "I'm checking up on you." I'd have been happy to see her, except I needed to talk to Logan, and the house looked like multiple bombs had gone off in each room. The kitchen sink was still full of dirty dishes, and a stack of unopened mail and flyers on the table leaned more precariously than the Tower of Pisa. Logan's toys and homework had rendered the floor of the den invisible, and the hallway had become clogged with abandoned jackets, boots and shoes. Even the stairs were covered in laundry— washed and folded, at least—but one look around and Lisa would know I was losing it.

When we got home, I tackled the kitchen first, working as efficiently as I could, and took out the trash while Logan picked up his toys and haphazardly pushed the vacuum around. As I was throwing away the junk mail, and waiting for Logan to come out of the shower so we could talk about Dylan, Ronnie called.

"You cut the drywall in the wrong place for the dimmer switches," he said, and by his hushed voice and the noise in the background, I assumed he was still at the office with Leila. "The client's pissed. Can you go fix it early tomorrow? Seven thirty?"

Christ alive, the day was going from shit to deep shit, and all I wanted was for it to end. "Got it," I said, then remembered Mrs. Banks telling me she was leaving early in the morning, and I couldn't spring looking after Logan on Lisa or Ivan at such short notice. "No, wait. I don't think I can get there before Logan's made the bus."

"Crap. I forgot," Ronnie said. "Okay, I'll handle it."

"You sure?"

"Yeah. I'll figure something out. Don't tell Leila, okay?"

When we hung up, I looked at my watch, decided I had enough time to talk to Logan about the bullying. But when he walked into the kitchen, hair still damp from his shower, dressed in his puppy-print pajamas and cuddling Biscuit, my resolve disappeared.

Tomorrow, I told myself. I'd tackle it all tomorrow.

CHAPTER SIXTEEN

When the doorbell rang a while later, I expected to see Lisa outside, but instead it was Ivan. I braced myself for his bear hug by planting my feet on the floor. It really did feel as if I was being pulled into a tree. A very well-dressed tree, with his charcoal suit and long black Armani coat.

He'd called most days, asked how I was doing, if I had news about the birth certificate, or if Harlan had heard from Vital Records. I gathered Harlan was waiting for me to share the details—or lack thereof—but I hadn't found the courage to mention it to Ivan or Lisa, nor had I said anything about the photographs, the note I'd thrown away or the tax returns. Although I told myself my discretion was because I wanted to figure out what was going on, the real truth was that I didn't want them to start judging Grace, doubting her, seeing her any differently in death than they had in life, and so I kept my mouth shut.

"Good to see you," I said to Ivan as he stepped inside. "How are you?"

"Ugh. Got off a four-hour conference call and I feel like my brain's been whizzing around a blender," he said. "I'm beat. Making sense, words are not."

"Alright then, Yoda. Still living the dream then?"

Ivan laughed, a sound almost too big for the narrow hallway and threatened to make the first floor come crashing through the ceiling. "If you call firefighting shit storms all day and finding creative ways to tell CEOs they're full of horse crap then yes, I guess I am."

I hoped I hid the pang of envy I felt whenever he talked about his career. He didn't deserve any of my jealousy, was easy to get along with, fun to be around, and I had a lot to thank him for. He was the one who'd struck up a conversation the first time I set foot in the boxing club, a place I'd walked past a dozen times and finally gone into with the hope it might make me feel better. I'd already dropped most of my drinking stints with JD, much to his annoyance, and with Lisa's help I'd found a part-time job as a general laborer on a building site. She'd told me if I stayed off the booze for more than two months and continued going to AA, she'd talk to her contacts about regular work.

That had further instigated my health kick, because whenever I walked up more than a flight of stairs I sounded like I was about to pass out, throw up or both. So, one night after work, I went to the boxing club, a somewhat dingy affair that smelled of years of encrusted sweat and blood, but they offered a free trial, which was about the most I could afford.

The owner, a short guy with ginger hair and an S-shaped nose, showed me around. When the club's phone rang, and he disappeared, a huge blond guy the size of a polar bear strolled over and introduced himself as Ivan.

"Thinking about joining?" he said. "It's a great place. You fought before?"

"Not legally."

Ivan grinned, quietly said, "Yeah, same."

An hour later we'd gone for a drink—cranberry juice in my case. Within a week he'd introduced me to Ronnie and Leila, and I got my first steady job in years, and then—I smiled at the memory—and then I'd met Grace.

"You alright, pal?" Ivan put a hand on my shoulder, making the memories scurry away.

"Yeah, yeah. Lisa's coming over, too," I said. "She should be here in a bit."

"Uh-huh, she texted." Ivan took off his coat and chucked it on the rack behind him.

"You guys are talking without me as your peacekeeper? Is World War Three coming?"

"Oh, ha-ha. Where's the squirt?" He lowered his voice. "How's he doing?"

"Not fantastic, to be honest. I had a call from—"

Before I could finish my sentence, Logan ran into the hallway and catapulted himself toward Ivan's arms. Ivan lifted him high, the top of Logan's head almost touching the ceiling.

"Squirt!"

"Viking!"

Ivan made a grunting noise and shoulder pressed Logan up and down until my son's face turned an off-white color, and he stopped giggling.

"You're not going to barf on me, are you?" Ivan said. "Squirts barf. Vikings don't."

Logan grinned and wriggled to be put down, ruffling Ivan's hair and tapping his shoulders. As soon as his feet hit the floor he disappeared into the den, where I heard the click of the TV followed by the unmistakable voice of Patrick Star.

Ivan followed me to the kitchen and settled down at the table, avoiding eye contact. I handed him a bottle of pop, and watched as he peeled the paper label away. He never usually had a problem speaking his mind. It's what annoyed Lisa the most about him.

"He's so bloody opinionated," she'd said once, after they'd spent an hour debating British politics. When I asked her if she'd looked in the mirror lately, she'd thumped me.

"You alright?" I said as Ivan tore the pop label into tiny pieces, arranging them in a pile.

He looked up. "Huh? Yeah, I'm fine. Work stuff. You know how it is."

Before I could ask anything else, the front door opened, and Lisa stepped inside. "Bloody hell, it's cold out there," she yelled. "Is Ivan here yet?"

"Kitchen," he called back, and within seconds Lisa hugged us both, her cheeks icy cold from the chilly breeze.

"Did you conspire to come over together or something?" I said. "Because you've been rumbled. I know you're checking up on me, and you don't need to."

Lisa rolled her eyes. "Is Logan asleep?"

"In the den," Ivan said. "Watching TV."

"I hoped he'd be up. I brought this for his collection." She held out a little gray-and-white Old English sheepdog plush, waggled it around midair. "Woof, woof. Cute, huh?"

"Since when do you think stuffed animals are cute? You chucked yours out when you were eight. Remember? Mom had a fit."

Lisa shrugged *so what* and left to look for Logan while I went to the washroom. "Want anything?" I said when the three of us were back in the kitchen.

"No, thanks." Lisa's eyes met Ivan's for a beat. She was about to say something else, but quickly got up and made a beeline for the hall without saying another word.

"What was that about?" I said, peering out the doorway. "She didn't look very well."

"She's worried about you," Ivan said. "We both are."

I rubbed my hands over my face. "Are you hungry? I've got leftovers."

"It's okay," he said. "Had takeout at the office. Besides, I'm here for moral support."

"Thanks, Goose," I said. "Maverick appreciates it."

"First of all, I'm Maverick." Ivan grinned. "And the support isn't for you, it's for—"

"Me." Lisa stood in the doorway, her arms crossed and, I now noticed, her face blotchy.

I laughed. "You? When did you last need any kind of support?"

"Right now." She didn't move, didn't blink. "I'm pregnant."

"Very funny," I said.

"About ten weeks."

I looked at her, then at Ivan, and back at Lisa again. Finally, not only the penny, but an entire row of piggy banks dropped as the images flooded my thoughts all at once. Ivan and her standing so close to each other in the kitchen after the funeral. Lisa only drinking juice and water that day—come to think of it, I hadn't seen her have a drink for weeks—and now Ivan's "moral support"? Grace would've clobbered me around the earhole for being so dense.

"The baby's *yours*?" I looked at the radiant smile spreading across Ivan's face. "But...but you barely *tolerate* each other. Ever since *you*—" I pointed at Lisa "—found out *he* slept with one of your friends and never called her again. You said he was... let me see, what was it again, hmm...ah, yes, a total bloody *wanker* who has his head stuck so far up his ass he could French kiss his own tonsils."

Lisa waved a hand. "Water under the bridge, as Dad would say."

"Actually, I had my tonsils out when I was five," Ivan added.

"But he's younger than you," I continued, smiling now, too. "You cradle robber."

"Grow up, Josh, it's by six months." She turned to Ivan. "Aren't you going to say anything else? Feel free to jump in anytime."

He held up his hands, shaking his head. "You're kidding, right? I know you two well enough not to get in the middle."

"Anyway," I said. "And spare me the details, obviously, but how long have you two been...carrying on?"

"*Carrying on?*" Lisa harrumphed. "Well, *Dad*, his fingernails are clean and I promise you his intentions were *never* honorable and—"

"A few months," Ivan said, and I couldn't help noticing the way he looked at her, all gooey-eyed and...in *love*. It wasn't an expression I'd associated with him and a woman before. He'd had a few girlfriends in the time I'd known him, sure, but none he'd raved about. I probably had a jar of strawberry jam in my fridge longer than he'd dated anyone. But he was going to be a dad, and my sister—the woman who'd stated she'd never have kids and hell would freeze over first, which was impossible because of global warming—a mom. It was a good thing she'd usually ended her antichild speeches with, "I love Logan, though. He's the best."

"You've been going out for a few *months*?" I said, finally registering Ivan's words. "Why are you only telling me now? I could've done with some good news."

Lisa said, "We weren't sure what you'd think, so—"

"What do you mean? I think it's fantastic. Congratulations." I hugged Lisa, then Ivan. "Honestly, two of my favorite people getting together...and having a baby? Wow."

"Thanks," Lisa said. "It just kind of happened, you know?"

"We ran into each other at a bar one night," Ivan said,

squeezing Lisa's hand. "And...well...I didn't go home for three days because we were—"

"I don't need to hear this," I said, stuffing my fingers in my ears.

Lisa laughed and pulled my hands down. "Because we were talking so much, you chump. Turns out we have more in common than we thought."

"I've been telling you that for years," I said. "Still, you could've said something."

"We had to be sure it wasn't a fling," Lisa said, "or it might've got...weird."

"Her idea." Ivan pointed at my sister. "And I supported it, of course. But then, well—" he put his hand on her still pancake-flat stomach, and she smiled "—surprise."

"Plus it'll be obvious in a few months," Lisa said. "Although I'm not sure you'd notice, because I've been here ten minutes and you still haven't asked me about *this*." She held up her left hand and wiggled her fingers. "We're engaged!"

"Engaged?" If my mouth opened any wider, it would have split my face in half. "You're having a kid? And getting married? That's...*fantastic*."

"I know," Lisa said. "I'm still freaking out about it all—"

"We both are," Ivan said. "I've had a secret crush on Lisa forever—"

"You never told me," I said.

"Bro code says sisters are off-limits," Ivan said. "But why do you think I've been hanging out with you all this time?"

"Very funny." I took in their happy faces, feeling envious and immediately hating myself for it. "I wish I could tell Grace. She'd be pumped," I said, and Lisa smiled, gave me a hard squeeze. "Wait until we tell Logan. He'll freak out. He wished for a baby brother or sister almost as much as a dog, so a cousin will be brilliant."

"Before we tell him," Ivan said, "I want to ask if you'll be my best man."

"And," Lisa added before I could answer, "will you be the godfather? Don't even think about saying no. Believe me, we need your expertise. I've been reading up about this baby lark, and I tell you, I'm the one freaking out. Ivan hides his panic well, but he isn't such a stoic Scandinavian when he's reading *What to Expect When You're Expecting*, let me tell you. So, will you, Josh, please?"

I held my hands up in surrender. "Of course I will, I'd love to. Yes to both. Have you already set a date? Before child or after child?"

"After," Ivan said.

"Ivan says we should get married here, but I want the wedding in the Bahamas, on a beach," Lisa said. "But he's a stick-in-the-mud and thinks it's much easier to stay local."

"It is," Ivan said. "For everyone."

"Well, it'll only be a few friends," Lisa said. "We'd have the christening there, too. And before you say anything, Josh, I'd pay for both you and Logan." She put her hand in front of me like a stop sign. "Don't even think about arguing, Joshua Stuart Andersen, because you'll lose."

I opened my mouth, but all my words scuttled down the back of my throat.

"You alright there, baby brother?" Lisa patted my shoulder.

"Uh, yeah." I coughed, blinked a few times. "I never argue when you use my middle name, and a trip to the Bahamas sounds fantastic. *Really* fantastic."

"Hold on, guys," Ivan said. "We haven't decided anything and I think—"

"I think you're overruled." Lisa laughed before turning back to me. "Don't worry, I'll make him think it was his idea in the first place. But you're okay with me paying for you?"

"Well…I could put up a fight and pretend to be too proud to accept," I said, "but every man has his price. And I guess you've found mine."

"See?" Lisa grinned at Ivan. "I told you he'd say yes."

As I watched my sister beam at me, I hoped she'd win the case about where to get married because a trip to the Bahamas couldn't come soon enough. I imagined tearing down the beach with Logan, whooping as we jumped in and out of the waves. We'd flop down on our towels, have ice-cold drinks and authentic Caribbean food, we'd… My good mood and smile vanished as if washed away by the tide.

Lisa must have noticed, because she leaned in. "What's wrong?"

"Logan needs a passport," I said quietly.

"That's why we'd have the wedding after the baby comes," Lisa said. "You'll have tons of time to apply and—"

"You don't understand," I said. "I, uh, there's trouble with the birth certificate."

"What kind of trouble?" Ivan said, his back straight.

I took a deep breath and told them about my conversation with Harlan and the letter from Vital Records, but still left out the bag of photos, the cryptic note and the tax returns. I couldn't go there yet. Not yet.

Lisa stared at me. "But that's so strange," she said as Ivan nodded, his frown deeper than hers. "It's got to be some kind of mix-up, it has to be. Honestly, I wish you two had sorted this all out before—"

"So do I, believe me, but you know how protective Grace was of Logan," I said. "And not just Logan, of herself, too. I think that's the reason why she wouldn't marry me. She worried I'd complicate things if we got hitched and I left."

"What are you going to do?" Ivan said. "What can I do?"

I checked over my shoulder, made sure Logan hadn't wandered up behind me, then lowered my voice, anyway. "I honestly don't know, but I keep wondering when someone from Child Protective Services is going to show up and take him away."

"Harlan said that wouldn't happen," Lisa said. "And he's right. Anybody with a brain cell can tell how much you love Logan. Where else would he go?"

"What about Grace's parents?" Ivan said. "Still no luck?"

"No, although to be honest with everything that's going on, I don't really have the courage to—" I noticed Lisa biting her thumbnail. "What?" She shook her head so I glanced at Ivan, but he looked clueless, too. I threw my hands in the air. "Out with it, sis. I don't have the energy to guess."

Lisa took a deep breath. "Well, doesn't it seem strange how Grace loved you so much, but wouldn't even talk about getting married?"

"Plenty of people don't—"

"Or how she never really told you anything about Logan's dad?"

Ivan spoke but didn't get very far. "Lisa, I don't—"

She held up a hand. "And you never met her parents."

"What exactly are you getting at?" I said. "You know what happened. She had a despicable family, a one-hour stand and trust issues. Sorry, but what's hard to understand?"

I could tell Lisa was treading carefully, as if she were on a thirty-foot-high tightrope with a venomous snake pit on one side, and a pride of famished lions on the other. I also knew if she was about to say something important, she'd have thought it through, gone over it in her head countless times. My sister's idea of spontaneity meant choosing between two movies after reading every single review on Rotten Tomatoes.

"Grace kept a lot of things close to her chest. Far more than most." She sat back in her chair with the expression of a poker player laying down the winning hand.

"That's a shitty comment to make," I said.

"I agree," Ivan said, ignoring my sister's death stares. "I knew Grace before either of you, and I didn't find her secretive."

"Course you didn't," Lisa said with a sigh.

"I loved her," I said. "Secretive or not, I loved her."

"More than life itself, you told me a million times." Lisa rubbed my arm in an unmistakable conciliatory gesture, but I shook her off. "I'm sorry, Josh, I shouldn't have said anything. Look, how about we get Logan and tell him our news?"

"I'll go," I whispered and walked out of the kitchen, pulling the door shut behind me. I didn't want them to see me in the hallway, resting my head against the wall as I tried to get it together. Because Lisa had managed to articulate all the things I'd barely dared to think about, let alone had the guts to say out loud.

CHAPTER SEVENTEEN

I woke up an hour before my alarm went off, one of Lisa's comments from the previous evening crashing around my brain like a Roller Derby team. She'd talked about registering their baby for day care, how she'd already looked into it because they wanted the best spot possible.

If I was being completely honest, I hadn't actively listened, made an off-the-cuff remark about rich people problems, which prompted Lisa to tell me to, quote, "Bugger right off." But as soon as I opened my eyes and remembered the conversation, I immediately thought about how Grace had signed Logan up for school, gone there alone despite my offer to come. Consequently, a visit to Winterhurst Elementary became my new, burning, priority.

I sent Ronnie a text, saying I might be a few minutes late. It was only five thirty, but his reply—A FEW is fine—was instant. Logan and I wouldn't need to leave for ages, ample time and opportunity to finally bring up what was going on with Dylan, but, I decided, I'd pick the moment carefully, make sure he didn't have the chance to storm off and hide out in his bedroom.

Once we were settled in the truck I put the radio on low, hummed along to a few bars of the Sam Hunt song, waiting for Logan to join in. I felt like the Child Catcher from *Chitty Chitty Bang Bang*, lulling him into a false sense of security like that. All I needed was the hat, bow tie and net, maybe the oversize nose. Apparently Logan was onto me, as well. When I glanced in the rearview mirror, I caught him staring at me, the worry in his eyes as plain as the zigzag scar on his forehead, the one he'd earned by driving his Bobby Car into a table when he was three.

"I heard there were problems at school yesterday," I said.

Logan stared out of the window. "I thought Mr. Shapran forgot to call you."

"He told me you've been picking on Dylan, not the other way around. Is that true?"

"Yes," Logan whispered.

"Why?" I said, but he looked away. "Can you tell me what the fight with Dylan was about yesterday? How did it start?"

"Pablo," Logan answered, and when I didn't reply he added, "Because he's mean."

"Pablo's mean? Okay...how so?"

"He just *is*."

"I'm afraid you're going to have to do better than that, kiddo. Talk to me, please. It's the only way I can help. Let's figure this out together."

Logan crossed his arms. "He said I'm a cast out."

"An outcast?"

"Yeah. An outcast. He said I don't have any real parents."

Trying very hard to keep my voice under control, I said, "Did Dylan say it, too? Is that why you tripped him?" A shake of the head. "Then why?"

Logan mumbled something I couldn't make out, and when I asked him to repeat it he said, "He's small. I knew I'd win."

I let that sink in for a minute. "Have you been mean to Dylan when someone else has been mean to you?" A guilty look and a slight nod. "And how does it make you feel when someone isn't nice to you?"

"Bad," Logan whispered.

"Exactly. You can't go around hurting people, especially not the ones who haven't done anything—"

"But—"

"*No*, Logan. It's wrong."

"But Pablo—"

"He's wrong, too. About everything. First of all, he shouldn't call you names. Second, you're not an outcast because that's someone who's been rejected by everybody else. Someone nobody wants around. Am I making sense?" I said, making myself calm down by exhaling quietly and counting to five. "But you have friends. Your teachers like you—"

"Mr. Shapran does, he's nice."

"—and you've got me." I smiled at him. "Forever and ever, remember? We're PB and J. Mac and cheese. Ketchup and fries. Crumpets and—"

"But what if you die, too?" Logan's voice went up a few notches. "Where will I go?"

Another glance was all I needed to see the tension etched on his face. There was no point trying to make light of his concern because it bothered me, too. For the next twenty years I could hardly avoid taking any and all risks, roll myself up in a hundred layers of Bubble Wrap, or find a way for both of us to hibernate.

"I'll speak to Aunt Lisa about it, okay? Sort something out so you don't worry," I said, thinking I'd ask Harlan to take care of it once we'd figured out the rest. "And I'll talk to Mr. Shapran about Pablo. In the meantime, I want you to apologize to Dylan when you get to class."

"I already did." Logan put his head down, hunched his shoulders.

"Well, saying sorry again isn't going to hurt anyone. Maybe you can be friends from now on? Look at Ivan and Aunt Lisa. They didn't like each other much and now they're getting married." Although Logan nodded, I think it was more to appease me, because he still didn't look convinced by the time we pulled up at the school.

"Josh, Logan, good morning." Vickey Longo greeted us with her trademark smile, wearing a wine-colored sweater vest, matching pleated skirt and glasses on a gold chain. "How are you, dear?" she continued once I'd said goodbye to Logan and he'd sped off to class.

I stuffed my hands in my pockets and head-bobbed. "I'm fine."

"Had enough of people asking you how you're coping yet? Especially when they do this..." She tilted her head to one side, let the corners of her mouth drop.

"Would it be rude to say yes? Everyone means well, you know?"

"They do. And when it stopped about two years after my husband died, I suddenly realized I missed it, let me tell you." She waved me into her tiny little office. Vickey had a thing for rabbit decor. Pictures and calendars, ornaments and stuffed animals, half a dozen homemade toilet-roll bunnies, gifts from the students she'd watched grow up. "The thing is," she continued as we sat down, "most of us aren't taught how to handle grief, or those who are grieving. We all muddle along, hoping to get it right."

"And that it won't happen to us."

"How true... I know it's not much help, but we all miss Grace. Every single one of us." We sat in silence, save for the ticking of her Bugs Bunny clock on the wall, both of us grappling with our emotions for a moment until she spoke again. "How can I help you today, Josh?"

"I'm applying for legal guardianship for Logan."

"Oh, how wonderful."

"Yes, it really is. We're both excited." I made sure I injected plenty of enthusiasm. *No problems here, Vickey, no trouble at all.* "But I'm having trouble finding his—"

"Birth certificate?" Vickey said with a knowing smile.

"I take it I'm not the first person to ask. It would really help if you had a copy."

"You'd be surprised at how often those things sprout legs. Happens all the time. Now, let's see." She walked over to her brown filing cabinet, pulled open a drawer, her lips moving as she silently read the labels on the files. "Ah, here we go." She removed a beige folder and flicked through the pages, went through them again, turning each one, slowly. "How strange. I should have a copy right here...but I only have Logan's vaccination records from Dr. Minhas."

"But wouldn't Grace have needed the birth certificate to register Logan?"

"Normally, yes," Vickey said. "But we accept vaccination records, although I always leave myself a note to follow up for the birth certificate. Why wouldn't I have done that?" She bit down on the tip of her glasses. "Let me check a few other files, make sure I didn't put it somewhere by accident, although I can't imagine so."

"Okay, thanks," I said, trying to disguise the worry gnawing at my bones.

"I'll call you if I find anything. I suppose you could ask Dr. Minhas if they have a copy. You never know." She continued rattling off suggestions, saying I should call the hospital where he was born, or maybe city hall, and I thanked her politely for her brilliant ideas.

Back in the truck I phoned Dr. Minhas's assistant, but her reply was swift. A few clicks on her keyboard and she informed me they didn't have a birth certificate copy; it wouldn't have been necessary for Grace to register Logan as a patient.

I'm not sure how long I sat there, my arms and legs filled with fast-setting mortar. Even after Ronnie called, demanding to know where I was because the client was going ballistic, I didn't start the engine. A trickle of sweat sank into the back of my jeans. I was no closer to understanding what was going on. Somehow Grace had managed to make it even harder, despite the fact she was gone.

CHAPTER EIGHTEEN

"**W**here the hell have you been? You're over forty minutes late," Ronnie yelled as soon as I got to the job site, and I knew all the placating in the world wouldn't work when he continued with, "You were the one with the drawings, remember? And a few minutes means five, maybe ten, not forty, Josh. Get your shit together, will you? *Christ!*"

We spent the next hour fitting kitchen cabinets in silence, highly unusual for the man who normally regaled me with the hair-raising stories about living with his four daughters. The disgruntled silence did little to stop me from thinking about Grace's secrets, and everything they implied. Then there was Logan's bullying, something so out of character even Lisa and Ivan hadn't had any great gems of wisdom to offer the night before.

"You know where Logan's behavior is coming from," Lisa had said. "He needs to talk to someone. You, me, Ivan, a friend, his teacher, a counselor. It doesn't matter who."

I told her she was right, didn't say I wished he would to talk to *me*, felt if he didn't, he was slipping through my fingers.

"I spoke to a grief counselor," I'd said. "I have to be his legal guardian to sign him up for sessions. Can you believe it?" I'd balled my fists at that point, worked hard not to put one of them through the wall.

As I screwed another cabinet door in place, I sneezed for what had to be the fifteenth time, wished the home owners had put the cages with their two guinea pigs in a different room, my sore, watery eyes warning me there was at least one cat around, probably a dog, too. Sure enough, when the home owner returned from her errands, a black Labrador trotted up and sat down beside me, a *gimme treats* expression on its face.

"You're allergic to dogs, aren't you?" Ronnie said, breaking the silence for the first time.

Grateful for the virtual bone he'd thrown my way I said, "Break out in hives when I touch them. My sister used to have one..." I almost snapped my fingers. Why hadn't I thought of it before? What had been the one thing Lisa swore got her through our parents' death? The one "person" she'd shared all her emotions with?

Rufus, a drooling, sandy-colored retriever she'd got after graduating from university, and who she'd touted as the best dog in the world. "He knows when I'm sad," she'd said. "He puts his head in my lap and looks up at me with his big eyes. I swear he won't leave me alone until I'm smiling again. And I mean properly smiling."

Damn Rufus must have sensed what a state I was in, too, because he'd followed me around. Every time I touched him I developed a bumpy rash, to the point where I'd considered showering in Benadryl, especially after I'd fallen asleep on Lisa's couch, forgetting it was Rufus's favorite spot, and woke up half an hour later looking worse than Jabba the Hutt.

But I'd dive into a vat of antihistamine if it meant helping Logan, and we didn't have to get a dog; it could be a smaller pet. Something that could stay in his room all the time, like a guinea pig or a lizard. Vat of antihistamine hopefully not required. I picked up a cabinet door.

"Everything okay?" Ronnie said.

"Yeah, I think so." A smile crossed my face, and at lunchtime I called Mrs. Banks, asking if she'd mind if I ran a little late.

"How was school?" I said to Logan when we walked back from Mrs. Banks's house. He'd barely uttered a word since I'd picked him up, clearly unimpressed I'd left him there to eat dinner again, and do his homework. I tried to keep my face even, and asked the question again.

"Fine."

"And Dylan?" I pulled out my keys, slowly opened the front door, savoring my anticipation. "Did you apologize?"

"Yep. We're friends now."

"That's excellent, well done. Want to know something? I made a friend today, too." When he didn't answer I added, "A really, really cool one." The minidrumroll I played on my thighs generated far less of a response than I'd hoped, so I gave in and opened the front door. "She's in the kitchen," I said, trying not to laugh at Logan's frown. "Go and have a look."

He took off his jacket and shoes and wandered down the hallway while I held my breath for his reaction. It was a loud squeal that lasted a full five seconds before he ran to the kitchen doorway. "You got a puppy?" he shouted. "A *puppy*!"

I legged it to the kitchen, got on my hands and knees in front of the plastic crate. "Do you know what breed she is?" I said as I lifted the animal out. She was a tiny little thing, the runt of the litter, brown and white, with huge eyes, floppy ears and a short, pointy tail.

"A Beaglier," Logan said, breathing hard and fast as he held out his arms, and I gently put the wriggling puppy in them. He looked so happy I wondered if he might pass out.

"That's right," I said. "They told me she's a cross between—"

"A beagle and Cavalier King Charles spaniel," Logan said quickly. "They come from Australia, they're good with kids and they live until they're about thirteen years old."

"My goodness, you're a walking, talking doglopedia." I laughed.

Logan joined in as the dog sniffed his face, let out a small yap. "Stop it, silly, that tickles," he said, stroking her fur, burrowing his face in it. "What's her name?"

"Well," I said, "you can choose whatever you want. But you'll never guess what the pet shop called her... Cookie."

Logan gasped, his eyes wide, his mouth open. "*Cookie?* Like *Biscuit*?"

"That's when I knew she was the one," I said. "What do you think?"

"I love her," he said, looking up at me. "I *love* her. Thank you, Dad, *thank you*."

"You're welcome, kiddo. But I'm counting on you to walk her and feed her, brush and wash her, too. And if she poops or pees in the house—"

"I'll clean it up. I'll do all of it," Logan said, cuddling Cookie. "Every single day."

I smiled. The pup and supplies had cost a small fortune, and I'd stocked up on anti-allergy pills, too, but as I listened to Logan giggle every time Cookie nibbled at his fingers, tried to lick his face, I knew it was worth it. I'd figure something out money-wise. Some guy had called about Grace's car, and he'd sounded serious enough to buy it. My plan had been to save the cash, but to hell with it. This was far better, and there was another solution if I got into a pinch—Grace's engagement ring. I pushed the idea away. No, I wasn't ready, not just yet.

"Cookie pants a lot, doesn't she?" Logan said.

"Yes, she does. You know she'll have to sleep outside—"

"But she'll freeze!" Logan said, hugging her tighter still.

"Outside your *bedroom*, silly. On the landing. Otherwise you won't sleep."

"Yes, I will," Logan said. "Cookie can sleep in my room. On my bed, with Biscuit."

"I'm not sure that's a great idea, Logan. She'll probably pee everywhere for a while."

"I don't care," Logan whispered. "I don't."

The two of them rushed upstairs, on a mission to decide where the best spot for Cookie's basket would be. It took a while for both of them to settle down, but when I sneaked inside an hour after they'd finally gone to bed, I noticed an unfinished drawing on his desk.

It was of Logan, me, Biscuit and Cookie, with Grace's face beaming from the sky. He'd written *My Family* underneath, and my heart ached, swelled and burst, all at the same time. I'd often found being a parent the most difficult job in the world, muddling through, hoping I'd made the right decisions, third-guessing them with alarming frequency, relying on Grace more than she wanted, or said I needed to.

For the first time since the accident, I didn't feel he was pulling away from me, that we'd been thrown together by a common tragedy and were now slowly drifting apart, despite our initial promises to hold on.

I went downstairs to the den, not even slightly wishing for something other than a drink of pop, buoyed by the knowledge I'd done something good that day. At the same time it felt fragile, delicate as newly formed ice, ready to crack, break and plunge me into the icy waters below if I didn't tread carefully.

CHAPTER NINETEEN

An hour later I sat in the den, staring at the ceiling. I knew Harlan was waiting for my instructions, but I didn't know what to do, where to begin. I flicked through the TV channels, barely registered the reality cooking show with the screaming chef, the blood-soaked, warmongering knights or the diametrically opposed strangers shoved together on an island.

Eyes closed, I willed Grace to burst in through the front door, rush to Logan's room and kiss him good-night before snuggling with me on the sofa. She'd put her head on my chest, stick one foot out from underneath the tartan blanket and explain everything.

I missed her so much. At any given time, in the space of a heartbeat, I'd go from empty and numb to feeling the pain ripping me in half. Whenever I thought I'd taken a step to accepting our new reality, a commercial that had made Grace laugh, a tune she'd always hummed or the smell of her shampoo threw me right back to the beginning. Despite it only being two months since she'd gone, I had trouble imagining her voice, and her face blurred when I conjured it into my mind, a camera lens going out of focus.

I had to do something about the guardianship, surely that would help make me feel better, and someone out there had to have answers. There was no doubt Grace's parents, Marcia and Albert Wilson, were a logical place to start—if only I could find them. Sure, they hadn't seen their only daughter in a long time, but maybe they could give me details about some of her old friends, people she may have stayed in touch with. But how would I find them?

Grace had no siblings, no social media accounts I could look through for old friends or clues. She'd insisted she had no time or interest in an online presence, and made sure I didn't post pictures of her, or Logan. I pushed away the nagging feeling about it being another oddity. She wasn't the only fiercely private person on the planet. Just because the rest of the world had jumped on the over-sharing bandwagon didn't mean she had to. But still…she'd gone to great lengths to hide Logan from his father, or—I swallowed—hiding who Logan's father was from me and everybody else.

When the commercials came on, I picked up the remote to continue my channel-hopping exercise, but stopped at the opening beats of a familiar advert. Instead of ignoring it, I turned up the volume, grabbed the tablet and binder with Grace's birth certificate and typed the genealogy website address into the browser. It seemed straightforward enough: enter some details, choose a plan, provide my credit card number and hope at least one of Grace's not too distant relatives had been interested in tracking the family's history.

A few swipes and double taps and there it was—Grace's extended yet still tiny family. I raced through the list, found myself nodding at the details I remembered her mentioning. Mother and father, a maternal aunt, a paternal uncle, two cousins…

The details had mainly been input by Elizabeth Gander, Grace's aunt who apparently lived in Salida, Colorado. Grace had talked about her Aunt Betty a few times, said how they'd always got along when she was a kid, but they'd lost touch. I opened up another tab, searched for Elizabeth's name and phone number, didn't get anywhere until I ran a search using Betty. One result came up. I looked at my watch. Still early enough to call out west.

"Hello?" a woman said, her voice thick and raspy, and I couldn't speak, my tongue somehow no longer fit my mouth. "Hello?"

"Is that Betty Gander?"

"Yes, this is she."

"Elizabeth Gander? Grace Wilson's aunt?"

"You mean Marcia and Bert's daughter? Yes. Who's this?"

I paused to take a breath. "I'm Josh Andersen, Grace's partner."

"Is she alright? Is she in some kind of trouble?"

I hesitated, briefly wondered if I should hang up, let Betty live on in blissful ignorance. But it wasn't right. "I'm so sorry to tell you she passed away in March."

"What? How?" Betty gasped, and when I told her, she dissolved in tears. "Oh, poor Gracie. My poor, poor sweet girl. I'd always hoped I'd hear from her again, but not like this. Never like this…" She took a few breaths. "And you said you're her husband?"

"Her partner, yes. We'd been together for five years."

Betty stifled a sob, so I encouraged her to take a moment, then gently explained how I'd found her, and wanted to locate Grace's parents to give them the news, too.

Betty sighed. "I can't help you—"

"Please. I really should talk to them."

"Well, that's the problem. Bert's got Alzheimer's. He's in a facility now. Doesn't know anyone anymore, thinks he's the president most of the time, or Luke Skywalker, depending on what's on TV. And my sister… I'm afraid Marcia died two years ago." A literal dead end.

"I'm so sorry," I said, thinking how strange that Logan would never get to know his grandparents, how sad I felt oddly detached from the fact Grace's mother had passed.

"Thank you. Poor thing had a stroke and never recovered," Betty said. "She went far too young. I'm sure Gracie told you I didn't always agree with Marcia, but she was my sister, you know? And I'd have contacted Grace, only nobody knew where to find her. My poor Gracie."

"She told me they weren't close."

"Exactly, and, goodness dang it, I wished they'd made their peace. My sister wanted to, I promise. Even on her deathbed she hoped Grace would come home or call. But she never did."

"When did you see Grace last?"

"Hmm…would've been about seven-and-a-half years ago," Betty said. "A few months before I moved out here with my fella. Grace turned up out of the blue, looking lovely as ever. Said she'd been living in Portland but had a new job, in Albany, I think. She was about to move there, wanted to come see me before I left, too."

"And, uh, was she…alone?"

"You mean was she with a boyfriend? No. She didn't bring anyone," Betty said, and I frowned. Seven-and-a-half years ago Grace would have either had Logan, or she'd have been heavily pregnant.

"I offered to take her to see her parents, but she refused," Betty continued. "Thought she was ready, but decided she couldn't face them. Such a shame. They should've talked about what happened back then. Marcia regretted how she handled everything. Really, she did." I heard the click of a lighter, the sucking in and exhaling of smoke. "I'm telling you, Teddy Barnes, the ugly, fat piece of *crap*, if you'll excuse my French, has a lot to answer for. Gracie tell you about him?"

"Yes," I whispered, remembering how the blood had rushed through my ears the day she'd mentioned his name. We'd gone out for a walk in the park, had settled down on a bench with Logan fast asleep in his stroller. I'd put my arm around Grace, taken a deep breath and asked her if she ever thought about having another child. We hadn't been together for long, but aside from Grace marrying me, it was the one thing I wanted, for us to have a son or daughter, a sibling for Logan.

"And I was wondering if maybe you'd introduce me to your parents," I said. "I could help you bury the hatchet. I know you didn't get along in the past, but maybe we can figure it out? My parents are dead. I'd do anything to have them here again. Don't wait until it's too late. Don't regret not giving them another chance."

Grace had looked up at me with a sadness I'd never seen before. She cried, tried to get the words out, but couldn't, so we sat on the park bench until her sobs subsided enough for her to tell me what the disagreement with her parents had really been about. Teddy Barnes.

She was seventeen when she'd taken a summer job at his store, stacking shelves, helping at the checkout. "I enjoyed it at first," she said. "It gave me a bit of money to spend and got me away from my God-fearing parents."

But Teddy's hands had started to wander, discreetly at first, a pat on the back here, a brush against her leg there, until the day he'd pinned her down in the storage room, and she'd lost her virginity to a man more than twice her age.

"He told me I'd asked for it," she said, fingernails digging into the palms of her hands. "My skirts and spaghetti-strap tops meant I was willing, and I hadn't put up much of a fight, which meant I liked it rough. He insisted my parents would agree if I told them. Then they'd know exactly how much of a dirty little slut I was."

Grace asked if I wanted her to stop because there was more, and I gently told her to go on, but only if she wanted to. "I got sick, had pains in my stomach, ran a fever," she said. "I ignored it, thought everything would go away, but it didn't… it got worse. By the time I went to the doctor, he said it was the worst case of pelvic inflammatory disease he'd ever seen."

Her parents demanded to know who she'd been whoring around with, and when she said Teddy raped her, they believed his word over hers, exactly as he said they would. Her mother called her every name she could think of, and her father didn't speak to her in over three months.

"That's why I left when I was eighteen," she said, swiping at her tears. "And when I got pregnant I never told them about Logan. How could I when I didn't know his father? It would only have proven everything they thought about me was true." She took a deep breath, held my hand. "Josh…about a year after he was born I had premature ovarian failure. I don't know if it was related to what Teddy did, but either way, we'll never have a baby of our own."

She told me she'd understand if I walked away, if I didn't want to be with her. I held her, kissed the salty tears away, told her I loved her no matter what, and I'd meant every word.

"Yes," I whispered to Betty now. "Grace told me all about Teddy Barnes."

She grunted. "Five years ago he was charged with raping a thirteen-year-old, and when six other girls told similar stories, Marcia and Bert knew Grace hadn't been the one lying."

"Did he get convicted?"

"Oh, yes," Betty said. "Rotting away in a cell somewhere, good and proper. I wanted to tell Grace, hoped maybe she and her parents could patch things up, but I didn't know where to find her. On her last visit she said she'd stay in touch, maybe come visit me here."

"She never contacted you?"

"No. I wish she had. She was a good girl, my Gracie." She let out another sob. "She'd been through so much. Her parents, Teddy and before that, when she found out she'd never have a family."

"Wait. What do you mean, *before*?"

"When they said her ovaries had stopped working and that she was barren. The only blessing from her condition was Teddy Barnes couldn't get her pregnant. But imagine hearing that at sixteen…"

I sucked in my breath. "No. That's not right. Sixteen? Are you sure—"

"A hundred percent," Betty answered. "Premature ovarian failure, the doctor said. I should know. I was in the room with her."

CHAPTER TWENTY

I barely made it to the bathroom before throwing up, the contents of my stomach splashing into the toilet bowl, the air filling with the bitter smell of digestive acids. Attempting to sleep after that was ridiculous, and by the time the sun rose the next morning, Betty's words echoed even louder in my head.

Premature ovarian failure, the doctor said. Imagine hearing that at sixteen.

Not twenty-four like Grace had told me. *Sixteen.*

I pushed myself through the motions of getting Logan off to school, and let Cookie sniff around the garden as my mind screamed at me to stop making excuses, I wasn't—had never been—confused by my grief, hadn't misheard, misinterpreted, misunderstood, *miswhatever.* When my phone beeped with an incoming text message, I snatched it up, grateful for the interruption until I looked at the screen and saw the note from Leila.

Come to the office. Now.

I hadn't showered the night before, or shaved in four days, but there was no time. Avoiding the mirror, I grabbed my keys, tried to smooth down my hair. There was nothing I could do about my stubble, but I ran upstairs to change my shirt, hoped it would mask the smell of cold sweat and vomit. As I drove to the office, a spiky ball grew inside my stomach. Leila's message meant I'd be eating a major portion of humble pie, and doing some serious groveling. Sure enough, when I arrived she sat at her desk, arms crossed, Ronnie standing behind her.

"Hey, guys," I said with a tentative smile. "I came as quick as I could. What's up?"

"Uh, look, we, uh," Ronnie mumbled. "You know—"

Leila cut him off. "We can't keep you on, Josh."

My gut lurched as if she'd kicked me in the stomach with her steel-toed boots. No, my performance hadn't been brilliant, that much was obvious, but I'd expected a warning, a sharp and fully deserved slap on the wrist. I searched her face, then Ronnie's, but he refused to look at me. "You said you wanted me to manage the summer crew this year, and—"

"Yes, that's true," Ronnie said. "Leila, uh, *maybe*—"

"We discussed this," she snapped at her brother before turning to me. "We've seen a dip in your performance and—"

"A dip in my...? Grace *died*," I said.

Leila stood up behind her desk, recrossed her arms. "We gave you time off."

"Yeah. Unpaid."

"You *have* been late, though. Quite a lot." While Ronnie sounded subdued and apologetic, him siding with his sister came as no surprise, their blood thick as molasses.

"It was always about Logan," I said. "And I texted."

"Then there was the wholesaler incident," Leila said.

"And you had those kitchen plans with you that time, Josh," Ronnie added. "You were the one with all the details. It made me feel like a total idiot."

"Did Ronnie tell you they threatened to withhold money?"

Leila said. "Give us a watered-down reference before we'd even started? Look, it's simple. We have a business to run, and I—*we*—won't carry nonperformers. Come back in the fall and we'll see where we're at."

"In the *fall*?" I forced a sharp laugh. "What am I supposed to do until then? I need to work. I need the money. Why didn't you come to me, Ronnie? Tell me—"

"I did, Josh. At least I tried. You seem to be—" he made butterfly movements with his fingers "—somewhere else."

"Don't forget I warned you the very first time, tardiness is unacceptable," Leila said.

"*This* is unacceptable." I tapped her desk with my index finger. "You can't do this."

"Speak to your lawyer if you want," Leila said. "We owe you two weeks. We're paying you three. But we both feel it's best if you leave immediately."

I put a hand to my chest. "I *need* this job. I have Logan to look after."

"Maybe both of you need time off," Leila said, her chin raised. "Ronnie mentioned there's something going on at school. Why not focus on him?"

"Shit," Ronnie muttered as a burning-hot flash shot up from my chest and filled my face like a giant thermometer, ready to burst.

"Who the hell do you—" I shouted. "Jesus Christ, Leila, why don't you go fu—"

"Careful, Josh." She held up a hand, her voice louder than mine. "Your hopes of a job in the fall are fading pretty fast from where I'm standing."

I opened and closed my mouth a few times, looked at them in turn. Without another word I stormed out before I lost control and told them exactly what they could do with their fall job. Back in the truck I took deep gulps of air and mentally added up the money I had in the bank. Enough to last a few months, if I was careful. But what then if I didn't find a job?

We'd have to cut down on expenses, maybe move to a flat. Our lease for the house was month to month, and nobody would blame me for leaving, although how Logan would take the news was another story. I'd seen a few places advertised, smaller than the house, and they cost a bit less. Then again it would mean moving Logan to a different school—which he might be okay with—but getting a flat without a job…

Everything was spiraling, spinning out of control, roadblocks popping up every way I turned, making my stomach lurch, my head swirl as if I'd spent a month riding an increasingly precarious roller coaster on a continuous loop.

My hands trembled as I started the truck and shifted it into gear. I tried to push the thought of a temporary solution away, the one thing I knew would let me escape from the craziness that had clawed at my life for the past months, tearing it to shreds with its gnarled hands and whispers of suspicion. I needed a drink. Just one. Something to take the edge off for a little while. I could almost taste the release, feel the fuzziness invading my head.

Just this once. *Only* once.

Nobody else needed to know.

CHAPTER TWENTY-ONE

I don't remember how I got home or exactly what happened after I arrived. Didn't hear anyone come in later, barely registered Logan's voice and him shaking my shoulders, trying to wake me.

Sound had disappeared altogether as I lay on the sofa in the den, the copious amounts of Jack's fogging my brain. I'd meant to have one drink, really, I had. But the taste of it, the smell of it… One had turned into two, and two into too many as I'd become impatient, impulsive. It was a good thing the barman cut me off, or I'd have been away with the fairies until Christmas.

The first thing I recalled was Lisa and Ivan arriving, her voice too loud, too shrill. "Josh. *Josh!*" she said, before the unmistakable muttering of colorful expletives, followed by, "Ivan, grab Logan and go for dinner and ice cream somewhere, okay? I'll text you when this idiot's come back to earth."

The smell of dog crap smuggled its way into my nose, making me retch. I struggled to get up, leaning on whatever furniture I could reach, crisscrossing the hallway to get to the bathroom. Splashing cold water on my face may have defogged my head a smidge, but when I opened the door and Lisa shouted at me again, all I could think of was pouring myself another drink.

"What the *hell*? No, actually, what the *fuck* are you doing? Really, Josh, *really*?"

I pressed my palms over my ears. "Please don't shout." How pathetic the protest sounded wasn't lost on me, but I still said it again.

"The hell I won't." She pulled my hands away, grabbed hold of my shoulders. "Logan said Mrs. Banks walked him to the door when you didn't pick him up. Lucky for you he came in, saw you and told her you were asleep on the couch—"

"I *was* asleep..."

"Yeah, because you're all pissed up to the eyeballs. Your truck's here. Did you *drive*?"

"I—"

"Have you gone completely insane? What if you'd got stopped?"

"I didn't. And how did you know I was—"

"Logan called." She pointed to the front door. "Your seven-year-old kid saw you lying on the sofa, eyes rolled into the back of your head, and he called *me*. I can't believe it. More than two thousand days, Josh. Why in the holy hell—"

"I got fired."

Lisa didn't miss a beat. "Well, I'm not bloody surprised. I sure as shit wouldn't keep you on in this state. Is this really the first time, or have you been drinking in secret? Tell me. Tell me right now because you're not going down this path again, Josh. Over my dead body and—"

"Grace isn't Logan's mom."

Lisa's mouth stopped midway. She stared at me, as if trying to decide if there was an iota of truth to my revelation, or if I'd given her some elaborate and messed-up excuse in an attempt to grab hold of her pity. "What are you talking about? That's absurd."

"Trust me, I wish it were." I sank to the floor, rested my back against the wall. Telling her was a relief, like releasing the pressure from overinflated tires, all the anger hissing from my lungs, filling the air around us as if it were poison. "I'm going mad. I can't focus on anything. Now I've been sacked and—" I gave a small shrug "—I needed something to help."

"*I* can help." She forced me back to the den, where she pushed me onto the sofa, quickly disposed of Cookie's mess and opened the window. When the puppy padded up behind her, Lisa lifted her onto her lap, rubbed her belly. "I'm not going to comment about you getting a dog right now, but you'd better talk to me, Josh. About everything."

I did. The hidden photos, the torn-up cryptic note, my extensive search for the birth certificate, the tax returns, the conversation with Betty and all of Grace's lies. By the time I'd finished, Lisa's eyes had grown stalks.

She shook her head. "Go back to the beginning. You're one hundred percent sure about where she said Logan was born? You didn't get it wrong?"

"No—"

"Because it would explain something. I mean, the whole ovary failure thing could've been a misdiagnosis or—"

"Betty was adamant about it, and Grace definitely said she had him in Maine."

"You're sure?"

"*Yes*, I'm sure. She even told Logan. Showed him on the map, spun a cute story about the magical bloody day he was born. Why, Lisa? Why would she do that if she didn't give birth to him? Jesus, what does any of this mean? He's her kid, right? Surely—"

She clicked her fingers. "She fostered him, or maybe adopted him—"

"Already thought of—"

"—and she didn't tell you because…because she was embarrassed or something." She clapped her hands, happy as Sherlock Holmes to have solved but the easiest of mysteries.

"If she fostered him, then why haven't there been any social service visits? Why didn't I find any adoption papers?"

"I don't know. Those visits don't go on forever, do they? Maybe she misplaced the adoption stuff, or hid it somewhere so nobody would know…"

"And the tax returns?"

I watched as Lisa's mind dashed off in all the different directions mine had already gone before admitting defeat and skulking back. When she spoke, her voice was quiet, yet filled with unmistakable big sister grit. "I'm sure there's a perfectly logical explanation for all of this. Can you search adoption records for New York, or Maine, maybe?"

"How do I do that without raising suspicion? What do I say?"

Lisa nodded. "Okay, this will sound ridiculous, but what if you did a—"

"DNA test?"

"Exactly. But only to be sure. Sure you're *wrong*."

"I could get one of those home kits. Send in the samples and—"

Lisa held up her hand. "I know someone. A friend of mine runs a private lab that does genetic testing and stuff. I'll ask her. She'll do it on the quiet, anonymously. I'll call her—"

"No, no, no." The panic rising alongside the words in my throat threatened to choke me. I wanted another drink. If only I'd stopped at the liquor store on the way back. Maybe I had. I couldn't remember. "I can't. I don't want to. What if I'm right? What if—"

"Josh," Lisa said gently, patting a whimpering Cookie. "Let's do the test. It'll come back showing Grace is his mom and we'll figure out the rest, okay?"

"No. I'll ignore it all. I can do that."

"Can you?" She raised an eyebrow and I looked away. "Josh, I know I let you down when Mom and Dad died—"

"No, you—"

"*Yes.* I did. I promised I'd look after you but when you derailed, when you ended up in such a state… If I'd been there for you, if I'd helped you—"

"You did. You paid for my flight back home, remember?"

"I mean *earlier.* Before you left the country, and after you came back. I knew you were drinking, but it was easier to kick you out, pretend tough love was the only thing I could do." She paused. "I know you. This'll eat you up from the inside out."

"It won't."

"How can you say that? It already is, and I can't let it happen. I won't. Promise me you'll think about the DNA test? Whatever the result, we'll figure it out. You and me, okay?"

"Lisa…"

"*Think* about it. I'll get the kit and you can—"

"You can't tell anyone," I said. "Not your friend at the lab, or Ivan."

"I'm pregnant with his kid, Josh. I'm going to marry the guy. I won't keep secrets from him. It's not the kind of relationship we have—"

"You mean like mine and Grace's—"

"—and he's a lawyer. Whatever's going on, we need his help."

"Fine. But for your lab friend you'll have to—"

"Make something up?" Lisa said. "Way ahead of you, kiddo. Way ahead."

CHAPTER TWENTY-TWO

Lisa dropped off the DNA kit a few days later. As I opened the brown envelope with the sample tubes, I recalled her instructions. Get a cheek swab from Logan. Hair from Grace's brush, the roots attached. Include her toothbrush, if I still had it. I didn't mention I still had all of her things, hadn't discarded a single lotion, potion or lip balm.

I closed the envelope without getting any of the samples, repeated to myself I was being ridiculous. Logan was Grace's son. Everybody said how much they looked alike. Lisa must have been right about Grace being misdiagnosed as a teen; she knew far more about these things.

When we told Ivan everything he agreed it was nuts, too, said maybe Grace gave birth to Logan at home, didn't register him because she was afraid the father might find out and want custody. He expertly and very convincingly argued it was a perfectly logical explanation for her not listing him as a dependent on her tax forms, too. That was the reason for all the secrecy; the father's identity, not the mother's.

It had therefore been almost easy to shove the kit in the top

drawer of my bedside table and ignore it for three days, focus-
ing on patching things up with Logan instead. I apologized for
my behavior, for him finding me passed out on the sofa, promised it would never, ever happen again and bit down hard on
my lip when he hugged me and asked if I was okay.

"Yes, I'm okay," I said, although what I really wanted was
to get wasted again. Although I considered going to a meeting,
I couldn't face it, didn't want to admit I'd slipped after more
than two thousand days, or explain why I'd derailed. I didn't
want to lie, either.

When Logan came home from school, grinning wider than
he'd done in a week, he held a piece of paper toward me.
"Look," he said. It was a drawing of him and Cookie in a field,
Logan throwing a stick, the puppy jumping into the air. Even
the sun had a toothy smile.

"Amazing, Logan. Well done." I tried hard not to examine
him like a specimen under the microscope. For days I'd been
comparing him to Grace at every opportunity—the slant of his
nose, the shape of his eyes, the precise location of his dimples,
the egg-shaped birthmark on his knee, the way he chewed his
inner lip—but whenever I saw similarities, I spotted differences.

"I got the best grade," Logan said. "Mr. Shapran thinks
Cookie's a good subject." With his chest puffed out, I could've
sworn his expression was precisely Grace's. He bent over and
picked up the puppy, who panted and squirmed, making him
giggle. "Can I eat? I'm starving."

His frame had started to fill out a little, and I wondered what
would happen to his body if my suspicions were true. Would
I tell him? If I found out Grace wasn't his mom, would I say
anything at all? I'd promised to protect him. Did that also mean
from her? As he washed his hands, I continued to observe his
every move, and put a plate of crackers and cheese in front of

him when he sat down. There had to be a different explanation. Something I'd missed.

"Logan," I said. "What do know about your dad?" He looked at me, stuffed a cracker in his mouth, but didn't answer. "It's okay," I continued with a nod and a smile. "You can tell me."

He hesitated a while longer, ate another cracker. Crumbs landed on his sleeve and he brushed them off. "Mom said he wasn't nice. She said she's glad you're my dad, not him."

"Me, too." When he looked away, my smile quickly faded. What was I doing, pressing him for information, trying to find answers to questions he didn't know existed?

We played some cards after dinner, and when Logan went to bed I opened the envelope from Lisa, read her note again.

You need to be sure.

No, I really didn't, I decided, and shoved it to the back of the drawer again. I'd sort out the house in the morning, tackle the laundry mountain before it turned into Everest, go food shopping and ask Lisa to refer me to her construction contacts. Harlan had left another message a few days ago, wondering if I'd made progress with the birth certificate. I'd call him back, make something up, tell him the project was on hold until I'd sorted out a job. Maybe he could refer me, too. Yes, I convinced myself, I'd take control wherever I could and ignore the rest.

My perfect intentions unraveled the next morning when the phone rang an hour after Logan left for school, my heart sinking when I heard Mr. Shapran's voice.

"Don't worry, Logan's not hurt," he said, "but he punched Dylan for no apparent reason and broke his lip. Dylan will be fine, thankfully, but it would be best if you picked Logan up."

"Now?"

"Yes. He's very upset. Honestly, I think you should take him home for the day, if at all possible." Mr. Shapran paused. "I had to call Dylan's parents. They're insisting I involve the principal. I'm seeing Mr. Searle later this afternoon."

I wondered how many more piles of steaming shit life could possibly shovel on top of my head, wanted to drive my fists into the wall, knock the plasterboard straight into the den. Instead I gritted my teeth, said, "I'll leave right now."

Forty minutes later we were back at the house. Logan had his head in his hands, cried quietly at the kitchen table as I shouted at him, unceremoniously ranting at a grieving seven-year-old boy, my voice an unstoppable crescendo, the blood whooshing in my ears.

"You might be suspended, Logan, do you get that?" I yelled. "And what will I do then? You have no right to punch people, *ever*. This is unacceptable, completely unacceptable. Who do you think you are, picking on Dylan? What gave you the right? You can't do this. You've got to learn how to control your anger."

Oh, I saw the irony in what I was doing, and for the briefest of moments my rage dissipated. But when I saw Cookie pissing on the floor, I shouted at her, too. I pointed a finger at Logan, more words spewing from my mouth as if it were a fiery volcano, and for the very first time I wished I'd never met Grace, never fallen in love with her and her doe-eyed boy.

Later, much later, when Logan was in bed, I cried, too, self-loathing, guilt and shame washing over me in sickening waves. I sat in the den, whispering soft apologies to Grace as well, and instead of pushing the memories of her away to save my heart, this time I rolled back the barbed wire and let them in.

CHAPTER TWENTY-THREE

With my thirtieth birthday looming, my health back on track and Ivan helping me land the job with Ronnie and Leila, it seemed my life had inched its way toward some much needed—but still wobbly—stability. Which was exactly why I'd fobbed Ivan off when he offered to introduce me to a girl he'd met at a local bookstore, particularly when he told me she had a kid.

"But I know you two would hit it off," he said. "Really. She's great."

"Thanks, mate, but I don't need somebody else's problem," I'd said. "I've still got enough of my own, and I bet you she needs none of those in her life."

"How's the program going?" he said, his voice low to ensure nobody else in the locker room heard. "You still going to meetings?"

I nodded. "Three times a week."

"Still off the booze?"

"Yeah. I'm done this time. I mean, really done."

"I get it," Ivan said. "But you don't have to do this alone. And maybe this girl—"

"Why don't you ask her out?" I said with a laugh.

He grinned. "I've got my eye on someone else. Anyway, she said I'm friend material."

That comment led to me teasing him for the next twenty minutes because Ivan certainly was not used to being stuck in the buddy zone. He'd given me her number anyway, and I popped it in my jacket pocket, forgot all about it within a few days.

The next Saturday afternoon I sat in the window seat of a coffee shop I'd dashed into when the clouds, heavy and looming all day, finally burst open, throwing an icy-cold April downpour onto the city.

As I held on to my steaming cup of tea, trying to warm up, a stroller outside caught my eye, its fabric cover a sun-bleached, peachy hue. One of the double plastic wheels on the front spun left and right like a break-dancer, and the kid in the seat, dressed in a pair of green corduroy pants, a sheepskin jacket and a stripy hat with moose ears, clutched the remains of a soggy-looking cookie in his hands.

When I looked up, I couldn't take my eyes off the woman pushing the stroller. Her red curls bounced past her shoulders, some stuck to her face thanks to the rain, and her hands gripped the stroller's handle so hard, her knuckles had paled. Her brown suede ankle boots had salt stains, her infinite, jean-clad legs disappeared underneath the thigh-long coat she'd pulled in at her tiny waist and her turquoise scarf flapped around her neck. The stony expression on her face sent the message that everyone should get the hell out of her way. Despite her uninviting glare, she was the most beautiful woman I'd ever seen, her wide eyes and Hollywood lips pulling me in. I watched her move to cross the street, turning her head and checking for traffic, but, in doing so, missing the pothole in front of her. The stroller lurched and sank to the left as a front wheel vanished into the underbelly of the road.

At first I thought it was a matter of her lifting the stroller out and plowing on, but the buggy now had only three wheels; the fourth snapped clean off. No one else noticed, much less attempted to help. Everyone was too busy holding plastic shopping bags, shiny briefcases or whatever else they could find above their heads.

Without as much as throwing her hands in the air, the red-haired woman picked up the broken wheel and put it under her arm, ignoring the stream of horns from harried drivers reminding her their light had turned green.

That's what did it for me, her serene "it's just another day" attitude. I abandoned my cup on the table, yanked the coffee shop door open and jogged over. By this point she'd almost steered the broken stroller to the other side of the road, talking to her kid in a low voice.

"…and we'll be home soon," she said. "It's only a bit of rain, baby."

"Can I help?" When she looked up, my feet stopped working properly, as if I'd magically donned clown shoes. I forced myself to blink. "Uh, here." I took the damaged piece of stroller from her. "Let me."

"Thank you." Her voice was quiet, soft as a hug. "That's very kind of you."

"Can you believe the weather?" Christ, any minute now I'd win the pathetic prat prize.

She looked down at the stroller, stroked the boy's cheek as he grinned up at me. "I don't mind the rain. We think it brings good things."

Sounded intriguing, but a car horn blared, a reminder we were still in the driver's way.

"We should move before they flatten us," I said, and we navigated the stroller under the black-and-silver awning of a trendy-looking French restaurant called Chez Marc, managing to avoid the incessant rain from above, but unable to stop it from bouncing off the pavement, speckling our shoes.

"Thanks again," she said. "I really hoped I'd be home before the storm."

"Do you live close by?"

"Oh, no, but I'll be fine. The bus stop isn't far."

"Are you sure? I could help you get wherever you're going."

She looked at me, head tilted to one side, probably trying to decide if I was a crazy ax murderer. For a split second I almost hoped she wouldn't take me up on my offer. Ronnie wasn't due to pay me until next week, my truck was too low on gas to get far and I certainly couldn't afford a cab. Except by that point I'd have given this woman my jacket, the shirt off my back and anything else she asked for, too.

"Well, I'd better get going," she said. "Bye."

"Wait," I said quickly. "Can I get you a cup of coffee? Or a tea? Juice for your son?"

She looked at me, her brow furrowed. "I don't think—"

"We could dry off." I pointed at the coffee shop. "Until the rain stops. Look, I'm not some nutter, honestly."

Her lips twitched. "Nutter...?"

"A crazy person," I said with a laugh. "But I'm soaked and a cup of tea works wonders in the rain. Trust me. I grew up in England."

She looked at the gray clouds rolling past in the sky. As if on cue, the rain spattered down harder, bigger, fatter drops making thud-thud noises on the awning, bouncing off the ground, bypassing our shoes this time and aiming for our knees.

"I quite fancy a bagel, too," I said with what I hoped was a charming shrug.

"Toasted, with lots of cream cheese?" She smiled, careful, wary, almost as if she'd forgotten how to do it, but then she shivered, rubbed her arms. "Is it true English rain is worse than ours?"

"Oh, yeah. That stuff seeps into your bones and sticks to them for weeks."

"Do you live there? In England?"

"No, we moved here when I was a teen."

"To get away from the bone-sticking rain?"

I laughed again. "It's not all bad. It has its charms."

She hesitated a little longer, seemingly letting her next words form slowly in her mouth, maybe considering them a third and fourth time before saying, "A coffee would be nice. Will you tell me more about England?"

"I'd love to. I'm Josh, by the way."

"Grace," she answered. "And this is Logan."

A bell went off in my head and I dug around in my pocket, pulled out the crinkled piece of paper with the phone number. "This might sound odd, but do you know a guy, well, a giant really, called Ivan?"

She looked at the piece of paper in my hand. "You're *that* Josh? Ivan's friend?"

"Pleased to officially meet you." I held out my hand.

I knew as soon as our fingers touched. Right there in the miserable, chilly April rain, I knew I'd spend the rest of my life with the girl who had fiery-red curls and green eyes, an air of mystery and a button-nosed son. Except I'd been wrong. It hadn't been the rest of my life, not even close, and most of what we'd had, quite possibly, had meant nothing to her at all.

As I sat alone in the den, resurfacing from the memory, my heart wrapped itself in another protective layer, shielding me from Grace. I couldn't ignore this. Any of it. Not anymore.

"I'm going to find out the truth," I whispered, the path forward crystallizing in my mind. "I promise you, Grace, I'm going to know everything."

CHAPTER TWENTY-FOUR

I clutched the envelope that contained the cheek swab from Logan—which I'd taken Monday morning under pretext of checking his teeth—Grace's toothbrush and hair. The pain I'd felt from touching her things, that I was somehow poisoning them with my doubt, or her me with her lies, had taken my breath away. As I let her silky strands glide across my fingers, it was too much to bear, almost, *almost*, making me change my mind.

"You sure about this?" Lisa said when I arrived at her office unannounced, looking like a hobo, making the receptionist jump as I skulked out of the elevator in dirty jeans and a baggy T-shirt. "We can leave it until you're certain you're ready."

I slid the envelope across her desk, no longer able to hold on to it. As I stuffed my hands in my jeans, I turned away and looked out of the window at the clear blue skies, the buds already visible on the trees in the park below. "Yeah. Let's get it over with."

Lisa texted after she'd dropped the samples off at her friend's lab, and I called my sister twice a day, every day, despite her reassuring me she'd tell me as soon as she heard. Now that I'd made the decision to have the test done, I wanted the results *yesterday*, then kept telling myself it was irrelevant anyway, because of course Logan was Grace's kid.

For the next week I tried to keep myself busy by helping Mrs. Banks with her yard—for which she insisted on paying me despite my protests—went for a couple of runs with Cookie and headed to the boxing club, where I pounded a punching bag so hard, I almost broke my wrists. More time got killed by surfing the web for jobs and applying for a handful. I helped Logan with his homework and school projects, talked to him about Dylan, was relieved to hear they'd been getting along. And then, early Tuesday morning as I walked around the grocery store trying to make what had been a weekly food budget stretch to two, Lisa's number flashed on my phone.

"Josh? Can you talk? I…I got the results."

The tremble in her voice gave it away, and my half-filled basket of groceries clattered to the floor, the three tomatoes bouncing across the shiny floor. "Jesus Christ, Lisa. Are you *sure*? Maybe your friend made a mistake? Maybe she—"

"She ran the tests three times," Lisa said. "I can't believe it…"

Even though I'd played out this conversation in my head a thousand times, nothing had prepared me for the pain, the anger that assaulted my insides, leaving me smack in the middle of the shop, stuttering, "But, but, maybe they're…I don't know…cousins, distant ones, or—"

"Josh," Lisa said gently. "I'm so, so sorry. They're not related. At all."

My breath came in ragged puffs, the aisle of fresh produce closing in on me. I wanted to let out the scream that had grown in my belly for weeks now, but the only thing that came was a strangled, "What do I do now?" When she didn't answer I said it again, louder this time. "*Lisa*. What the hell do I do?"

"I...I don't... I'm sorry, Josh. I didn't think..." She exhaled, the emotion in her voice dripping through the phone. "I thought you were wrong. I was so bloody sure you were wrong."

Tears stung my eyes, and I swiped at them as I pretended to ignore the elderly gentleman in a black cap staring at me as he tentatively reached for a head of lettuce. I forced air into my lungs through my nose, expelled it from my mouth, tried to stop my head from spinning. The only result was my heart racing even harder, so fast it was in danger of exploding in my chest like a bloody, rage-filled grenade.

"He's your kid," I heard Lisa say, the phone still somehow pressed to my ear despite the fact my arms had gone numb. "*Yours.* You've spent every day with him for the past five years. He calls you dad. *You.* Who else is going to take care of him?"

"But—"

"But nothing," she said as a jolly announcement about the low, low, *low* price of beef came on over the speaker. "Where are you?"

"Picking up some goddamn groceries," I said, "'cos life goes on, right?"

"Okay, listen," she said. "I'm calling Ivan. We're coming over to your place and—"

"No, Lisa. I can't ask you to drop everything—"

"You're not asking, and there's no way I'm leaving you alone. I should never have told you over the phone, but I was so shocked and—"

"Shocked doesn't even begin—"

"—if the three of us put our heads together we can figure this out. I'm heading over now so go straight home, Josh, please? Forget the groceries. I'll go shopping for you later."

I nodded, mumbled a thank you and hung up, tried hard not

to look at the shelves of beer as I strode past, trying to leave my nemesis, and all her pretty sisters, behind.

Lisa and Ivan arrived within the hour, both in full caretaker, roll-up-your-sleeves-and-get-this-done mode, and I was grateful. My brain hadn't yet managed to accept Logan wasn't Grace's biological child, let alone process the implications. After Lisa fed Cookie and settled her in the den, we headed to the kitchen and sat at the table.

"I made a few calls on the way over," Ivan said, pulling out a notepad filled with scribbles. When he caught my look he said, "Don't worry, I didn't mention names."

"Thanks, man," I whispered. "And you, Lisa. I don't know what I'd do without you."

"It's okay." Lisa gave my hand a squeeze and turned to Ivan. "What did you find out?"

"Well, the adoption angle seems the most logical, right?" Ivan said, and we nodded. "Except if Grace adopted Logan in Maine, there would've been an amended birth certificate with her name on it, and that means Harlan would've got a copy when he wrote to Vital Records." He took a breath. "I was thinking maybe she adopted him here, in Albany."

Lisa shook her head. "Remember what Mrs. Banks said after the funeral? When Grace arrived here she already had Logan, and she came directly from Portland."

"That's true," Ivan said.

"Is it?" I looked at them. "At this point we should take everything Grace ever said with an entire salt mine."

"Josh…" Lisa said.

"Let's ask Vital Records here for Logan's birth certificate, to be absolutely sure," Ivan said. "Are you okay with that, Josh? I can handle the paperwork."

"Sure, sure," I said. "I'll sign whatever you need."

"Okay, so that's adoption partially covered, for now at least," Ivan said.

"What about fostering?" Lisa said. "That's still a possibility, isn't it?"

"Not from the conversations I've had," Ivan said. "There's no way there wouldn't have been any caseworker visits since Josh moved in with Grace. Besides, he'd have needed a background check, too. Then there's the money Grace would've received."

"There wasn't any, not that I saw, anyway," I said.

"Right. Not fostered then—" Ivan tapped his notepad with the tip of his pen "—unless Logan slipped through the cracks in the system somehow. I mean, it can happen."

"What if she fostered him in Maine and brought him to Albany?" Lisa said.

"I don't know," I said. "Can you just move out of state with a foster kid?"

"I don't think so," Ivan said. "But just because something's illegal doesn't mean people won't do it. I've got some contacts in Portland. I'll make some calls, see if there's a warrant—"

"A warrant?" I said. "What kind of warrant?"

His eyes darted over to Lisa. "Uh, for her arrest. For leaving with a foster kid or unlawful restraint or something. I'll call them now."

Ivan got up and headed for the den, his voice too low for Lisa and me to hear from the kitchen. I didn't know what to say. The entire situation felt as if it were happening to someone else. This couldn't be my life, a tangled, mess of lies and half-truths, mysteries and secrets tripping me up at every turn. How would we ever find our way back to any kind of normal? How would I tell Logan that Grace wasn't his mother?

"Are you going to be okay tonight?" Lisa asked quietly.

"Yeah." I clenched my teeth, forced a smile. "I'll be fine."

She shook her head, let out a sigh as she leaned forward to

rub my arm. "You don't look fine, and I don't blame you. Uh, you don't think you're going to have a—"

"Drink?" I shook my head. "No, I'm not, Lisa. I mean, I want to, believe me. A bottle of Jack's or whatever is looking very sexy right now, trust me, but I won't. I can't."

"Are you sure?"

"Yeah. I know that's hard to believe considering the amount of times I said I wouldn't and got shit-faced five minutes later. But I've got Logan to look after—"

"But the other day—"

"A one-off, I promise. I can't let myself fall apart. For him."

Lisa nodded, the question of what I'd do if Logan was no longer there, if he were taken from me, a rotten lingering smell in the air we both ignored. I couldn't face that possibility, not ever. As I busied myself with making yet another cup of bloody tea, Ivan returned.

He shook his head. "No warrant. Nothing. Not even an outstanding parking ticket."

"Well, that's good news." Lisa crossed her arms, furrowed her brow. "Okay, this might sound crazy but...what if a friend had a baby but couldn't look after him, so Grace stepped in?"

"Then why lie?" I ran my hands over my face. "Why *all* the lies?"

"To protect Logan?" Lisa said. "Maybe she didn't want him to know."

"Yeah, maybe," I said, and I wanted to believe it, I really did, but I'd done a lot of thinking since I'd given the samples to my sister. At first I told myself the DNA results would come back proving Logan was Grace's, but as the days passed, puzzle pieces kept slotting together in my brain, even though I tried to keep them quarantined in separate parts of my mind.

Some were what I'd considered smaller, trivial things. How she'd always refused to take out a loan, barely used her credit card, paid off the bills every month—early—even if it meant we'd scrimped to get by. Her driving had been careful, deliberate, always a mile under the speed limit, never running a red light, stopping properly at crossings, following every rule of the road. She'd been so respectful of the law she wouldn't even jaywalk, for God's sake, and I'd praised her for it, teased her, and she'd replied she'd never been one to get into trouble.

Other things had frustrated me, too; how she wouldn't consider marriage, or discuss buying a place of our own one day, saying she didn't want to be tied down. It had been more than that. Way more. She'd had secrets. Secrets she'd been petrified of anyone finding out. Things she'd been ready to run from at a moment's notice.

"What if she stole him?" The weight of my words threatened to crush me flat, right there in the kitchen as Ivan and Lisa looked at each other. "Come on," I said. "Are you going to sit there and tell me it hasn't crossed your mind?"

Ivan answered first, choosing every word slowly and deliberately, sidestepping the question like any good lawyer might. "It's a little premature to jump to that kind of conclusion."

"Then what do I do?" I said, slamming my palms on the table. "What the hell do I do?"

"Nothing right now," Lisa said. "You—"

"What do you mean, *nothing*?" I threw my hands in the air. "How can I do nothing?"

"What option do you have?" Lisa said.

"The *police*?" I said.

"Are you crazy?" Lisa said, her voice bouncing off the ceiling. "What will you say? 'Hello, Officer, can you help me? This kid isn't who his mom said he is and I've no idea who—'"

"I don't know. I don't know," I said, shouting now, too. "But surely the right thing to—"

"The right thing to do?" Lisa scoffed. "The honorable thing?

Think about it. If Grace—I can't believe I'm saying this—if Grace *took* Logan they'll investigate you, as well. What about your record, your DUI—"

"That was years ago—"

"Maybe, but what if they take Logan away from you immediately?" she said. "Keep him until they figure out who he is? You're not his legal guardian, remember? Wasn't losing Grace enough? And what would you tell Logan if—"

"Yes, but—"

"Josh, listen to Lisa for a sec," Ivan said, his tone calm, even. "Imagine what this will do to the poor kid."

"Please don't call the police, Josh," she said. "We don't know anything for sure yet, so you can't. You just *can't*. Grace must've had a reason to—"

"*Fuck* Grace." I ran a trembling hand over my face.

"You don't mean that, man," Ivan said. "We know you don't."

"I bloody well do," I spat. "I don't know who she was. I mean, if she lied to me about Logan, what else did she lie about? What did we mean to her? What did *anything* mean to her?"

"She loved you!" Lisa said. "You know she did, Josh, you're not thinking straight."

"Damn right I'm not."

"Please, don't make a rash decision. No one's going to come looking for Logan—"

"But that's exactly it," I said, my shoulders sagging. "That's exactly how it'll be from now on, me worrying someone's going to figure this whole mess out."

"*We'll* figure it out," Ivan said. "And until then, nobody else knows."

"Somebody does," I said quietly. "I think somebody out there is missing a kid."

CHAPTER TWENTY-FIVE

The night was long and full of research. Articles and videos, news reports and dedicated websites about children who'd vanished—some found, many still missing—and once I'd set foot on that mine-filled road, I couldn't bring myself to tip-toe back.

Even when I had triple vision and headed to bed at 3:00 a.m., sleep danced on my pillow, taunting me, refusing to let me rest because of information and caffeine overload in equal measure. My body finally won the war, succumbing to exhaustion, but all my dreams were about Logan; him disappearing through a crack in the wall, sucked into quicksand or snatched away by hooded figures.

A few hours later I stumbled to Logan's room like an extra on a zombie show, hovering in the doorway as I watched him stir, thinking, *Who are you? Who are you really?* I tried a smile that threatened to break my face as I reached out and touched his shoulder, but I had to keep pretending. There was no other choice. "Hey, sleepyhead, time to get up for school."

Logan yawned and immediately bounded out of bed. "Come

on, Cookie," he said, urging her to run behind him. Despite my insistence, the puppy hadn't spent a single night in her basket, but instead had settled on Logan's bed, sandwiched between her young master's legs. I wished Cookie's sleeping spot were the only thing I had to worry about.

"Will you be home again after school?" Logan called out on his way to the bathroom.

"Sure will," I said, wanting to give myself a round of applause for sounding so normal. I hadn't even told him I'd lost my job yet. At this point it almost felt irrelevant.

After he'd gone to school I returned to the den, went through the pages of notes I'd made the night before, still talking myself into believing Logan had been adopted or fostered. But my mind kept on asking if Grace had stolen him, telling me that if she had, and I didn't do something, I'd be denying Logan and his actual parents the right to be together. In turn that meant if I didn't act on my suspicions and seek the truth, I would be complicit in Grace's lies. For the millionth time I asked myself if I could live with that, if it was something I could handle for any length of time. The answer was no.

On the flip side, if I did what I thought was right, what Lisa had blasted as the honorable thing, I could lose Logan. There was no guarantee I'd get any kind of parental access, and if Grace had kidnapped him—the thought made me want to vomit—I'd be investigated, our faces splashed all over the news. Could I be charged as an accomplice despite my innocence? Thrown in jail? If I asked Harlan for help now, would he call the police? Was destroying the only life Logan had ever known something I could live with? Again, the answer was a resounding no.

I spent more than an hour wandering around the house, then went for some badly needed fresh air with Cookie, but my mind kept circling back to the questions on a loop. Day or night, wherever I was, no matter what I did, there was no escape, no release.

A short reprieve came in the form of Mrs. Banks, who rang the doorbell midmorning. "Can I ask you for a favor, Josh?" she said, a deep shade of crimson creeping over her cheeks while she fiddled with the button hanging from her bright orange jacket that had turned her into a clementine on legs. "I'm going away for a few days, to New York."

"How fantastic, Mrs. Banks. Have you been before?"

"Never," she said, lowering her voice and smiling brightly. "Want to know a secret? I met someone on one of those dating sites two months ago, and he's taking me."

"You met someone online?"

"Oh, don't look so surprised. Everyone's doing it these days." She had the giggle of a woman a third of her age. "Although I feel a little old for this dating game, to be honest, it's been a long time. Anyway, would you keep an eye on the house while I'm gone?"

"It'll be my pleasure," I said. I'd have agreed to rebuild it from broken matchsticks if she'd asked. Anything to stop my mind from disintegrating.

"Thank you. Well, I won't keep you. You'll be late for work."

"No, I won't. They fired me," I said, figuring she was going to find out from someone soon enough and it may as well be me. "I wasn't focused, apparently."

Mrs. Banks shook her head before muttering what I could have sworn was "assholes" under her breath. "It's hardly surprising you weren't on top form, given the circumstances," she said. "It hasn't even been three months. What did they expect?"

"A robot?"

"No doubt. Maybe Grace will come back to haunt them." When she saw my expression her face fell. "My goodness, I'm sorry. That was incredibly insensitive, but...oh, Josh, I miss seeing her. She was always smiling, always happy… Anyway, I'd better let you get on with your day. I don't want to intrude so—"

"You're not," I said. "I could do with some company. Do you have time for a coffee?"

"Are you sure? Well…a quick drink of juice would be lovely, please," Mrs. Banks said, and followed me to the kitchen, where she sat down as I poured her a glass. "I can ask around, see if I can help find you a job?"

"You would do that for me?"

"Of course. And between us, I never cared for Leila or Ronnie much. I only hired their company because of you, just like I continued shopping at Ruby & Rose's because of Grace."

"She told me you were a regular."

"At least two trips a month. Ruby was an acquaintance, so I was delighted when I introduced her to Grace, and she got hired." Mrs. Banks drank some juice and smacked her lips. "Is this orange?"

"Pineapple, Logan's favorite. Grace never mentioned you helped her find a job."

"Well, it was nothing, really. She had a job lined up here, but when she arrived from Portland, her childcare fell through."

The hair on the back of my neck stood on end and I tried not to shiver, forced my voice to stay politely interested. "Really?"

"Didn't she tell you? The boss didn't wait for Grace to make other plans and gave her job to someone else. That's the corporate world for you, I suppose. So there's Grace, a single mom, money tight, no family to help with the baby… I had to do something."

"And you got her the job at Ruby & Rose's?"

Mrs. Banks waved a hand. "Took me two minutes. I did Ruby's hair every other week until we both retired. She was looking for someone, Grace and I had already discussed books a few times, and I knew how much she loved reading…it was simple."

"So that's when you started looking after Logan…"

"To be honest I needed the company as much as Grace needed the help. My daughter had moved away, my husband had left and I missed my grandson, so—"

"Do you remember where Grace had the initial job lined up?"

"I'm not great with dates, but I never forget a name. Mayor and Mayor."

"The insurance firm?"

"The one and only. Never did enjoy their annoying commercials." She drained her glass and stood up slowly. "Well, I'd better get going. I still have to pack. Broadway here I come."

"Thanks," I said as we moved to the front door. "And have fun in New York."

After she'd left I grabbed the tablet. Fresh mug of tea in hand, I opened the browser, typed in Mayor and Mayor, called the main number and asked for the HR department.

"Hi, I'm, uh, Ronnie Thompson," I said to the man who answered. "We do homebuilding and landscaping. I need a reference for someone who worked at your company… Grace Wilson." I gave him her date of birth and crossed my fingers.

After a lot of clicking on his keyboard and a string of sighs he said, "I don't have any record of… No, wait…she said she worked here?"

"Yes," I lied. "For, uh, ten months, seven-and-a-half years ago."

"I'm afraid that's incorrect," he said. "Ms. Wilson never joined the company."

Injecting as much fake surprise as I could muster I said, "Are you sure?"

"Uh-huh. Didn't show up on her first day. Note here says

she called a week later, told us she was no longer interested. But if she put us on her résumé, well…not a good sign, you know what I'm saying?"

"You're right. I should check the other companies she's listed," I said. "What do you have on her résumé? I wonder if they're the same." I jotted down the names and dates he gave me, thanked him and hung up. Three minutes later I confirmed where Grace had worked right up until October thirtieth, weeks after Logan was born. No mention of any absence, she'd been there full-time until she'd left. If she'd already had Logan then, what would she have done with him during the day? She'd have needed an accomplice, and if someone else had been involved, where were they now?

I hung up the phone and pulled out my research notes, looked at the timeline and facts I'd written on the pad. I added October thirtieth, circled it three times in red pen, did the same with November eighteenth, the day I remembered Mrs. Banks saying she'd met Grace in the rain. A possible gap of nineteen days where something might have happened. Only nineteen.

I went back to my internet searches, reopened the FBI's missing children site I'd found, studied the details of a baby who'd disappeared months before Logan was born. *Supposedly* born. Had we celebrated Logan's real birthday, or was it a day Grace had plucked out of thin air?

I leaned closer to the screen, tried to determine if the baby was Logan, my pulse pounding as I read his name: Carter Jeremiah Polisano. I wasn't an expert in baby sizes, but the dates didn't match. If Logan was Carter, he'd have been almost a year old when he and Grace arrived in Albany, and there was no way she could've passed him off as a newborn. I opened the missing person's sheet and read about Carter's mother, who'd been found dead in a field, the boy's whereabouts, and that of his older sister, still unknown.

Sweat collected underneath my armpits, and a cold trickle sneaked its way down my back. When I'd—however tentatively— imagined Grace as a kidnapper, I'd focused on her stealing an infant, hadn't stopped to consider the parents, other than to imagine the terror they'd felt when they'd found out their child was gone. What if Grace had *hurt* someone? What if she'd decided she wanted a child so badly, she'd been prepared to do anything? Even kill for one.

I picked up the photograph of Grace, a black-and-white picture I'd taken two summers ago when she wasn't watching. She'd sat on the deck reading another book, so deeply engrossed she hadn't noticed me. I'd watched her turn the pages, the breeze gently blowing the loose strands of hair around her face. Over a dozen photographs had been taken on my mobile before she'd looked up. I'd promised to delete them, which I had, except for my favorite one I'd printed, framed and put in the den despite her objections, because in it she'd seemed so serene, at peace and content.

How could she feel that way if she'd taken a child? If she'd harmed his parents? How was it possible for Grace to be the best partner, the most loving mother in the world, and have done something so despicable? Did she feel remorse? Shame? Did she have nightmares?

"Nobody should die with this many secrets," I said out loud. "Nobody should be allowed to do what you're doing to us."

A swell of anger made it from my brain to my hand. In an instant I'd launched the picture hard, sent it smashing against the wall with a dull crunch. As it fell to the floor in pieces, I did, too, and I stayed there for a long time before daring to reach for the tablet, and expanding the parameters of my search for other missing kids.

CHAPTER TWENTY-SIX

"This is for you." Lisa shoved a piece of paper into my hands as I sat across from her over a Thai lunch she'd insisted on inviting me to. It was packed, the minimalist decor barely absorbing any of the noise. Thankfully our booth was tucked away at the back, close to the kitchen doors, the waft of satay and lemongrass filling the air every time the waitstaff hurried by.

"Is this a check?" I unfolded the paper, my forehead scrunching into a frown. "Five grand? I can't—"

"You can," Lisa said. "You need cash. I've got cash. Don't make it a big deal."

"It *is* a big deal. How did you know I needed—"

"I'm not daft, Josh. I see things, and I knew you'd never ask. You're too bloody proud."

"But—"

"Take it for Logan. I won't have my nephew eat ramen noodles and ketchup—"

"It was once. And only because I'd run out of—"

"Food?" She paused. "Well, now you won't. I'll give you

more if you need it, no problem. But so help me if you spend even a cent of it on booze I'll—"

"I won't." I shook my head, trying to convince her as much as myself. "I promise."

"Good. Okay, I'm going to clumsily change the subject now, and you'll be fine with it."

"Thanks, Lisa."

She waved a hand, dabbed her lips with her napkin, whispered, "What's going on with the *other* situation?" When I looked down, she grabbed my hand again. "What did you do? Please don't tell me you went to the police."

"No, I mean... I'm still thinking about it. Did Ivan tell you Vital Records came back with nothing?" Lisa nodded so I said, "I don't know what to do about the cops. Not yet."

"Good," Lisa said. "That's good."

"I've done so much research, it's all I can think about, and I keep coming back to the same points." I counted on my fingers. "Not the birth mother. Not fostered. Not adopted. Not listed as any kind of dependent."

"I know, I know. It's crazy."

"I have to find out where he came from, Lisa. I need to know if Grace...if she..."

"Took him...?" Lisa said gently.

"Yeah. I mean, could there have been a valid reason?"

"What, you mean if she rescued him because he was in some sort of danger?"

"Exactly. You know Grace. She took in every waif and stray when she had the chance."

"Remember the robin?" she said with half a smile.

"Jesus." I rubbed my forehead, tried to unfold the creases that had claimed their permanent place, making me an old man. "I'd forgotten about the bloody bird. She hand-fed the thing for three days straight."

"Uh-huh, until the stray cat ate it."

I grimaced, put down my fork, my *gaeng dang gai* no longer appetizing. "That was unfortunate. Anyway, if Grace was a… *psycho*, surely I'd have noticed the signs? No, there's got to be a logical explanation why she had Logan. But I can't work it out."

Lisa kept quiet. I knew what she was thinking: How many people had no idea what kind of heinous crimes their partner carried out behind their back? How easy had it been for Grace to get me to believe anything? Nice, placid, gullible Josh, such a good little lie-eating boy. The anger inside me bubbled up again, so I forced it back down my throat with a forkful of food.

"I get it, I do," Lisa said. "You need to know. Tell me what you've found out so far."

"Quite a lot, I think, but there's a crap lot of speculation, too." I told her about my conversation with Mrs. Banks and the two HR people where Grace had worked. "Basically there's a window from October thirtieth to November eighteenth when Grace left her Portland job, where I don't think she had a kid, and showed up in Albany with a baby."

"And Logan would've been what…six or seven weeks old?" Lisa said.

"Tops. We're talking about something happening in under three weeks in a relatively small area. Unless she went out of state or traveled abroad, but as far as I know she didn't have a passport. I couldn't find one anywhere, but that means exactly shit."

My sister stared at me for a while. "You're scary, you know? Maybe you should forget landscaping. Be a private detective instead." She pushed her pad thai away.

"Not hungry?"

She pouted. "Still feeling sick."

"Jesus, Lisa. I haven't asked you about the baby. I'm pathetic."

"You're not. I'm fine, baby's fine. It's a few inches long and weighs less than an ounce."

"How's Ivan?"

"God, he's distracted. Yesterday morning he left without his work bag, then he came back to pick it up and I noticed he was wearing odd socks." She grinned. "Talk about baby brain. He's going to be a total mess before it's born. And after. I think he's freaking out a bit but trying to hide it."

"When's he moving in?"

"A couple of weeks. Did he tell you he sold his place? He's in the middle of packing up. It's cardboard city over at his flat... Anyway, never mind us. What else did you find out?"

I exhaled deeply. "Three missing kids fit my timeline, but two of them are a long shot."

"Why?"

"They disappeared from the same town within a few weeks of each other."

Lisa let out a gasp. "You're talking about the Faycrest boys."

"You've heard of them?"

"You hadn't?"

"I wasn't exactly in a good spot seven-and-a-half years ago."

"No, I suppose not. It was all over the news, though. The first boy disappears from a house in the middle of the day. Then another one goes missing and the police go into overdrive because that kid's dad's a cop."

"Tyler Rhodes, married to Emily."

"Yeah, that was it. Didn't they reckon the first boy was a case of mistaken identity? The target had always been the Rhodes kid? And it was personal?"

"Exactly." I looked down at my plate, trying to stop a shudder from creeping up my spine. "It can't have been Grace. I mean, what would that mean? She was in some kind of kidnapping gang or something? I'm sorry, but that's insane."

"Yeah, I agree," Lisa said. "But you said there were three. Who's the third boy?"

"Charlie Abbott. Disappeared November twelfth from Sturbridge in Massachusetts. His mom put him to bed at eight, the dad checked on him after midnight, and when they went to his room the next morning, he was gone."

"You think Grace sneaked into the house and took him?"

"Possibly," I whispered, clenching my paper napkin in my fist, turning it into a tight ball. "The parents both had rap sheets as long as my arm. Theft, drugs, illegal gun possession. Two of their kids had been taken into care already, and the cops thought they were involved in Charlie's disappearance, but they categorically denied it."

"Sure they did…"

"What if they were telling the truth? I mean…the kid's age, the dates, the town—"

Lisa waved her hands around. "Back up. Didn't you say they live in Massachusetts?"

"Yeah. Sturbridge is on the most direct route from Portland to Albany. Lisa…" I could barely bring myself to say the next words. "I…I think Logan's Charlie Abbott."

I'd pulled all the details together the night before, my mind refusing to believe them at first, but it made up stories reaching blockbuster proportions all on its own. Grace and Charlie's mom were friends. They conspired for her to take the child because the mom was sick, the dad a monster. Or Grace and the dad had been lovers, and this was her revenge for a bad breakup. Perhaps Charlie's mom and Grace had some other history… On and on it went, my mind becoming a blur of images, converging into a single giant, cinematographic explosion.

"What did you do, Grace?" I'd whispered last night as I looked at the photograph lying on the floor in the shattered frame. "What's Logan's real name?"

"Josh?" Lisa's voice pulled me back to the restaurant. "What shall we do next?"

Thankfully my phone rang so I didn't have to answer, but I grimaced when I saw it was Logan's teacher. Before Mr. Shapran had a chance to speak, I said, "Let me guess. There's been another *issue*."

"Another fight, yes," Mr. Shapran said. "It got ugly real quick, and when a teacher intervened, Logan punched her."

"He did *what*?"

"It was an accident, and she's okay, but this is still serious. The principal wants you to come in. Now, if at all possible."

I closed my eyes and exhaled, trying to come up with a polite enough response. It wasn't Mr. Shapran's fault, although the reminder didn't help calm me much. "Alright."

"I can't imagine how stressful this whole situation is for you," Mr. Shapran continued, then lowered his voice. "You should know the word *expulsion* has been thrown around."

"You can't expel a seven-year-old!" I said, and Lisa's eyes widened.

"I agree and I can't see it getting to that point," Mr. Shapran replied quickly. "Suspension, maybe. But Mr. Searle needs you to come in. I can tell him you're delayed, give you time to collect your thoughts?"

"There aren't many to collect. I'll be right there." I stood up and Lisa looked at me.

"Want me to come with you?"

"No, thanks. I'll manage. I've been through worse, right?"

She hesitated before whispering, "Don't do anything stupid, okay? Please?"

"Like punch the principal?"

"Like go looking for Charlie Abbott's family."

"I won't, promise, and thanks again for this." I broke eye contact and tapped my pocket, ensuring I'd slipped her check in there. If she got a whiff of my plans, she'd wrestle me to the ground before tearing her generosity into a million pieces, but I couldn't do nothing.

As I walked to my truck, I thought about what the school's consequences for Logan might be, figuring that this time, perhaps, things might actually work out in my favor.

CHAPTER TWENTY-SEVEN

I sat opposite Mr. Searle, who was usually a kind and generous principal, one who'd been complimentary about Logan, and his behavior, on many occasions. The way he looked at me now, the overhead light bouncing off his naked skull, his mouth set in a straight line, hands clasped in front of him, praise clearly wasn't on his agenda.

"Well, Mr. Andersen," he said, "it seems we're having some trouble, doesn't it?"

I wondered if talking to adults in the same way he did to his students was an occupational trap every principal fell into. He'd offered me a small wooden chair, automatically seating me lower than him, and when I put my hands in my lap and kept my head slightly bent, it reminded me of the time I'd been caught smoking when I was twelve.

After I'd been unceremoniously marched into the headmaster's office by one of the teachers, they'd called Mom, who'd stormed down to the school within six minutes flat. Her voice had been loud, her dressing-down so severe, it became the stuff of legends, creating the "don't get Andersened" expression that survived in the school's halls well after we'd left for the States. She'd stopped my pocket money for six months, too, and if that hadn't been enough, my father, a great believer in old-school techniques, made me smoke one cigarette after the other until I puked all over Mom's prize geraniums. When I was finished, he'd told me wipe them off with a damp cloth, leaf by leaf, which had made me retch some more.

Now in Mr. Searle's office, I shifted in my seat, reminding myself I was the parent this time around.

"As you're aware, this isn't the first incident," he said. "I understand things have been escalating. We're lucky our teacher isn't injured."

"I'm very glad she's okay."

"Yes, but I hope you understand I have to suspend Logan." Mr. Searle held up a hand despite the fact I hadn't said anything. "I know it may put you in an awkward position, but—"

"It's okay," I said quickly. "I agree. With the suspension, I mean."

Mr. Searle's brow furrowed. "That's not usually the reaction I get from parents."

I shrugged. "I, uh, I'm thinking of taking Logan away for a bit. Give him a break."

He let out a snort-laugh. "Good one," he said before clocking my expression. "Oh, you're serious? Are you sure that's a good idea? We find rewarding a child when they get suspended—"

"It's not a rewa—"

"I can't help but wonder if some stability would be better, Mr. Andersen."

I straightened my back, bringing us almost eye to eye. "Suspending him is hardly stable."

"Touché." Mr. Searle paused, drummed his fingertips on his desk. "However, we can't simply let this go and send Logan on vacation. It would set a dangerous precedent and—"

"Then give him compassionate leave. Give the kid—and me—a break. He lost his mother, I've lost my partner, my job and now this…" The empathy angle was my trump card, and he knew it.

"There's not much time left until the end of term," he said, rubbing his clean-shaven chin. "We'll suspend Logan for a week. I'll arrange compassionate leave for the rest. You can correspond with Mr. Shapran about his lessons and finishing any projects or assignments."

"Perfectly acceptable," I said, getting up and shaking Mr. Searle's hand. "I'll pick Logan up right now. And please apologize to the teacher on my behalf."

"I will, and we'll be very pleased to welcome Logan back at the start of term," he said, tightening the invisible noose around my neck that little bit more.

With what I was about to do, there was no telling where Logan would be in the fall.

CHAPTER TWENTY-EIGHT

"I thought you'd be really, *really* mad." Logan sat at the table with Cookie by his feet, occasionally feeding her scraps when he thought I wasn't looking. "You're not going to shout?"

I put another scoop of rice on his plate. "No, and I'm sorry I did last time. It was wrong."

"It's okay, Dad, it's—"

"No, it really isn't…" I said. "Do you remember me telling you I lost my mom and dad when I was young?" He nodded. "I know how tough it can be, how angry you must be inside."

Logan leaned over to pat Cookie's head, but didn't say anything. He'd cried on the way home, bawled his eyes out and fled to his bedroom from where I'd been able to coax him out only by insisting Cookie had to eat, too—she'd get sick if she didn't.

"Logan," I said, pushing my plate away, "ever heard of Massachusetts?"

"Uh-huh. The Boston terrier is the official state dog."

I shook my head. "Where do you get this stuff from?"

He gave me a *duh* look. "Books."

"Silly me. Well, how about going on a trip there with me?"

"Are there roller coasters? Or a water park?"

"I don't think that'll work with Cookie. Plus it'll probably still be too cold, but there might be an indoor one somewhere."

Logan pumped his fist up and down and jumped off his seat, heading for the door.

"Where are you going?" I said.

"To pack."

"Seriously?" I couldn't help grinning at him. "Are you sure you're seven, not seventeen? You'll be bringing your girlfriend next." Although I'd meant it as a joke, Logan's face fell, his excitement evaporating.

"Are *you* bringing a girlfriend?" he said quietly.

"What? No. I don't have a one, I—"

"But what will happen when you do? Will she be my mom?"

I got on my knees and pulled Logan close, gently pushing a jumping, barking Cookie away. "Right now it's you and me, kiddo, and that's how it's going to stay."

"Promise?"

"Pinkie promise." It was out before I could stop it, before I remembered there was no guarantee I'd be able to keep my word, not with what I was about to do. I imagined the agony of losing him, of us saying our final goodbyes, and as the pain threatened to rip me apart, I had to inject a giant syringe of fake enthusiasm into my voice. "About this road trip. We'll leave in the morning and head for a cool campsite I found by a lake. We can swim and fish."

"For real?"

"Yeah, for real."

"Thanks, Dad," he whispered, giving me a hug. "You're the best. I love you."

"I love you, too," I said, blinking hard as I pressed my lips on the top of his head.

★ ★ ★

We loaded up the truck the next morning with our overnight backpacks, a cooler full of food and drinks, sleeping bags, my old tent and a set of beach toys. Logan was still yawning and rubbing his eyes when we stopped at a drive-thru thirty minutes later.

"Want anything?" I said.

"Chocolate donut?" He gave me a goofy smirk, wiggled his eyebrows à la Kevin McCallister in *Home Alone*, a movie that had made the three of us laugh so hard we'd cried.

I grinned at him. "What is it with Americans and their donuts? I was going to suggest white milk and a multigrain bagel… but whatever. Double chocolate with sprinkles?"

Logan's mouth dropped open, probably willing me to get the food in it so he could gobble it down before I changed my mind. Grace would've crucified me for feeding Logan crap before ten in the morning, hell, at any time, but she wasn't there, and in the case of double chocolate donut versus kidnapping, I'd take the sugar sin, thanks very much.

As I picked up our order from the window, Ivan's number flashed on my mobile. I hadn't told him or Lisa we were going away. If I answered, he'd quiz me about where we were and what we were doing, plus he'd mentioned us going over there tonight for dinner, said he'd make his famous Swedish meatballs. Tempting, because he was as much of a beast in the kitchen as he was in the ring, but our camping aka fact-finding mission took priority over everything.

I switched my phone to silent and settled into my seat, listened to Logan humming along to the country radio station tunes, enjoyed the warmth from the sun streaming in through the windshield, the temperature uncharacteristically high for the time of year.

This was the calm before a monstrous, category five hurricane, which had the potential to rip our lives apart, change them forever. And still I pointed the truck east and drove, knowing full well I was heading directly for the eye of the storm.

CHAPTER TWENTY-NINE

Although the Happy Families Campground on the shores of East Brimfield Lake sounded cheesier than a family-sized bag of Cheetos, it appeared a safe bet for a night or two, and a few hours later we pulled up to our designated spot, next to a tent the size of a small county. A gray-haired woman dressed in fluorescent pink shorts and a neon green T-shirt looked up, and as soon as Logan and Cookie got out of the truck she clapped her hands and said, "Oh, my stars, I'm in love."

"Good morning," I said, wishing the office had given us a space farther away from our neighbors so I didn't have to engage in chitchat. With my luck she was a retired schoolteacher who'd give me the third degree about why Logan wasn't in class.

"Glorious day, isn't it?" she said, tilting her head to the blue skies. "Are you on vacation?"

I nodded. "Kind of. One night. Maybe two."

"How lovely, me, too. I'm about to meet my sister at the café for lunch. Have you been? The ribs are delicious, but you've got to get there early. Want me to save you a spot?"

"Thanks, we're all set."

"You'll regret it, trust me, but suit yourself." She waved at Logan. "Bye, cutie."

Logan helped me unload the truck, and before long we made a first attempt at setting up the ancient tent I hadn't used since I'd backpacked around Australia more than a decade earlier. Cookie's idea of assistance consisted of gnawing on the strings and poles, but eventually the decrepit two-sleeper stood firm, albeit leaning somewhat to the left. We sat on the ground, ate sandwiches and drank a can of pop from the cooler.

"Want to check out the lake?" I said after we'd finished, handing Logan his bathing suit. Before I had a chance to slip off my shoes, Logan had already dashed into the tent to change, and took off in the direction of the water with a whoop and a squeal.

He jumped in and leaped straight out again. "Argh! It's freezing, Dad."

I chuckled as he ran up the beach, jumping around in an attempt to get warm. "Maybe you should've dipped a toe in first?"

"Toes are for losers," Logan yelled. "Charge!" He disappeared beneath the surface while Cookie barked at him and ran around in circles.

When Logan resurfaced he laughed out loud, a deep belly sound I hadn't heard in months, and it was all I needed to entice me into joining him. Logan was right; the water was freezing, tiny ice picks piercing my skin, but it felt pure and cleansing, almost as if it could wash the last three months clean away. I swam the few yards over to Logan, picked him up and lifted him above my head.

"Throw me," he said, waving his arms around. "Please, Dad, throw me!"

We'd played the game before at the local swimming pool, got growled at by one of the lifeguards for being unsafe. The shores were empty here, nobody to stop our messing around.

I scanned the lake and launched Logan like a human missile. He dived into the clear water, hooting and splashing as he resurfaced. "Again. Again!"

I didn't stop until my biceps burned and had to practically crawl to the beach, where I flopped down on a towel. Cookie ran over, shook her coat, covering me in speckles of sand and water. I rubbed the dog's belly and watched Logan play on the shore for a few minutes. He was on his hands and knees, a yellow plastic bucket with a picture of a starfish by his side, an orange shovel in his hands, the tip of his tongue peeping out from between his lips.

"Whatcha doin'?" I asked.

"Diggin' a moat. Anybody who attacks my castle will be eaten by crocodiles."

"Crocodiles? That's a tough break. Want some help?"

Logan looked up. "Yes, please. But I'll be the king."

"As you command, Sire. I am but a subject." I gave a short bow, which sent Logan off into another fit of giggles as he whispered "butt subject" under his breath.

Over the next hour we fashioned a castle Logan declared better than Disneyland's, decorating it with pebbles, twigs and a flag made of candy wrappers. More people arrived, older couples, some younger ones with small children, no doubt on vacation before the summer rush and mandatory high-season price hikes.

I lay back on my towel, stared up at the sky as my body warmed in the sun and thought how quickly my life had changed after I'd met Grace in the middle of the street on a rainy April day. We'd spent the next two hours in the coffee shop before going our separate ways, her phone number safely tucked away again in my pocket, where I wouldn't forget about it this time.

I'd called Ivan that evening. "You're never going to believe this. This afternoon I met the woman I'm going to marry."

Ivan groaned. "Pass me the barf bucket, man. You had a fight in the ring today? Someone smack you in the head or something?"

"No," I answered, too high on the memory of Grace to be offended. "She's amazing, mate. Really. So is her son."

Ivan made a choking noise. "What happened to not wanting someone else's problem?"

"You'll never guess who it is…" I said, ignoring his dig.

"No way. You met Grace? You finally called her, huh?"

"Not exactly. We met in the street by accident."

"Get out of here. Isn't she great? I knew you two would get along."

"You're right, but I'm not the one you need to convince."

"What do you mean?"

"She seems…hesitant," I said.

"Maybe, but she's a great person. She deserves to be with someone who cares about her. Anyway, leave it to me. I need a new book. I'll stop in at Ruby & Rose's, and—"

I laughed. "Back away, my friend. I can manage this on my own."

I'd called Grace the next day, asked when I could see her again. She'd seemed surprised to hear from me so soon, maybe surprised to hear from me at all.

"Let me take you for lunch today," I said.

"Josh, I'm flattered. But I have Logan, and I can't get a sitter that easily—"

"We could go to the aquarium," I said. "The three of us. There's one in Schenectady."

Grace didn't answer right away, but when she did, I heard a smile in her voice. "You want our first date to be at an aquarium… with my kid?" And then she'd laughed, a gentle sound, making me feel strangely breathless, and I'd laughed, too, before we arranged for me to pick them up. I'd begged Lisa for cash, and she'd been happy to oblige when I told her why.

Logan accepted me within twenty minutes of us arriving at the aquarium. One chocolate ice cream later, and I felt his sticky hand slip into mine as he pointed at the clown fish, then at my shoulders and said, "Up?"

I'd often wondered if people thought we were a regular family that day; a mom, dad and son on a fun day out. I hoped so, because I already felt I was exactly where I belonged, as if I'd finally found my purpose. It might not have been building the winding roads or physics-defying bridges I'd dreamed of as a kid, but when Logan giggled as a seahorse grabbed hold of another's tail, and Grace squeezed my hand, I knew I was finally home.

It had taken a while to gain Grace's trust, even longer for her to tell me she loved me, but I wasn't after a fling, much to Lisa's delight, who declared Grace the sister she'd always wanted.

"What do you see in me?" I asked Grace on more than one occasion. "I'm a broke thirty-year-old with a crappy job and no real prospects."

She'd simply answered, "You're a good man. You love me, you love Logan. It's all we'll ever need."

"It's okay, Dad." Logan's voice startled me and I opened my eyes, so lost in the memories I'd forgotten we were by the lake. "I get sad, too."

I looked at him, confused until I felt a tear leak out of my eye and slide down the side of my face. Logan leaned in, his eyelashes tiny fluttering wings against my bare arm.

"I get the saddest when I'm having fun," he whispered. "Because I'm happy and then remember Mom's gone, and I don't want to have fun anymore because it makes me feel bad."

I pulled him in for a hug. Lisa had often accused me of becoming emotionally stunted after our parents had died, incapable of feeling anything, or worse, refusing to, and she hadn't been wrong. Their deaths were something I still couldn't talk about, didn't want to talk about. Grace had pulled me from that deep, detached state, and I never wanted to disappear into it again. At least the raw, stabbing pain of grief I felt in the core of my heart meant I was still alive.

We moseyed back to the tent, pulled out the cooler and set to work grilling hot dogs to absolute perfection in the nearby firepit. Logan got a kick out of the telescopic forks I'd bought at the Dollar Tree in the fall. Grace had laughed at them, called me a "silly sausage," an expression Logan had borrowed since.

While I ate one hot dog, Logan devoured three, including one that fell on the ground despite my insistence he throw it away. Cookie chewed her kibble, throwing us an occasional look of disappointment, drool running out of her mouth as she eyed the food. Once we'd cleaned up and brushed our teeth, we settled down in the tent, zipped into our sleeping bags as the temperature outside slowly dropped. We lay on our sides, facing each other with Cookie between us, as we listened to the chirping crickets.

Logan reached out, rubbed his hand over my cheek. "This was the best day *ever*."

"Really? You enjoyed it that much?"

"Yes." His mouth turned into a yawn, and he closed his eyes. "It's been my favorite since Mom left." He looked at me. "Can she see us? From heaven?"

"Yes," I whispered back. "I bet she's looking down at you right now thinking how brave you've been. And how well you're taking care of little Cookie." I watched him smile and close his eyes again, listened as his breathing slowed, his chest moving up and down with increasing regularity. I took in the pattern of the freckles on his nose, his long eyelashes, the little dimples on his cheeks, barely visible now he was almost asleep.

"I love you, Logan," I said, and kissed him softly on the forehead, forcing the lump back down my throat. "I love you."

CHAPTER THIRTY

I'm not sure what was louder, the clap of thunder roaring right above our heads, or the sound of Logan's retching. Either way, I grabbed the flashlight and leaped to my feet. My head bounced off the roof of the tent, making me crouch back down. Cookie cowered in the corner, and Logan was on his hands and knees, a pile of fresh vomit pooling on top of his sleeping bag.

"I don't feel well." He clutched his belly, his face like old scrunched-up newspaper.

I swallowed the saliva running down the inside of my mouth, grabbed a plastic bag and handed it to him. As Logan was sick again, the wind picked up, and drops of rain hit the tent at an increasingly alarming speed. A flash of lightning lit everything up, illuminating Logan's crumpled face, the sound of intense thunder echoing above us.

Cookie whined, and when Logan threw up a third time, I poured him a cup of water, rubbed the back of his sweat-soaked pajamas. He brought up whatever he drank, until he pushed the cup away, refusing to try again. With the next flash of lightning I noticed the leak, rivulets of water traveling down the tent seams and dripping onto our sleeping bags.

"This is hopeless." I wrapped a towel around Logan. "We have to get out of here."

He didn't argue as I piled him and Cookie in the truck, shoved the cooler in the trunk and threw together a backpack as they waited. I drove up the road to a motel I remembered passing on the way to the campsite. The rain splashed against the windshield when we pulled up, the flickering neon lights of the Keyes Motel sign making the place resemble something Norman Bates would have reveled in. I shuddered, but Logan had already used the plastic bag I'd given him, the tent might have been washed into the lake and we needed a dry place to sleep. If Psycho was in the Keyes Motel and wanted a fight, he'd picked the wrong guy.

I lifted Logan up, praying to the Intestinal Gods he wouldn't barf down my back, and grabbed Cookie's lead. We made a mad dash to the motel's office, where I chucked the vomit bag in the trash can outside and yanked the door open, only to be greeted by the rank smell of damp, mixed with stale cigarettes. A portly man sat at the counter, dressed in jeans and a plaid shirt, a sweat-ringed, red baseball cap askew on his head. He threw us a disinterested look before returning to his tablet.

"Hi," I said. "We need a room. My son's really sick."

The man grunted, got up and reached for a panel full of keys, but when he took a second look at us, he shook his head. "No pets."

"It's only for the night. She won't be any trouble."

"Motel policy." He pointed to a yellowing, hand-written sign on the wall: *No Pets Aloud*.

I tried hard to keep my voice even. "Fine. I'll leave her in the truck."

Logan tugged my sleeve. "No, Dad—"

"We have to follow the rules. I'll leave the window open a tiny bit and check on Cookie every couple of hours, okay? We have to get you warmed up and into bed."

"Your kid's not going to puke everywhere, is he?" the man said, and it was all I could do to stop myself from vaulting over the desk and pinning him to the wall.

"Don't worry," I said through clenched teeth. "I'll clean up whatever mess we make."

I signed the paperwork, handed over my credit card for the fifty-dollar charge I hadn't budgeted for and grabbed the keys to room 4. It turned out to be the size of an old shoe cupboard, and smelled only slightly more appealing, but by that point I didn't care.

Once I'd laid Logan on the bed I made a show of going back to the truck and putting Cookie inside. The man from the front desk was eyeing me through the window, I was certain, but as soon as I turned my back I scooped the puppy up and hid her inside my jacket before grabbing the backpack and returning to the room. No more than thirty seconds had passed, but Logan had already rushed to the bathroom, knelt in front of the toilet, groaning as he held his stomach.

I got down beside him, rubbed his back as he retched until there was nothing left to bring up. "It hurts, Dad," he said, crying hard. "It really, really *hurts*."

I hugged him, carried him to the bed, where he slipped under the thin, scratchy blankets as Cookie snuggled up next to him. As I pressed down on the lower right side of his stomach, I prayed it wasn't appendicitis, something I'd had when I was ten. I didn't want to imagine what would happen if Logan was that ill. The lack of medical insurance, my unemployment… it was enough to make me gag, too. I mopped his brow with a cool towel and coaxed him into taking some sips of water, hoping he'd hold them down.

"Take this." I pressed a Pepto-Bismol tablet into his hand, grateful when he agreed, and when he finally fell asleep, the grimace on his face eased. Cookie curled up between us, panting and whimpering until she drifted off, too.

As I looked at Logan, I couldn't help wondering about his parents, what they would've done in my situation. Would they have been out partying somewhere, too shit-faced to give a crap? Would they have taken care of him the way I was? Were they terrible, despicable people, or perfect parents who could offer him far more in life than I ever could?

I stroked Logan's hair, made a silent vow that had been building inside me for days. If I found his family, if they were good people, the kind who'd love and cherish him the way I did, I'd consider telling them who Logan was. If they weren't, I'd silently retreat, never talk about the situation again. Not to anyone. Not ever.

CHAPTER THIRTY-ONE

By the time the first signs of dawn slid in between the tattered curtains, I'd already been staring at the ceiling for an hour, listening to Logan, who was still fast asleep, sprawled out on his back with his mouth open. I got off the bed, pulled on the clothes I'd chucked in a heap on the floor and crept to the window without making a sound. The weather hadn't brightened, but the rain had morphed into a constant drizzle, extending from the sky as if it were a net curtain. So much for the uncharacteristically warm weather.

When Cookie let out a quiet bark and hopped off the bed, I unlocked the door and we walked to the truck. My stomach grumbled. "You hungry?" I said, and she wagged her tail. "Yeah, me, too."

I dug around the cooler for some bread and peanut butter, and a pack of puppy food. Once I'd checked Logan was still asleep, I pulled on my jacket, sat on the plastic chair underneath the covered deck outside the room, gave Cookie kibble and water, and watched the Saturday morning come to life as we ate.

The noise of the traffic on the main road slowly picked up,

and bleary-eyed people emerged to load up their cars, moving on to what I hoped were pleasanter destinations. When a couple about my age walked out of the room two doors down, holding hands, kissing and laughing, an immediate pang of jealousy hit me. I looked away, envious because of what I'd lost, angry because I'd always question if it had ever been as real for Grace as it had for me and downright furious because I'd never know.

"Okay," I said to Cookie, ordering myself not to dwell. "Let's check on your master." She yawned, looked at me with one eye and rested her head on her front paws. I smiled. "Come on, little lass."

Logan sat up as soon as I opened the door, his face a mixture of sleep and confusion. "Where did you go, Dad? I woke up and you weren't here. I was scared."

"Right outside. Thought I'd let you sleep. How are you feeling?"

He stretched before flopping back down, burying his face in his pillow. "Better. But I stink," he said, the words muffled.

I walked over and ruffled his hair. "Yes, you do a bit. Want to shower and see how you feel afterward? I'll get some clean clothes ready for you."

Ten minutes later, a citrus-smelling Logan emerged from the bathroom, his wet hair sticking up in a chicken-feathery mess. "I'm so hungry I want a whole pig for breakfast," he said.

"No can do. You're on water and crackers today," I said as Logan stuck out his tongue. "Don't pull a face. We have to be sure you've got rid of your tummy bug."

He snuggled with Cookie on the way back to the campsite, and I made them both stay in the truck while I gathered the rest of our things, grateful the tent next to us was empty, too, so I could prepare myself for our next stop, one only I knew about.

When I'd told Lisa I wouldn't go looking for Charlie Abbott's family, I'd lied. I'd deliberately chosen a campsite near

Sturbridge, and as we'd got closer the day before, I'd wondered if I'd change my mind. If anything, I'd become more determined, even more so as I packed everything up, and we set off in the truck again, driving south.

"Look! There's a water park." Logan's yell made me jump, and he pointed at the huge sign of kids on inflatables, their grins ten feet wide. "Can we go? Can we?"

I shook my head. "You were bringing up a lung last night. We definitely can't—"

"But I feel fine now, and—"

"*No.* We can't—"

Logan crossed his arms and glared at me in the mirror. "Mom would let me. She's—"

"She's not *here.*" I hadn't meant to say it, not as harshly at least, and I wished I could pluck the words out of Logan's ears and stuff them in my pocket.

His eyes narrowed, and when he spoke again he could have been a kid twice his age. "Yeah, and it's your fault."

It took every ounce of effort to keep looking straight ahead. The veins in my temples throbbed as I took the next exit, where I pulled to the side of the road, switched off the engine and turned around. "What do you mean it's my fault?"

"You forgot the salt!" Logan shouted. "I heard her say not to. But you did!"

I saw the resentment in his eyes, the hatred transforming his face into an ugly mask. I couldn't blame him. When I looked at myself in the mirror, I couldn't stand who I saw, either. In his place I'd feel exactly the same, would've directed way more venom toward me. I'd never been my greatest fan, but now... being responsible for Grace's death and not daring to admit it, finding out about Logan but not having the balls to go to the cops...

Maybe that was the answer; drive to the nearest police station and tell them everything. Wouldn't Logan be better off in the long-term without me, a lying coward, a pathetic excuse for a role model? If he hated me this much now, it could only get worse. His resentment would build and grow inside him, a destructive disease that would erupt, leaving a shell of a person behind.

I wanted to talk to him, tell him I was sorry and beg him for forgiveness, but the words caught in my throat, threatening to strangle me as I slumped down. After wrestling with my seat belt forever, I got out of the truck, had to bend over by the side of the road, my chest heaving as I gulped in lungful after lungful of humid air. I don't remember how long I stood there, only that Logan suddenly slipped his arms around my waist.

"Please don't be mad, Dad. *Please*," he said. "I'm sorry, I'm sorry."

The red-hot pain in my chest was only a fraction of what he must have felt in his, and I deserved every last shred of his anger. "I'm sorry, Logan," I whispered, kneeling and pulling him close. "I'm the one who's sorry."

Our shoulders trembled as we stood by the side of the road, the increasingly fragile bond between us straining and writhing, threatening to break us apart forever.

CHAPTER THIRTY-TWO

We'd been back on the road for a little while, and neither of us had talked much since we'd got in the truck. I knew where I was going, had memorized the exact route to take and turned right as soon as I saw the cookie-cutter hotel on the corner. You could only go so far with Street View, and as soon as I got onto the dusty path flanked by towering oak trees, I entered unseen territory.

My intention was to slow down when we passed the Abbotts' house, get a quick look, park the truck and have a walk around, keep my distance. That changed when I saw the Harley-Davidson standing in the driveway, the opportunity too good to miss.

I doubled back and parked. "I'll be a minute," I said. "Stay in the truck with Cookie."

"Okay." He reached for the *101 Amazing Facts About Dogs* book Ivan had given him, ready to read out loud to Cookie.

As I walked up to the house the front door opened, and a woman I recognized from the news stepped outside, a cigarette between her lips and a beige, chipped coffee mug in her hand. She put the mug on the broken plastic table, and pulled her two-toned hair into a tight ponytail, her pink, tie-dye shirt rising up over her swollen baby-belly. When we finally made eye contact, I stumbled, recovered as fast as I could.

"Can I help you?" she said.

"Uh… I saw your bike. It looks great."

"You'd better believe it." She arched her back, and I suddenly had an image of her going into labor on the front steps. "Gotta love America's finest."

"What year?"

"Early '90s." She took a drag of her cigarette, blew the smoke from her nostrils before reaching for her cup.

"I'm Josh," I said, holding out a hand, but she made no effort to move.

"Jen."

I knew exactly who she was. Jennifer Abbott, twenty-seven, mom of Charlie Abbott, wife of Derek. I'd watched and rewatched the news reports of when Charlie went missing from this exact spot. A tiny bungalow, its roof now in even more desperate need of repair than it had appeared on TV, boarded-up windows on every floor, and rotting wooden steps that didn't look sturdy enough to carry a child's weight, let alone an adult's. The garbage can to the left side overflowed with bags of trash, the pungent smell of rotting food wafting past me in the breeze. I told myself to stop feeling superior. If I hadn't had Lisa's help years ago, I'd probably have ended up in a similar place.

"We might sell the bike." She took another drag. "You interested?"

"Why are you getting rid of it?"

"Need the cash." She picked a piece of tobacco from her lip and flicked it away.

"Who doesn't, right?"

"Tell me about it." Her smile took years off her face, almost made her a teenager. "Factory closed few months ago. Both me and my husband got laid off."

"Jeez, that's rough."

"Yup." She pointed to her stomach. "Nobody gonna hire me with this."

"You got more kids?" I said, and when she raised an eyebrow I quickly added, "Only, I know how tough it is. Got laid off, too. Few weeks back. Still need to take care of my boy, but they didn't care."

"Powers that be never give a shit," she huffed. "What kind of work d'ya do?"

"Construction. Been tough for me, but I worry more for my son, you know?"

"Yeah." Her face softened some more. "I've got a girl. Huge pain in the ass already and she's only two." She took a final drag on her cigarette and flicked the butt onto the dusty driveway, where it landed a couple of yards from my feet. "You interested then? Only, it's fine chatting and all, but I got stuff to do."

"No, I'll have to pass," I said. "Thanks, though. Nice meeting you."

When she turned and went into the house, I took a quick step forward, dropped to my knees, feigned interest in the bike's wheels. I snatched up the smoldering cigarette butt and tapped the tip in the dirt, hoping I wouldn't contaminate any of Jennifer's DNA. They made it look easy on the crime shows, but apart from the list Lisa had given me about items I could collect to get a sample, I didn't have a clue what I was doing, felt more like Johnny English than James Bond. A trickle of sweat slid down my back as I opened the trunk and quickly located a small, empty, paper sandwich bag I'd left in the cooler.

"Who was that?" Logan said when I'd stowed away the cigarette and got in the truck.

"Just someone selling a motorbike," I answered, heading back the way we'd come in, looking over my shoulder, expecting to see someone tailing me, yelling at me to stop.

"Did you buy it? Can we go for a ride?" Logan pouted when I didn't answer. "You're no fun anymore," he said, staring out of the window, lips pressed together.

I was grateful for the continued silence as my brain shifted into overdrive, the encounter with Jennifer Abbott whirling around my brain. If Logan was Charlie Abbott, could I send him to live with them? Could I really give him up, knowing what kind of a future he might have? That he, like two of the other Abbott kids, might end up in care? No, I decided. I couldn't do that to him. They'd have to kill me first, pry Logan from my cold, dead hands before I'd let that happen. If it made me a bastard because I'd be depriving a mom and dad from knowing what had happened to their child, so be it. Logan's happiness and future had to come first, not theirs.

I wrestled with the thoughts for the entire trip home, and by the time we pulled into our driveway, I almost hoped Logan *was* Charlie Abbott. If he was, it meant I could perhaps justify the guilt of keeping quiet, and holding on to him in secret, forever.

CHAPTER THIRTY-THREE

Lisa and Ivan brought two monster-sized pizzas over for dinner the next evening, along with what appeared to be their overnight kit. I pointed at it, eyebrows raised in a silent question.

"We're sleeping over." Lisa plonked a kiss on my cheek. "Didn't think you'd mind."

"I don't," Logan said.

"Neither do I," I said. "I know how you two love nothing more than bunking on the old, crappy sofa in the den instead of your huge bed."

"The sofa's actually quite comfortable," Ivan said, and Lisa coughed in an attempt to disguise her laugh.

"You don't need to keep checking up on me," I said. "Either of you."

"Sure we do." Lisa lowered her voice to a stage whisper. "That's what you get when you don't answer your phone in almost two days."

I threw my hands in the air. "Whatever."

"We went camping," Logan said. "We swam in a lake and made a castle."

When Lisa frowned and turned, I shrugged. "Spur of the

moment thing. Change of scene because of the stuff at school, you know?" I told them about our trip, took some creative liberties about the location, but gave enough detail to stop them from asking too many questions.

Logan regaled them with his stomach bug story. "I barfed so much it came out of my nose. And it was yellow at the end. Dad said that was bile because I was completely hollow."

"Ugh." Lisa's face turned a peculiar shade of green. "Well, you must be back to normal. You've scarfed two slices of pizza already and I haven't eaten one."

Ivan laughed. "Change the subject, squirt, or your aunt Lisa will show you a magic trick with her food. Speaking of tricks, have you taught Cookie any new ones? Want to show me?"

Logan turned to me. "Can we go to the backyard?" he said, jumping up and knocking over Lisa's glass of water, which splashed onto my plate and into my lap.

I leaped up. "Sh…oot."

"Sorry, Dad," Logan said.

"Don't worry about it. Accidents happen, right?" I froze as he looked at me, wondered whether he might say something about Grace. Whatever he was thinking, he let it go. I pushed my chair back. "I'd better get changed."

I headed for the bedroom, where I caught sight of my reflection in the mirror and winced. The person staring back at me was almost unrecognizable, my face yet again an overgrown, woolen mess. Despite that, I could see my cheekbones, mountain peaks jutting out, accentuating the valleys of my sunken cheeks. The bags under my eyes could've been made by Samsonite, and I didn't want to know where the indecipherable stains on my T-shirt had come from, or how I'd failed to notice them until now. But, as I examined my reflection in the mirror, what was going on inside bothered me far more.

I'd first noticed it a few weeks ago, but had pretended it

wasn't happening, had ignored it until the drive back from Sturbridge when Logan had asked me to turn up Grace's favorite
song on the radio. When I did, it hadn't hurt quite as much as
I'd expected. Although I didn't want to admit it, wasn't ready
to say it out loud to anyone, my feelings for her had shifted. I
no longer wanted to collapse in a heap when I thought about
her. I'd stopped feeling a rush of love when I pictured her face;
instead it was replaced by a simmering, growing rage I didn't
know how to stop, or what to do with. Everybody knew there
was a fine line between love and hate, and I seemed to be dangling my toes closer and closer to the other side.

I grabbed clean underwear and walked across the landing to
the bathroom. "Mind if I have a shower?" I called out.

Lisa's voice floated up the staircase. "Good idea. And lose
the beard, Santa."

I dropped my crumpled clothes in the bathroom hamper and
turned the water on high. After a well-needed scrub, I wrapped
a fresh towel around my waist and reached for my razor, almost
resembling something human again as I hacked away the fluff.
Back in the bedroom I pulled on a T-shirt, the Superman pa-
jama bottoms Logan had given me for Christmas and padded
downstairs to the den.

Ivan and Lisa sat on the sofa, Logan and Cookie snuggled between them. An unfamiliar, downright ugly green-eyed monster snarled within me as I stopped to look at them. Very soon
they'd have a baby of their own, *their* kid, who nobody could
take away from them. They'd be a happy family, fantastic parents, and I suddenly hated—no, not strong enough—*loathed*
the prospect of them having everything I thought was mine a
few short months ago.

Lisa noticed something was up because she turned down
the volume on the telly. "You alright? We thought you'd
passed out."

I bit down my anger, patted my cheeks. "It was a lot of fuzz."

"You look better, Dad," Logan said. "Very handsome."

"Thanks, but you know flattery won't delay your bedtime, right?"

Logan tried to burrow his way behind Ivan's back. The result was him ending up being dangled by the ankles. "I've got him, I've got him," Ivan said as he tickled Logan's belly. "Give it up. Surrender to the mighty Viking. Bid adieu to your most awesome, most favorite aunt."

"Sh-she's m-my only a-aunt," Logan stuttered through fits of laughter, his face turning red, arms flailing around.

"Yes, she is," Ivan said. "Come on then, Sleeping Beauty—"

"Hey! I'm not a princess!"

"—and say good-night to the best dad in the world." Ivan turned him the right way up, and Logan's arms went around my neck, squeezing me hard.

"Night, Dad. I love you. Night, Aunt Lisa." He clapped his hands. "Come on, Cookie. I'll read to you."

"And to me," Ivan said as they walked out of the room, Logan still in his arms, pulling on Ivan's ears and nose as they headed for the stairs. "Tell me more interesting dog facts."

Lisa flopped onto the sofa. A smile crossed her face, but as soon as our eyes met, it vanished. "I'm so sorry," she said.

"What for?"

"For being happy, and—"

"You shouldn't—"

"—that you're in this impossible situation. It's not fair because—"

"No, it's not fair. But it's not your fault, either. You have every right to be happy, and you *should* be happy. It's still a bit odd it's with Ivan…"

She let out a leisurely sigh. "He's such a great guy."

"I know. What the hell took you so long?" I laughed and

shook my head as Lisa threw a pillow at me, which I promptly caught and threw back. "You're my favorite people in the world, and the fact you've hit it off is brilliant."

"You're sure it doesn't piss you off?"

"Not even a little bit," I said, because it didn't, not in the way she meant.

"And it doesn't gross you out?"

"Lisa, I'm not ten." I paused, crossed my arms. "But I'm *very* worried about you."

"Me? Why?"

I pointed to her slightly rounding stomach. "There's a kid the size of a giraffe in there."

"Ugh, don't remind me." She rubbed her belly. "I'm going to be stretched out like bubble gum. I refuse to think about how I'll push the little bugger out."

"*Big* bugger."

"*Mammoth* bugger." Lisa chucked the pillow at me again before looking straight at me, her eyes narrowing. "How's the drinking going?"

"And here we were, having such a nice chat."

"Stop being facetious, Josh."

"Oooh. There's a big word—"

"Stop. I mean it. Have you been drinking again?"

"*No.* I haven't. I told you, it was a one-off."

"You sure?"

"Yes. I've got my priorities in order. Don't worry."

"I do worry. All the time. I'm worried you're going to crumble."

"I'm not."

"Could have fooled me when we arrived tonight. I wasn't sure who smelled worse, you, or the poor homeless man I gave my sandwich to."

"Gee, thanks a lot. But I'm fine, I promise."

She looked at me and must have decided to let it go, for now at least, and we settled on the sofa to watch TV like we were kids again, neither of us needing to make conversation. When Ivan walked back into the room, he sat down, staring at me.

"What's up?" I said when I couldn't ignore him any longer.

"You went camping close by, huh?" he said.

"Uh-huh. Close-ish." I turned to my sister. "Hey, do you want to watch—"

"You went to Sturbridge," Ivan said.

Shit. I'd been deliberately vague when Logan has asked me where we were going, but the kid was smart, reading road signs hardly a challenge for him, and Cookie and his books not nearly enough of a distraction.

"You went *where*?" Lisa said.

I ignored her and looked directly at Ivan. "Yeah. It's a great campsite, so—"

"Bullshit," Lisa said. "I know why you went. You said you'd leave it alone."

"You went looking for the Abbotts without telling us?" Ivan said. "What the hell—"

"Why are you getting so bent out of shape?" I snapped.

He waved his hands around. "Because I care about you and Logan, you moron. Haven't you figured that out yet?"

"It was just curiosity, right?" Lisa said. "You didn't...*do* anything there?"

I mumbled something about putting the kettle on, but she wasn't having any of it.

"What happened?" she said, lowering her voice. "What did you find?"

I drummed my fingers on the armrest, trying to figure out how much I should reveal, decided I'd better tell them everything. They wanted to help, both of them. Maybe it was time I let them in completely. Once I'd finished recounting the events in detail, I got up and retrieved the paper bag with the cigarette butt and held it out to my sister. She looked at it for a second, then reached for it and dropped it in her purse without saying another word.

"Do you need another sample from Logan?" I said.

She shook her head. "But my friend from the lab is on holiday. It could take a while."

"Christ, I need a drink," Ivan said.

"Make mine a triple," I said.

"Sorry," he said. "That was stupid. Look, all this is moving so fast. Why not stop—" he held up a hand as I opened my rebuttal-ready mouth "—just for a bit. Give yourself time to think, room to breathe. And us, too."

"He's right," Lisa said. "Or better yet, forget about it completely. I'll help you find a job. You can get back to normal, move on—"

"Move *on*?" I said, trying to keep my voice down. "Can you two hear what you're saying? Do you have any idea how this feels? No, you don't. Because your lives are bloody storybook perfect, aren't they?"

Ivan's jaw clenched and Lisa looked away.

"How can I move on with this looming over my head?" I continued. "Whatever the truth, my conscience keeps telling me Logan has a right to know. Besides, at some point he'll need a social insurance number, a passport or some kind of government documentation, won't he? It's not a question of *if* I'll have to face this shit show, but *when*. What will I do when he comes looking for his birth certificate, and—"

"Maybe the next step is getting a fake one," Lisa said so matter-of-fact, she could have been ordering takeout.

"Golly gee-whiz with sprinkles on top," I said, slapping my forehead with the palm of my hand. "Why didn't I think of that? Hold on. I'll go print one off the internet right now."

Lisa raised her voice. "You don't need to be an asshole, Josh. I swear you—"

"Guys," Ivan said. "Faking a birth certificate...that's some serious shit right there."

"Because this isn't some serious shit right here already?" I fired off, leaping from the sofa and pacing the room, trying to keep my expanding temper in check yet again. I seemed to spend most of my time angry these days. Angry, defeated and confused. I was sick of it, all of it.

None of us spoke for a while until Lisa said, "Josh, if he's Charlie Abbott what will—"

"Then I'll have a decision to make," I said quietly, closing my eyes and pinching the bridge of my nose. "An absolutely impossible one."

CHAPTER THIRTY-FOUR

At first, Jennifer Abbott's pending DNA comparison hung over me like a gleaming ax, ready to slice off my head in one clean swoop. Despite—or probably because of that—I savored every precious moment with Logan, wishing time would slow down, or stop completely.

We went for walks and ice cream, dug out his kite and flew it at Lincoln Park one gusty morning. The next day we took a trip to Great Sacandaga Lake where the fish successfully dodged all of our attempts to catch them. We ended up lying in the grass, eating peanut butter and jelly sandwiches, staring at the clouds, pointing out fluffy faces, dragons and boats.

A few hours were spent bookmarking job listings and checking out flats online. The rent for my favorite one cost significantly less than the house. It had two bedrooms, was right next door to a recreational center and a massive park where we could take Cookie, and fell within the catchment area for Winterhurst Elementary. Not that I was ready to make the decision to move yet, not until I'd secured work, but it felt good to know we had options.

Logan's smile returned as he slept in longer each day, the dark bags under his eyes a little smaller and lighter every morning. I had to loosen my belt, thanks to my sister's best efforts at fattening me up. She and Ivan came over every evening, and little by little I managed to relax. Toward the end of the week, the test results were no longer the very first thing on my mind when I woke up, or the absolute last before I fell asleep, and I gradually let myself imagine my future with Logan still in it.

Lisa's comment about the forged birth certificate continued to dance around my brain, and the more I thought about it, the more logical it seemed. I called Ivan when Logan was in the shower. "Do you think it's possible to get one?" I said quietly.

"Anything's possible," Ivan said, "but I can't imagine it'll be easy, or cheap. It's highly illegal, too, I might add. Are you sure that's a road you'd want to go down?"

"To protect Logan from a life with the Abbotts? *Yes.*" When Ivan didn't reply I added, "Wouldn't you?"

"Other than the fact it would probably end my career if I got found out? I don't know, man," he said. "I've been thinking about how you said Logan has a right to know, and I think that's fair. Whatever the truth is, it's Logan's truth. Do you understand what I'm trying to say? Ultimately it's his life. He should be able to decide—"

"What? Whether to live with a deadbeat family that's already had two kids taken from them? Possibly end up in danger, and definitely without a future?"

"That's exactly what Lisa said. She says he won't *have* a choice because the law will be on the Abbotts' side." He sighed. "Let's wait and see what the DNA result is."

"He's Charlie. I know he is. Everything fits. I even think he looks like his mom."

"In that case are you sure you're ready to lie to Logan for the rest of his life?"

"Wait until Lisa has your baby," I said, "then ask me again. You'll do anything to protect your kid, trust me. You'll have emotions you didn't even know existed."

Ivan backed down after that, but my conscience didn't. Of course I knew my intentions to keep Logan's true identity a secret were wrong, plain and simple. Consequently, my less than steely resolve to keep the lies going warped and bent, a pendulum swinging back and forth between my options.

Swish... *I don't have the right to keep Logan from his family.*

Swoosh... *I can't send him to live there. I have to do what's best for him.*

When Lisa came to the house that evening, I could tell something was up as soon as she walked through the door. Once she'd made sure Logan was in the yard with Cookie, she pulled an envelope from her bag and handed it to me. "I got the results."

"Have you looked?" I said.

She shook her head. "I wanted to but I couldn't, not without you."

The front door opened again and Ivan walked in, dumping his coat and bag by the banister before coming through to the kitchen, planting a kiss on my sister's cheek. "What's going on, guys? What's with the long—" His eyes went wide when he saw the envelope in my hand. "Is that what I think it is? What does it say?"

My fingers trembled as I held my breath, pulled out the sheet of white paper and unfolded it. This was it. The moment I'd have to decide how to move on, knowing Logan was Charlie. My brow furrowed as I took in the words, read them over and over.

"It's not him," I said. "He's not Charlie Abbott."

"Are you sure?" Lisa grabbed the paper so she could see for

herself. "Jesus, I don't know if I'm relieved or upset. I really thought it was him."

"Me, too." I sat down before my legs gave out. All I'd focused on was the choice I'd have to make about telling Charlie's family, and now that decision was gone, I almost smiled. "This is better, surely? Logan isn't Charlie, and the chances of him being either of the other two missing kids—the Faycrest boys—frankly, that's so remote…"

"So what now?" Ivan said. "Getting a birth certificate? Because I—"

"No," I said, shaking my head. "I have to be sure."

"Sure?" Lisa looked at me wide-eyed. "Sure of what, exactly?"

"That he isn't a Faycrest boy," I said. "I…I think I have to go there."

My sister's eyebrows shot up, a look of absolute horror spreading across her face. "The hell you are! No. No way. You're insane."

"What do you want to do there?" Ivan said.

"Stop encouraging him," she said. "Whose side are you on?"

"The same as with the Abbotts, I guess," I said. "Get their DNA somehow. We'll have to stay there for however long—"

Lisa made a choking noise. "We? What do you mean, we?"

"Me and Logan." I held up a hand as she tried to jump in. "Chances are neither family is Logan's, but I have to be sure."

"And if you're right?" Ivan said. "If he's not one of those boys?"

"Then I'll come back and I'll stop looking."

"You won't go to the police?" Lisa said. "At all?"

"No," I whispered. "I won't, but if I don't go to Faycrest, every time I look at him I'll wonder what if… I know you don't get it, but I have to know. I need to."

Lisa's face flushed a deep red. She opened her mouth to say something else, but instead got up and stormed out of the kitchen.

"Is there any sense in my trying to sway you?" Ivan said.

"No," I answered slowly. "I've already made up my mind."

CHAPTER THIRTY-FIVE

Lisa, Ivan and Logan were eating homemade, face-sized blueberry pancakes when I got up the next morning. Cookie lay on the kitchen floor with half a bowl of abandoned food by her side, and only bothered to cock one ear, give her tail a single wag when she caught sight of me. It was a more enthusiastic reception than I got from Lisa, who barely threw me a glance. In contrast, Logan bounced off his chair and flung his arms around me.

"Dad! Aunt Lisa said she'll take me swimming today."

She forced a smile I could only presume was for Logan's benefit. "I thought it'd be nice to spend as much time with him as I can," she said, shooting me a withering look.

"Can I go, can I?" Logan hopped from one foot to the other. "Please, Dad, please?"

"Sure," I said. "Let me wake up for a sec. Dang it, I forgot my socks."

"I'll get them." Logan dashed off, thundered up the stairs.

"Brush your teeth and get dressed while you're up there,"

I called after him, and once he was out of earshot I turned around. "About yesterday—"

"I hardly slept," Lisa said. "But it gave me time to think. A lot. And I've decided—"

"*You've* decided?" I said.

She sighed. "Don't make this another argument, Josh. Listen, if you go to Faycrest, Logan should stay here because—"

"Excuse me?" I said. "You're not his mom, Lisa. And you sure as hell aren't mine. You don't get to tell me what I can do with my kid so—"

"Josh, she's not trying to tell you what to do," Ivan said as he pushed the plate of pancakes and the bottle of syrup toward me. "Just hear her out."

I sat back and crossed my arms. "Go on, then."

"It'll be much quicker," Lisa said. "Think about it. If you're there on your own, you can get in, get the DNA samples and get out. It'll be easier without Logan there."

"And what if he *is* one of the Faycrest boys?" Ivan added. "And looks like the parents?"

"He doesn't," I said. "Not that I could tell from the photos and all the footage. I mean, there are some similarities, sure, but nothing blatantly obvious. And I told you, the chance of him being either of them is so small—"

"Well, you'll still need a cover story for being there," Lisa said.

"A cover story?"

"Yeah, maybe something about looking for work or thinking about moving to the area," she continued. "Worst case you say you're a writer, researching missing kids for a novel."

I picked at a pancake, wondering how Logan would cope without me, decided he'd be fine. He loved Lisa and Ivan; he might even be glad for the change. The real question was how I'd cope without him, knowing it could be some of the last weeks we might spend together. "I can't leave him. You're working, and—"

"I run my own business," Lisa said. "I'll work from home for a week. Two if need be. It's not going to take you longer, is it?"

"I'll help her," Ivan said. "I'll do whatever it takes."

"I looked at summer camps last night," Lisa said, pulling out her phone. "Found loads of them Logan will go crazy for, and he'd be gone for most of the day, so you can stop worrying."

"But—"

"Let him have some fun," she said. "It'll do him good to be with kids his age."

"You agree with this?" I said to Ivan. "Or has my sister expertly manipulated you like a giant piece of Play-Doh?"

"Whatever," he replied. "But for what it's worth, I think she's right. About everything. Nobody will know him at camp, or what happened to his mom, or at school… Maybe it'll give him a break, help him make new friends."

"What about fluff ball here?" I said. "What'll we do with Cookie?"

"Leave her with us, too," Lisa said. "If Logan goes to camp, I'll take her to the office. The guys there love dogs."

"You're such a great boss." Ivan put his arms around her, pulled her toward him.

"Get a room you two," I said. "Actually, don't. That's what got you into this trouble."

"*Actually,*" Lisa said, raising an eyebrow, "it was a faulty diaphragm."

I stuck my fingers in my ears, closed my eyes. "La-la-la-la-la. Not listening."

She pulled my hands away. "So we've agreed? You go on your trip, if you must, but Logan stays here?"

"You're going away?" Logan was behind us, his voice small, frightened. "Dad?"

I spun around. He stood in the doorway looking up at me, a deep-set frown on his face.

"Maybe," I said as I knelt down in front of him. "We're just talking about it, and it wouldn't be long. A week, two at the most."

"But why are you going?" Logan said.

"It's for work," I said quickly, hating myself for the lie, not seeing any alternative. "There might be a new job, so I thought I'd check it out. See if it's any good."

"Can I come?" Logan said.

"We thought you could stay with me," Lisa said. "Ivan will come, too…"

Logan looked at him. "You will?"

"Uh-huh," Ivan said. "I'll take you to a football game—"

"And you can go to a summer camp," Lisa said. "I found one where you can try lots of different sports. There's basketball, football, soccer, archery—"

"Like Katniss in *The Hunger Games*?" Logan said.

"When did *you* watch *The Hunger Games*?" I said.

Logan rolled his eyes. "I read it."

"Aren't you supposed to be reading that diary of a puny boy or something?" Lisa said.

"Wimpy Kid," Logan said. "I did. All of them."

"In that case I'll take you book shopping, or to the library," Lisa said. "Both if you want."

"You'll only go for a week, Dad?" Logan asked.

"Maybe two," I said.

He shrugged, grabbed an apple from the fruit bowl and sank his teeth into it, a trickle of juice running down his chin. "Okay. Can I watch TV?"

"Sure you can," I said, a sudden stabbing pinch jabbing my heart as I watched him leave the kitchen, Cookie by his side.

"He's a great kid," Ivan whispered. "Really. A great kid."

"I know," I said.

"Are you sure about this, Josh?" Lisa said. "Aren't you afraid of what you could find?"

"I'm terrified," I said quietly. "Absolutely bloody terrified."

CHAPTER THIRTY-SIX

A few days later—all too soon—it was time to drop Logan and Cookie off at Lisa's. We'd decided I'd take him over the evening before I left for Faycrest so they could catch a movie, and I'd get an early start the next morning. Or, as Lisa had put it, "Hurry up and get it over with."

"I'll call every day and I'll be back next weekend," I told Logan as I kissed him and hugged him tight. "Friday at the latest. A few sleeps, okay?"

He nodded and threw his arms around me, my heart yelling at me to stay while my head ordered me to go after those answers so we could move on once and for all. I gave him another squeeze. "Call me anytime, kiddo. I'm only a few hours away."

Ivan clapped me on the shoulder, almost looking more miserable than I felt. "Good luck, man. Promise you'll be careful, you hear me?" he said quietly. "You're not Sherlock Holmes. The first sign of anything weird and you come back here, stat."

I could tell Lisa was fighting hard not to well up as she hugged me, too. Anyone watching would have wondered what the fuss was about. I was hardly going off to war, although on some accounts it felt like it. I patted Cookie, gave Logan a final embrace, another kiss, and headed back home for the night, where I tossed and turned, finally falling asleep well after midnight.

Impatience had me up again at five, and I went for a run to offset the long drive ahead. That's what I told myself, anyway. In reality, I was too nervous to get going, and needed to delay the journey a little while longer. My legs and lungs soon burned as I pushed them harder than I'd done in years.

Tiny dew crystals sparkled on the trees. Birds chirped, squirrels chattered, an engine backfired in the distance. It seemed a reawakening of my senses of sorts, as if I'd been on standby for the past few months. Fresh energy filled my veins, pumping more adrenaline through my body, making me go faster until my sweat-drenched T-shirt stuck to my back like a second skin. Finally, when I couldn't go any farther, I stopped and closed my eyes, turned my face to the sky. This was it. In a few hours I'd be in Faycrest, scouting out two families, somehow getting DNA samples from the mothers.

"Or from the dads," I'd said to Lisa a couple of days ago. "Might be easier. Chances are I'll befriend the blokes more quickly than the women, right?"

Lisa shook her head. "What if they're not the dad?"

"God, Lisa," I said, "that's so twisted it's not something I'd even considered. But you're right." I frowned, shook my head. "Getting Jennifer Abbott's cigarette butt was simple enough. Maybe it'll be the same."

"Yeah, course it will," Lisa said, although I could tell from her tone she considered my statement almost as naive as I did. Nothing in life was that straightforward.

Back at the house I showered, packed my bag with a week's worth of clothes, and had an uninspired breakfast of toast and jam, trying to rid myself of the impression it was some kind of last supper. I looked around the kitchen. This was how it would be if I found Logan's family and gave him up. The empty seats around the table, the absolute silence in the house. Me, alone. Sure, Lisa and Ivan would invite me over all the time if I didn't end up in prison for kidnapping, obstruction of justice or whatever the hell other charge I hadn't thought of, but I knew from experience how wrapped up people became with their own families. In a short while they'd want it to be the three of them, or the four of them, if they had more kids. Where did that leave me?

Maybe I'd meet somebody else, but as far as trusting them the way I'd done Grace, well, it wasn't going to happen—how could I trust anyone again?—although I didn't want to spend the rest of my life alone. Perhaps in time the pain of betrayal would ease, and I'd be ready to try again with someone new, a person who didn't have secrets. Someone... I exhaled sharply. Whoever I met, I'd never be able to tell her the truth about Logan if he stayed with me. Goddamn it, lying by omission meant I'd make her a part of the lie, like Grace had made me.

Sitting there wasn't going to solve anything, and it was time to move. I shoved my mug and plate in the dishwasher, and checked the route on my phone for the third time. Faycrest was a small town southeast of Portland on the banks of the Saco River. It would take four hours to get there, if traffic cooperated, so I settled in for the drive with the radio blaring, a deliberate attempt to drown out the voices in my head.

If Dad had been there, he'd have talked in clichés, said I was completely *off my rocker* and I should *let sleeping dogs lie*. Trouble was, over the years I'd found when those sleeping dogs eventually woke up, they'd grown into oversize, snarling beasts that bit me in the ass. The only way to tame them was to get in control, and that would happen only if I had more of the missing pieces to Grace and Logan's puzzle.

And so I drove, the trip uneventful save for some jerk cutting me off and giving me the finger, which I replicated before easing off the gas and letting him speed ahead. At one time I'd have challenged him, driven up his backside flashing my lights, but now it felt insignificant, ludicrous, even.

My mind drifted back to Grace, and I tried to conjure up the feelings I'd had for her what seemed a lifetime ago already. Each time I thought about a happy memory, an accusation popped into my head, like the time we went to Niagara Falls, and how jumpy Grace had been when I'd suggested crossing the border so we could see the views from the Canadian side.

"We don't have passports," she'd said.

"Do you need one for Canada?"

"Yes, definitely. I looked into it once. He needs one, too."

"Are you sure? Well, I suppose we could apply for them, come back another time."

"What for?" she snapped. "The view of the falls isn't going to be that different."

"No, but we could make a trip out of it. Visit Toronto. I've always wanted to go."

She shook her head. "Passports are ridiculously expensive and my car's about to die, remember? We can't afford to spend money on a trip. It wouldn't be sensible."

"Maybe not sensible," I said, pulling her in for a hug, "but it would be fun to explore another city. There's the CN Tower and an aquarium. Logan would love that. I'm sure I can find a cheap place to stay."

She wrinkled her nose. "I know you love traveling, but money aside, crossing the border's a nightmare. I've heard it takes forever. I'm not doing that with Logan."

"But—"

"And think about the crowds and the traffic. No, if you really want to get away, let's go somewhere closer. What about a day trip to Finger Lakes? And we can go back to the aquarium in Schenectady. It's not like Logan remembers our first time there."

Although I'd mumbled something about there being more to life than just the state of New York, I hadn't put up much of a fight. I'd have done anything to make the love of my life happy. Now I wanted to go back in time, slap my cheeks, give my shoulders a good shake, tell myself to wake up and see what was right in front of my sodding face the entire time.

When I looked down, I saw my hands had wrapped around the steering wheel so tight, my knuckles were a ghostly white. I released my grip, flexed my fingers, tried to force my brain to go in another direction, think about the fact I'd be an uncle soon. There'd be a difference in age, sure, but I had no doubt Logan would be a great cousin and... I couldn't stop the shudder from zipping down my spine. Would I have Logan when the baby came? Five months down the line would he still be with me?

The scream that filled my truck was a primal roar, and I slammed my palm on the dashboard a couple of times before hitting the brakes and pulling over. My head dropped as I breathed heavily, ordering myself to get a grip, and desperately failing. I sat there for a long time before I finally found the courage to nudge the truck into gear, and set off, thinking if I'd once believed Grace was my salvation, I was now certain she'd be my undoing.

CHAPTER THIRTY-SEVEN

Faycrest turned out to be smaller than I'd imagined, despite the hours I'd pored over it on Street View. The town's clunky website proclaimed it a "handsome place," and to a certain extent that was true, what with the wide streets and the tall, thick trees on either side, indicating the length of history. It seemed a quiet, rural place, the type of area one might settle down with a family to escape from the city, or retire to once the kids had left home.

The houses were modest in size, but well-maintained, front yards beautifully manicured, white picket fences pristine. Even the shopping plaza, with a grocery store, a coffee shop, a pizza joint and the local barber, looked tidy and clean. No stray plastic bags flying around, no overflowing garbage bins, or abandoned shopping carts. It all indicated a certain standard, a relative wealth, but also law and order. Was it a reaction to the missing Faycrest boys? People trying to keep everything under control because of the one terrifying event they hadn't been able to prevent? Or perhaps paranoia was setting in, had me interpreting everything as another clue.

I pulled into the mall's parking lot, took out my research file and went over the details again, despite knowing them by heart.

Felicia King and Gavin Sommer's son, Alex, had gone missing on November first, a little over seven-and-a-half years ago, while their friend, Emily Rhodes, babysat him at her house. I'd watched the YouTube videos and the news channel archives, the teary-eyed couples huddled together, faces blotchy, the bags under their eyes dark as storm clouds, both women holding on to each other, the husbands standing sentry either side.

"I took Hunter upstairs to change him," Emily said, unable to look at her friends, her lips wobbling, shoulders shaking. "When...when I came down, the back door was open. Alex was gone. He was *gone*. I'm sorry, I'm so sorry."

She'd been unable to speak after that, and the lead detective had taken over to give more details, fielding questions from the dozens of reporters who'd already invaded the small town.

The general public immediately concluded it was an outsider. No way had this been an act carried out by one of their own. Faycrest was the kind of place where everyone knew everyone, people helped their neighbors and doors were left unlocked. No longer, I suspected.

The initial investigation showed no useful leads. Not only had the rain been torrential on the day of Alex's disappearance, but Emily and Tyler's house was being renovated, the multitude of footprints in and out an overwhelming blur.

The search of the Rhodeses' house hadn't revealed any useful prints, there were no security cameras and the canvassing of the neighborhood yielded nothing. Sniffer dogs eventually became available, and brought in, but by then the scent had literally gone cold, the crime scene too contaminated by the well-intentioned people rallying around both families. It was something Tyler said was one of his biggest regrets. As a police officer, he felt he should've done more to protect it, but everybody understood.

Emily and Tyler's house backed onto a dense, gnarly forest and a rugged ravine, so the Faycrest community came together to comb the area, but no trace of Alex turned up, not even after the Amber Alert was issued.

The next abduction happened two weeks later, during another series of violent storms. Emily had been driving back from Portland with Hunter when she'd been forced to stop.

"A black Ford SUV was in the middle of the road," the investigator said at the press conference. "Mrs. Rhodes was forced out of her car at gunpoint by two masked men, and her son, Hunter, was taken from the vehicle." He'd paused, looked around the room. "Mrs. Rhodes was unharmed, but the assailants threw her phone and car keys into the Saco River. She was stranded eight miles from the nearest house, in the decade's heaviest rainfall. She's now in hospital, recovering from the trauma. An Amber Alert has been issued, and we're hopeful for some results very soon."

There were none.

Tyler Rhodes was a cop, and had been instrumental in the arrests of several high-profile Portland-area criminals. The focus of the investigation shifted when the police began to suspect Hunter was the original target, making Alex's disappearance a terrible case of mistaken identity. As the days and weeks passed, and the theory went from ransom to revenge, the lead investigator was forced to admit the situation did not bode well for either child.

I put my notes away, recalling the rest of my research without them. Felicia still lived in Faycrest; she was already a veterinarian when Alex disappeared. She and her husband Gavin had a girl a little over a year after Alex vanished, but the couple divorced a while later. From what I'd been able to find out,

Gavin had moved to Boston, where he'd remarried, and worked as a software engineer for a telecoms company.

By the looks of things, Tyler and Emily had stayed together, still lived in town, too. He'd left the police to become a consultant, devoting his time to cases of missing children, traveling the country, assisting police departments in over a dozen states as far away as Alaska. Emily had her own art studio in Gorham, the next town over, her website a colorful affair offering commissioned work and after-school classes for kids. There had been no mention of them having any other children, and I'd wondered what made them stay in the place where their son had been taken from, but concluded I'd do the same. Had it been me, I'd have put Logan's white-and-purple kite in the window, hoping it would somehow help him find his way home.

As I drove back up the sleepy town's main street, both sides flanked by the two-story buildings clad in whitewashed wooden siding, my stomach grumbled, begging for food.

Casa Mama looked interesting, with its chunky sign and specials chalkboard outside, and it had to be popular because most of the tables I could see from my vantage point in the truck were taken. No matter. I couldn't face a huge meal, anyway. Since I'd first seen the street signs for Faycrest, my appetite had shriveled away. I continued my drive, planned on grabbing something from the gas station as I filled up the tank.

A few hundred yards later, the large, treat-filled windows of a place called Ethel's Café caught my eye. From the outside it appeared harmless enough, and a homemade sandwich would be better than a prepackaged one, but I had another stop to make first.

I'd kept quiet about my next move for fear both Ivan and Lisa would try to talk me out of it, so I crossed my fingers, hoped things would work out exactly as I'd planned. If they didn't, I ran the risk of it all tumbling to the ground faster than a set of dominoes, except with far less elegance and way more unpredictability.

CHAPTER THIRTY-EIGHT

The main road led me out of town, where the space between houses widened and turned into lush green fields. I drove until I spotted the rustic sign with the four carved pine trees I'd closely examined online: Bill Langham Landscaping. I switched on my indicator, pulled over and stopped next to a second notice, a cheap MDF one, handwritten and hastily thrown together, and which hadn't been on Street View when I'd looked the night before.

URGENT! LANDSCAPER WANTED!

This was an opportunity I couldn't afford to mess up. I swallowed, wiped my hands on my pants, waited ten seconds before getting out of my truck. The gravel scrunched beneath my feet as I walked over to the large red barn located about twenty yards from a generously proportioned farmhouse with bright blue window boxes filled with pink geraniums.

"Hello?" I said, sticking my head inside the barn, surveying the multitude of landscaping supplies. When nobody replied I called out again, and a man came out of a room on the right-hand side. He stood a little shorter than me, but was much broader, his hair a mass of gray, tight spiral curls. His jeans were dotted with dirt, but his blue T-shirt with the quadruple pine tree company logo looked pristine.

"Can I help you?" He walked over and smiled, the dark skin on his face thick as leather, his crow's-feet running into deep gullies that traveled midway down his cheeks. You could tell this man had worked outside all his life, and my bet was he'd enjoyed every minute.

I pointed behind me. "I saw your sign. About the help."

"Bill Langham." He grabbed my hand, gave it an iron shake. "You looking for work?"

"Yeah. I was driving by and, well, here I am."

"You local?" Bill said with an inquisitive frown, giving me the once-over.

I was glad I'd practiced the answer on the way to Faycrest. "UK but Albany for a long time now. I've always loved Maine, so I'm having a look around. Might move here if it suits."

"Been here all my life, if that's any recommendation. Town's a great place to be."

"It seems it, and when I saw your sign…"

Bill crossed his arms, his expression neutral, although when he spoke I couldn't help but notice the excitement seeping into his voice. "Got experience in the landscaping business?"

"I was with the last company for over five years."

Another smile spread across his face. "Five years, huh? In that case, let's grab a pew and we'll talk. I could do with giving my back a break. Got time now?"

"Sure do."

We settled into two beaten-up, slightly wobbly chairs in a lackluster-beige room on the right side of the barn, filled with kid drawings of all shapes and sizes: finger-painted turkeys for Thanksgiving, cotton wool Santas and what appeared to be potato-stamped Easter bunnies.

"You've got kids?" I said.

"How could you tell?" Bill laughed. "Four of 'em. Not seeing them as much since my guy upped and left last week, and I've been working sixteen-hour days. Clara, my wife, she's nagging me crazy. Put my back out last year, see. She's worried it'll happen again."

"Whatever I can do to help."

"Appreciate it," he said. "People are understanding around here, but I have a reputation I need to maintain, not to mention the promises I want to keep. The excuse of being short-staffed only works for so long." Bill tapped his index finger on his desk as he looked at me.

I didn't want to afford him the chance of raising any objections, so I jumped straight in, told him about my experience, detailed the stuff I'd done for Ronnie and Leila. He interrupted me occasionally to ask a question, nodded enthusiastically at my answers, jotted some notes on a pad stained with coffee mug rings.

"I'll need a reference," he said when I'd finished. "Speak to your previous employer. You okay with that?"

I'd anticipated his request, decided to be as forthcoming as possible. Otherwise there'd be too many fibs to keep track of, too many lies to remember. "I'll write down the details. But before you call them, you should know they asked me to leave."

Bill sat back in his chair, his earlier enthusiasm sliding from his face like melted cheese from a plate. "They fired you?"

"Yes. I had to take some time off because my partner died and my son was having a ton of trouble at school—"

"Woah. They let you go when you had those kinds of family issues to deal with?" He huffed. "That's big-city syndrome, right there. No wonder you want to get away. Trust me, it's not how we do things around here. Family's got to be number one." He indicated to a picture on the wall: him, a petite woman and four young boys dressed in identical football jerseys. "Clara and the gang."

The tension in my neck eased as my shoulders retreated from my ears. "You've got your business development plans covered then."

Bill laughed, the deep crinkles in his cheeks reappearing. "They were born with shovels in their hands, that's for sure. They're nine, ten, twelve and fourteen. How old's your boy?"

"Seven. He's staying with my sister while I get things sorted."

"How long are you in the area for?"

I shrugged. "As long as it takes to find a job, I guess. After that, permanently, I hope."

He tapped his foot a few times, no doubt running over the options in his mind. I wondered how many other people he had to choose from, hoped it was none, and that he'd be sufficiently desperate.

"You know what?" he said. "Forget the reference. I need help and I'll make up my own mind. What do you say I take you on for a week, see how things go and then we decide?"

"Fantastic, thanks."

"Is cash okay for now? It'll cut down on the paperwork until we're sure."

"Cash is king." We agreed on an hourly rate and shook hands. "Thanks, Mr. Langham."

"Sweet jellybeans, call me Bill. So, last question for today. When can you start?"

"Tomorrow morning?"

"I was hoping you'd say that. Come here for seven thirty?"

"Great. It'll give me a chance to find a place to stay this afternoon. Any motels you can recommend? Cheap ones, preferably."

"There's a Travelodge a few miles east, although maybe you should stop in at Ethel's."

"The café on the main street?"

"Yup. She mentioned her empty cabin the other day. Said something about wanting to rent it out again. You might be in luck. But fair warning, it's isolated and you'll most probably end up bunking with some kind of wildlife."

"Thanks," I said, getting up. "I'll be sure to check it out. I'll see you tomorrow?"

"You bet," Bill said. "Can't wait to see what you've got."

I drove off, pulled over as soon as I was out of Bill's sight and had to sit on my hands to stop them from trembling. Things had worked out better than I'd imagined. Playing tourist for more than half a day in Faycrest would have been impossible, but now I could work for Bill, blend in for the week, at least. The town had a population of around four thousand, and Bill had said all his work was local, the perfect cover to get closer to that DNA as he showed me around and introduced me to his clients.

By now it was almost three, and my stomach let out another loud growl. I headed for Ethel's Café, hoping my good fortune would stick with me for the rest of the afternoon, fully aware I shouldn't get even remotely comfortable because things could easily blow up in my face well before the sun set.

CHAPTER THIRTY-NINE

The woman behind the counter looked up as soon as I walked into the café. She was older, late sixties or so, petite with short silver hair and thin, wrinkled lips that revealed a set of white teeth when she smiled. "Good afternoon, sir, and welcome to Ethel's."

"Hello." I went to the counter, smiling broadly, too, greeting the couple sitting at a table near the back with a wave. First impressions were important at the best of times. Right now they were crucial. The woman's name tag said *Ethel*, and the café had rung a far and distant bell as soon as I'd seen it, but I struggled to make any kind of connection despite the fact it resonated more loudly in my ears. I indicated to a table near the counter. "Is this one free?"

"Please, sit wherever you choose." Ethel's immaculately made-up face broke into another dazzling smile as she pushed her fringe out of her eyes. "Coffee?"

I gave her a hopeful look. "Tea? With milk and sugar?"

"Coming right up." She was about to turn away, her long, black, sparkly earrings wobbling as she moved, and added, "I'm sure you've heard it a hundred times, but your accent's lovely. Very charming and exotic."

"Exotic?" I laughed. "That's kind of you, but you know, if you went to England, they'd say the same about yours."

"Oh, if only." She touched the gold locket hanging from her neck. "My Al promised we'd go to London one day, but we never got there before he died. Anyway…how about something to eat? It's all homemade. Nothing artificial, guaranteed."

"A sandwich would be great. Ham and Swiss on whole wheat, if you have it."

"Fully loaded with lettuce, tomatoes and pickles? Good choice. Make yourself comfortable and I'll bring everything over."

As Ethel disappeared through a doorway into the back room, I glanced around. The place was small, ten tables at most, surrounded by an eclectic collection of mismatched wooden chairs that gave it a homely, comfortable feel. Every shelf behind the white counter overflowed with a variety of cups, saucers and mugs, all different shapes and sizes. Bright, abstract paintings of multicolored trees hung on the lilac walls, and the scent of toast, cinnamon and brown sugar lingered in the air. It felt as if I'd stepped into my grandmother's front room for a chat.

"Are you passing through town?" Ethel said when she brought my tea and food on a blue-and-white-striped plastic tray she set in front of me.

"No, actually I've got a job with Bill Langham."

"Have you?" Ethel indicated to the empty chair opposite me, sat down when I nodded. "I bet he's thrilled. Poor man's been rushed off his feet. Oh, bye, you two lovebirds, see you tomorrow." She waved at the couple who'd made their way to the door, and after they left, Ethel and I were the only people in the café. She turned back to me. "I take it you're a landscaper?"

"Yes, but I've worked construction for years, too, renovations, extensions, that kind of thing." I poured some milk into my mug, added a spoonful of sugar. "Bill's hired me for the week to see how things go. He seems great."

"Salt of the earth," Ethel said. "You won't find a better boss around here. Not unless you know how to make scones and pies."

"Ah...not so much." I grinned. "But I'm always willing to learn. I'm Josh, by the way. And as your name tag says Ethel, this must be your place?"

"Forty years and counting, if you can you believe it, because I can't."

"That's a lot of tea and coffee." I took a bite of my sandwich. "This is delicious."

"Thank you," she said. "And yes, more cups than I care to count. But I'm still here, despite the fast-food joints coming in. So, are you planning on moving here, or...?"

"Very possibly," I said, covering my full mouth with a hand. "You have a family?"

"A son. He's staying with my sister in Albany until we've decided what we're doing."

"My daughter's about your age. She lives in California with my grandkids. It's hard being away from your children, whatever their age. You must miss your son, too."

"I'll go back next weekend, but we won't move until I'm sure things will work with Mr. Langham." Except I'd make sure they wouldn't, I thought as I ate my food. I'd find something to mess up enough for him to fire me once I had what I'd come to Faycrest for, or tell him I didn't like the area after all.

Ethel wagged a finger. "You'd best call him Bill or you won't last a day."

"Yes, he mentioned that," I said with a laugh, putting the rest of my sandwich down. As casually as I could, I added, "Anyway, I'm heading to the Travelodge after lunch. I need to sort out a room for the week." I hoped she'd bite, tell me about her cabin, but instead her gaze flickered to my left hand.

"And, uh, would it be you and your son coming here, or…?" My hesitation made Ethel's face fall. "I don't mean to pry. Ask anyone and they'll tell you I'm too chatty for my own good." She wiped imaginary crumbs from the table and slid her chair back.

"No, it's alright," I said, gesturing for her to stay seated. "Logan's mom passed away in March."

Ethel gasped, put a hand to her throat. "My goodness. You poor thing. And your poor boy. I'm so sorry. Was she sick?"

"An accident."

"What a terrible shock that must have been. No wonder you're thinking of moving." She paused. "I don't mean to speak out of turn, and while I know it's a terrible cliché, time does help. Goodness knows you don't believe it at the beginning, but it's true, and I'm not only saying that because I lost Al." She sat back in her chair and as I drank my tea, I thought that was the end of that part of our conversation, until she said, "If you're thinking of moving to Faycrest, you must have heard what happened here?"

I felt my pulse throb. "Are you talking about the missing boys…?"

"That's right." Ethel nodded, her face falling. "One of them was my goddaughter's son."

CHAPTER FORTY

The café spun as if I'd jumped on a merry-go-round, the tree paintings, cups, saucers and Ethel's face all becoming a blur until I pushed my heels firmly onto the floor. This was Ethel Byrne, Felicia King's godmother.

I put down my tea, fingers trembling, unsure how to handle the revelation, deciding stunned silence was hopefully the most believable approach. It wasn't far from the truth, but I'd never been a good actor, or a particularly convincing liar. Within a couple of hours of arriving in Faycrest, I was already being pushed well beyond my natural abilities, and this was but the start.

"It's alright," Ethel said. "Most folk don't know what to say. Goodness, when it happened some people I'd known for decades crossed the street to avoid talking to me. Went to get their coffee from a drive-thru for a while. Sad really. Anyway—" she clapped her hands together "—speaking of coffee, I need one, and let me get a treat for you."

"No, that's—"

"I insist."

As she busied herself at the counter, I sat quietly, my head a mess. I pulled out my phone, pretended to read the Faycrest articles I'd already seen a hundred times, slid my fingers over the screen without taking in a single word. Ethel returned with a coffee, and a gooey chocolate brownie the size of a brick she put in front of me.

"There you go."

"Thank you." I didn't want her to turn away so I added, "I've been reading about what happened here. And your god-daughter…"

"Felicia," she said. "Baby Alex's mom."

"I'm so sorry, Ethel, really."

She nodded. "It rocked the whole community when he went missing. Then Hunter disappeared, too… The town hasn't been the same since, and for a long time more families moved out than in. People just didn't want to live here anymore, you know?"

I needed to keep her talking, pretend I was a regular guy, interested, not gawping, there to give empathy, not collect gossip. "And they think the other boy, Hunter, was the real target?"

Ethel smoothed down her apron. "That's the conclusion they came to, that taking Alex was a mistake. A *mistake*, that's what they said, if you can believe it. But we all feel responsible. Everyone wishes they'd done more, been more vigilant."

"You can't blame yourself," I said, as Grace's face loomed in my mind.

"Anyway," Ethel said. "I won't take up more of your time."

"It's okay," I said, willing her to sit down. "I'm not in a hurry."

She looked at me for a while before shaking her head and lowering herself back into the chair. "I suppose you'll find out sooner or later as you'll be working with Bill. He talks more than me. You see, Felicia asked if I could watch Alex that afternoon."

"The day he went missing?"

"Yes. She's a vet and they had an emergency at work. Gavin, that was her husband, he was traveling, I was at a trade show and Al had gone on a fishing trip a few hours away." Her hands trembled as she slid the locket up and down its chain. "Emily offered to look after Alex."

"You mean Emily Rhodes, Hunter's mom?"

"That's right. They'd known each other for a few years. Had been pregnant at the same time. Alex was taken from Emily's house when she was upstairs with Hunter."

"How awful, Ethel," I said, trying to detach myself from the situation, from what Grace might have done. My hunt for the truth would produce results only if I stayed focused, analytical, almost unemotional. Easier said than done when I looked at Ethel, saw her watery eyes filled with pain and regret I could only hope to ease somehow.

"We were all praying Alex would be brought back to us safe and sound," she said, "but a few weeks later Hunter vanished. The stress of it brought on Al's stroke, I'm sure of it."

"But how do you manage?" I said. "How do you keep going?"

"A minute at a time, at first. Then an hour, then a day. That's the best I can do, even after all this time." Ethel's gaze drifted away until she waved a hand. "My goodness, I really should clean up the lunchtime mess or I'll be here all afternoon."

My stomach almost forced Ethel's food straight back up my throat. Reading about the disappearances had been one thing— hearing from the people involved, how it may have sent Ethel's husband to an early grave, was sickening. I drained my cup of tepid tea and wondered if I should get in the truck and leave, pretend I'd never suspected a thing. But then what?

As Ethel got up she turned and said, "It does get better, I promise. The pain of losing someone never goes away, but it does stop hurting quite so much. Give it time."

I didn't ask how much time in case she said years. Not because it seemed long, but because Grace hadn't been gone four months, and sometimes I thought I hardly missed her at all.

CHAPTER FORTY-ONE

When Ethel brought the bill over and put it on the table, she rested her weathered hands on the back of the chair. "Did you mention something about the Travelodge…?"

"Yes, I'm heading there now."

"Well, I've been thinking. This may sound kooky, but I have a cabin outside town."

"Do you know, I believe Bill may have mentioned it," I said. "I can't believe I forgot." Shameful how swift the lies came, but Ethel needed to think it had been her idea. The voice in my head berated me for being such a manipulative piece of shit, so I shoved it to the back of my mind and taped its mouth shut with a roll of heavy-duty duct tape.

"…it's not much, and it's a couple of miles outside town," Ethel was saying. "Two small bedrooms, a deck. Even got air-conditioning that's fairly decent, although it needs a good kick from time to time. And as you work landscaping and construction…"

I crossed my arms and grinned at her. "I sense there's some huge disadvantage coming, but I'm too intrigued to stop you."

"We used to rent the cabin out, but I haven't done much to it since Al passed. Don't worry, it's clean and not in too bad a shape. Nothing elbow grease and a lick of paint can't fix. How do you feel about that? Do you think you could help?"

"Not a problem. What kind of rent are you looking for?"

"Five hundred bucks a week."

"Woah. There's no way I can—"

She put her head back and laughed. "You should see your face right now. I'm joking. You help fix it, and you stay for free."

"Free? I can't—"

"Why not? It'll give you a chance to decide if you want to move here. Why not bring your son, too, let him have a look around? What was his name?"

"Logan," I said quickly. "But, uh, for the time being I'll go back to Albany at weekends. It's more stable for him, at least for now."

I couldn't stand who I was becoming. It was too reminiscent of the person I'd been when I drank, the guy who'd often lied, albeit badly, and continually let his sister down. The difference was back then I'd lacked a certain sense of direction—not the world's best excuse—but now I knew exactly what I was doing, which made it about a million times worse.

"Tell you what," Ethel said. "I need half an hour to clear up here, then I'll show you the cabin so you can make up your mind, if you have time?"

"I'd love to."

"Want to wait inside till I'm ready?"

"I'll step out, work off that lunch." I gathered my things and went outside, grateful to stop pretending for a few minutes. Back in the truck I dialed Lisa's number, bracing for impact.

"You've done *what*?" she yelled when I told her not only about the job with Bill, but the cabin and who it belonged to. "Have you gone completely *mad*? I know it was my idea to say you're looking for work, but this is crazy." She calmed down a little once I'd explained the size of the place and my cover story logic.

"If anything I can get the DNA samples more quickly," I said. "And come home."

"Okay, I get it, I think. What are you doing tonight?"

"Depends on the cabin, I guess, but I'll probably check out the town. There's an Italian restaurant here that looks good. Casa something or other."

"No booze, right?"

"How's Logan?" I said. "Is he ready for tomorrow?"

"I'll take that as 'I'm having none, sis, don't worry,' and Logan's fine. He's so excited for camp I keep thinking he'll pee his pants."

"Text me tomorrow when he gets home. Let me know how it went, okay?"

"About that," Lisa said. "Don't forget we said we'd keep our messages to a minimum and always open to interpretation. If you have to plead ignorance, you can't be sending anything proving otherwise."

"Got it," I said, before exhaling sharply. "I hate this. I really do."

"Then come home," Lisa said. "If you leave now you could be back—"

"Ethel's waving at me," I lied. "Kiss Logan for me. Tell him I'll see him Friday night. Who knows, with the way things are going it might be before."

I stayed in the truck for another fifteen minutes, thoughts going through my head at warp speed. Was going to the cabin, intruding in Ethel's life, really what I wanted to do? Clearly she was still suffering from her godson's loss. Who was I to play puppet master? If I casually showed her a photograph of Logan, would she gasp and press a hand to her chest because she could see Felicia at the same age? I knew I couldn't risk it, which was why I'd left my photos of Logan at home, and stuffed a picture of a brown-haired, green-eyed boy I'd found on the internet in my wallet, just in case someone asked. That had been Ivan's suggestion, and although it was a good one, it made me feel as dirty as pond scum on the inside. Lisa said I should leave Grace's photos, too, but I'd kept one hidden because I still needed her with me.

When all the thoughts invading and colliding in my brain became too much to handle, I returned to the café, where Ethel had a green-and-white-striped cloth in her hand, wiping down the counters, humming a Rolling Stones song.

"Bill called," she said as soon as I walked in. "Asked if you'd stopped by. He's very impressed and said you really know your stuff. He also warned you should, and I quote, mentally prepare yourself for a week of hell. I told him I know you'll do absolutely fine."

"Thanks for the vote of confidence. I hope it works out."

Ethel winked. "Bill's got a ton of work coming up for the summer. You could be at my old cabin for a while." She picked up a burgundy tassel with a single key dangling from it, held it up toward me. "Ready?"

"Yes, definitely."

"Great. Bill's meeting us there to see what kind of tools you might need to borrow if you stay. Oh, and—" she passed me a paper bag "—I almost forgot your gift."

The smell of fresh bread invaded my nostrils, making my stomach rumble again despite the fact I'd just eaten. "Ethel, are you trying to bribe me with a homemade loaf?"

"And some lemon drizzle scones." She lowered her voice to a stage whisper. "You haven't seen the state of the cabin yet. I'm hoping those will stop you from running away."

I wondered if rescuing whoever happened to stumble upon

her café was something she did on a regular basis. Had she always been this way, or was it since the Faycrest boys had disappeared? Could the point of her kindness be more about easing her own pain than helping me? I thought of Grace and the injured bird and stray cat she'd taken care of. Had that been to quieten her guilty conscience, an attempt at erasing one terrible deed with a multitude of smaller, good ones? And could one act define you, make you a despicable person for the rest of your life, even if nobody else knew about the original sin?

"I'll get my car from around the back." Ethel's voice drowned out the impossible thoughts, got rid of the tortured souls screaming for attention. "It's the red one with the caterpillar bumper sticker. Follow me and we'll be at the cabin in no time."

We drove out of town, past Bill's, and another two miles beyond, where Ethel took a left turn up a dirt track so narrow, it would have been easy to miss. We kept going another mile or so until we came to a dead end and a small clearing surrounded by pine trees and dense brush. I spotted Bill's truck immediately, and when Ethel parked her car and got out, I looked around, wondering if she'd got the wrong place.

While the wooden cabin was small, it was bigger than the dinky little shack with a leaky roof and broken windows I'd imagined. Although tired and somewhat neglected, the place was almost charming with its small front deck and tin roof sitting on top, a well-worn, lopsided hat. Its shutters had been a dark blue once, but had since chipped and faded, the wood gnarled and worn. The matching, centered front door bulged slightly in the middle, and the first three letters of the word WELCOME lay in a brassy heap on the leaf-covered mat. The grass, shrubs and bushes at the front threatened to overtake the pathway, thorny monsters reaching out, clawing at our clothes as we walked by.

"Hey, guys," Bill said, coming round from the back of the

cabin. "Good to see you again already, Josh. Ethel told me you might patch this place up."

"I have my tool bag with me," I said as we walked up the steps, the deck creaking underneath our collective weight. "Rumor has it you can lend me the rest, Bill?"

"You bet."

"Sounds like the perfect plan," I said, vowing I'd at least do some of the work to repay Ethel for her generosity before running off.

"You ready?" Ethel unlocked the door and gave it a good shove, and as she swung it open it let out a loud groan. "Gosh darn it, I keep meaning to oil those hinges," she muttered.

"It'll be the first thing on my list," I said, and followed her inside.

We stepped directly into the living room, which was about the size of the den in Albany. I took in the wooden floor, the lumps in the faded floral sofa, and hoped there weren't any dead animals buried underneath the cushions. A dented pine coffee table stood on a pale paisley rug, and the dilapidated chest of drawers in the corner had a vase of dusty plastic roses on top. The walls had probably been light pine once, and had turned to a burnt yellow over the years.

I wondered if I'd send bats or birds to their fiery deaths by lighting the little wood-burning fireplace nestled between the two windows on the left wall, and decided I wouldn't chance it. I squinted down the short, narrow hallway leading to the back of the cabin, realizing the whole place had a musty smell, as if I'd walked into a room with a year's worth of unwashed gym kits.

On cue, Ethel gently opened a window, then pointed at another that went almost from the floor to the ceiling. "Al insisted on putting that thing in after the doc told him to slow down.

Loved to sit and observe the wildlife going by. Be careful with it. The caulking's brittle. I should have replaced it already."

"I'll take care of it, no problem," I said.

"Thanks, Josh. Now, the kitchen is to your left," Ethel said. "The bathroom is on the right, and both bedrooms are at the back. Tiny, but enough for one or two."

"We used to hang out here as kids," Bill said. "Got up to all kinds of trouble."

Ethel laughed. "Bill's mother and I went way back. Believe me, Josh, I don't think I want to know what our children did in here. My hair is already gray enough, thank you very much. Anyway, Al used it as a base for hunting before we rented it out a few summers."

"It's great, really," I said.

"*Great* might be a bit of a stretch," Ethel said with a smile. "The more I look at it, the more I see wrong. I won't be offended if you don't want to stay. The Travelodge—"

"No, it's perfect. More than perfect." Not only could I be away from prying eyes out here, but staying at Ethel's cabin meant even more opportunity to mix with the locals, especially Felicia. Maybe this way we'd be introduced.

Ethel was still observing me. "Are you sure you really want to take this on?"

"Positive. Do you have a list of everything you want me to do?"

"Buckle up," Bill said. "I bet you it's as long as your legs."

"He's right," Ethel said. "But I don't expect you to do it all."

"Really, it's no problem," I said. "Tell me, and I'll do whatever I can while I'm here."

"Okay… I've got floorboards to fix the broken ones—"

"Check."

"The bathroom and kitchen need painting. The bedroom

carpets should be replaced. The new ones are rolled up at the back. Al bought them before he died. I hope they're still okay."

"Consider it done. What about electrical and plumbing?"

"Checked them and they're fine," Bill said. "The roof is, too, but out back the trees and bushes are trying to climb in through the windows."

"I'm sure I've seen worse, believe me," I said with a grin.

"You don't scare easily, do you?" Bill said.

I looked at Ethel, kept the smile on my face. "What you're doing is very kind."

"Same as you. The way I see it, there's nothing wrong with people helping each other out," she said. "Alright, why don't you have a proper look around? Really make sure you want to take this project on."

"I'm already sure," I said. "Really."

"Excellent," Ethel said. "There's a cupboard in the hall where I packed away the linens. They're in bags, but let me know if they smell funny. In the meantime, here's the key, and enjoy making yourself at home."

Bill shook my hand and whispered a "thanks for doing this" in my ear, and I watched them go back to their cars, laughing and chatting as longtime friends do. I closed the door and rested my forehead against it, listened to them back up and drive away, holding my breath until the sound of the engines faded into the distance.

"This is it," I whispered, my throat tight. "You're in the dragon's den now."

CHAPTER FORTY-TWO

I brought my bags in from the truck and dumped them in the bedroom before heading outside to the back. Bill hadn't exaggerated; those trees and shrubs alone would be enough work to keep my mind off things for a while. I decided I'd prepare whatever I could for kindling and firewood, a goodwill gesture of sorts for Ethel. It was the least I could do.

Back inside I located the paint supplies and rolls of carpet, retrieved my tool bag, measuring tape, pen and notepad, and jotted down calculations. By the time I'd finished planning and roughly scheduling the work, I'd developed a literal case of cabin fever.

The mid-June sun was still warm, although not quite enough for a T-shirt as evening drew near, so I grabbed my jacket, jumped in the truck and drove toward Casa Mama. Ethel and Bill had mentioned it, too, said it had the best tomato soup they'd ever tasted, apparently a recipe handed down for generations. "Rumor has it they add a tin of Campbell's," Ethel said. "But whatever they do, it's delicious."

The restaurant wasn't too busy, and I settled at a table at the back, taking in the red-and-white gingham tablecloths, fake green plants, multitude of Italian flags and old-fashioned family portraits on the walls. A curly-haired waitress bounced over, introduced herself as Wendy, handed me the menu and offered me a drink. What I really wanted was a large beer, but I asked for a Coke instead, half of which I gulped down as soon as it arrived.

"Have you decided what to eat?" Wendy said. "The pesto linguine's my favorite, if you're looking for a recommendation."

"Sounds perfect."

"Are you the guy staying at Ethel's cabin?" She laughed at my startled look. "Bill Langham's my uncle. And we don't get many British people here."

"News travels fast," I said, hoping my voice didn't betray me.

Wendy leaned in. "Everyone knows what everyone's up to around here," she whispered, and as she retreated to the kitchen, the galloping of my heart grew as loud as thunder in my ears, culminating in a deafening crescendo when the front door opened and a couple walked in. I slid down in my seat a little, grateful for the low lighting and fake ivy partially obscuring me as I watched the people I'd never met, yet instantly recognized. Tyler and Emily Rhodes.

As they were escorted to their table, I couldn't help but stare. It was almost as if I knew them, that's how hard I'd studied their faces and gestures as I'd played and replayed the press conferences, scoured the articles online for clues.

I could see their profiles perfectly from my vantage point, and Tyler was far more imposing than he appeared on television. He was tall, trim and fit, his brown hair short and neat. He wore a dark suit, the sleeves of his blue shirt rolled up, his tie slightly askew. The way he'd casually slung his jacket over his shoulder made me think he'd come back from a long day at work, fighting crime and helping to chase down the bad guys. Intimidated didn't even begin to cover how he made me feel.

His wife, Emily, was breathtakingly beautiful in an effortless girl-next-door kind of way. Strands of her golden-brown hair had loosened from her ponytail and fallen past her shoulders. Her pastel dress, long and flowing with large blue tulips, skimmed her curves. I couldn't take my eyes off hers, almond-shaped and filled with melancholy so deep it would take years to get to the bottom.

Was Grace the cause of Emily's sadness? What would she say if I could show her the look on Emily's face? Had she already seen it? During my research, I'd read somewhere perpetrators sometimes returned to the scene of their crimes, so I'd zoomed in on each photo, paused the footage every few seconds to study the crowds, held my breath in case I came across Grace's face, tried to imagine what I'd do if I did. I hadn't, but that didn't stop me from examining everything again, and then a third time.

Wendy came over to ask about my food. "It's delicious," I said, taking a forkful to demonstrate, pushed my plate away once she'd left.

This was another fight-or-flight situation, except I'd voluntarily put myself here, and already felt way, way in over my head. I had to stay, which left me no real choice but to spend the week in Faycrest. No longer, I told myself. A week had to be enough for me to get what I needed and prove the nagging possibility Logan was Alex King or Hunter Rhodes a hundred million times wrong.

When I looked over at Emily again she turned her head, her eyes staring straight into mine. I didn't look away, found it impossible to drop my gaze, and she didn't, either. For the briefest moment it felt as if we were the only ones in the room, the only people who mattered. Neither of us blinked, smiled or moved until Wendy reappeared in front of me, blocking my line of sight with another glass of Coke. After she left I glanced at Emily, but she and Tyler were silently perusing their menus. The spell—or whatever had happened between us—broken.

CHAPTER FORTY-THREE

I practically crawled back to the cabin, exhausted from the long day and the sugar crash induced by the peach cobbler à la mode Wendy insisted was on the house. While sitting on the deck with a bottle of water, I tried to identify the source of the strange noises around me but couldn't decipher where all the squeaking, rustling and some kind of light snorting came from.

I hadn't asked Ethel about the animals in the woods, not wanting to appear too much of a city slicker. Now I had what were—hopefully—unrealistic images of me waking up to a ravenous, toothy bear on the deck, or a pissed-off moose outside the window. The cabin had electricity, but no phone or internet, and the cell reception was spotty. If I needed help with pesky four-legged visitors, I was very much on my own. Still, it wasn't an unpleasant sensation, sitting in the dark, letting it settle over me, an unfamiliar but surprisingly comforting blanket.

My thoughts went back to Tyler and Emily, well, Emily mainly, if I was being honest. Despite my attempts not to, I kept picturing the curve of her neck, her toned arms, the heart-shaped birthmark on her shoulder. Most of all I thought about the look we'd shared, which led to me wondering how it might feel to touch her and...taste the softness of her lips. Where the hell had that come from? I'd never cheated on Grace, never had any desire to be with another woman since we'd met. I wasn't supposed to be imagining these things about anyone, certainly not now, and least of all Emily Rhodes.

The more I fought to conjure a memory of Grace, the more her image kept being replaced by Emily's, the two merging into one, to the point where I couldn't distinguish either of them. As I sat on the deck, trying not to think about anything at all, loneliness climbed out of my heart and settled on top of my chest, its heaviness crushing me. Enough. I pushed myself up and headed to bed, knowing full well my mind would remain a jumble of questions, the answers to which still felt light-years away.

I woke before my alarm the next morning, showered with cool water in the thimble-sized bathroom, shaved and pulled on clothes and work boots. The weather had warmed up again, leaving only a slight but welcome chill in the air. Outside on the deck, accompanied by the other early birds, I drank a mug full of instant coffee I'd found at the back of the cupboard. The best before date was from two years ago, a reminder I needed to get groceries, which would have to wait until after I'd spent the day with Bill.

"Welcome, welcome." He grabbed my arm when I arrived, pumped it up and down before letting me go. "Worried I'd hallucinated yesterday and you were a figment of my imagination. Thank the sweet Lord you're not. First good night's sleep I've had since last week. Alrighty then. You up for some fun?"

"I'm ready." I followed him into the barn and over to a row of neatly stacked bags of lava rocks, mulch and rolls of sod.

"These all have to go in the back of my truck, and man, am

I pleased I don't have to do this alone today," Bill said, grabbing the sod.

"Where did your other guy go?" I threw a bag over my shoulder and followed him.

"Got himself another job as a foreman. Good for him, I say, I'm not one to stand in anybody's way." He walked ahead, talking over his shoulder as he went. "Company's only small. Him and me most of the time, plus a few people here and there as and when we needed them. Knew he'd move on at some point. Shame on him for putting me in the pooper when we'd shaken on two weeks' notice." Bill dumped the sod in the back of his truck and looked at me. "Josh, if there's one thing you should know about me it's that I try extremely hard never to let people down."

"Got it. You're a man of your word."

"That's right, and I expect the same courtesy in return."

"Understood," I said, trying not to think about how pissed he'd be when I downed tools and disappeared, too, by the end of the week, if things went the way I intended.

He looked at me for a second, then nodded. "We'd better get the rest of the supplies and head out. We'll start on Hampton Street first. Got a few upkeep regulars there. Ride with me and I'll show you the area. You should give me your cell number, too. I forgot to ask you for it."

"Yep…" I felt around the pockets of my jeans, crossed over to my truck and had a look inside, hardly believing I could have been so stupid. "Crap. I must have left it at the cabin. You mind if we stop in? If my son or sister need to reach me…"

"Sure thing. Family first."

Within ten minutes we were on the road, heading up the dirt track toward the cabin. About thirty yards away something caught my eye, a dark shape disappearing into the bushes. Bill didn't seem to notice, but when I got out of the truck I stood still, squinted into the brush, listened for the sound of snapping branches, but heard none.

"You okay?" Bill called over.

"Yeah. Thought I saw an animal or something. Probably a trick of the light."

"Or a deer. Plenty of them around Faycrest. Al fed them. Drove Ethel crazy because they did their business all over the place. She says nowadays she'd let him feed them all day long if it meant he was still alive and—" his mouth dropped open "—oh, man. You lost your... I'm sorry. Clara always says I'm about as tactful as a fart in a crowd."

"It's okay, Bill, don't worry," I said, and walked over to the cabin.

The front door was locked, the front windows intact. From what I could tell, nobody had tried to get in. It was another case of my overactive imagination seeing potential enemies and threats where there were none. The whole world wasn't against me, certainly not the population of Faycrest, who thought I was a down on his luck landscaper with nothing to hide. I pushed the door open, found the rest of the cabin in order and retrieved my phone from where I'd left it on the kitchen counter, a text message from Lisa twinkling on the screen.

Hey. How's it going? Made progress?

The message was innocuous enough. "Progress" could refer to any number of things, and while it didn't scream *impostor*, I quickly changed the settings so none of the alerts would be visible, cursing myself for not doing so earlier. A criminal mastermind I certainly was not.

"You set?" Bill asked when I returned to his truck and got in.

"Yes, thanks again," I said, although unable to quite shake the feeling of unease.

He put the truck in Reverse, turned and drove back down

the dirt road, country music blaring from the radio, both of us tapping our feet to the tune.

"I didn't know you Brits listened to country," Bill said with a grin.

"I prefer the more recent stuff," I said, "but Mom had all the Dolly Parton and Kenny Rogers records before we even came to America."

"Ah, she'd be a woman after my own heart," he said. "Love the classics."

We drove the rest of the way listening to the music, Bill occasionally pointing out things: the school, the brand-new community center and a range of his clients. He waved to a handful of people as we drove past, a mother jogging with her stroller, an elderly couple walking toward the town hall, which was a small building clad in yellow siding with a huge American flag outside, gently flapping in the breeze. Once again it struck me as a good, old-fashioned town, a place where knowing your neighbors' names mattered, and the community supported one in good times, and in bad. Somewhere, I realized, I could see Logan and me living an uncomplicated life, away from the hustle and bustle of the city, unencumbered by problems. I doubted if Lisa would agree. After I'd fled when Mom and Dad died, she said moving never sorted out your issues. They sneaked inside your suitcases when you weren't looking and jumped out when you arrived.

Before long the conversation turned to when I'd moved to the States. I answered most of Bill's questions carefully and truthfully, just as Lisa, Ivan and I had agreed. If I did end up finding Logan's real parents here, and made any kind of official contact, I'd have to work hard to maintain my "what an incredible coincidence" story. Without evidence to the contrary, Ivan had suggested, what could anyone prove?

We mowed the lawns and tended to the yards of three clients that morning, and all of them offered us copious amounts of food and drinks. It didn't take long to figure out Bill was practically a local institution. No wonder; he extended everyone the professional courtesy and respect I'd seen from Ronnie and Leila, but he also treated them as extended members of his family. He inquired about their health, their children's school grades, how their grandkid's birthday party went, rattling off names and ages as if he had a database for a brain. At one o'clock we ate curried chicken sandwiches Clara had made, and headed to another part of town where the old bungalows had been torn down and replaced by large two-story houses.

"All of my customers are important," Bill said as we drove into a large court with five properties, "but this one I'm especially keen to keep happy."

I looked at the houses, each with its own vast front yard, all of them jostling for some kind of dwelling-of-the-year nomination. They could easily have featured as a backdrop for a celebrity shoot in a glossy magazine, the kind Lisa read despite her claims they were trashy and dumb. While my sister didn't design rural dwellings, I'm sure she'd have appreciated the craftsmanship of the pillars and bay windows, the wraparound porches and Juliet balconies. One of the houses had a pond in the front yard, complete with a red-and-white miniature lighthouse perched on top of a rock.

"See that?" Bill said, nodding toward it. "The owners are from Nova Scotia in Canada. Asked me for something to remind them of home. You should've seen their faces when I suggested a Peggy's Cove lighthouse. I swear they were about to elect me mayor."

"Is that our next client?"

"Nope, come on."

He parked the truck and we walked up the path of a stone, colonial-style home. Although it was as large as the others, it came across less intimidating, even with its twelve-foot front door, gabled dormers and a raised deck that wrapped around the back. The place felt familiar, like the face of someone you've met but can no longer remember when or where. It wasn't until Bill rang the doorbell—a low-sounding chime echoing way beyond the front door—that I inhaled sharply as the memory emerged from the depths of my brain.

I'd seen the front of this house before. Except I hadn't focused on the bricks and mortar, but on the owners begging for their child's safe return. Well before the door opened, I knew exactly who lived there.

Tyler and Emily Rhodes.

CHAPTER FORTY-FOUR

I blinked at Emily, who stood in front of us dressed in work-out gear, a pair of fluorescent pink earbuds hanging around her neck. As soon as she saw Bill her face broke into a smile, which made her even more beautiful than she'd been at Casa Mama, and she stood so close I could have counted the freckles on her nose.

"Good to see you, Bill." She looked at me, her smile broader still. "Hi, I'm Emily."

"This is Josh," Bill said, and I gave her some kind of ridiculous wave I immediately wished I could erase from her memory.

"You're Bill's new guy?" she said, her voice soft as she extended a hand to shake mine. "Nice to officially meet you. How are you enjoying Faycrest so far?"

"I like it," I said, forcing myself to let go of her fingers. "It's great."

"Alright then." Emily turned to Bill. "You don't need me around, do you?"

"No, ma'am," he said. "Know where everything is."

"Okay. See you in about an hour." She popped her earbuds

in and took off down the path, her ponytail swish-swishing behind her as she ran.

"Big yard," Bill said, and I hoped he hadn't caught me staring at Emily as she disappeared around the corner. "You handle the mowing, I'll prune. We'll be done in no time."

Before we'd taken half a dozen steps, his cell phone rang. He fished it from his pocket, his expression darkening as he listened. "You've got to be kidding me? What? *Now...?* Okay, yes, *yes.* See you in a few minutes." He slipped his cell back in his pocket. "Supplier delivered the wrong trellises. Client's going crazy. You alright to handle this one on your own? Weekly tidy-up, same as the others. Mow the lawn, front and back. Use their machine, not ours. Trim and clip whatever needs it."

"Sure, no problem. You go ahead."

He gave me the thumbs-up. "Sweet. Make sure you sweep the paths when you're done. Tyler hates getting stuff on his shoes. He's really fussy about that. Messed them up once when my other guy left a pile of topsoil in the rain. Thought he was going to fire me."

"Got it," I said, ignoring the tingling sensation that crept into my gut when I realized I'd be alone at Tyler and Emily's house. Could I somehow find a pretext to get inside? Was this already my opportunity to get my hands on the first sample of DNA? I pictured myself sneaking around the rooms, examining Emily's things, and my pulse quickened.

"Baptism of fire for your first day." Bill gave me a slap on the back and retreated toward his truck, talking as he went. "Call me if you need me. Otherwise I'll pick you up in two hours. No need to ask for payment. They have a standing order, so no sweat." He raised a hand and jogged the last few yards, got in and lightly honked the horn as he drove off.

I made my way around the back of the house to Emily and Tyler's sprawling yard I estimated at least eighty feet deep. The tall trees at the back, which led to the woodlands and ravine behind, swayed gently in the breeze, the subtle scent of jasmine in the air. When I stood with my back to the house, images of Grace peppered my mind. I saw her sneaking through the pouring rain, up through the garden and into the house, where Emily was upstairs with Hunter. Had Grace grabbed Alex and disappeared into the forest while an accomplice—but *who*?—waited in a car nearby? How had Grace known the baby would be there in the first place, or had she meant to steal Hunter all along?

Despite the warmth outside I shivered, and another scenario played out in my mind. Logan—Hunter—spending the first few weeks of his life at this very house, a place where he'd been loved and cherished before he was snatched from Emily on a deserted road in the rain. Revenge remained the theory about his disappearance, but revenge for what? Had the Grace I'd known—thought I'd known—really been involved in something so sinister?

When the answers I desperately wanted didn't leap out from behind a tree or a bush, I made myself shove the questions a little farther back in my mind, and pressed on with work. As per Bill's instructions, Emily and Tyler's riding lawn mower was in the shed, the keys hanging from a metal daffodil on the wall. I hopped on, started it up and reversed it onto the grass.

The sun beat down as I worked, the wrath of a fiery god. It scorched my neck, made my shirt glue itself to my back and chest. Within half an hour I'd guzzled the rest of the water I'd brought, cursed myself for not bringing more, moved on to the forsythia, rhododendron and lilacs, before shaping a set of junipers. When I mopped the sweat from my brow, I heard someone's footsteps behind me, and spun around to see Emily, her arms and face glistening.

She surveyed the yard, a hand on her hip. "You're fast. And neat. Thank you."

"My pleasure." Before she could turn away I added, "How was your run?"

She grimaced a little. "Planned to do eight miles, but it's way too hot. Are you thirsty, too? I'm having some iced tea."

The way Emily moved her hands when she talked, the upward curve of her lips, the smallest of dimples that appeared on her cheeks when she smiled; it was difficult not to notice all of those, and I hated myself for it. Here I was, already staring at another woman, betraying Grace and unable to justify it, even with everything she'd done. When Emily raised her eyebrows because I hadn't answered I said, "Iced tea would be great."

"I'll bring it outside," Emily said. "Back in a minute."

As she walked over to the deck, I tried very hard to keep my focus no lower than the middle of her back, and when she disappeared into the house I took a deep breath. I dried the sweat from my face with my T-shirt and flattened down my hair, hoping I didn't look like too much of a dirtbag, and tried to think of something intelligent—and marginally witty—to say. Then I told myself to cut the crap, remember the reason for me being there, the—albeit remote—possibility of who Emily might be, and also on the fact she was married. *Married*. I repeated it to myself a third time, thinking I'd do well to focus on that, too.

CHAPTER FORTY-FIVE

"It was so hot out all I wanted to do was collapse in the shade," Emily said when she returned with a pitcher and two tall glasses on a tray. She set them on the garden table, poured the iced tea and held one out to me. "Here you go."

"Thanks. Do you run often?"

"About four times a week, but it depends on work and I don't bother much in the winter. I'd rather be a hermit with a stack of good books and a box of chocolates. Do you run?"

"Yes, not as often, though." I drained half my glass. "This is delicious."

"My mother's recipe," she said, and poured me some more. "Which reminds me, were you at Casa Mama last night?"

I drank again to buy myself time, secretly enjoying the knowledge she'd remembered me from the restaurant. The feeling lasted only a split second. Apparently, I couldn't hiccup in Faycrest without it being noticed.

"Yes," I said. "I thought I recognized you, too. I've never lived in a small village—"

"Town," Emily said, a smile playing on her lips. "Don't let

anyone hear you call this place a village or they'll ban you for life."

"Thanks for the tip," I said with a laugh.

"When did you move to the US? It hasn't been long, has it? Your accent is still so—"

"British?" I said with a grin. "It's been twenty years and I can't seem to shake it, or put on an American one. People think I'm from Texas whenever I try."

She gently pushed a stray lock of hair from her eyes. "Keep the one you have. Ethel was right when she said it was very charming. She's over the moon you're helping with the cabin, by the way, boasting about you all across town and beyond."

The heat rose to my face as I digested the fact she and Ethel had talked about me, then worried they'd suspected something and looked into my background to check out my story. "It's nothing, really."

"But it is. She's had a rough time these past few years," Emily said. "It's nice you can give her a break, and Bill, too, of course. I ran into his wife, Clara, at the store this morning. Have you met her?"

"Not yet."

"Well, she's singing your praises, too." She smiled. "You've made quite the impression."

"No pressure then," I said, and she laughed.

I didn't want our conversation to end, didn't want her to tell me she had stuff to do, places to be, and disappear into the house. I opened my mouth again, about to ask if Faycrest had changed much since she'd moved there. At the very last second I remembered I wasn't supposed to know anything about her, and quickly said, "Did you grow up here?"

She shook her head, refilled both glasses again. "My husband and I are from Portland and moved here when we got married. Secretly I think there was always a small-town girl inside me, desperate to get out. I hardly go back to the city now." She touched her wedding band, spun it around her finger with her thumb. "Are you're moving here? Ethel said you might."

"I'm considering it, yes."

"If you love a strong sense of community, you'll feel right at home. Do you have kids?"

My stomach lurched, the iced tea churning around my gut, threatening to come rushing up my throat like a tidal wave. "Logan. He's seven," I said, not wanting to reciprocate the question because I knew how much it would hurt her.

She seemed fragile, a china figurine on a shelf. I knew Lisa would have kicked me for thinking something so macho, except it had nothing to do with gender. I was broken, too, smashed to pieces by my grief, trying to slowly put them all back together again, knowing the cracks would always be there. It was as if my soul could sense the fragility in hers, was reaching out, wanted to offer solace. Or maybe it was a case of pure guilt. I didn't mention any of this, of course, for fear she'd think me insane and ask me to leave.

"You have a lovely house," I said instead. "Your garden's amazing."

"Thanks. It's still a work in progress. I'm not a hundred percent happy with it, but I can't figure out why."

I looked at the perfect symmetry, the symphony of colors all expertly placed. "Really?"

"Yeah. I guess I wish the path was more of a feature. I mean, it goes to the back and then it's kind of, I don't know—" she waved a hand "—*blah.*"

"Ah, the most technical of landscaping terms." I grinned and rubbed my chin, thinking it was a good job I'd made an effort with the razor that morning before immediately kicking my-

self and sprinting back into yard-pro territory. "You know...
you could line the path with lavender."

"Would that look good?"

"Definitely. It'll go well with the colors you already have.
The stuff's practically indestructible, too, and it's deer resistant.
I hear there's quite a few of them around." I pulled a face. "At
least I hope it's deer. There were some peculiar noises outside
the cabin last night."

"Could've been a b—"

"Please don't say bear," I said. "Or I'm off."

"In that case I was going to say Bambi." Emily laughed.

She gave no indication she was in a hurry to be somewhere
else. Neither was I, and I hadn't expected to meet Emily so
soon, certainly not speak to her alone for so long. Yesterday
morning I'd have jumped at the chance, but getting her DNA
now almost felt too rushed. Unlike Jennifer Abbott, I wanted
to spend time with her, find out more.

"So you think lavender is the way to go?" Emily said, forcing me to regroup.

"We could build an archway for you," I said. "Let morning glory grow over it. It'll really draw the eye to the back.
You mentioned books. What if we built a bench to put at the
far end?"

"Long enough to lie down on? With thick pillows?" She
tapped her lip with her finger as she looked toward the tree
line. "I love that. Why didn't I think of it?"

"I could discuss it with Bill, do some drawings?" If I'd been
a dog, I would have wagged my tail, jumped around and barked
for her, too. Getting myself in check I added, "Maybe your
husband would use a reading bench, too?"

She finished her iced tea and popped her glass on the tray
with a clunk. "Tyler won't care." Her eyes widened slightly

and she cleared her throat. "I mean because he travels so much, he doesn't have time to enjoy the yard nearly as often as I do."

"He's a cop, right?" I said, feeling a complete fraud.

I'd read so much about her and Tyler, I could practically recite their life stories. She was thirty-four, Tyler thirty-eight. He was the only son of a highly successful, now deceased investment banker, and a schoolteacher. Her parents had retired to Miami, both of them already too old and too sick to travel far when Hunter had been taken, and his disappearance had almost killed them. Knowing all these things was dangerous, and I had to be careful not to divulge anything someone in Faycrest hadn't told me. It was as if I had to play a gigantic game of chess, constantly be on the defensive, think ahead, plan my next ten moves.

"He used to be a state police officer," Emily said, exactly as I'd expected her to. "He consults for the police now—for the last few years, actually."

"What about you?" I said, wondering how professional con artists manipulated people for a living and still managed to sleep at night.

"Me?" she said, sounding surprised. "I paint. My studio's in Gorham."

"Not in Faycrest?"

"No. I'd have loved to open one here, but the place is too small, you know? Not enough clients. I teach art classes to kids, too. If you move here, maybe your son would be interested. Does he draw?"

I thought of the stacks of pictures Logan had brought home, how Mr. Shapran had praised him and gone out of his way to mention Logan's budding talent. Were those kinds of traits hereditary? I wasn't sure. Neither of my parents had been handy, much to Mom's dismay. Until I'd been old enough to wield a hammer and a screwdriver, she'd usually asked a neighbor whenever she needed DIY work done.

"Yes, he loves drawing," I said. "Dogs mainly. They're his favorite thing in the world."

"I love dogs," Emily said, and I worked hard not to flinch. "But Tyler's allergic, so we've never had one."

"Me, too," I said. "So what do you paint?"

"Commissioned portraits." She smiled. "Humans, though, not dogs, unfortunately. Sometimes I think they'd be far more patient. I paint landscapes, too, but they're usually more abstract, especially my trees."

"Trees? Are the ones at Ethel's yours?"

"You've seen them?"

"Yesterday. They're spectacular, very…enchanting."

A blush crept up Emily's cheeks, and for a few moments she looked away. "Thanks."

"So…why trees?"

"Well, most people see the same thing depending on the season, you know, a birch is a birch, a maple is a maple, buds in spring, bare in winter. But for me, how they evolve and change and grow each year…it represents strength and wisdom. Harmony, peace." She laughed. "See? It's a bit abstract."

"I understand what you mean," I said. "I think that's why I enjoy landscaping so much. You can come back the next day and notice something new."

"Exactly," Emily said. "You should visit my studio if you have five minutes to waste. It won't take longer than that to look around, I promise."

"I'd like that," I said, and when she smiled and glanced at her watch, added, "I'd better finish up before Bill gets here and finds me slacking off on my first day."

Emily chuckled, both of us reaching for my empty glass, our

fingers brushing lightly. She pulled her hand back, her cheeks taking on another rosy hue.

"Thanks for the tea," I said quickly.

"My pleasure," Emily said quietly before picking up the tray, slipping into the house and closing the patio door softly behind her.

CHAPTER FORTY-SIX

When Bill picked me up twenty minutes later, he showered me with more praise than Leila and Ronnie had given me in all the years I'd known them. After visiting another couple of his regular clients, we drove back to his barn and pulled up next to my truck.

It was a few minutes before seven o'clock, and my stomach growled. I needed to pick up some food, decided it could wait until I'd had a shower, then I'd pop to the store, get some grub, kick back on the deck in the peace and quiet, and call Logan. I felt like a total ass. I'd been so busy, he'd barely crossed my mind all day. Maybe it was some sort of self-preservation mechanism, my brain's way of extricating itself from his life with the minimal amount of damage. I berated myself for being defeatist, for deciding the battle was lost before I was certain there'd be one to fight, or knowing who my opponent would be.

"See you in the morning?" Bill said when I got out of his truck. "Seven fifteen?"

"Absolutely. Looking forward to it," I said. "Thanks."

"No, thank *you*." His phone beeped and he pulled it out

of his pocket. "Text from Emily. Says she's thrilled with your work and excited to see your yard designs." He grinned at me again. "Let's go over them when you're done, and price them out. Then you can show her and let her decide."

"Sounds good, Bill. And thanks again. You know, for giving me a try."

"Don't thank me. We're not out of the deep, dark woods yet. Today was the easy stuff. Wait until you see what I've got lined up tomorrow. Better get a good meal down your gullet. Shoot, that reminds me…gimme me a second." He jogged into the house and returned with a tinfoil-covered dish a minute later, and pushed it into my hands. "Clara texted before she took the kids to soccer practice. She made shepherd's pie. Saved you some."

Inhaling deeply, I let the smell of beef and potatoes take over my nostrils as my stomach growled again. "This is amazing. Will you thank her for me when she gets back?" I shook his hand and got into my truck, and as I drove I almost, *almost* convinced myself being in Faycrest was normal, a feeling that stuck with me only until I arrived at the cabin.

I first noticed the box when I parked the truck. The unmistakable red-and-white case with twenty-four cans of Budweiser, a silver bow stuck on top. My pulse quickened as I sprinted to the cabin, leaped onto the deck and snatched up the booze, holding it in my hands, staring at it from all angles. Had Ethel left the beer for me as a thank-you gift? Or Bill? Wouldn't he have said something?

I scanned the area slowly, the hairs on the back of my neck standing on end. As far as I could tell, nobody lurked in the shadows, or behind the bushes and trees. There were no strange sets of eyes—animal or human—observing my every move. The booze was now a deadweight in my hand, but I could taste the liquid slipping down my throat. *Nobody needs to know*, the little voice in my head whispered. *You've had a long day. A long few weeks. A can or two will help take a load off.*

Loneliness and alcohol had never been a good combination. Right now it was a downright dangerous one. I closed my eyes, silencing the urgent whispers of how good I'd feel, how relaxed. Only one thing would keep me on track. I pulled my phone from my pocket, quickly dialed Lisa's number, frustration growing when I had to repeat the process three times to get an adequate signal, and told her about the gift.

"Come home, Josh," she said, and when I heard her voice, high-pitched and emotional, a tone I hadn't heard her use in a long time, I wished I hadn't called. She had enough going on with the pregnancy, work and Ivan moving in. Lisa was strong, yes, but it wasn't fair that she was always the one watching out for me, cleaning up my mess.

"Josh?" she repeated. "Did you hear what I said? Pack your stuff and leave."

I stared out of the huge window, the one with the dodgy caulking I'd promised Ethel I'd repair, looked at the thick foliage, watched the leaves moving gently in the breeze, a hundred thousand waving hands. Maybe they were a signal for me to do as Lisa said, and despite it being light outside, I pulled the curtain shut, but it did little to convey any reassurance.

"It's just someone welcoming me to the area." I sat down on the lumpy sofa before leaping up again, deciding to check the doors and windows in case I'd missed something. "We're being paranoid. Nobody knows I have…issues."

"Can you be absolutely sure? What if it's Grace's accomplice and they still live there? What if someone in that town took those kids and passed them on to desperate families? Think about it, Josh, what if they *sold* them?"

"That's crazy," I said, rubbing a hand over my face in an attempt to rid myself of the possibility. "First of all, Grace didn't have any money—"

"Not when you met her," Lisa said quickly. "What if she spent it all on getting Logan?"

"I can't see it, Lisa. Can you?"

"I don't know." She sighed. "But I'm so bloody glad you didn't take Logan with you. I mean…what if there's some kind of organized crime going on in that village?"

"You mean the Mafia?" I laughed. "Yeah, maybe Ethel's place is a front for a billion-dollar money-laundering business. I bet you she's hiding blow in her scones. And it's a town, by the way. Don't let anyone hear you call it a village."

"This isn't funny, Josh."

"Sorry, but if you were here you'd know how ludicrous it sounds."

"You're sure there wasn't a note?" Lisa said. "Something from one of these friendly neighbors of yours? Could it have blown away?"

"Maybe. I'll check, okay?" I ran a hand through my hair, noticed the sweat on the back of my neck despite the cool temperature from the rickety air conditioner. "If anything else happens, I'll let you know. How's Logan? Is he really bummed out I'm not there?"

"Uh…sure," she said, and we both laughed at her blatant fib. "Speak of the devil, he just walked in. Hey, Logan, guess who's on the phone?"

I heard footsteps charging over and the phone exchange hands. I imagined his goofball grin as he stood next to my sister with the new Spider-Man backpack she'd bought him for camp firmly clenched in his hand. "Dad! Dad! Camp was so *cool*!"

I smiled. "Tell me everything. Did you make friends?"

"Yeah, loads. This girl Brittany picked up a frog and pretended to eat it. It was so funny and Jack said he was going to be sick. We went swimming, and Brittany showed me how to dive properly. Her dive is the best." He sniffed, sneezed twice.

"So now you're a big fish?"

"That's what Brittany said."

"Sounds awesome, kiddo. So you're having fun with Aunt Lisa and Uncle Ivan?"

"Lots and lots and—" Logan's third sneeze muffled his words.

"Is your hay fever bothering you again?"

"Uh-huh. I sneezed a million times today."

"A million, huh? I bet that sucked. Did Aunt Lisa give you your antihista—"

"Yep, and I have to take more before camp tomorrow." He paused, a little of the excitement draining from his voice. "Aunt Lisa said you'll be back on Friday. Can you be here before? I miss you."

"I miss you, too. I promise I'll try, but I'm not sure. I might be late on Friday night, so—"

"Wake me up when you get back, *please*, Dad. I don't care."

"You will the next morning. How's Cookie?"

"Great and—uh-oh. She's got the remote. No, Cookie, *stop*." The phone clattered to the floor. When Logan picked it up again he said, "Gotta go. Aunt Lisa wants you. Love you, Dad!"

"I love you, too," I said, but he'd already gone.

"If my kid turns out half as brilliant as him, I'll be all set," Lisa said when she got back on the phone. "He's fabulous."

"How's that tiny tot of yours behaving?" I asked. "Are you still feeling sick?"

"Not today although yesterday afternoon I thought I'd bring up a kidney. I tell you, whoever named it morning sickness and said it lasts only for the first trimester was full of crap." She lowered her voice a little. "I'm worried about Ivan, though. I caught him watching a nappy advert three times in a row last night."

"That's true love," I said. "You've got nothing to worry about there."

"I know," she said, after a few seconds added, "Josh, what will you do with the beer?"

"Throw it away."

"Promise me?"

"All of it. I promise."

"It's really freaking me out. You're there, all alone. You still haven't spoken to a new sponsor, have you? Could you find a meeting close by—"

"No. I don't want anyone around here finding out. I'll be okay."

"Will you? You've always been a good person—"

"Except when I was a lying drunk—"

"*Stop,*" Lisa said. "You lost your direction for a while, and you got back on track. But all this lying, the secrecy, snooping around. I'm scared it's going to derail you again."

"Don't worry." I picked up the beer and headed for the kitchen, opened the first can and, after a moment's hesitation, emptied it down the sink. "Everything's going to be alright."

After we hung up and I'd disposed of the rest of the booze, I thought about her advice to pack up and leave, knowing I'd be no closer to the truth if I did. I had to stay strong, stay on track, and although Grace had started all of this, it was now very much mine to finish.

CHAPTER FORTY-SEVEN

Another day of working with Bill sped by. I didn't see Emily again, and I hadn't yet met Felicia, despite popping into Ethel's café, hoping I'd run into her. Unless she was one of Bill's clients—and so far I hadn't had the opportunity to ask without it seeming odd—I wondered if orchestrating a believable encounter would mean bringing Cookie back with me after the weekend, and taking her to Felicia's animal clinic.

In the meantime, no more gifts—alcohol or otherwise—had showed up on the deck, and that evening after I'd been shopping for food, I decided to concentrate on the cabin updates. It didn't take long to fix the front door hinges, take up the bedroom carpets, and prime the tiny bathroom and kitchen for their first coats of new paint. At around eight o'clock I heard a vehicle come up the dirt track, my senses going into overdrive until I saw Ethel's car.

"Thought I'd come and see how you're doing," she called out, waving at me. "Bill said he's working you to the bone, but I see you're still standing."

"It'll take more than that," I said, thankful I'd had the foresight to stuff the beer cans in a bag and drop them in the recycling on the way to work. I didn't need Ethel spotting twenty-four empties and drawing incorrect conclusions. "Did you stop by the cabin yesterday?"

"No, I've been rushed off my feet at the café. This weather has brought more customers than usual, not that I'm complaining. How are you settling in?"

"Very well, thanks."

"Music to my ears. I hope you'll stay in Faycrest. We need people like you."

"Me?" I said as we walked up the front steps.

She patted my arm, gave me another smile. "Hardworking, trustworthy and… My *gosh*." Ethel pointed to the rolls of old, dusty, blue carpet I'd stacked outside the window. "You've taken it all up already? Don't tell me you've painted, too, because it smells like it."

"Only primed so far."

"You've been here five minutes."

"It helps when you have no internet. I never knew how much time I wasted on YouTube. Glass of water?"

"Please. I don't deal with the heat so well anymore." Ethel fanned her face with a hand. "Have you heard a bad storm's brewing? Can't come soon enough if you ask me. At least it'll clear the air. You'll let me know if there are any leaks, won't you?"

"Once I've fixed them."

Ethel laughed. "You see? Hardworking and trustworthy. I hope you're not finding it too cutoff out here?"

"Not at all."

"You're sure? I mean, I know we're not far from town, but you can't tell, looking out of the window. Always seemed I was in the middle of nowhere. Al would've lived here, if I'd let him. In fact, he did once or twice when the old chump was in the doghouse."

"Uh-oh. Sounds serious." I chuckled and filled two glasses with water. The way Ethel talked about her husband made me think how my parents' relationship would have been, had they grown old together. Or mine and Grace's…

"Ah, well. It's bound to happen once in a while over forty years." She took the drink from me. "Thank you. I thought you might be lonely out here, being used to the city and all."

"Not really."

"Are you sure?"

"Yeah, honestly, I'm too busy."

She looked at me, wrinkled her nose and let out a sigh. "Alright, Josh. You're not taking the bait and I'm not getting any younger, so I'm just going to have to come out and say it. Do you recall me mentioning Felicia?"

"Your goddaughter? Yes, of course," I said, unable to hide a look of surprise.

"I was wondering if you two would want to go for dinner."

I laughed at her directness until the implication of the suggestion hit me. "I'm not sure—"

"Before you say anything else, I'm not matchmaking. Trust me, I know you lost your partner and I'm not that uncouth."

I quickly batted the images of Emily away. "I'm not ready for anything—"

"Of course not, but you and Felicia are about the same age, and…well, to be perfectly honest she could do with going out once in a while. She's only ever at the clinic, or at home. I can't remember the last time she did anything else despite my offers to babysit."

"Well, I—"

"I think you might enjoy each other's company, that's all.

And don't forget Felicia can fill you in on the schools around here, so you'd know what to expect for young Logan."

I leaned against the wall, crossed my arms as I felt my pulse quicken. This could be my shot at getting Felicia's DNA, and with a bit of luck, I'd be back in Albany for good by the weekend. Taking her for dinner under false pretenses was wrong, but my entire reason for being in Faycrest was hardly saintlike. How much difference could adding another lie to the steaming pile really make?

Ethel held her hands up, palms facing outward. "I'm sorry. I shouldn't have suggested it. It was just a thought. Forgive me? I—"

"Nothing to forgive and you're right. I could do with the company."

"Marvelous," she said, handing me a piece of paper. "Felicia's number. Why don't you phone, text or do whatever it is young people do these days? She'll be glad you called. Now, let's have a look at those paint colors."

After we'd said our goodbyes, I stayed on the deck until the sun went down, the cold nibbling at my fingertips, and all that time, the piece of paper with Felicia's number felt as if I'd filled my pocket with embers.

CHAPTER FORTY-EIGHT

Bill filled the next day with back-to-back landscaping appointments that kept my mind busy, and my time limited. By midafternoon I still hadn't called Felicia, and when I finally pulled out her number, Bill offered to go over the yard sketches and estimates I'd put together for Emily after I couldn't get to sleep the night before. Thirty minutes later I was on my way home, but changed my mind and continued past the turnoff to the cabin and toward Emily's house instead.

I drummed my fingers on the steering wheel, telling myself the strange fluttering I felt in my stomach was indigestion from the pulled-pork sandwich Bill had split with me for lunch, and which had almost been the size of my head. Truth was, I could have been a kid on a trip to the fairground, and I found myself changing into my pair of clean shoes when I parked the truck. I rang the bell, attempting hide my disappointment when Tyler opened the door.

He looked slick in his dark suit, black shirt and tie, his hair newly cut, his stance assertive. The role of police consultant suited him, and I had no doubt he commanded the room, had people literally on the edge of their seats, listening to his every word. From what I'd read, the number of cases he took on where they found the missing kid alive was incredibly high. Knowing I might have his son, was doing this tenth-rate detective crap, filled me with exactly zero self-confidence. If Logan was Alex King or Hunter Rhodes, I might well face Tyler in an interrogation room, or at the very least he'd be watching my every move from behind a two-way mirror. Quite frankly the thought scared the shit out of me.

"Yes?" he said with a frown.

"I'm Josh Andersen. I work for Bill Langham."

He held out a hand, his grip the kind that oozed authority, and flashed a smile. It made him look completely different in an instant: the kind, generous next-door neighbor, a person you could trust, someone to rely on. "Tyler Rhodes. Pleasure."

"Same. Uh, is Mrs. Rhodes at home?"

"Not yet. Can I give her a message?"

I held out the white envelope with the drawings. "These are the yard designs for her."

"Yard designs?" Tyler frowned again.

"She and I talked about them the other day."

"Oh, yes. Emily mentioned something." He took the documents and set them on the chest of drawers behind him without a further glance. "I'll let her know you stopped by."

"Thanks." Maybe it was a sudden flash of inspiration, or the fact I'd suddenly remembered my reason for coming to Faycrest in the first place, but I added, "Would you mind if I check your mower? It didn't start properly the other day and I should—"

Tyler's phone rang. "I'd better get this," he said as he looked at it. "But go right ahead."

He flashed his perfect teeth again, and it irked me. His confidence and suave appearance felt slick, too practiced. I recalled one of his recent interviews in which he'd been asked if he'd ever consider running for government, and now I knew why. He'd be perfect. Although I was man enough to admit seeing his expensive house while I lived on my own in a decrepit cabin in the woods was making my male pride roar, not to mention the fact I had a bit of a pathetic crush on his wife. Like him or not, I reminded myself as I walked to the back of the house toward the shed, the guy was a hero.

"Finding missing children helps with the pain of losing Alex and my son," he'd said in another interview I'd seen. "Making sure other parents can be spared what we've been through, what we're still going through. Knowing their little ones are back at home, tucked up in bed… Trust me, there's no better feeling."

He'd also said he'd never give up searching for Hunter or Alex, regularly held appeals for witnesses, maintained the websites and social media profiles he'd created, begged people to send anonymous tips, organized poster drives, had updated sketches of the boys drawn. I'd studied each one in detail, showed them to Ivan and Lisa, and we'd agreed they didn't look like Logan, no more than many other brown-haired seven-year-old boys did. The eyes were too far apart, the forehead too big, the nose too narrow. "Because Logan isn't Hunter or Alex," Lisa had insisted. "He can't be."

As I opened the shed door, I decided I was being an obnoxious asshole for taking an unjustified disliking to Tyler. His son had been *kidnapped*, for Christ's sake. I couldn't imagine what the guy was going through, how he'd carried on when each of his words and gestures were scrutinized and judged, not only by his family and friends, colleagues and the press, but also by the court of public opinion. And me.

I wondered if Tyler had ever blamed Emily for what had happened to the Faycrest boys, or even suspected her of somehow being involved. Had he tapped her phone, lifted her prints, insisted she take a polygraph? Although, as I'd discovered in my hours of research, plenty of innocent people failed lie detector tests, especially when a child vanished. It was the guilt that did it. Not because they'd had anything to do with the disappearance, but, as Ethel had said, because they felt they should have been there to stop it from happening, or at least sensed the danger somehow.

Parents, I'd learned, were almost always suspects when kids went missing. Emily and Tyler, Felicia and Gavin, they'd all been interviewed, questioned and requestioned. Nothing suspicious ever came to light, and when the police uncovered one of the handymen who'd been working on the renovations at the Rhodes house had a record, the focus shifted to him for a while, despite his rock-solid alibi and repeated claims of innocence.

Walking toward the mower, my animosity tipped a little to pity before settling somewhat closer to admiration. The fact Tyler and Emily were still together was a testament to their relationship. Through all of this they'd somehow managed to keep the shreds of their marriage together, which had to count for something. And, I repeated to myself, it also meant I had to stop thinking about another man's wife.

I knelt down in front of the mower, pretending to check it out for a few seconds. It had started fine the other day, but I'd hoped I might get Emily's DNA from something in the shed, a glove maybe, or a stray hair band. After a few moments I knew it was a lost cause, and I didn't have the guts to wait until Tyler left and attempt a burglary of their home. It was Thursday, which meant I'd been in Faycrest for almost a week and hadn't yet accomplished either of my goals. Time to change that. I closed up the shed, pulled out my phone and dialed.

"Felicia King."

"Felicia, hello. It's Josh Andersen. From Ethel's cabin."

"Oh, hi. I didn't think you'd actually call..." Her laugh was warm, friendly. "Oh, boy, that sounded lame. Look, I'm sorry Ethel's been interfering. First she offers you the cabin—"

"For which I was grateful…"

"Sure. Until you saw the work it needs." She laughed again. "Now she's organizing us 'young kids' as she called me earlier… Josh, no doubt you'll find my godmother, witty and charming as she may be, is extraordinarily meddlesome. God bless her. And her scones."

"Especially her scones," I said, and forced a grin. "I'm sorry, I didn't mean to—"

"Oh, no, you misunderstand," Felicia said quickly. "Ethel is also annoyingly right, because I'd love to go out for a bite to eat."

"You would?"

"With the living legend of Faycrest? Yes. Plus it'll shut Ethel up, and it'll make a change to talk to someone who doesn't look up an animal's backside for a living."

"Can't say that's ever been a burning desire," I said, pausing for a second before deciding I had nothing to lose. "I'm heading back to Albany for the weekend tomorrow. I don't suppose you're free this evening? I know it's short notice, but—"

"I'm sure it's fine. Ethel's always bugging me to spend more time with my daughter. Shall I choose a place? Is there anything you don't want to eat?"

"Tripe, liver and kidneys?" I offered.

"Ugh, tell me about it," Felicia said. "Take it from me, being a vet puts you off meat. I'll check with Ethel and text you my address. Can you meet me there at seven?"

"That works. I'm looking forward to it."

"Me, too," she said. "And I promise I won't bore you with a million animal stories."

I laughed. "No worries. See you later. Bye, Felicia."

When I hung up and slipped my phone in my pocket, a small

movement caught my eye. I looked toward the house, my gaze darting up until it settled on Tyler, who observed me from the open window upstairs. I raised my hand in a wave, but instead of returning the gesture, he looked at me for another few seconds, turned away and disappeared.

CHAPTER FORTY-NINE

It was almost five thirty when I left Emily and Tyler's house, more than enough time to head to the cabin for a shower and change of clothes before meeting Felicia. I rehearsed a number of topics and questions in my mind as I drove to ensure we didn't run out of things to say. Her cutting the evening short before I'd completed my mission would be a disaster. I cataloged the ways of getting a DNA sample, too: a straw, a cigarette butt or discarded gum.

The various scenarios sped through my mind as I drove to the other side of town, past Bill's and toward the turnoff to the cabin. About four hundred yards farther on I slowed down when I spotted a white Toyota stopped by the side of the road. Emily, wearing another long, pastel flower-patterned dress, was crouched down, her hair up in a ponytail, her arm stretched out underneath the vehicle. I got out of my truck and jogged over.

"Hi, Emily," I said.

"Oh, hi, Josh." She smiled as she put a hand above her eyes to block out the sun.

I knelt down beside her. "Car trouble?"

Emily nodded and stuck her hand back underneath the car. "Heat shield fell off again. It's stuck." She wrestled with the offending object some more, finally pulling it free. "The damn thing came off last week already, and the garage didn't put it back on properly. It punctured my tire when it came off this time." She stood up and opened the back passenger door, shoved the shield behind the seat. "Were you on your way home?"

"Yeah, I just came from your house."

"Really?"

"Uh-huh…" The heat prickled the back of my neck. Damn it, her gaze was intense, her eyes—a deep shade of turquoise—almost rendering me incapable of formulating coherent sentences. "You know, for the yard designs. I gave them to Tyler."

"Tyler was home?" she said with a frown.

I shrugged. "Let me know what you think of the designs, and we'll go over them whenever you're ready."

"We could grab a drink at Casa Mama, if you're free?"

"That would be… Oh, no, I can't." I shook my head. "I'm having dinner with Felicia." I have no idea why I told her. The words had a will of their own, spilling from my mouth like floodwater over a riverbank, and I felt the urge to justify. "Ethel suggested it so she can fill me in on the schools."

Emily nodded. "You'll have a great evening. Felicia's lovely and very involved with the school, so you'll definitely get the inside scoop. Anyway, I'd better get this tire changed."

"Can I help?"

"That's okay. I don't want to keep you. I've been doing it since I was twelve."

I grinned. "You've got me beat. I was thirteen."

"My dad taught me. He said he never wanted his daughter to be a damsel in distress."

"He's a wise man."

She smiled. "Yes, he is, so how did you learn about cars? Was it your dad, too?"

"God, no, he only cared about knowing how to drive, not how the car worked," I said, laughing at the distant memory. "Mind you, he had the same philosophy about the tin opener. Although I'm pretty sure he'd be very unhappy if I abandoned someone by the side of the road with a flat. Want to take the lead and tell me how to assist?"

"Sure, why not?" She smiled as she walked to the trunk of her car and took out the jack. "Watch and learn. You might be able to teach your dad a trick or two after all."

"I wish I could. He's been gone almost twenty years."

Emily's eyes widened. "Oh, gosh. I'm so sorry. What happened?"

"It's a very long story, and not a particularly happy one," I said.

"We've got time," Emily said. "If you want to talk about it."

I hesitated for only a moment, then found myself telling her the entire story as we worked on changing the tire; the real reason why we came to America, and how Mom and Dad died when I was still in high school. When I finished, she lowered the wrench and turned toward me.

"Have you ever stopped blaming yourself?" she said quietly.

"I never…" I sighed. Grace had asked me the exact same question. "No, and thank you."

"For what?"

"For not saying I shouldn't feel responsible."

"Only you can decide that," Emily said softly, that sadness creeping back into her eyes, a silent ghost emerging from the shadows. "We all have our regrets, things we wish we could go back and change. Some of us more than others."

She stared at me. A little smudge of dirt from the tire had

found its way to her cheek, and I wanted to reach out and gently wipe it away. "Do you want to talk about yours?"

Emily shook her head, looked away. "You'll be late for your date with Felicia—"

"It's not a d—"

"—and I'd better get going. It was nice seeing you again. Thanks for your help."

A minute later she was back in her car, leaving me standing on the side of the road, wishing she and I were going out for dinner instead.

CHAPTER FIFTY

Back at the cabin I had a quick wash and changed my clothes, noting I was down to my last clean shirt. Once done, I followed Felicia's directions to her house, an unassuming bungalow with a low pitched, gable roof and a yellow-and-green swing set that stood next to an abandoned pink space hopper on the lawn. A copper umbrella stand in the shape of a swan guarded the front steps, making the place look even cozier, quite the contrast to Emily and Tyler's place. *Emily.* I had to stop thinking about her, so I took a deep breath and rang the doorbell.

Within two seconds the door flew open and a blue-eyed, blond-haired girl stood in front of me. I took in her corkscrew ringlets, her Wonder Woman costume, rubber boots and the plastic sword in one hand, the other on her hip.

"Do you come in peace?" she said, pointing the sword at me. "Or are you the enemy?"

"In peace, of course," I said, trying not to laugh, "and I surrender, Your Highness."

Her hands flew to her face as she covered her mouth, burst

into a squeal and took off down the hallway as Ethel appeared with a deck of cards in her hands.

"Hello, Josh, how are you, dear?" she said, a wry smile playing on her lips. "I see you met Lydia. She'll rule the world one day, let me tell you. In the meantime, we lesser mortals have to try to keep up." Without taking her eyes off me, she called out, "Felicia, Josh's here."

"Be right there," I heard Felicia call back from somewhere inside the house.

"No rush to get home," Ethel said, leaning toward me. "I taught Lydia how to play chess a few weeks ago. Now I have to practice after she goes to bed if I ever hope to win again. Mind you, chasing after a superhero is exhausting. I'll end up falling asleep in front of the TV."

"I don't think we'll be late. It's just dinner."

Ethel smiled. "Want to come in while you wait?"

"No need. I'm ready," Felicia said, appearing behind her, wearing a pair of jeans and a blue-and-white-striped T-shirt that made her wide eyes pop. I knew she was attractive, but the online pictures hadn't done her justice. Her face was perfectly symmetrical, her cheekbones high, and the way she'd cropped her blond hair into a bob suited her way more than the longer style I'd seen her with. She looked younger, healthier and happy.

"Weren't you going to change?" Ethel whispered, still loud enough for me to hear.

Felicia rolled her eyes. "Bye, Ethel." She kissed her on the cheek before calling out, "Bye, munchkin!" and closing the door behind her. As we headed to our vehicles, she stopped and turned to face me. "So you know what you've signed up for, most people will tell you I'm very blunt but I need us to be clear about something."

"Okay..."

"Ethel has always been more of a mother to me, really—"

Felicia tucked her hair behind her ears "—but she doesn't understand, or accept for that matter, that I'm not interested in anything, you know, romantic."

"Thank God, because me neither," I said with a grin. "And, by the way, I don't think there's anything wrong with your being blunt about that."

"Great." Felicia smiled. "So now that awkward bit is out of the way, what do you say we get out of town and away from the gossipers? Faycrest can be a bit of a viper's nest at times."

"Lead the way. You're in charge."

"Oh, I like you already," Felicia said. "But don't tell Ethel or she'll bake the wedding cake. Anyway, I have to stop at my clinic after dinner, so can you follow me to The Storyteller? Have you heard of it?" When I shook my head she added, "I think you'll enjoy it. It's a pub a few miles out. Best food I've ever tasted, and don't tell Ethel that, either."

"My lips are sealed." I opened her car door for her, and then got into my truck.

It had been a long time since I'd been out to dinner with a woman other than Grace, and I'd never been particularly talented at dating before that, either. Most of the time I'd stuff my big feet into my even larger mouth, or my dark and rather obscure English sense of humor missed the mark completely. Then again, it didn't matter this time, and I was relieved Felicia had been clear about her expectations, or the lack thereof. Even if the circumstances had been different, if we'd met at a bar or through work, I doubt there'd have been a spark. While Felicia was obviously smart, attractive and, from the little I'd seen so far, funny, too, she also reminded me way too much of Lisa. I let my shoulders drop as I drove, told myself to relax. I should at least try to enjoy the evening despite my highly questionable motives.

I followed her out of town, past Bill's and a farther ten miles past that. One turn and another narrow lane later, she pulled into a small but busy gravel-filled lot surrounded by cornfields. My eyes widened as I looked up at the pub, taking in the smooth, white stone walls and thatched roof. For a moment I thought I'd been teleported back to the English countryside, half expected a man in a flat cap and a pair of wellies to stroll past with a shotgun, offering to take us clay-pigeon shooting.

"Quaint, isn't it?" Felicia said as I walked over. "An American built it for his English fiancée over a hundred years ago, but on her way over the ship sank and he never got over it. Rumor has it his ghost roams the house at night, waiting for his true love to arrive." She shuddered, rubbed her arms. "Don't let that put you off. The fish cakes are fantastic."

"Didn't you say you don't eat meat?"

Felicia wrinkled her nose. "I'll eat anything I don't operate on, so I'm good with fish."

The pub was dark inside, and it took my eyes a few moments to adjust to my new surroundings. Its low, pale ceilings and dark-stained beams, the swirly patterned carpet, brown leather seats, deep mahogany tables and delicious smell of comfort food reminded me of The White Swan, a place Mom and Dad had taken Lisa and me for Sunday lunches when were kids.

While The White Swan had been a somewhat dark and dingy affair, The Storyteller's bar was lit with twinkling fairy lights that made the bottles, glasses and mirrors sparkle like a crystal cave. A large clock with Roman numerals hung above the empty fireplace on the back wall, and it was easy to imagine how the place would feel at Christmas, decorated in all its festive glory, the pub-goers boozed-up and warm as an unrelenting snowstorm raged outside.

"Felicia!" A tall, wispy woman with olive skin and long black hair and a collection of silver hoop earrings rushed over for an embrace. "Good to see you. How have you been? And how's your gorgeous girl?"

"Lydia's great, thanks," Felicia said. "Found her at the top of our tree again over the weekend with a penknife. Honestly, she'll be the death of me, I'm sure." She laughed and turned to me. "This is Miranda, proud owner of The Storyteller and chef extraordinaire. Miranda, this is Josh. He's thinking of moving to the area, and he's helping Ethel."

"Welcome, welcome." Miranda shook my hand. "Lovely to meet you. I've prepared a table for you inside, or would you prefer the terrace?"

"Inside," Felicia said. "Do you mind, Josh? My hay fever's really bad at the moment."

My mind raced back to how Logan had sneezed on the phone, how I'd heard him sniff a dozen times in the few minutes we'd spoken. The pollen this time of year always bugged him. Grace had never suffered from allergies, so I'd assumed Logan had either inherited them from his dad, or it was simply one of those things. But…what if it was from Felicia?

An image of her discovering Logan was her son surged from the middle of my brain and hurtled around my mind. I imagined Felicia falling to her knees in front of him, pulling him in for a desperate embrace. She'd hug him tight before examining his face, unable to believe he was truly Alex, her aching sorrow and yearning turning to disbelief at first, and then to unbridled joy. She'd take him home, watch his every move, unable to sleep until he was back from school or soccer practice, safely tucked up in bed. There wasn't just Felicia to consider, but her ex-husband, Gavin, too, and Lydia. Did she know about her older brother? How would she react to his return? Would she accept him with open arms, make room for him in their lives?

I'd hardly spent any time with Felicia, but one thing was becoming crystal clear. If Logan was Alex King, I'd have no choice but to step up and confess. I had no right to stop them from being reunited. Felicia wasn't like the Abbotts. As far as I could tell, there'd be no valid objection, nothing but my own selfishness and heartache standing in the way of them being together again, and that wasn't the kind of person I wanted to be.

"Josh?" Felicia touched my arm. "You okay with a table inside?"

"Sure, sure," I said, plastering a smile on my face I hoped would somehow cover the cracks within me, too. "That would be great."

"Perfect, follow me." Miranda guided us to a table at the back of the pub, next to a window with the best views of the rolling fields and gentle hills beyond. Clouds had partially obscured the blue skies, and they looked gray and heavy. Miranda followed my gaze. "A storm's coming," she said. "It's supposed to rain for the next three days straight, at least. I hope summer isn't over already. Anyway, I'll be right back with menus."

"This is a great place, Felicia," I said as Miranda left. "I feel right at home."

"It was the obvious choice when Ethel told me you're British. I've been coming here for years. I love it…" She paused, tucked another stray lock of hair behind her ear, looked like she might say something before reconsidering.

"What is it?" I asked gently. "Is everything okay?"

She nodded, and her smile might have accentuated the fine lines around her eyes, but it still made her look younger. For the first time since we'd met, I was close enough to notice the smattering of freckles on the bridge of her nose…a pattern almost identical to Logan's.

"Do you think we should let the elephants in the room loose?" she said.

"The elephants…?" I said, my eyes darting to hers. "I don't think I understand…?"

Felicia opened her mouth but closed it again when Miranda came over.

"Here you go," she said, setting glasses of water on the table and handing us a rolled-up, parchment paper menu each. "Would you—" The sound of porcelain shattering on the floor filled the air, and Miranda pulled a face. "Uh-oh. New dishwasher started yesterday. Not going so well. Be right back."

After she'd dashed off, Felicia looked at me and I shifted in my seat. "I know Ethel told you about Alex," she said. "She told me you lost your partner, too, in an accident?"

The breath I hadn't realized I'd been holding rushed from my lungs. Of course that's what she'd meant. She wasn't onto me, or my secrets. If she were, she'd have called the cops, not agreed to have dinner. I nodded. "Yes, last March."

"I'm so sorry for your loss, Josh. How are you coping?"

I shrugged, drank some of my water while deciding how to respond. "I'm doing okay."

"Is that why you're living in a tiny town in the middle of nowhere, hiding out in a cabin that smells of rotten feet?"

I couldn't help but laugh. "When you said you were blunt, you meant it, didn't you?"

Felicia smiled and set her glass on the coaster. "After Alex disappeared I wanted to hide, too, believe me, but it was all about keeping him in the public's mind, constantly reminding them he was missing. Appeals, TV shows, interviews, candlelit vigils…" She paused. "None of it helped, in the end."

"I wish it had," I said, a pathetic offering in a desperate attempt to disguise how uncomfortable I felt. As I tried not to squirm in my seat, I almost wanted to open up, tell Felicia everything, get her DNA and run a test right there, in the middle of The Storyteller.

"What was she like?" Felicia said. "Your partner?"

I tried to erase the last few months from my mind, think

about the Grace I'd thought I'd known, the woman I'd fallen in love with and declared my soul mate to anyone who'd listened. "She was incredible," I said, which had been my truth not that long ago, and fell silent again.

"But you don't want to talk about her?" Felicia said, and when I didn't answer she nodded, gently aligning her silverware with her fingertips. "Then we won't."

As Felicia sipped her water, it reminded me I'd need a strategy to steal her glass before the end of the evening, seeing as she didn't smoke and hadn't chewed gum. Taking the glass from the table during the meal would be too obvious, so I discreetly pulled my phone from my pocket and set it on the bench beside me, ready to put my plan into action.

"How do you know Miranda?" I said.

"Oh, we go way back. We both grew up here. Went to the same high school."

"And did you always want to be a vet?"

"If my parents were to be believed. I operated on all my stuffed animals from the tender age of five. What about you? Have you always been into landscaping?"

"Well, the fresh air and the physical side are great—"

"Not the original dream then? What did you want to be when you were growing up?"

"A civil engineer."

"Really? How come?"

"We went on holiday to Wales a lot when I was a kid, and we'd drive over this massive bridge that goes over the River Severn—"

"The Severn Bridge," she said. "I've heard of it."

"I thought it was the most amazing thing. It was the highlight of my trip, and I always dreamed of building one."

"So why the landscaping?"

I shrugged. "Life threw me a few curveballs and instead of

running with them, as they say, I dropped them all, and that was that. Game over."

"Totally understand," Felicia said. "I had the perfect life, everything I'd ever dreamed of until Alex disappeared. Then it all fell apart until Lydia came along and glued me back together."

"She seems quite the character."

"Honestly, I wouldn't have made it through without her." Felicia put an elbow on the table and rested her hand under her chin. "I found out I was pregnant five months after Alex was taken. And you know what? Back then I worried he'd come home and think we'd tried to replace him. That was when Gavin and I were convinced he'd be found."

"Were?" My hands trembled, so I put them palms down on the table. "You've lost hope?"

"I know I should say I haven't," Felicia answered. "It's what the parent of any missing child is supposed to say, how they're sure their baby is alive, that one day they'll be found."

"It does happen," I said gently, wanting to lean over and touch her arm, but worried what she might make of the gesture. "I've read about cases where the kids have been found years, or even decades, later. He could still come back."

"Yes, I know that, technically, but I don't feel it—" she put a hand to her chest "—in here. I can't feel my little boy anymore."

I didn't speak, could barely look at her, couldn't bring myself to see the sorrow that had been etched into her eyes, and I bit down on my tongue, hard, tasted a hint of blood.

"God, Ethel was right," Felicia said suddenly. "You *are* easy to talk to. But this is getting very heavy for what's supposed to be a fun night out, isn't it? We haven't even ordered yet." She picked up her menu, let a breezy smile slide across her face. "Let's take a minute."

I perused the choices of fish, steak and pasta, which all would have sounded amazing if I hadn't a lump the size of a baseball lodged in my throat. Felicia pointed out her favorite dishes, and I followed her recommendation by ordering the fish cakes, lamb and homemade, thick-cut fries I already knew I'd mostly leave on my plate. We moved on to other subjects, which led to me tiptoeing around her questions about Logan, telling her more about England and asking for details when she mentioned a trip to Europe a decade earlier.

"I fell in love with Paris," Felicia said, sipping her Sprite. I'd been relieved when she'd declined a glass of wine because she was driving, and heading back to work later. If I'd ever had a reason for not being tempted and making sure I kept a clear head, then having a casual dinner with Logan's potential mother was definitely it. "I always wanted to go back to France," she continued, "but then life happened, you know? Within a few blinks I'd got married, opened the practice and had Alex."

"I've never been, but it looks great." I took another bite of the fish cakes Miranda had put in front of us, and which truly were spectacular, and was about to ask what Felicia's favorite part of the trip had been when my phone sprang to life.

"Go ahead." Felicia dabbed the corners of her mouth with a napkin. "I don't mind."

I frowned at the number, tapped the screen. "Hello, this is Josh."

"Hi, Josh, it's Emily. Emily Rhodes."

"Emily? Hello." My voice took on this weird falsetto pitch, and I cleared my throat in an attempt to dislodge my tongue, which had become stuck to the roof of my mouth.

"Bill gave me your number," she said. "I know you're busy, but I just wanted to call quickly and say thank you for the designs."

"Do you like them?"

"Like them? I love them, I really do. I was wondering if you could stop by tomorrow morning. Not just for the designs, but for a sprinkler problem. I'm not sure what's wrong, but a couple of them aren't working properly. Could you take a look, too?"

"Sure," I said, trying not to let an idiotic grin spread across my face. "Bill doesn't need me until eight thirty. I could come over an hour before. Or is that too early?"

"Not at all. I'll put some coffee on, or boil the kettle. I hear you prefer tea."

"I do, thanks. See you tomorrow." I hung up, worked harder to keep my face straight. Feeling the need to explain, I said, "That was Emily Rhodes. I did some yard designs for her."

"I can't wait to see what she chooses," Felicia said. "Emily's so creative, too, a real artist. Have you been to her studio yet?"

"No. Not yet."

"It's fantastic. Lydia's been going to her after-school art classes for six months, and absolutely loves it now. It was a struggle getting her to go at first."

"How come? Isn't she a fan of painting or something?"

"Oh, no, not at all. It was the building. For whatever reason it freaked her out. You know how kids can be. It's this big, old, redbrick thing, lots of corridors and creepy spaces. It was a clothes factory years and years ago, then they made printers—"

"Printers?" I frowned. "You mean for offices?"

"Yeah. Those early models where the paper was all connected with the holes down both sides? They were really successful, but missed the boat for the digital trend and went out of business eventually. Shut the whole company down overnight about ten years ago, laid everybody off."

"That must've hit the town pretty hard."

"It did. The building was empty until Emily and Tyler bought it, and they rent out the spaces to artists now. They have a photographer, a couple of sculptors, a glassblower and a recording studio on the top floor." She grinned. "Meanwhile I can't sing, play an instrument or draw to save my life."

"Ah, but you save animals instead. That's got to count for a whole lot of something."

"You're very sweet." Felicia pushed back her chair. "Excuse me for a minute?"

As she got up and headed for the washroom, I took a deep breath. They'd made printers in that building? It was a total long shot, but what if that note Grace had hidden—TELL NO ONE—had been printed there? It was definitely done on one of those old machines... I shook my head. A machine from there or anywhere else on the planet, and I still didn't know if it had even meant anything.

Felicia wouldn't be gone long, and I reminded myself I had to get her DNA. I reconsidered pocketing her glass, but the couple at the table next to us was too close; they were bound to see. Instead I bent over, pretended to fix my shoelaces, all the while quietly sliding my phone onto the floor—volume off, display side down—and nudging it under my seat.

An hour later I paid for dinner despite Felicia's insistence on splitting the bill. "You showed me a fantastic pub," I said as we made our way to the front door. "Buying you a meal is the least I can do." We said goodbye to Miranda, making promises to visit again soon, and as we stepped outside into the crisp air, I patted my jacket pocket.

"I think I dropped my phone. I'd better check..."

"Do you mind if I head off?" Felicia said. "It's far later than I thought it would be. A sign of good company."

"Likewise. Thanks for a great evening. It was good meeting you."

"You, too, Josh," she said with a smile. "Really lovely. I hope I'll see you around."

I waved her off, quickly walked back to the front of the pub, ready to retrieve not only my phone, but Felicia's glass, too. My plans derailed as soon as I stepped inside.

"Thank goodness you came back," Miranda said, rushing up to me. "I found this on the floor." She pressed my phone into my hands and looked over my shoulder. "Did Felicia leave?"

"Yes, she's heading back to work."

"Dang it," Miranda said. "She forgot her cardigan here last time. I meant to give it back."

"I could drop it off at Ethel's in the morning."

"Really? Thanks so much. It'll save me the trip into town. Let me get it for you."

As soon as she disappeared into the kitchen, I walked back to our table and made a big deal of checking the floor for anything else we might have dropped. By the time Miranda returned with the cardigan, Felicia's glass was rolled up in a napkin, safely tucked away inside my jacket pocket.

CHAPTER FIFTY-ONE

Grace's presence filled my dreams that night, the kind of dream where I'd have bet everything it was real. We sat in a field of tall, green grass that smelled of summer, the sun high up in the cloudless sky. Grace smiled, whispered, "I love you," and I smiled back, said it, too, before remembering what she'd done. Within an instant the skies turned dark, filled with purple, menacing clouds that made the grass wither and die. I tried to ask Grace who Logan was, and why she'd taken him, but found I couldn't speak, my lips held together with sticky caulking.

When I finally managed to talk, Grace answered as if speaking through a two-inch-thick pane of bulletproof glass. I watched her lips move, cupped a hand to my ear, and still heard nothing. She shook her head and got up, slowly drifted across the barren fields in the pouring rain. My boots became as heavy as concrete when I tried to follow her, and they disappeared into the earth, sucking my body farther and farther down until only my head was clear. A high-pitched noise filled my ears as a monstrous lawn mower raced straight toward me, tearing up the dirt, about to rip me to shreds.

As I struggled to break free, squirming and writhing my entire body, I woke myself up with a loud yell. I wasn't about to die a horror-movie death, but had become tangled up in a mess of sweaty sheets instead. It took my brain another second to figure out the loud screeching wasn't still a figment of my imagination, but my truck's alarm.

Within a heartbeat I'd leaped out of bed and legged it to the front door, my feet pounding over the bare living room floorboards. Despite being dressed only in a pair of boxer shorts, I yanked the door open just in time to see a dark shape disappear behind the trees and out of sight.

I sprinted inside, grabbed my keys and cut the alarm, pulled on my jeans and sneakers, and ran back outside. Freezing drops of rain thudded onto my torso, the smell of wet forest filling the air. The light from the cabin cast eerie shadows while I stood perfectly still, my chest heaving as I strained to listen for something, *someone*, scrambling over roots, tripping over rocks. The only sounds were muffled thunder in the distance, the raindrops hitting the leaves and the swish of the trees as they bent in the wind.

Ignoring the frigid downpour, I checked the truck and walked around the cabin, found everything as it had been before I'd gone to bed. I told myself an animal had bumped into the truck, setting off the alarm, or the local teens had paid me a visit, curious to see if the newcomer had anything interesting to steal. When I went back inside, I grabbed a towel, then wedged the back of a chair under the door handle.

Only eleven thirty yet it could have been the depths of the night. I stretched out on the bed in the darkness, my mind going back to Felicia's glass, which I'd sealed in a plastic bag and hidden behind the coffeepot in the kitchen. In under twenty-four hours I'd give it to Lisa, and if I could manage to get my hands on a sample from Emily in the morning, I'd be able to return to Albany for good. The thought of not seeing Emily again stung more than I expected, so I pushed it away, but it refused to leave as I replayed our phone conversation, and wondered if there was another reason she wanted me to come over so early. I told myself to stop being ridiculous. This wasn't high school; there were no mixed signals. There was a problem with the sprinklers and she wanted to discuss the yard plans. End of story. I had to get a grip before I lost it completely.

Maybe Lisa and Ivan had been right; I should've left things alone. Spent all this time concentrating on how to get my hands on a fake birth certificate to secure both Logan's and my future. I tossed and turned some more, the damp sheets a cold squid wrapping around me as I realized I'd all but forgotten how to have a normal life, couldn't imagine it ever feeling normal again, whatever happened with Logan.

I still couldn't bring myself to believe he was one of the Faycrest boys, but even once we had confirmation I wasn't sure I could keep my promise to Lisa and stop looking. Alex's and Hunter's disappearances had shaken the town—and that of the people in it—to their very core, changing lives forever. They all deserved to know what had happened to those boys, just like whoever Logan's real parents were deserved to know where he was, too.

Admittedly, it wasn't quite the same, but I couldn't imagine my need to learn who Logan was, or that the thirst to understand what Grace had done, and why, would ever go away, either. Without that knowledge I'd never be able to make sense of who Grace truly had been. The question still remained what I would do once I'd discovered her secrets, and after another hour of endless roundabout debates in my head, it was a relief when I fell asleep again for a few hours, escaping from reality for a while.

The rain had stopped when dawn finally came, although the

sky still billowed with clouds, the air colder than it had been all week. After a cup of strong tea I threw my tools in the truck, made sure my research file and Felicia's glass were locked safely in the glove compartment, and set off.

My heart beat a steady rhythm until I got to Emily's house. At that point it practically bounced out of my chest and fled down the street when I spotted her ancient Toyota parked in front of the garage, Tyler's flashy Mercedes nowhere to be seen.

After not getting an answer when I knocked on the door, I walked around to the back. Emily stood in the middle of the yard, what had once been a tartan pattern on her rubber boots now a sludgy, muddy mess, and her blue shorts and green sweatshirt were caked with dirt, too. I forced my gaze away from her tanned legs and up to her face.

"Hi, Emily."

"Fuck." She spun around, narrowly avoiding my knees with her shovel, and put a hand to her throat. "Heck, you spooked me. And I said fuck. Twice." Her laugh and the sparkle in her eyes made my stomach flip as my mind headed straight back to places it had no business being.

"What are you doing out here?" I said, looking around, anywhere but directly at her.

"Getting a head start. I think I found the problem." She pointed to the holes in the grass. "The pipe is broken over there, and there, too."

"How long have you been out here?"

"Awhile." Emily grinned. "That's what happens when your husband leaves the house at five thirty and you can't get back to sleep."

"That's an early start," I said, taking the shovel from her. "Is he on a trip?"

"No, he's at the gym. He was supposed to go to Boston this week, but it got canceled, I think. I lose track to be honest."

"He travels a lot then?" I said.

"Boston, New York and Portland most of the time, although he went to Florida in the spring. Actually, he's been to Albany a few times. That's where you're from, isn't it?"

I looked at her, shifted my feet. "Yes, that's right."

"Anyway, the best invitation he ever got was a speaking engagement in Hawaii."

"Lucky you. How was it? Did you get to see much?"

"Oh, no, I didn't go. I rarely travel with him. I had a commission to finish."

"You chose painting over sandy beaches? Spoken like a true artist." When Emily's only reply was a tight smile, I looked around the yard. "Thanks for doing most of the work for me. The rest won't take long to fix. I'll patch up the grass for you, too."

"Great. I hope the weather holds for you. There's more rain in the forecast. The weekend is supposed to be terrible, too. If you'll excuse me, I'd better go and clean up. People won't be impressed to find a mud monster in the studio."

"Tell them you're trying something new. You could say you're the latest Salvador Dali."

Emily held out a foot, turning it from side to side, and laughed. "Surrealist rubber boots? Hmm… I think I'd better stick with my trees."

Thirty minutes later I'd replaced the parts, patched up the grass as best I could and texted Bill about getting a roll of sod to finish the job. As I packed up my tools, Emily reappeared, dressed in a long white skirt and silky teal blouse, accentuating her eyes, her hair still damp, smelling of strawberries.

"You're done already?" she said. "Can I get you some water, or that cup of tea I promised? I've got time if you want to go over the designs, too?"

"I'd love a tea," I said. "But do you mind if I wash my hands first?"

"The bathroom is through the kitchen and the hallway, first door on your right."

I took as much time as I dared walking through the house, surprised at how different it looked from what I'd imagined. I'd thought the place would be warm and inviting, the same as Emily's personality, but it was the complete opposite. Save for a few monochromatic photographs of moody, barren landscapes, the stark white living room walls were almost bare, the pristine, cream leather sofa cried out *I'm uncomfortable* and the spotless black granite countertop in the open-plan kitchen appeared practically unused.

Moving through the hallway, I took in another gloomy piece of abstract artwork—an oil painting this time—that I knew was Emily's because of the signature in the bottom right corner. It had none of the colors, none of the pure joy the tree paintings at Ethel's conveyed. While expertly done, it looked soulless, as if all the happiness had slid off the canvas, or had never been there at all.

Three other pictures adorned the walls. The first was a photograph from Emily and Tyler's wedding day—bride and groom complete with deliriously happy smiles—the second, more recent, taken somewhere warm. A third photo stopped my feet moving all together. A picture of a newborn, Hunter; it had to be. My throat dried up as I peered at the baby's fluffy head and blue eyes. This had to have been taken a few days, weeks at most, before he'd disappeared. I shuddered. How his parents had functioned, held it together and continued for over seven years without knowing what had become of their boy, where he was, whether he was even alive, was anybody's guess.

I used the bathroom and washed my hands while staring at my reflection in the mirror. The late nights had caught up with me, the dark circles under my eyes the color of bruises, and I could have sworn my temples had turned a shade grayer since I'd arrived in town. Deceit had never felt or looked good on me.

When I heard the coffee machine running, I softly opened the bathroom cabinet, searched for a toothbrush, hairbrush or anything else that might belong to Emily. Other than a few rolls of tissue, some pills and a pair of tweezers, there was nothing useful, and I reluctantly moved on.

Back in the hallway I spotted Emily sitting in a chair on the deck with her book in her hands, two mugs in front of her. I figured I had another minute before she'd wonder where I'd got to, and the opportunity to check the room directly opposite was too good to miss. The door was slightly ajar, and I pushed it open slowly, ready to stop if it creaked.

The first thing to hit me was the light streaming into the room from the floor-to-ceiling windows, the next, the colors— yellows, purples, greens, oranges and blues, splashes and dots on abstract paintings lighting up the room, a hundred fireworks going off at the same time. There was something about how the colors merged, the way the kaleidoscopic patterns swirled, that made me feel six years old again, standing in front of Mrs. Button's sweetshop. When my eyes landed on a row of paintings hanging on the right wall, my excitement disappeared.

There were seven separate portraits of a child. Hunter, no doubt, and they all had the same date in the bottom right corner: October fifth. In the first one the swaddled baby slept in a crib, in the next he lay on a teddy bear blanket and in the third he knelt in the grass, blowing on a fluffy dandelion, the seeds carried away in the wind. As the paintings became more recent, he appeared bigger, older, his face changing and growing from baby, to toddler, to young boy.

They didn't resemble Tyler's composite pictures, neither did they look much like Logan, save for the shade of his hair, which was spot-on. Hunter's eyes were blue, not Logan's deep shade of green, weren't enough of an almond shape, either, and his face was too round.

"What are you doing?" Emily's voice made me jump, and I almost lost my footing as I spun around, immediately taking in her clenched jaw, her hands in fists by her side. "The bathroom is on the *right*," she said. "This room is private. Nobody comes in here." She grabbed hold of the doorknob, her eyes narrowed. *"Nobody."*

I mumbled an apology and walked past, kept my head down as I disappeared back into the bathroom, where I splashed my face with cold water, cursing myself for being nosy. When I found the courage to emerge, Emily sat on the deck again, staring out toward the tree line. I headed outside, wishing I hadn't been so stupid, gave myself an even harder time when I realized what bothered me the most wasn't that I'd no doubt blown my chances to get her DNA, but what she might think of me.

"I'll be going then," I said. "And, uh, I'm sorry to have intruded. Really sorry."

"Sit." A clear order, not an invitation or something up for debate. "I made your tea."

I hovered around the table, trying to read her expression. Her brow had unknitted, but there wasn't a trace of a smile to be found. If she played poker, she cleaned up every single time.

"Are you sure?" I said. "I can go."

"There's no need," Emily said. "It's my own fault. I usually keep that door locked and—"

"You don't owe me an explanation—"

"They're of Hunter," she said quickly, as if she needed to get the words out of her mouth before her brain stopped her. "My son. I'm sure by now you've heard he went missing."

"Yes, I've heard."

She nodded. "Nobody's seen the paintings, except for Tyler.

He says they're too raw, too emotional. He won't look at them anymore, and I don't think he's seen the most recent one."

"Well, for what it's worth, I think they're beautiful."

"Thank you," Emily whispered.

A long moment passed where neither of us spoke, and yet, it didn't feel uncomfortable, but like the silence between old friends who understand each other without having to say a word.

"I didn't pick up a brush for almost two years after…after he went missing," Emily finally said, gesturing again for me to sit, and I sank into the chair, unable to take my eyes off hers. "I used to dream about him every night, but when it became every second, and then every third, I painted two of those portraits in a week, because I was scared they'd stop."

"Did they?"

"No. But since then I've only painted him once a year, and I always start the day after his birthday. That's all my heart can manage."

"I wish I could say something to make you feel better," I said.

"You can't," she whispered. "I don't think anybody can."

We stared at each other in silence again, and neither of us moved until the sound of a phone ringing in the distance drifted out through the doorway and Emily got up.

"Please stay, Josh," she said before slipping inside.

This was my chance, her mug a mere foot away. I could grab it and go, let her think I'd been embarrassed to be caught snooping and dashed off. Except I didn't want to leave. What I wanted was to sit on the deck with her, and talk, all day if she'd let me. Before my brain could convince me to snatch the mug, Emily reappeared with the yard design envelope in her hands.

"I hope I haven't made you feel uncomfortable," she said. "I'd hate that."

"Not even slightly, but I hope I didn't upset you, either?"

Emily shook her head slowly. "No, I feel…okay with you seeing my paintings. I'm not sure why, but I do."

"Does that mean you still want me working here?"

"Yes. Yes, I really would, Josh. But…I'd be grateful if you didn't mention the paintings to anyone. I'm not ready to share them with anybody else."

"Not a word, I promise," I said, and Emily smiled before pulling her chair to the head of the table and sitting down, putting us at a right angle, our elbows almost touching.

"Shall we go over your designs now?"

"Sure, yeah." I coughed to release the tension that had immediately caught itself in my throat at her nearness. Once I'd laid out the designs on the table, she traced a finger over the sketch of the rounded archway that framed the long reading bench I'd drawn at the back of the garden. "I think those colors are beautiful, Josh. And you're right, lavender would work well. It seems…peaceful." She looked up; she was so close I could smell her perfume, see the faintest of scars on her right cheek, a small line shaped like an arrow. I wanted to reach out and touch it, ask her to tell me the story of where it had come from, and the stories behind any other scars she had, too.

"It's my favorite one, as well," I said instead, trying not to stare at the plumpness of her mouth and its delicate cupid's bow. I imagined how it might be to lean in and touch her lips with mine, cup her face in my hands as she slid her arms around my neck. I wanted to find out, was a mere heartbeat away from doing exactly that. The way she looked at me, her lips slightly parted, her eyes staring straight into mine, unwavering, full of…what was it? Not desire, not the sexual, rip my clothes off kind, anyway. It was a longing, a yearning, the need to connect I'd felt from her before—and which I had inside me, too—as if by doing so we could help one another heal.

It had happened to me before, when I'd met Grace that rainy

afternoon, and it wasn't something I'd expected to experience even once in a lifetime, let alone twice, and definitely not here, not now, not with Emily. We hadn't moved, there hadn't been the slightest touch, and yet the air between us shifted, crackled; the promise of something...

"Emily? Are you home?" A deep voice from inside the house startled us both, and Emily pushed her chair back as she stood up, almost sending it flying.

"On the deck," she called out as Tyler appeared a second later dressed in workout gear, a towel slung around his neck, his skin shiny with sweat.

"Oh, hey, man," he said when his eyes settled on me. "Josh, isn't it?"

"Yes," Emily said, her face in a tight, professional smile. She smoothed down her shorts, touched her ear. "We were going over the designs. Want to see?"

"Maybe later," Tyler said, pulling out a chair and sitting down.

"I'd better get going," Emily said. "Do you mind seeing yourself out, Josh? I'll let you know about the yard after the weekend, if that's alright?"

"No problem," I said, avoiding eye contact with either of them before reconsidering. "Thanks for the tea, Emily. Nice meeting you again, Tyler."

He didn't answer, but when Emily looked at me she gave me the slightest of smiles and paused before looking away, and quietly going back into the house.

CHAPTER FIFTY-TWO

Despite having a DNA sample, getting away from the incessant rain that had come down again since midmorning, and the opportunity to spend the weekend in a relative sense of normalcy with Logan, leaving Faycrest didn't come as a relief.

My mind kept replaying the moment at the house with Emily, how we'd looked at each other, the silent connection we'd shared—more than once—and the way she still made me feel, hours later. My guilt toward Grace for thinking of another woman came and went in waves. One minute I hated my own guts, and the next I reminded myself I hated parts of Grace, too.

I sighed when I pulled into the driveway and parked the truck, said a quick hello to Lisa and Ivan who were in the den— deftly avoiding their immediate onslaught of questions—before creeping upstairs to Logan's bedroom. A smile spread across my face as I saw another drawing of him and Cookie stuck to his door, and as soon as I stepped inside his room, Logan whipped off the covers, jumped out of bed and flung his arms around my middle.

"Dad!" He hugged me, let me go so I could drop to my

knees, then squeezed me again over and over, pushing the air out of me as if I were a human accordion. "I missed you, Dad," he whispered as Cookie put her front paws on my thighs, her little wet nose snuffling around my fingers, licking and nibbling them with her sandpaper tongue.

"I missed you, too, kiddo," I said, giving him a one-armed squeeze while patting Cookie with my free hand. "I can't believe we almost went a week without seeing each other. Did you forget my face?"

"Da-*ad*." Logan laughed. "Don't be a silly sausage."

"Why aren't you asleep? It's way past your bedtime."

"I was waiting for you." Logan grinned again, climbed back into bed and patted his Avengers duvet. "Can you stay with me, Dad? For a bit? Please?"

I made an exaggerated grunt as I climbed onto his bed before letting my head fall on the pillow and lifting Cookie on my chest. His room felt comforting, familiar and warm with its glow-in-the-dark moons and stars on the ceiling, the Lego figurine men neatly lined up on his shelves above the desk, and the space-ship curtains we'd chosen together. Within seconds my body melted into the mattress, daring me not to move until morning, or ever. How could I even imagine him not being in my life?

"Wake me up if I fall asleep, will you? Or roll me onto the floor."

"Nope," Logan whispered. "You'll stay with us. We don't mind, do we Cookie?"

"You will when I turn into the snore monster," I said with a laugh, and Logan giggled, his hair tickling my nose as he snuggled up closer. I put my arm around him, breathed in the scent of his berry bubble bath. "You've had a good week, huh? How was the rest of camp?"

"Awesome." Logan twiddled the fabric of my shirt between

his fingers, something he used to do when he was tiny, and fighting to stay awake. "I made so many friends, and we went swimming, and we did archery—"

"Like Katniss?"

"Uh-huh. I got a bull's-eye."

"I wish I'd been there to see that. Did you meet any cute girls?"

"Da-*ad*." Logan rolled his eyes and clicked his tongue so hard I had to stifle a laugh at the maturity of his disdain. "That's what Ivan said. Aunt Lisa told him to shush. I'm a seven-year-old kid, for goodness' sake."

"Yes, my sister would say that, wouldn't she?"

"She's nice. And Ivan, too. We had fun." He fell silent, his brow furrowing.

"What is it, kiddo? You've got that look…"

"Is it true you're going away again? Aunt Lisa said you will."

"Yes, but hopefully just for another week—"

"That's what you said last time and—"

"No, Logan. I said one week maybe two. And I'm not leaving until Sunday night. Don't forget you'll be at camp, so time will fly by, you'll see." My words of reassurance missed their target because Logan's eyes narrowed even more. "What camp did you choose for next week? Alien studies?"

Logan's pout slowly lifted. "No."

"Lion taming? Dragon flying?"

"Ultimate sports."

"Again?"

"Uh-huh. And Ivan said he'll take me swimming." Logan shut his mouth again, tried—and failed—to contain a yawn.

I hugged him, kissed his head. "You get some rest. I'll see you in the morning, alright?"

"Okay," Logan whispered, his eyes blinking slowly. "Night, Dad. I love you."

"I love you, too," I said, lingering in the doorway as he gave me a final wave.

"You can shut my door now," he said, rolling onto his side and putting a hand under his cheek. "I don't mind the dark when you're home."

Back downstairs I grabbed a glass of water and padded to the den, where Ivan immediately switched off the television and Lisa leaned forward, waiting to speak until I sat.

"Did you get them?" she said. "The samples?"

I pressed my palms over my eyes before silently going to the hallway, where I pulled out the research file and Felicia's glass from my bag. Back in the den I held them both out to Lisa. "This is Felicia's. And can you burn these papers? I don't need them anymore."

Lisa nodded. "What about Emily?"

"I met her a few times," I said, "but, uh, it didn't work out."

"Jesus," Ivan said. "You met her, too? Why didn't you tell us?"

"I'm hardly going to give you a blow-by-blow account of my day," I said. "I've got enough going on as it is."

Lisa stared at me for a second. "You're going back then?"

"Yes."

"But what did you think?" Ivan whispered. "Could she have taken one of those boys?"

I looked away, thought about Felicia's hay fever, Emily's gift for art, Tyler's allergy to dogs. While I hadn't met Felicia's ex-husband, Gavin, it would come as no surprise if I found some similarity between him and Logan. After all, there were commonalities between Logan and Grace, and Logan and me, too. But as to how much of each was nature versus nurture...

"I don't know," I said.

"I don't know how you can do it," Lisa said. "It must be so

incredibly odd thinking one of them might be his mom. What were they like?"

"Felicia's smart and funny," I said. "She reminded me a lot of you, Lisa."

"I'll take that compliment. What about Emily?" she said.

"She's...broken," I said.

Lisa looked at Ivan, stared at me. "I know that look. Be careful. She's not yours to fix."

"Yeah, I get that, thanks," I snapped. "And you're missing the point."

"Then what is the point, Josh?" Lisa said, her voice calm. "What happened?"

"Nothing. There was..." I rubbed a hand over my face and sighed. "The only way I can explain it is that there's this... *connection*."

"Connection?" Ivan said. "Are you saying you like her? Christ, Josh. That's crazy—"

"Yeah, and hello, she's married," Lisa added, jumping in. "Or have you forgotten that bit?"

"I know," I said. "Nothing happened."

"That doesn't mean you didn't want it to," Lisa fired back. "Have you thought that maybe this isn't about Emily at all? That it's got nothing to do with her?"

"What are you talking about?" I said.

"Think about it. You're angry at Grace, you feel guilty that you do, so you're latching—"

"I'm not *doing* anything, Lisa," I said. "And, for the record, you're really pissing me off."

"I'm looking out for you, Josh," she said. "It's not real, it's rebound. Just remember that."

"It's a shit lot worse than rebound," Ivan said. "The woman's husband is an ex-cop."

"For the last time, nothing happened, okay?" I said, raising my voice as much as I dared without waking Logan. "Calm the hell down, both of you. The whole situation is messing with my brain enough already, and I didn't drive four hours to be given a hard time by you two."

"Okay, man," Ivan said.

"No, it's not okay," I said. "Because I don't need this crap. What I need is a good night's sleep, so whatever else you have to say about a whole load of nothing, save it, yeah?"

Lisa's eyes narrowed as I got up and headed for the door, but for once she didn't say anything when I walked away.

Instead of sleeping in the next morning, I was up before seven and headed out for a run. The summer heat was already bearing down on the city, grabbing at me with its giant, sweaty hands, the humidity levels zooming past comfortable, straight to excruciating. I pushed myself hard, took increasingly long strides, arms pumping by my sides. I headed to the park, tried to deafen the voices in my head, the ones insisting Lisa was right; whatever I felt for Emily was rebound, or generated by the fear of losing Logan, making me grab on to whatever—whomever—I could find.

No matter the reason, it was a complication I didn't need, something best left ignored, and yet, every time I closed my eyes I pictured Emily. The dimples in her cheeks, how her hair fell over her shoulders, the diamond-shaped beauty spot on her left cheek. Her voice, her laugh, the way she blushed when I paid her a compliment. The list was bloody endless. For goodness' sake, it was only Saturday morning and I was counting the hours until I might see her again.

"You're being a stupid idiot," I said, running faster, stumbling on the curb as I crossed the road, almost plowing into a trash can and a man with three dogs. "An idiot."

Why? the voice in my head whispered. *Can't you tell she's not happy with Tyler?*

The next image I saw was of Emily, Logan and me sitting around a breakfast table, eating French toast and telling jokes. A happy, picture-perfect family. Ludicrous to feel that way about someone I'd just met, but we'd both felt something between us, I knew we had. I stopped running and put my hands on a bench, breathed heavily.

Although I hadn't known what to expect from my trip to Faycrest, one thing was absolutely certain. Falling for someone— especially the woman who could be Logan's mother—sure as hell hadn't been part of the plan.

CHAPTER FIFTY-THREE

Lisa and Ivan took off on Sunday, and I spent most of the day with Logan at Lincoln Park. We flew his kite, played catch and chucked a Frisbee around as Cookie bounced between us. The fact I'd soon leave my son behind again settled over me like the Faycrest storm clouds, refusing to shift despite filling the day with as much fun as humanly possible. All too soon it was time to go, and Logan's eyes filled with tears when he watched me pack up my things.

"But *why*?" he said. "Why do you have to leave again?"

"I'll be back as soon as I can, promise." I didn't dare look at him because he couldn't change my mind, and I worried he'd see it in my eyes, think it was something he'd done. That realization pumped anger into my veins, which I took out on Grace's puppy slippers that still, pathetically, sat under the armchair in the bedroom, as if she'd come home.

I picked them up and launched them to the back of the wardrobe, deciding none of her things had a place in our house anymore. Not a single piece of her clothing, none of her jewelry or any of her books, everything needed to disappear. If I'd had the time, I'd have yanked all of her stuff out of the wardrobe, cleansed the entire place of every single one of her possessions. I sank down on the bed, breathing hard knowing I couldn't erase her from my life, or from Logan's, even if it was the best thing for both of us. Not for the first time over the weekend I felt the need to escape, craved my life in Faycrest, which was, paradoxically, simpler because it was a place where I could pretend everything was somewhat normal.

Ivan grabbed my arm as I walked to my truck. "Hold up a second," he said. "Why don't you just take a minute and think about staying here, for good. I looked into getting a fake pa—"

"I thought you understood," I said, trying to shrug him off, but his grip stayed firm.

"I'm trying, seriously, I am," he said quietly. "But this isn't just about you, and I'm worried about Lisa. I know she won't tell you any of this, but she's having constant nightmares, okay? And when those aren't happening, she can't sleep properly because of this insomnia that keeps her awake half the night. She's still feeling sick, she's dizzy all the time…"

I shook him off. "She'll be fine."

"Jesus, you don't get it, do you?" Ivan's voice got louder with every syllable, one of the veins in his neck throbbing as he towered over me. "I'm worried about her, and our kid. Meanwhile she's freaking out about what'll happen to you and Logan." He paused, shaking his head. "She's sure it'll push you to drinking again, do you understand?"

"It won't."

"Then make sure by staying here. For once in your life, put your sister first."

"Fuck you, Ivan." I regretted the words when I saw the look on his face, as if I'd scorched him, but I wasn't done. "It's easy to talk down to someone when you're sitting pretty on the highest rung of the privilege ladder, isn't it? When you've had everything handed to you?"

Ivan put his hands up, took a step back. "Whatever, man, just be sure you're going to Faycrest for the right reasons. Because, let me tell you, this...*connection* you think you have with Emily, it's bullshit and—"

"Seriously?" I spat. "You've got a woman to put up with you for more than five minutes and now you're an expert at relationships? Why don't you mind your own fu—"

"Guys?" Lisa and Logan stood behind us. She glared at Ivan and me in turn, while Logan frowned, his expression a mixture of confusion and alarm.

"Are you okay, Dad?" he said.

"Yes, yes, of course, kiddo." I forced a smile. "All good."

Although I didn't want to say it out loud, I knew Ivan had a point. Whatever I felt for Emily was irrelevant. I had to refocus, get her DNA and come home. It was the only way to move forward, and hopefully leave Grace—and all of her excess baggage—behind.

When I got to the cabin I trudged up the front steps, ready to collapse for the night, but something stopped me as soon as I opened the door. I looked around, the hairs on the back of my neck standing on end. At first glance nothing seemed out of place, nothing had been moved, and yet the air felt electric, as if the ceiling swirled with dark clouds from which a thunderstorm could break out any second. Perhaps my brain was playing tricks on me, the lack of sleep and the spats with Lisa and Ivan messing with my mind, but in case someone jumped out at me, I kept my fists clenched as I walked through the hallway. The kitchen and bathroom were both empty, as were the bedrooms, everything still exactly how I'd left it, the windows shut, the air-conditioning unit's hum unchanged when I switched it on.

It wasn't until I looked at my tool bag that I noticed some of my things were out of place. For years I'd kept all my tools meticulously lined up for speed and efficiency, an impossible habit to break, always returning them to the same place so I could practically work blindfolded. It was something Ronnie and Leila had complimented me on. One quick glance told me my pliers, screwdrivers and measuring tape had all been moved—only an inch or two—but enough for me to notice. The remaining doubt evaporated. Someone had been in the cabin, gone through my things, searching for...what, exactly?

Maybe Ethel had stopped by to check on the work I'd done, no doubt she had a spare key, but in my gut I knew it was unlikely. She was old school, not the kind of person to let herself in without permission and besides, why would she have searched through my tools?

After emptying my bag on the floor and inspecting each item twice, I felt around the empty pockets. Nothing. I did the same with the cabin, checked every drawer, every cupboard, looked under the mattresses and behind the curtains, and still came up empty-handed.

Doubt crept back in through the cracks in my mind. I knew stress made people do odd things—leave car keys in the fridge or put salt in coffee—maybe I'd misplaced my tools after all, and yet my nerves wouldn't settle.

By now I wished I'd kept one of those beers that someone had left on the deck, thought about how easy it would be to get in the truck and drive to the liquor store. I didn't need to get plastered, just buzzed enough to stop the questions rolling around my head, and to have a proper night's sleep. Was that too much to ask? Would it really be that bad? After the last blip

I had no trouble staying dry. I picked up my wallet and keys, made it as far as the front door before I stopped myself.

"Don't do this," I whispered, my fists clenched. *"Don't."*

A good ten seconds went by before I grabbed the chair and shoved it under the door handle. Whether it was to keep people out, or me in, I wasn't sure. Either way, as I headed to the kitchen for a glass of water, I already knew this would be yet another excruciating night.

I spent the next day with Bill, but none of his clients were Emily. Although I'd given myself strict instructions not to think about her, my gaze swept the streets as we drove through town, hoping I'd catch a glimpse of her. I wanted to call her, pretend to inquire about the yard designs just so I could hear her voice, even caught myself running through our imaginary conversation in my mind. Bill asked me three times if everything was okay before I managed to pay attention to what I was doing, and even then I found my thoughts drifting again.

After the last lawn had been mowed, the final tree clipped, I drove to the grocery store and filled a basket with supplies to last me another few days. I didn't quite manage to walk past the beer without as much as a sideways glance or a pinch of desire, but I didn't touch the stuff. Although it beckoned me, I put my head down and strode on, turning the corner in search of milk, almost bumping into the person coming in the opposite direction. *Emily.*

"Uh, hi," I said. "How are you? How was your weekend?"

A shade of pink crept up her neck as she smiled. "It was okay. Rainy. You?"

"Fine. Good to be back," I said. "Uh, because of the amount of work, you know?"

"I do," she said with a nod. "I'm supposed to be submitting ideas for a commission—"

"A new one?"

"Yeah. Trouble is, I'm drawing a blank. No pun intended."

"Painter's block?"

Emily grinned, rolled her eyes. "Yeah, sure. It's for one of the banks in Portland. They have this huge lobby and they want to see designs for some—"

"Trees?"

"Dear God, please don't tell me I've become that predictable." She covered her eyes with a hand, the dimples in her cheeks growing more visible than ever. "But yes, trees. And they have to be huge. The space is a hundred and forty square feet."

"That's massive, practically life-size."

"Exactly, and not only that, but they're looking for a different spin, and so far I haven't come up with anything, so—" she lifted her basket, which was filled with bread, cheese and white-chocolate-chip cookies "—I'm procrastinating. Besides, a girl's got to eat. Then I'll work."

"Want to help paint Ethel's cabin kitchen? You can doodle all over the primer."

I'd meant it as a joke, kind of, and at first Emily laughed, too, until she said, "You know, that might be exactly what I need. A bland and boring job so I can let my mind wander. Okay, why not? I'll cook you dinner."

In the back of my mind I heard Lisa's comment about playing with fire, decided I should tell Emily I wasn't doing any painting, had other plans for the evening. There would surely be another chance of getting her DNA that didn't involve us being alone in the cabin in the woods on a rainy Monday night. Yes, I should tell her... "You want to help paint *and* cook dinner?"

"Don't tell anyone, but I'm buttering you up for a good deal on the yard." She shrugged. "And I make a mean pasta sauce."

"As do I..."

"Oh, yeah? Well, does yours have chorizo, basil and fresh tomatoes?"

I held my hands up in surrender. "You win."

Emily laughed again. "Good decision. Shall I come over in about half an hour?"

"Are you sure? I mean…won't Tyler mind?"

"Why would he mind?" she said, and looked at me as some kind of strange protective bubble formed around us in which nothing but she and I mattered, and everything else seemed to disappear. "I'll see you in a bit?"

"Yes," I replied, nodding slowly. "See you later."

CHAPTER FIFTY-FOUR

Depending on the situation, thirty minutes can feel like thirty seconds or thirty years. In this case, it was the latter. Time had slowed right down, moving at a glacial pace despite my trying to speed it back up by jumping in the shower once I got to the cabin, and calling Logan, deciding not to tell Lisa about my expected visitor.

After I hung up, I tried to convince myself Emily coming over was nothing but an opportunity to finally get what I needed to prove she wasn't Logan's mother. All that did was make me feel like even more of a traitor, so I paced the deck, whispering, "Rebound, rebound, rebound." When she still hadn't arrived after forty-five minutes, I presumed she'd changed her mind. Disappointment sneaked into my chest, but then I heard the sound of an engine, and Emily's car appeared from between the trees, big fat raindrops bouncing off its roof. I remembered seeing a tiny pink-and-blue-striped umbrella stashed away in the hall closet with the linens, and dashed toward the car with it as she pulled up.

"Sorry I'm late," she said, getting out with a bag of groceries in one hand. "Car trouble again. Battery this time."

"Want us to have a look?" I took the bag from her, held the umbrella over her head.

"No need. I made an appointment at the garage tomorrow."

"You sure?"

"Yes, thanks, Josh. Can you believe this weather?" she said as we walked back to the cabin, the cold water dripping off the canvas and trickling down the side of my neck. "The amount of rain we've had is ridiculous. We might as well cancel summer. It's fall already."

I smiled and held the door open for her. "But it makes everything so green."

Emily smiled back, wiped her sneakers on the mat. "You would say that, wouldn't you? Okay, what's first, food or work?" At the mere thought of a meal, my stomach let out a high-pitched whine. "There's our answer," she said with another laugh. "Great, because I'm starving, too. Let's see what we can rustle up in this tiny kitchen."

"You've been here before?" I said, setting the groceries on the serving tray-sized kitchen counter, wondering how both of us would fit in the space without our bodies touching.

She opened the cutlery drawer and peered inside. "Enough to know my way around to find...aha, there you are." Emily grinned as she held up a corkscrew. "I wasn't sure if you preferred red or white wine, so I got both."

I could feel my face falling, and she must have noticed it, too, because she frowned and gently said, "Are you okay, Josh? Did I do something?"

My usual response in this situation was to fib, say I had an allergy or was taking medication, but I didn't want to lie to Emily. Not more than I already had. "I used to drink a lot. Far too much, in fact, so I don't touch anything now."

She looked at me for a moment and then pulled two bottles from the shopping bag. "In that case, I won't, either. Tell you what, let me put these in the car and it'll be like it never happened."

"Thanks for not making it a big deal," I said when she got back inside. "And for not asking me a ton of questions, because most people do."

Emily squeezed my arm, her touch light, fingers soft. "No problem, although I do have to ask you one thing... Want to chop the onions or the basil?"

Within thirty minutes the cabin smelled better than Casa Mama. We settled down at the rickety old table in the living room, plates of steaming hot pasta in front of us, the rain coming down even harder outside. As far as I was concerned, we could have been stranded in the Rockies or the Alps somewhere, miles from civilization, and it wouldn't have bothered me in the least. Once again there had been a sense of familiarity, of ease, as we worked in the kitchen, chatting and moving together in the tiny space, her asking me to try the sauce for seasoning, me telling her it was perfect just the way it was, as if we'd been cooking supper with one another for years.

"This is delicious," I said, taking a first bite. "Much better than what I'd have made in double the amount of time."

"I find that hard to believe," she said with a grin. "But I'm glad you're enjoying it. I'd better not eat too much or I won't want to move afterward, let alone pick up a paintbrush. Although I brought some chocolate mousse, in case we need some energy for later."

"Pasta and chocolate mousse?" I said. "I wish all my helpers thought that way."

"Ah, but would you ever get anything done?"

I laughed. "Fair point."

"So tell me about your weekend. I bet Logan was happy to see you."

When my smile tried to slide off my face, I had to make a mammoth effort to keep it there, and to make my voice stay even. "Yes, he was."

She looked at me, quietly said, "I know why you won't talk about him, Josh."

"What do you mean?"

"You're not the only one who doesn't want to mention their kid in front of me because of Hunter," she said, making the pasta turn into a clump in my stomach. "But...it's okay, I promise. It helps me picture where he might be, what he might be doing. It hurts, but at the same time I can imagine him having a good life. Does that make sense?"

"Yes," I whispered, not daring to look at her.

"Then tell me something about him," she said. "Please?"

"He's amazing," I said. "Clever and generous, and whip-smart, too. Since Grace died...he's the one who's been holding me together rather than the other way around. He's the best thing that ever happened to me. Honestly, I don't know what I'd do without him. I love him with everything I have."

"He's very lucky to have you," she said quietly, "and from what you've said, he sounds exactly like you. Like father, like son, right?"

"Except he isn't," I said. "I met him when he was two."

"I didn't know you adopted him," Emily said, and I let the assumption sit there without comment. She twiddled her napkin between her fingers, hesitating before she continued. "I was adopted, too. I was six."

There hadn't been anything about that in my research. The articles had only ever mentioned her parents being an older couple in Florida. It almost felt strange for her to share details about her life that I hadn't read about, and which I didn't have to pretend not to know.

"So when you said your dad taught you all about cars—"

"I meant my adoptive father, Malcolm. Best man in the world."

"What about your parents?" I said. "Do you know who they are?"

"I remember a few things," she said, smiling slowly as if she were watching the memories play out on a screen somewhere in her mind. "My dad taking pictures of my mother, my little sister, Morgan, and me, the three of us twirling in the garden. We had the same dresses my mother had made, a light green gingham, I think, and I had a blue satin ribbon in my hair… I'm not sure how much of it is real, though."

"Can I ask what happened?" I said. "Why did they give you up?"

Emily didn't reply for a long time, and when she did, she whispered. "My father."

"Your dad didn't want you?" I said. "Why?"

"It wasn't that," she said, her eyes welling up as she spoke, and I could tell from the strain in her voice that each of her syllables took an increasing amount of effort.

"You don't have to—"

"I was at a friend's house one day. A sleepover I'd begged my mother to let me go to, and she'd finally given in an hour earlier. Morgan wanted to come, but I told her no, she was too small, even when she cried." She paused, took a deep breath. "When my father came home after work, he went straight to the kitchen, picked up a knife and slit my mother's throat—"

"What?"

"—and then Morgan's, who was playing in our bedroom."

I leaned forward, grabbed her hand. "Jesus, Emily, are you saying he killed them?"

"Yes," she whispered. "And then he hung himself in the basement. Nobody knew until my mother didn't pick me up the next morning. That's another memory I have, sitting on the staircase, wishing she'd come and get me. I hated the sleepover after all. The girls made fun of my dinosaur pajamas, and I'd wished I'd stayed at home." A tear slid down her cheek and she brushed it away.

"But why did he—"

"They said he had so much debt he couldn't see a way out, didn't want to let us down. I think my father loved us, as bizarre as it sounds. He couldn't see a future but wanted to keep his family together. I can only imagine what he went through when he realized I wasn't home, that he couldn't take his other daughter with him. I'll always wonder what he would have done if Morgan hadn't been there, either, if they might all still be alive."

I didn't speak as I stared at her, unable to imagine how a single person could endure so much pain and not collapse entirely. The intolerable regret she must have felt for not letting her sister go with her to the sleepover and, later, the agonizing guilt for not being able to keep either Alex or Hunter safe, her entire life annihilated not once, but three times.

"I've never told anyone," she said. "Only Tyler when we first met."

"Why now?" I whispered. "Why are you telling me?"

"I don't know," she said. "Maybe because when I'm with you, it reminds me of who I used to be a long, long time ago. And because you understand what it's like to blame yourself when everybody around you tells you not to."

Thunder echoed above our heads as a second passed, then two, then three. We didn't dare breathe for fear it broke the bond between us, made us change our minds and come to our senses. I pushed my chair back and walked toward her, not tak-

ing my eyes off hers. She looked breathless, beautiful. I reached
for her hand, gently pulled her toward my chest, wrapping my
arms around her waist as she slid her hands over my shoulders
and let them settle around my neck. Slowly, ever so slowly,
our mouths came closer, her breath sweet and intoxicating, her
fingers in my hair drawing me nearer still, our tongues taking
their time to find one another, her touch softer than butterfly wings. I hadn't felt such desire, hadn't wanted—needed—
someone so much for so long, I'd forgotten how it felt, but I
didn't want it to stop.

"Emily," I whispered and kissed her again. "Emily."

She pulled away and gently put a finger to my lips before
taking my hand and leading me to the bedroom, where she un-
buttoned my shirt, slipped it over my back and let it fall to the
floor. As she reached for my jeans, I slid my hands under her
cotton T-shirt, let them wander, slowly exploring and caress-
ing as I kissed her neck, breathed in the flowery scent of her
perfume. The rest of our clothes discarded, we lay down on
the bed, neither of us saying a single word until she was ready
for me to be inside her, and we lost ourselves in another embrace, crying out each other's names. Afterward we lay there
until our hearts stopped pounding, my chin gently resting on
her shoulder, her legs wrapped around mine.

"I'm sorry," she whispered.

I rolled onto my side, kissed the crook of her neck, could
already feel her retreating, inching away from me with every
second that passed. "You don't need to—"

"I've never done anything—" She sat up quickly and reached
for her underwear, her other hand over her naked breasts.
"Please believe me, Josh, I've never been with anyone since I
met Tyler and—"

"Emily, you don't have to justify—"

"I have to go."

Before I'd buttoned up my jeans she'd already slipped on her clothes and rushed out of the room, with me following behind. "Stay," I said. "Please, Emily. You don't have to—"

"You don't understand," she said, grabbing her bag from underneath the table. "If I don't, I may never want to leave."

As she turned around, her bag swung out and caught the empty water jug, sending it, along with both of our drinking glasses, crashing to the floor. Emily jumped back, gasping as her naked foot sank straight onto a broken piece of glass. She limped to the chair as I snatched paper napkins from the table, gently pressing them against the cut, her ankle on my thigh.

"It's not deep," I said. "I have a first-aid—"

"Please, Josh." She put her hands on my shoulder, pulled her foot away. "Let me go."

My world imploded for three reasons as I watched Emily walk out of that cabin. One, because I now knew for certain my feelings for her had nothing to do with any kind of rebound. Two, because the bloody napkins I held in my hand meant I no longer had a legitimate reason to stay. And three, because I'd already betrayed her.

CHAPTER FIFTY-FIVE

B ill called at seven the next morning, worried he may have woken me when, in fact, I hadn't slept for the past three hours. "Take the day off," he said. "Pray to the weather gods the rain will stop before we abandon landscaping in favor of building ourselves an ark."

"You sure you don't need me?" I said. "Want me to pick up any supplies or—"

"Really, Josh, don't worry about it. Chill for the day. The work will still be there tomorrow. Rumor has it we may even see the sun," he whispered, "but let's not jinx it."

And so I became stranded in the cabin in the ongoing rain, all of my thoughts returning to Emily, and the night before. Eyes closed, the images came thick and fast, invading every single part of my mind. Hands and fingers, mouths and tongues, hungry and desperate, her back arched, pulling me closer toward her, deeper. I wanted to call, needed to see her, hear her voice, but each time I picked up my phone I thought of the napkins, and all my lies.

My brain ordered me to leave Faycrest, pack up my things

immediately now that I had what I came for, but my heart stubbornly refused. Not yet. There was too much unfinished business between us, too many things to say. If I disappeared, she'd think it was because of her, of what we'd done.

I retrieved the napkins in the plastic bag I'd hidden in the kitchen. The test would come back negative, of that I was certain, but for a fraction of a second I allowed myself to think what I'd do if it didn't. I'd have to tell Emily that Logan was her son, and not only her, but Tyler, too. And once she knew, once she and Tyler had made their family whole again, could there be a place for me after what had happened between us? What would I do if I lost both of them, lost everything?

I imagined keeping the result to myself, taking Emily away from Faycrest, so she, Logan and I could build a future together. Within a nanosecond the illusion shattered around me like the water jug. How could there be any kind of "us" if I'd be willing to keep a secret of that magnitude from her? I shuddered, grateful it wasn't something I'd have to face, and as I listened to the rain belt out its own tune on the roof, I decided I wouldn't run away from Faycrest, but do things right. I'd wait for Lisa to confirm the results—a formality at this point to ease my conscience—then give Bill at least a week's notice, finish up the cabin for Ethel and, somehow, convince Emily to see me again because I was certain we could have a future together, one in which both of us were happy again.

Would I share my real reasons for coming to Faycrest? Tell her what I'd learned about Logan? For the first time I got a glimpse of how Grace had felt when she'd been confronted with the same question. If she'd told me from the beginning that Logan wasn't hers, would we have become involved? I wasn't sure of the answer, still didn't know who Logan was, and I didn't want to think about Grace, not anymore.

I called Lisa, quickly explained I had Emily's DNA, lied about how I'd come about it.

"Jesus," she said. "Are you on your way home? Please say yes."

"Uh, no. Listen... I'm going to send the napkins to you. Express or something."

"In the *mail*? Don't be crazy. You don't have to be there anymore. Let's just get this—"

"Not yet. I need to stay. Can you get the results of both tests by the end of the week?"

"Why won't you come—"

"I'm not getting into it, Lisa. Can you get the results by the end of the week, yes or no?"

She exhaled, took a few seconds before she answered. "I don't know. Yes, maybe."

"Then I'm going to the post office right now."

"This is about Emily, isn't it? Has something happened you're not telling me?"

As I closed my eyes, I gently said, "Get the results, Lisa, please? Then I'll come home."

"Okay," she said quietly. "Okay."

Within a couple of minutes, I'd packed up the napkins in an envelope I'd found in the bowels of the living room, and on which I hastily scrawled Lisa's address, and ran to the truck, getting soaked again. I drove down the muddy track and turned left. Faycrest didn't have a post office, so I headed to Gorham, where the chirpy clerk assured me the envelope would arrive on my sister's doorstep by morning.

The weather had got steadily worse during the short drive, and by the time I'd made a trip to the hardware store for the caulking to fix the large window at last, the clouds had become thicker, blacker, with deep thunder rumbling in the not-too-far-away distance. Unlike me, most people seemed to have decided to stay at home, and the roads were deserted until I spotted a car about a hundred fifty yards up ahead, immediately recognizing it as Emily's.

I slowed down, debated whether to follow her, dropped back and kept my distance, buying myself time to make up my mind. She'd said she had an appointment at the garage. Maybe I could ask her to have a cup of coffee with me while it was being repaired.

Another few miles ahead and the road curved to the right, the corner covered by thick trees. By the time I'd made the bend, Emily's car had disappeared. I slowed down, strained to see the three hundred yards ahead. It was empty, nothing out there but trees, not a single vehicle anywhere, but a car couldn't simply vanish. When I passed a narrow turnoff on the left-hand side, I doubled back, squinted as I read the letters on a broken sign on the ground. Monty's Pond.

Something inside my gut told me to keep going. If the weather had been different, I might have assumed there were great running trails around Monty's Pond, although I couldn't imagine going for a jog in this weather. Surely Emily would have left directly from her house, at least chosen somewhere less muddy for her runner's high.

I pressed on, driving eight, nine hundred yards or so, up the bendy trail that looked like it hadn't been used in years, coming to a stop when I caught sight of the left taillights parked up ahead. Someone was sitting inside the car, but it wasn't Emily, I decided, the person was too tall, too wide. I kept my distance, my truck enveloped by the thick foliage that hung down, obscuring most of my view, but also protecting me from being seen. The car door opened and when the driver got out, I didn't need to see his or her face to know who it was.

Tyler.

CHAPTER FIFTY-SIX

He wore jeans, boots and a thick, black rain jacket, a far cry from his usual groomed look. Raindrops bounced off his shoulders as he flipped the hood of his coat over his head and opened the rear passenger door. I leaned forward, my hands clamped on the steering wheel. He slipped something light blue over the bottom of his boots, grabbed a khaki duffel bag and slung it across his shoulder. After a quick glance around, he strode toward an overgrown path and disappeared into the woods.

I sat for a moment, watched the spot where he'd gone into the thicket in case he came back. What was he doing out there? Was he hunting, and if he was, why did he cover his boots? Could this be a clandestine meeting to do with his work? A secret rendezvous with his lover? And if it was the latter, did Emily know he was seeing someone else? Curiosity spread throughout my body as if it were infected, and before I could stop myself or properly consider what I was doing, I'd already got out of my truck and dashed halfway toward the trees.

It didn't take long to spot a flash of Tyler's dark jacket up ahead despite the path being so overgrown. I had to fight my way through parts of it, the noise I made drowned out by the rain. The smell of damp pine needles sat in the misty air.

As we moved farther, I avoided the muddy puddles, made sure to stay far enough behind so I could crouch down at a moment's notice and stay hidden by the bushes. I needn't have worried. Tyler's strides were double the length of mine, and he didn't turn around. When we got to a fork in the trail he turned right, then stepped off the path and carried on toward the pond I could now make out in the distance as the trees thinned.

It was too open there, too exposed, so I continued parallel, twenty yards inside the brush, and watched him head closer to the water—a murky, shallow patch the size of a football field—and into another clump of thicker trees.

I sprinted across the open forest, ducked down when I spotted Tyler again ten feet from the water, his head and knees bent, surveying the ground. I frowned as I noticed his gloves for the first time, thick and dark, not the kind you'd wear in June. My gaze dropped to his feet, and I saw the shoe protectors—booties someone who worked in a lab or a hospital might wear—were covered in mud and dirt.

He pulled a small shovel from the bag, and at first I thought he was going to dig into a small patch of sunken soil. Instead he rearranged it, making the earth even again, his lips moving silently as he worked. After another few moments he stood up, took a few steps back and nodded, seemingly satisfied. That was my cue to leave, and fast. Now wasn't the time to figure out his reasons for being there, and if he got back to Emily's car before I made it to my truck he'd see me. Instinct told me that would be a very, very bad idea.

I fought my way back to my truck, hoping the rain would continue to cover the noise, and the trees still gave me enough camouflage. There was no room to turn my vehicle around, so

I reversed down the track, hit the main road and headed right. I sped into the first driveway I found, went as far up as I dared, cut the engine and lay low, peeking over the dashboard until Emily's car zipped by.

I let five minutes pass before doubling back, returned to the spot at Monty's Pond where Tyler had stood. The soil was sodden but didn't look displaced, to the point where I second-guessed if I had the right spot, walked around until I was sure. What had Tyler been searching for? Unless, I reasoned, he hadn't been looking for anything at all, but instead making sure something wasn't found. With almost a week of heavy rainfall, had he been worried someone might come across something he'd hidden? Something illegal, like drugs or cash? Perhaps Tyler was a dirty cop turned dirty cop consultant, and he'd come to check on his hidden stash. It was the perfect place to hide wads of money—outside the house, off the beaten track, but where you could still pretend you were on a hike if anyone saw you. Not too far from his house, either, I realized. By my calculations, Monty's Pond was directly behind Emily and Tyler's place, about three miles away, four, tops.

Fired up by the need to know Tyler's secret, I sank to my hands and knees, pulling at the heavily drenched ground with my fingers, digging faster and harder until the mud reached my elbows, and covered my pants from my knees to my groin.

Two feet down and I was about to give up when my knuckles scraped something hard. Not another rock, I decided as I felt around with my fingers; it was too smooth. I wiped the mud away from the surface, frowning when I saw the metal box. It must have been military green at one point but was now covered in rust and mud, the hinges worn. Another minute of wiping and digging, and I managed to free the box and lift it out. It was about twenty inches long, fifteen wide and ten deep, big enough to hold a serious amount of drugs or money, particularly if it was packed with hundred-dollar bills, although it felt too light to be full. I lifted the lid, my heart thundering in my neck.

I couldn't stop the cry that expelled itself from my throat, or the way I leaped back, my feet scrambling, pushing my body away, putting more distance between me and the box. There were no illicit substances and no money inside. Not a dollar bill. Not a single coin.

It was bones. Human bones.

My hands shook as my breath came in ragged gulps, making my fingers and cheeks tingle. I tried to get back in control. Couldn't. Scrambled back another few feet, my hands now almost numb, my breathing faster. A panic attack. I'd had one when I was a kid, freaking out about a nuclear war documentary. Mom had me breathe into a paper bag to stop the hyperventilating, but my mother wasn't there, and I had no paper bag, it was only me and a rusty, metal box. And the body of a child. A *baby*.

I reached for my phone, dialed 9-1- and paused, my finger hovering over the last digit. The cops would ask questions, lots and lots of questions. Even if I explained how I'd seen Tyler drive up here, there was no way to be sure there'd be any evidence linking him back to the body. He knew the system, had contacts. It would be the case of an outsider's word against a trusted ex-cop's, a local hero. I'd watched enough TV shows to know my prints would be on the box, and other biological evidence in the dug up soil. Tyler had worn gloves and booties; no doubt he'd done the same when he'd put the box in the ground. How easy would it be for him to twist things around, pin it all on me? Whatever I did, they'd look into me, into my family. How would I protect Logan then? But I couldn't do nothing. These bones were someone's child and—the thought hit me with such force, it expelled all of the air from my lungs—

what if it was one of the Faycrest boys? What if these were the remains of Emily's son?

Emily. The thought of her being in the same house as Tyler made me retch. Could this really be Hunter? Or Alex? Maybe another child if Tyler was somehow involved in the abduction and killing of kids, his consultant job offering the perfect cover. He traveled all the time, could pick and choose his victims, knew the police's exact procedures, would always be at least three steps ahead.

Was Emily in danger? She'd been married to him for years, continued to live with him since the boys' disappearance, and was very much alive, but still... Tyler was a child killer, a baby murderer, or at the very least *somehow* involved. I had to get to her, warn her. But the box. What the fuck would I do with the box? There was no way I could drive to the cabin with it on my back seat, and I couldn't leave this poor baby in the ground, abandoned by Monty's Pond in the wretched, soaked soil. What kind of a person could do that?

"Tyler," I whispered. "Motherfucking *Tyler.*"

My fingers tingled again and I forced myself to take deep, slow breaths as I ran through my noose-like options. I'd put it back, I decided. Leave the box in the ground until I'd found Emily, managed to get her away from Tyler and made sure she was safe. Then I'd figure out what to do, who to call.

I took off my shirt, wiped the box to remove my fingerprints before gently lowering it back into the hole, whispering pathetic-sounding apologies, telling the baby not to worry, that he—she?—would be home soon, that it wouldn't be long. Once I'd covered it back up with the soaked soil and rearranged the pine needles, I took a few steps back, saw how I'd rendered the grave practically invisible again. That was when I finally acknowledged my tears. This was someone's child, their tiny, tiny child, left in the ground, abandoned by Tyler, and now by me.

"I'm sorry," I whispered. "Someone will come back soon. I promise."

My strides became increasingly determined as I walked back to the truck, my spine more rigid and straight as anger coursed through my body, zapping from nerve to nerve, muscle to muscle with the power and speed of a lightning bolt.

Tyler was going to pay.

CHAPTER FIFTY-SEVEN

"Pick up," I yelled into the phone as it rang. "Pick up, pick up, pick *up*."

"Emily Rhodes."

"Emily," I shouted, running through the trees and back to my truck. "Where are you?"

"Josh, is that you? What's wrong? Are you okay?"

"Are you at home? Is Tyler there?"

"He just got back from the garage—"

"Listen to me," I said. "Make an excuse and meet me at the cabin, right now."

"What? Why?"

"*Right now*. Can you do that?"

"Josh," she whispered. "I can't. Last night—"

"This isn't about last night. You have to come to the cabin. Please."

"I'm hanging up now—"

"*Don't*. I've found out some things about Tyler—"

"What kind of things?" she said. "What are you talking about?"

"I'll be at the cabin in ten minutes. You have to come," I shouted, and when she still hesitated I lowered my voice, quietly said, "I need to tell you about what I've found. It's...bad, really bad, but I can't do it over the phone. *Please*, please, Emily. Promise me you'll come."

"Yes, yes. I promise," she said as I jumped into the truck and floored it down the trail, overtaking another car that was already going well over the speed limit, trying to figure out how I'd tell Emily, knowing I'd be tearing her life apart, hoping I'd somehow be able to help her rebuild it whenever she was ready, and if she let me.

I'd been at the cabin for only sixty seconds when I heard a car coming up the dirt track, and I leaped off the steps, running toward it, yanked open the door before Emily had come to a complete stop, a deluge of rain pounding my skull as I did.

"What's going on?" She pulled the keys from the ignition and tossed them in her bag. "Josh, why are you covered in mud? What the hell happened?"

I looked down at my clothes, forced a mental note somewhere in my mind to throw them—and my shoes—away as soon as I could. There were so many things to think about, so many bases to cover. "Come inside," I said. "Please, come inside."

"You need to tell me what's going on, right now, Josh, because I shouldn't be here," she said, walking into the cabin, crossing her arms over her chest. "Not after what we did. It was a mistake, and if Tyler finds out it'll kill him—"

"He's not who you think he is," I said, taking a step toward her. "He's dangerous. He—"

"What are you talking about?" Emily said, her voice raised. "Is this some kind of mind game? Some crazy attempt to make me leave him for you?"

"No—"

"Then tell me what's going on or I'm leaving, and I swear you'll never see me again."

I rubbed a hand over my face, trying to buy time, realized it didn't matter if she graced me with a decade. I had to tell her what I'd seen, what I'd found; she needed to know. "Earlier today...I saw Tyler, in your car."

She nodded. "I told you. He took it to the garage. So?"

"I followed him."

"You followed Tyler? Why?"

"Because I thought it was you at first, and I needed to talk to you. He turned up a trail, the one that goes to Monty's Pond."

Her eyes flashed at me. "Monty's Pond?"

"Yes. I thought he was meeting someone, I don't know, a lover, maybe. But when I followed him..." I took a deep breath, pressed my palms over my eyes. "Emily, there's no easy way of saying this, there really isn't. Look, he buried something up there—"

"*What*—"

"Not something. Someone." As I went to grab her hands, she took a step back, her fingers flying toward her mouth. "I saw. It was a baby, Emily. A tiny skeleton in a metal box."

"You saw?" She shook her head, let out a moan as her legs buckled, sinking to the floor, her hands clawing at her shirt, pulling and tugging as if she couldn't get enough air. "No. *No*."

I dropped to my knees, put my arms around her, but she scrambled away. "We need to figure out what to do," I said, trying to hold her close, calm her down. "Call the police."

"The police? *No*. We can't."

"Emily, please, we have to. What if...what if it's Hunter—"

"It isn't," Emily whispered, getting up slowly, her eyes empty. "It's not my son."

"But we have to make sure—"

"I am sure," she said.

"How?" I frowned, pushed myself up, legs unsteady, but she wouldn't answer. "Emily?" I said, the panic making my voice boom around the cabin. "Do you know who that baby is?"

She nodded, her lips taking a hundred years to utter a single word. "Alex."

All the air got sucked out of the room at once, leaving me gasping. "It's Alex? Felicia's boy? But…but how do you know?"

She looked at me, her eyes wide, terrified. "Because…because I killed him."

CHAPTER FIFTY-EIGHT

"No," I said, taking three steps back, trying to escape the confession that seemed to grow inside the cabin, taking over the room, pushing down on me, making me suffocate. "No."

"I didn't mean to," Emily sobbed, looking at me as if this was a story she'd needed to share for years, something bottled up inside her for so long, she had no choice but to set it free. And still, I didn't want to know, didn't want to hear.

"I don't believe you," I said. "You wouldn't have—"

"It was an accident. I promise you, it *was*," she cried, unable to stop. "He was on the play mat in the living room, fast asleep, and Hunter vomited. It went in my hair, down my clothes..." She closed her eyes for a second, whispered, "I went upstairs to change him."

I sank down on the armchair, my legs folding beneath me as if they'd been broken.

"Hunter wasn't sleeping well," she continued, tears streaming down her cheeks. "Which meant I hadn't been sleeping well, either. And after I cleaned us up and put him in his crib,

I felt dizzy and needed to lie down. I told myself it would just be for five minutes, but I fell asleep—"

"What happened to Alex?" I said. "Did he cry? Did you shake—"

"*No*. It wasn't... I'd never hurt him. *Never*."

"Then—"

"Tyler came home and found him with...with..." She stared at me, her eyes begging for understanding, for mercy. "Alex wasn't breathing. He had a cushion on his face, one of the heavy ones from the sofa. I knocked it off as I jumped up when Hunter was sick." She let out another loud moan, balled her fists as she spoke. "I should've checked Alex was okay before I went upstairs. I should've looked back. Why didn't I look *back*?"

"But...but you said he was kidnapped. You said someone came into the house..."

She shook her head. "It was a lie."

"You made it up?" I whispered.

"We panicked. I might have gone to jail. And even if everyone understood it was an accident, Tyler's career would never have been the same, and his...*our* reputation... He'd always planned on going into politics. Senator, maybe, or even governor." She looked away. "The lies were easier than they should have been. We were renovating, people coming and going all the time. Our house backs onto the woods, the torrential rain—"

"Tyler took Alex—" I pressed my fingers over my eyelids until I saw stars, but the images of the tiny baby in the cold metal box came all the same "—and he buried him by the pond. But how could you do that? How could you lie? What about Felicia?"

Emily covered her mouth with a hand, but the sobs escaped from between her fingers as the remaining color drained from her face, leaving her skin ashen. "I couldn't bear it, Josh, you have to believe me. That night I wanted to go to the police, turn myself in, but Tyler begged me not to. He'd lied for me, covered for me, buried Alex for me..."

I looked at her, all the feelings I'd thought I'd had for her now dissolving like they'd been thrown in a tub of acid. "What about Hunter?" I said quietly. "Did you hurt him, too?"

Emily cried harder. "Please, Josh, you have to understand, all I could think of was Alex and what I'd done. What a terrible, despicable person I was. I didn't deserve to have a child—"

"What did you do, Emily? Where's your son?"

"I don't know," she shouted, "because I gave him away. I gave my baby away."

"What do you mean you—"

"It rained that day," Emily said, talking over me. "It came down so hard, worse than now. The roads were deserted, I could barely see. I stopped on a bridge, took Hunter out of his car seat, sat there as I cuddled him and cried." She gulped, her breath rapid and shallow. "I don't remember getting out, or walking to the edge of the bridge. But I stood there, holding my baby, staring down at the river, thinking how easy it would be for us to disappear."

"You were going to jump?" I said. "With Hunter?"

"Yes." Emily gasped for air, almost as if hearing someone say it out loud had suddenly made it real, that up to this point, she'd managed to tell herself it had all been in her mind. "I wanted to keep him safe, exactly how my father had done with my mother and Morgan. But then I saw the headlights, and a woman got out of her car—"

"Who?" I whispered. "Who was she?"

Emily shook her head. "She said she'd got lost in the rain, but I don't think that's what happened, not really. It was a sign. She was Hunter's guardian angel, and—"

"What was her name?" I said. "Emily, please, *tell me her name.*"

"I don't know," she said as I fumbled for my wallet. "I don't know. But I'll never forget her red hair, and she had the greenest eyes I've ever—"

"Was it her?" I said, pulling out the picture of Grace and pushing it into Emily's hands. "Is this the woman you gave him to?"

Emily gasped. "But...but...who... Why do you have—"

"It's Grace," I said. "This is my Grace."

"*Your* Grace? But...but that means—"

"Are you sure she's the one you gave Hunter to? Absolutely sure?" I said, and Emily nodded. "But how could she do that? How could she just take a kid?"

"Because I made her," Emily whispered. "I told her if she wanted him and me to live, she had to. I said if she went to the police, if she dropped him off somewhere, I'd convince everyone she kidnapped him, I'd make sure she went to prison for the rest of her life."

I closed my eyes, saw Grace pleading with a hysterical, suicidal woman, begging her to let her help, before giving up. Had she seen it as her only chance to have a family, a baby of her own? "She drove off with him? Left you alone on the bridge?"

Emily shook her head. "Not at first. She tried to convince me to go with her, said we could get help, and she wouldn't leave me. She told me she'd been through terrible things, but she was in a good place now, and I could get there, too. I almost believed her."

I looked at her, didn't dare say anything until she was done.

"I knew she was hoping somebody would come by to rescue all of us," she said, "but nobody did. She wouldn't leave, she still wouldn't take Hunter, so I held him over the edge of the bridge, screamed at her if she didn't do as I said I'd let him go." She swallowed, her voice hoarse. "She had no choice. I gave her no choice. She promised me she'd look after him. I made her promise."

The image of Grace, holding a boy in the rain, driving away with Hunter—*Logan*—rolled around my brain, and with it came an incredible surge of relief. She hadn't stolen him. She'd taken him because she feared for his life, for Emily's life. She must have been petrified, agonized over going to the police, or leave the baby somewhere, in both cases risk being arrested for something she hadn't done. Would anybody have believed the truth if she'd told them? And how could she have been sure Emily wouldn't make good on her promise to harm herself, and the baby, if he was ever returned? In her situation, what would I have done? What would anyone have done?

"And the story about the men forcing you off the road...?" I said, and Emily looked away.

"I threw my keys and phone in the river so I couldn't go after her," she said. "Don't you see? I had to keep Hunter away from us. Away from *me*. It was the only way I could make things right. The only way I could live with what we'd done."

I imagined Grace watching the news, wondering if the police were closing in on her. Had she understood she'd done the right thing when she'd heard Emily's fake account of what had happened on the bridge? A secret message from one woman to the other, an instruction to keep her baby safe?

"I never stopped thinking about him," Emily said. "Every second of every day I've wondered where he was, if he was alright. I wanted him back from the moment she drove away with him in her car and I realized I would never see him again. And all this time—" she smiled faintly "—all this time he was with *you*."

"Who else knew?" I said. "Who else did you tell?"

"Nobody," Emily whispered. "Only Tyler. He looked for

him. He's been searching for Hunter—for Grace—but he couldn't find them. And now you found us."

"We have to go to the police," I said. "We have to tell them—"

"Tell them what? What's going on?" a voice said behind us, and we spun around.

CHAPTER FIFTY-NINE

"Tyler!" Emily rushed toward him. "Oh, my God, Tyler. We've found Hunter. We've found him. He was with Josh. Can you believe it? The woman I gave him to, she was his partner. She was Josh's partner, Grace."

"Are you sure?" Tyler said before staring at me. "Is this true? You have my boy?"

Something in his voice wasn't right. As I looked at him, puzzle pieces started clicking and fitting, slotting together one by one, a picture, clear as Alpine water, emerging. The cryptic note I'd found with the old baby photos, made on a defunct printer Tyler could have had access to in the old building they owned. The snooping around the cabin and my truck, someone trying to find out why I was there. The beer on the deck, a gift, not from a welcoming neighbor, but a person who had the means to find my DUI record, who'd maybe hoped I'd drive drunk again, be arrested and made to disappear. Ivan would have argued circumstantial evidence at best, except for the final piece, the killer blow. Tyler was the only other living soul Emily had told about giving Hunter away to a red-haired woman on a bridge in the rain.

"You already knew," I said, taking a step toward him.

"What do you mean?" Emily looked at us both, her head shaking. "That's impossible."

"How did you find him?" I said. "How long before you figured out where he was?"

Tyler looked at Emily, grabbed her hands. "I'm glad I followed you here. He's insane—"

"Did you frighten her?" I said, my fists clenched. "Threaten her? Did you follow her, too? Is that why you'd go to Albany? To see Grace?"

"What are you talking about?" Tyler said, his shoulders back, chin raised. "Until thirty seconds ago I'd never heard of Grace Wilson."

Emily slowly turned toward Tyler. "How did you know her name?" she whispered.

"What do you mean?" Tyler said. "You both said it."

"Her *last* name," Emily said, and Tyler swallowed, his silence both revelatory and deafening. "You said you couldn't find her. You promised me—"

"Baby, I—"

"—but...but you *knew*?" she cried. "You knew where Hunter was?"

"You recognized me the first night, at Casa Mama, didn't you?" I said. "But you couldn't say anything because you didn't know if it was a coincidence."

Emily's sobs grew louder as she begged him, "Tyler, why didn't you tell me—"

"Because if I brought Hunter back," Tyler said quietly, "even if the police believed Grace had taken him, I knew the guilt would push you over the edge. You'd confess and—"

"You should have *told* me," Emily wept. "Tyler, I want my baby back, I need—"

"You *will* have him back," he said. "We're going to sit down with Josh and talk. Figure out—"

"He knows about Alex," she said, her voice empty, hollow. "He saw you at Monty's Pond. I told him everything. He *knows*. It's all over. We're going to prison."

Tyler frowned at me with almost an apologetic look as he removed his gun from its holster and pointed it at me. "No, we're not."

Emily jumped back as if electrocuted. "Tyler, what are you doing?"

"Think about it, sweetheart." He stared at her as if she was the only thing in the entire universe that mattered, his voice quiet, gentle, but the gun still on me. Emily took a step back and he moved closer. "Only the three of us know about Alex. We'll say you were having an affair—"

Despite myself, and the situation, I laughed, but Tyler ignored me.

"—and I came to the cabin to confront you, but he went crazy." He kicked over a chair, brought his knee up under the rickety dining table, flipping it to the floor. "I had no choice. He attacked me. It was self-defense."

Emily shook her head. "No. No, we can't, we—"

"We can, baby, we can. Then we'll wait, just for a while, before an anonymous tip will lead us to Hunter, and we'll get him back. It'll be the three of us again, the perfect little family you've always dreamed of."

I took a step forward. "You can't let him—"

"Don't move," Tyler said. "Emily, listen to me. If we don't do this, we *will* go to prison, and you'll never, ever see Hunter again. It's the only way."

She looked at me, and I could see the decision taking shape

in her eyes. Whatever affection she'd had for me over the past few days evaporated, the feelings she'd lost for Tyler reclaiming their ground. I finally understood what she'd meant when she said I reminded her of a former version of herself—it had been the woman she was when she'd met Tyler, when they were happy and in love. She'd been trying to recapture that with me, the way I'd been trying to recapture something I'd once had with Grace, too. And now I'd die if I didn't find a way to escape, and while Logan would be reunited with his parents, their despicable secrets would still be intact. I had to fight, I had to win. They didn't deserve to have him back.

"Emily," I said. "You're not a bad person. Don't let him do this."

"I'm sorry, Josh, I'm so sorry," she said, her voice flat, her eyes dark, bleak. "I'll have my son back. I'll have Hunter again."

"That's right, sweetheart," Tyler said. "That's right."

I calculated the risk of lunging at him, attempting to grab the gun from his hands. But I knew he'd put a bullet in me before I got to him, could then actually say it was self-defense. As I prepared myself for Tyler's shot, a flashing alarm signal went off in my mind, something about Emily's story that didn't make sense, and I clutched at the wispy thoughts, trying to piece them together, grabbed hold of an idea and didn't let go.

"Emily, wait," I said. "If he lied to you about not knowing where Hunter was, what else did he lie to you about?"

She looked at me, and I saw a flicker of doubt in her eyes. "What do you mean?"

"Shut up," Tyler seethed. "Shut the fuck up right now."

This was it, my way in, the chink in Tyler's armor. I didn't know what I'd uncover by chipping away at it, or if it would lead to him shooting me faster, but at this point, I had nothing left to lose. "Are you sure Alex suffocated? Did you see the cushion? What if Tyler wasn't protecting you? What if he was protecting himself? What if that's all he's ever done?"

"Don't listen to him!" Tyler yelled, and Emily grabbed his arm, moving the gun away.

"What did you do to Alex?" I said, staring at him, watched his jaw clench over and over. "Did you manipulate Emily about that, too? Did she give Hunter up for *nothing*?"

"You're insane," he said, shaking Emily off and pushing her away. "I never—"

"You're lying!" she shouted. "I can see it in your eyes. What happened, Tyler? Tell me!"

"Nothing, I—"

"Goddamn it, Tyler, tell me or I'm going to the police," Emily said.

She was about to shout at him again when he finally whispered, "I fell asleep with him."

"What?" she gasped. "With Alex?"

"Yes," he said, hands and lips trembling. "When I came home he was crying and you weren't around, so I picked him up and lay down on the sofa for a few minutes. It was no more than ten, I swear. But when I woke up…he'd slipped. His face… it was against the back of the sofa…and…he was already gone, Emily. Alex was already gone."

Emily's entire body shook, and I thought she would collapse until she reached for a chair and clung to it, her knuckles as white as her face. "You blamed me!"

"I'm sorry," Tyler said. "I'm sorry."

"You're *sorry*?" Emily shouted, spit flying from her mouth, eyes wide, filled with rage. "How could you do this? You said you loved me. You said you were protecting me from—"

He lowered his gun, took a step in her direction, arms open. "Emily—"

"Don't touch me," she spat. "You let me believe I'd killed my best friend's child. Because of you I almost jumped off a bridge with Hunter. My God, I gave him *away*—"

"But I kept track of him," Tyler said, his voice thick, eyes brimming. "Don't you understand? I always knew exactly where he—"

"That makes it worse," she screamed. "It makes it all so much worse."

"You'd have hated me. You'd have turned me in." Tyler was begging now, the gun waving around in his hand as he spoke. "Look at me and tell me you wouldn't. I loved you so much. It was the only way for us to stay together. But it doesn't matter now. We'll get Hunter back, and we'll—"

Emily wasn't listening anymore. Instead she rushed at Tyler, lunged at him with such force she sent him flying backward, straight into the living room window. A sickening crunching sound filled the air, mixing with yells of rage and surprise as they both sailed through the glass. I almost didn't hear the gunshot, a single popping firecracker noise, exploding as they fell onto the deck. It took me no more than a second to scramble through the shattered window and reach her, see the patch of red spreading across the front of her dress.

"Josh," she gasped, her chest barely moving. "Help me…"

"Emily," Tyler shouted as he staggered to his feet. *"Emily."*

Despite the steady stream of blood trickling from the deep gash on his arm, he still clung to the gun in his hand. "Don't touch her," he said, yanking me to my feet with his free hand, shoving me toward the broken window. "Don't you touch my wife."

"She's hurt," I said, raising my hands, palms facing him. "We need an ambulance."

"No." He swayed slightly, blood dripping from his wound. "You're not calling anyone."

"Tyler, please, she's *bleeding*. What if she dies—"

"Then I'll tell them you killed her," he said. "I'll shoot you and—"

Whatever he was about to say next died in his throat when Emily plunged a long shard of broken glass into the right side of his neck. He fell to his knees and toppled onto his face, and she hovered, dazed, beside him. And all that time, those two, three, four seconds, I said nothing. Didn't make a single sound.

The gun dropped from Tyler's grasp, and before I could move, Emily grabbed it.

"Hunter." Her eyes became unfocused, glassy as she staggered backward, the blood, so much blood, on her hands, arms, over her chest, splattered across her cheeks. "My baby couldn't choose his parents," she whispered, "but I can. Protect him from this, Josh. Keep him safe."

And then she put the gun in her mouth and pulled the trigger.

CHAPTER SIXTY

Five months later

My niece, Rachel Grace, arrived one cool November afternoon, kicking and screaming as she entered the world. As soon as we got the news, Logan and I rushed to the hospital, burst into the room with teddy bear balloons and an armful of stuffed dogs.

"Congratulations." I kissed Lisa's glowing cheeks and looked down at the perfect baby snuggled on her chest, fast asleep. "Well done. She's looks so much like you."

"Can I please hold her?" Logan asked, and I watched the excitement on his face as he perched on the edge of the chair with my sister, the woman who'd agonized over being a terrible mother already expertly showing him how to support Rachel's head.

When Ivan walked into the room, he pulled me in for a bear hug before quietly asking me how I was doing. They worried about me, him and Lisa, had checked in every day since my return from Faycrest, two fussing mother hens.

I'd rehearsed what to say before I got a cell phone signal

and called the police that night, decided to stick as close to the truth as possible. Lying by omission was easier than fabricating an entirely separate story, and Tyler had done the work of coming up with the most plausible lie, anyway.

"Tyler suspected us of having an affair," I'd said, and when the police asked if we were, I'd nodded. "He threatened us. I'm sure he'd have killed us both if Emily hadn't pushed him through the window. She was protecting me, and he didn't mean to shoot her. It was an accident, but afterward, when she stabbed…"

They concluded that was why she killed herself. She'd been acting in shock when she'd stabbed Tyler, and then the horror, the guilt, the regret, it overtook her. It was all too common. They questioned me for hours, had me sign a statement and eventually let me go. I kept up the pretense by moving into a room at the Travelodge, an act of good faith, an open display of innocence for all to see.

Ethel visited, as did Bill and Felicia, all of them expressing concern for my welfare, saying it wasn't my fault, I wasn't to blame, but their eyes betrayed them. When I told Bill I couldn't stay in Faycrest more than another few days, he told me not to worry, he understood. I thanked him for being so understanding, made all the right noises, kept all the right lies.

Two months after I returned to Albany, Ivan came by the house on his own. He handed me an envelope, and I immediately knew it was the birth certificate for Logan. I pulled out the document, my eyes darting over the details, confirming they were what I'd asked for—Grace's name as the mother, the father's unknown. I'd scrimped together every penny I had to pay for it, sold Grace's car and pawned the engagement ring I no longer needed, but still it hadn't been nearly enough. Lisa covered the rest, pushed the cash into my hands as we agreed we'd never speak of it again.

"It says Portland, Oregon," I said now, looking at Ivan, wondering if this was a moment I'd point back to, remember it as the second everything changed—for the better this time.

"That way you can tell Harlan you mixed up the state," he said. "Or don't say anything at all because it'll pass muster. I promise. You've got nothing to worry about. It's over."

I still held my breath until the guardianship application went through, and couldn't relax when we went out for dinner to celebrate. In time, I hoped I'd stop looking over my shoulder, panicking when the doorbell rang, expecting to see the police with a warrant for my arrest. Then again, I didn't have the right to forget. That's the price we pay for our lies, not knowing if, or when, everything will come crashing down.

I looked at my son as he handed Rachel to Ivan, both of them beaming at her, laughing, their eyes full of love. Logan was doing well in grief counseling, he'd been praised at school, hung out with new friends—even nonbully Dylan—with whom he shared his fascination for dogs. My boy was slowly finding his way back to the happiness he deserved, and as long as I lived, I would protect him from the truth.

Lisa walked over slowly, grimacing with every step. After making sure Logan was still preoccupied, she leaned in and said, "Did you see the news about Alex?"

"The anonymous tip worked," I said. "Felicia can bring her son home now."

"Are you sure you're okay with her not knowing what really happened to him?"

"No," I whispered. "And a big piece of me dies each time I think about it. But I can't say anything without revealing what I know about Logan, and who's to say they'll believe it."

"Maybe they'll figure it out when they examine the metal box, tie it back to Emily or Tyler somehow."

"Maybe," I said, trying not to think about them finding my DNA, too.

"Let's hope so," Lisa whispered. "Because they might decide they killed their kid, too."

I glanced at my son again, listened to him chatting with Ivan, watched him gently stroke Rachel's bald head, the perfect big boy cousin. Forevermore I'd worry he was destined to become a manipulator, a murderer like his parents, a liar like me. Although I'd come to understand everyone had morals and principles, things we said—and genuinely believed—we would or wouldn't do. Those morals and principles held upright until the moment we were faced with a situation we could never have imagined, put in front of an impossible choice, exactly as Grace had been. How she must have suffered over the years, agonized over her decision in secret, right up until the day she died.

I'd never know what might have happened if Grace hadn't taken Hunter from Emily on the bridge in the rain that day. Would Emily have jumped with her baby in her arms? Driven to the police to confess what she believed she'd done to Alex? In either case, would I have met Grace? Might she be alive?

It was something I couldn't dwell on. A boy named Logan came into my life one stormy afternoon. It no longer mattered how. What mattered was that we kept moving forward, together, and never, ever looked back. My darling Grace could rest easy now, because from this day onward I would forever keep my promise, and make sure her boy was safe.

★ ★ ★ ★ ★

ACKNOWLEDGMENTS

Such a huge amount of work goes into birthing a book, and I often think I have the easiest part—sitting at my desk (at times in my pajamas), making stuff up—so three thousand cheers to everyone else involved!

To all the readers, librarians, reviewers, bloggers, book clubs and bookstore staff—I would be nowhere without you picking my novels. Thank you for wanting to get to know my characters, and their lives. I am forever in your debt and will work hard to keep earning the time you choose to spend in the worlds I create. Big shout-outs to new social media friends, including Kristy Barrett, Toni Callan, Michelle Dunton, Linda Levack Zagon and Kate Rock. You *all* rock!

This third novel wouldn't have happened if Cassandra Rodgers hadn't signed me based on an early and slightly dodgy draft of my very first book—thank you. Thank you also to Carolyn Forde for accepting me into the Westwood family, and encouraging me to stretch myself as a writer. You've both had a huge hand in shaping me into the author I've become.

A gigantic thank you to my editor, Michelle Meade, who

has the most amazing insights, an incredible knack for "getting" my characters and more enthusiasm for my stories than I could have ever hoped for. You work tirelessly to make my scribbles and musings better, and I am so thrilled we tackled another novel together. I miss you already.

To Nicole Brebner, Meredith Barnes, Randy Chan, Sean Kapitain, Miranda Indrigo, Linette Kim, Suzanne Mitchell, Lauren Nisbet and the entire HarperCollins/MIRA team—you are fabulous. From championing to PR, audiobooks to library relations, marketing to cover designs, copyediting to proofreading—what more could an author ask for? Thank you for your support, hard work and making my dreams come true.

Where would I be without my family? Mum and Dad, Joely & Co—you've always believed in my writing and insisted from very early on that I don't give up. Thank you. To my mother-in-law, Jeanette, who has become one of my biggest fans; thank you for bragging about my novels to anyone who'll sit still long enough to listen. Thank you also to my other extended family members for reading my books (and rearranging them in the stores so they face outward).

My long-term friends Becki and Emma have encouraged and helped me for years. You're the best gal pals a girl could ever ask for. I'll see you both in Switzerland very soon.

An author needs local writing friends and I'm very fortunate to have found mine. Thank you to Brian Henry and the Quick Brown Fox community, and especially Donna, Lyanne, Mary and Shauna for the laughs and giggles along the way. Thank you to Amy Dixon for your support and encouragement, and to Karma Brown and Jennifer Hillier not only for forging the path ahead but also for encouraging me to follow.

To my new writing friends—and there are many—Sam Bailey, Kimberly Belle, Emily Carpenter, Tish Cohen, Rebecca Drake, Kimberly G. Giarratano, Heather Gudenkauf, Robyn

Harding, Wendy Heard, Karen Katchur, Shannon Kirk, Mary Kubica, Bianca Marais, Laura McHugh, Mindy Mejia, Kate Moretti, Roz Nay, Jill Orr, Kaira Rouda, Marissa Stapley, Paula Treick DeBoard, K.A. Tucker, C.J. Tudor and Wendy Walker—you all inspire me so much. I can't wait to see you again soon.

Special thanks to everyone who offered their advice and expertise as I wrote this novel, in particular Claudia Darcy, Harlan Gingold (love that name), James Hayman, Vickey "with an *e*" Longo, Theresa Roberts, Melissa Yuan-Innes, Jackie, Amanda and Donna. Huge thanks to Ed Adach and Bruce Coffin for taking the time to answer my strange questions, and for not immediately reporting me when I asked how to get away with kidnapping a child. All errors and omissions in the book are entirely my own fault, either because I lost the plot, or because I had to make things fit it.

And finally, a huge thank you to Rob, the best and most supportive husband in the world, who said right from the start I should follow my dreams and "write those books," and to our sons, Leo, Matt and Lex, who always believed I could. You are the greatest loves of my life, now and forever. Being with you just makes everything so much better.

HER
SECRET
SON

HANNAH MARY McKINNON

Reader's Guide

mira

1. At what point in the story did you suspect Grace wasn't hiding the father's identity, but the mother's? What tipped you off, and how did you feel about that twist?

2. If you were Josh, what would you have immediately done when you realized Logan wasn't Grace's child? What would have pushed you to make that choice?

3. Josh blamed himself for his parents' and Grace's deaths. What kept him from spiraling downward after Grace died, and how hard do you think he had to fight not to spiral again? What might have happened if he did?

4. Josh intended to give Logan up only if his parents were good, decent people. What did you make of that decision? If Logan had been Charlie Abbott or Alex King, what should Josh have done, and why?

5. What scene was the most pivotal in the story for you? How would the novel have changed if it had been different, or hadn't taken place? What did you expect to happen?

6. Given Emily's circumstances—her family history, and what she thought she did to Alex—how did you feel about her giving Hunter/Logan up?

7. What might have happened if Grace refused to take Hunter/Logan from Emily? What would you have done if you'd been Grace on the bridge that day?

8. Emily's father and husband betrayed her in different but devastating ways. Did that betrayal justify her attacking Tyler, and why? What do you think ultimately made her take her own life?

9. How do you think Josh will cope with the lies in the long run? Will he ever be able to move past them, and if so, how? What about when he finds a new partner? Do you think he'll share the truth about Logan?

10. How do you feel about Josh not telling Logan about his true identity? Can a situation ever justify hiding someone's reality from them? What might happen if Logan found out five, ten, twenty years later?

11. If Grace hadn't died, do you think her relationship with Josh would have survived long-term? What do you think he'd have done if she'd confided in him about Logan?

12. If Josh hadn't found Alex's bones, but had discovered Logan was indeed Hunter, what do you think he'd have done? Could he and Emily have found happiness, why or why not, and if yes, how?

What was your inspiration for *Her Secret Son*? Did the story start and end the way you first imagined, or did it evolve along the way?

I was at the gym one morning, watching a news report about a young woman who'd been kidnapped at birth, and lived a lie for the first eighteen years of her life. Initially I thought about crafting a story where a young boy was raised in a healthy, happy home before discovering he wasn't their child—how would that affect his love for them? What if he much preferred his kidnapping parents to the real ones, and wanted to stay with them?

However, as I sat down to plot the story, I started wondering what if the boy's birth mother had secretly given him up instead? First of all, I imagined the scene with two strangers— Grace and Emily—on a bridge in the rain, one of them begging the other to take her child. Then Josh strolled up to me (well, in my head, anyway) and said, "How about if I was Grace's partner and had no idea her son wasn't hers until she died?" That was it—I needed to tell his story.

What did you enjoy the most about writing the novel? Any seemingly insurmountable hurdles?

I adored writing the relationship between Josh and Logan, the bond between father and son. We have three boys, so I drew a lot of inspiration from watching them with my husband. I also thoroughly enjoyed writing an entire novel from a male character's perspective—something I'd never done before, and which stretched me as a writer.

As for the hurdles—there were a few. Strangely, I found having a whole story with only one viewpoint character more challenging (there were four in my previous book, The Neighbors). In fact, at the beginning I took the novel in a slightly different, more "conspiracy plot" direction, and gave Ivan a few of his own chapters. My editor, Michelle Meade, suggested I strip them out, allowing me to develop Josh and Emily's relationship more. She was right (she's brilliant!), and doing so helped me rewrite the ending, too, something else I'd struggled with for a while because I couldn't decide who to kill off!

You set the story in Albany, New York, and Faycrest, Maine, but your protagonist, Josh, is British. Can you tell us what was behind those choices?

I'd tried a North American setting while drafting The Neighbors, but found myself second-guessing whether the "voice" was right, if the expressions I used and the way the characters talked were American enough. It slowed me down, so I moved the setting to the UK. Consequently, when I was writing the proposal for Her Secret Son, and Michelle asked if I'd consider setting the story in the US, I was hesitant. However, I decided if I made Josh a Brit, I wouldn't worry about the voice, so it was an entirely strategic decision based on my comfort levels and abilities. Maybe for the next novel I'll feel confident enough to make it all-American.

As for setting Her Secret Son in upstate New York and Maine, I wanted it to be somewhere I'd been, and could easily return to. On the other hand, Faycrest is an entirely fictional place, which meant I could take whatever creative liberties I needed, and not upset any residents of a real town.

In reality, I believe my stories could happen almost anywhere. The novels are about everyday people and their relationships rather than the geographical location.

Speaking of everyday people, you throw them into difficult circumstances and place them under immense pressure. What draws you to writing family dramas?

I'm fascinated by the resilience and strength of people, how they cope when faced with tragedy, what they do to survive— including the lies they tell themselves, and each other. Our experiences, both good and bad, shape who we become, and shape us differently, which is equally interesting to explore. Creating difficult but entirely fictional circumstances for my characters provides the opportunity to think about how, and why, people have varying reactions to the same situation. I hope my stories also make the reader wonder what they would do if they found themselves in my characters' shoes.

What's your writing process like? Do you outline, or dive right in? Do you write the chapters consecutively, or jump around?

The more I write, the more I plan. My novels start with an idea—something that pops into my head, a radio segment, a newspaper article or a discussion I overheard somewhere. I noodle the thoughts around my head for a while as the main characters slowly take shape. The next step is to write an outline. I start by jotting the main plot points on sticky notes, which I then use as stepping-stones to build and write the rest of the outline. I fill out personality questionnaires for my main *characters to understand them better, and search for photos on the internet to build a gallery I stick on my pin board. By this point I'm raring to go.*

Whether I write the chapters consecutively or not depends on if I get stuck—if I do, I jump ahead and trust myself to be able to backfill later. I write a very basic, largely unedited manuscript that's about two-thirds of the final word count, then layer and develop until I'm happy calling it a first draft, and send it to Michelle. That's when the real editing work begins, which is fabulous because I know the story will become a thousand times better with her expert input.

What's been the biggest surprise since becoming an author?

Hands down the writing community. I've never, ever worked in an industry that's so supportive. Having an entire publishing team that's rallying behind my novels is incredible. It also amazed me to discover how authors don't see one another as competition, and are genuinely excited about, and interested in, helping each other—it's truly wonderful. I've made so many new friends and feel very fortunate and privileged to have become part of the community, and be able to help others in return.

What can you tell us about your next project?

My fourth novel is another family drama/suspense story about two half sisters who don't know the other exists. When one of them finds out, she decides she wants the life she sees as rightfully hers—the other sister's—and will stop at nothing to get it, even if it means destroying her sibling. I can't wait to introduce these new and messed-up people to the world. I should also mention my sister, Joely, is fabulous, so this novel is definitely not based on personal experience!